CHARLYYK
BOOK 2

Spencer Carvil.

SPENCER CARVIL

authorHOUSE®

AuthorHouse™ UK
1663 Liberty Drive
Bloomington, IN 47403 USA
www.authorhouse.co.uk
Phone: 0800 047 8203 (Domestic TFN)
       +44 1908 723714 (International)

© 2019 Spencer Carvil. All rights reserved.

No part of this book may be reproduced, stored in a retrieval system, or
transmitted by any means without the written permission of the author.

Published by AuthorHouse 08/20/2019

ISBN: 978-1-7283-9109-0 (sc)
ISBN: 978-1-7283-9108-3 (e)

Print information available on the last page.

Any people depicted in stock imagery provided by Getty Images are
models, and such images are being used for illustrative purposes only.
Certain stock imagery © Getty Images.

This book is printed on acid-free paper.

Because of the dynamic nature of the Internet, any web addresses or
links contained in this book may have changed since publication and
may no longer be valid. The views expressed in this work are solely those
of the author and do not necessarily reflect the views of the publisher,
and the publisher hereby disclaims any responsibility for them.

CONTENTS

Chapter 1   The Change in Charlyyk............................ 1
Chapter 2   The Sky at Night.......................................14
Chapter 3   The Arrival 23
Chapter 4   Charlyyk's House Guest........................... 39
Chapter 5   Christmas Invite 50
Chapter 6   Getting Ready for Christmas................... 66
Chapter 7   Winchester...81
Chapter 8   Christmas Day... 96
Chapter 9   Ringing in a New Year...........................112
Chapter 10 Home Truths 132
Chapter 11 Chelsea Pensioners 145
Chapter 12 Analysing Charlyyk...................................162
Chapter 13 The Scent of an Alien..............................191
Chapter 14 They Leave their Calling Card 200
Chapter 15 A Change of Mind.................................223
Chapter 16 The Light Consumed Them..................235
Chapter 17 The Silent Visitor....................................252
Chapter 18 Setting the Date......................................271
Chapter 19 Which Dress... 299
Chapter 20 The Intent...325

CHAPTER 1

THE CHANGE IN CHARLYYK

Janet Stokes quest to tell Charlyyk's story as she was a real person, and not as an Alien was paying off. To now follow Charlyyk efforts at school was quite a feather in her cap. Janet was becoming a friend of Charlyyk and this influenced Janet, to show off Charlyyk personality to win over the young reader.

In Miss Vasey's art class, Janet soon was asking permission to video Charlyyk's reactions to her attempts to paint. Charlyyk was no artist and did not pretend she was. But the sheer pleasure of splashing acrylic paint onto cheap paper was her idea of heaven. She was always upset when the lesson was over.

Mrs Landon would now and again sneak a view of Charlyyk while she was painting. The headmistress felt that she would like all her students to enjoy their days at school as much as Charlyyk enjoyed art class.

Alice Vasey told Janet what she needed to do for Charlyyk. "I dress her in a smock to save her clothes from the drips and splashes she always created when she paints. I also keep her well away from the other students. Otherwise their work would be covered by her over-enthusiastic endeavours. I encourage her as much as I can. Art is not about how well you can draw or paint, but what you have got out of it. The portfolio of Charlyyk's work proves just that. Her choice of colours is especially imaginative. There is much you can see in Charlyyk's paintings."

Alice Vasey showed Janet some of Charlyyk's paintings. Janet remarked, "Change the acrylic to oil and the paper to canvas, and these could be worth a small fortune."

One picture stuck out more than all the others. Charlyyk had painted Dippers Meadow from memory. She had seen the sun's rays hitting the trees and how it caught the water in the babbling brook. There were butterflies and rabbits, and birds on the wing. that used thermals to keep them afloat, drifting about in a sea of air.

Alice was interested in Janet's reaction. "Does that picture ring bells?"

Janet nodded. "It's her favourite place. She took me there one morning while we were jogging. It's called Dippers Meadow. Those splodges are the weeping willows. That streak there is the babbling brook. The flicks of paint are the sun's rays coming through the trees. I can see it because I've been there." Janet showed Alice a photo she had taken with her phone.

Alice Vasey had always tried to see through Charlyyk's eyes. Here was a key to help her interpret how Charlyyk expressed herself. Previously it had seemed that Charlyyk was simply slapping paint to paper. Now Alice knew she was painting a scene from her mind.

Alice spread other paintings over the table. It was easy to see which way they should be oriented, because of the paint runs. Alice saw them with a real artist's eye. The more she looked, the more she saw. Soon she was making notes and attaching them to each painting. She was so engrossed in what she was doing that she did not realise the lesson had ended.

Later at the cottage, Charlyyk and Janet helped to prepare dinner. They told Helen about the day at school. Helen knew Charlyyk liked art. "So you liked watching Charlyyk paint, then, Janet?"

Janet gave Charlyyk a playful nudge. "She really gives it her all. There is no holding back. She wields her brush like Joan of Arc going into battle. She takes no prisoners. But it's the joy in her face that tells the real story."

Holding a wooden spoon in her hand, Charlyyk spun around, waving it about. In a mock French accent, she declared, "En garde, or I shall cover you in paint."

The three of them could not stop laughing. Janet said, "You should tell the class that when you go into your art lessons."

Janet left the cottage to stay with James at the farm. Helen, Bryn, and Charlyyk settled in to watch *Dirty Dancing*. Helen had not watched it before she met Bryn. Romance had not been on her to-do list. Wendy Bailey had given it to Mace, who had given it to Charlyyk to give to Helen. Bryn was a little wary. How would Charlyyk would respond to the innuendo of "dirty" dancing? But Helen reckoned it would be OK.

Charlyyk began by sitting between them. Then she sat on Helen's lap. Then she sat between them again. Then she sat on to Bryn's lap. And so, it went until, when the film ended, Charlyyk was sitting on Helen's lap. Helen had her arms wrapped around Charlyyk. "Well, did you like that, Charlyyk?"

She looked at Helen. "I thought he was going to drop her, but I'm glad, he didn't. They are not like Janet and James. She was bigger than Janet—well, she *looked* bigger than Janet, and James is bigger than Patrick Swayze. Julia said it was her favourite film it's all about girl meets boy. But I'm trying to understand, why it's called Dirty Dancing?"

Hellen slightly biting her bottom lip. "Its…more to do in how they are dancing, the sexual orientation it implies."

Charlyyk nodded, the time it took thinking what Helen had said. "I understand, It saying that this type of Dancing is like sexual foreplay?"

Helen thought that near enough and quickly change the subject. "What homework have you got, sweetheart?"

Charlyyk reached into her satchel and pulled a paper. "Shakespeare, *Romeo and Juliet*. Mrs Thompson wants a synopsis of it for Tuesday. Mr Waverley needs the difference between farm workers, office workers, 15-year-old boys, 15-year-old girls in terms of their needs for nutrients and energy."

The cold air Helen was breathing in hurt her throat and made her cough during their run. She was pleased to be back at the cottage and to get a little extra attention from

Bryn. Charlyyk lay in a hot bath; she enjoyed the relaxed feeling.

As Bryn and Helen prepared breakfast, a worried looking Charlyyk arrived, still wet, in a bathrobe Helen had given her. "What's the problem, darling?" Charlyyk showed her a bath towel. It had blood on it. Opening her legs, she showed Helen where it had come from. Helen wrapped her in a big cuddle. "It's what we have been expecting, sweetheart. It's a part of what Michel has been saying about you changing from a girl to a woman."

Bryn placed his arms around her. "It's a regular thing that girls go through, darling. Women on this planet endure it on a monthly cycle, but we do not know how you will respond to it. Would you like to talk to Michel about it? I could phone him now if you want me to."

"Yes, please, Dad." Charlyyk looked at Helen, her face still showing concern.

Helen again pulled her in and cuddled her. She felt more and more like a mother towards her. "There, there, sweetheart, don't fret. You will see there's nothing to worry about."

Bryn had phoned Michel and passed the phone to Charlyyk. "Michel, I'm worried."

Michel's voice was calm and collective. "That's OK, Charlyyk. We do understand. Ask Helen to get you some pads to wear. She will know what I mean. But don't discard them—keep them so I can test them. Do you understand?"

"Yes. Thank you."

Charlyyk explained to Helen what Michel had said. "We had expected it, darling, and I already purchased the pads. Let's go and get you sorted."

When Helen and Charlyyk returned, Charlyyk was in a better place. Her smiling face showed Bryn she had got over her fears. She wrapped her arms around his neck and gave him one enormous squeeze. "Love you, Dad. I'll talk to Catherine about it. She will want to know."

Bryn was proud, seeing how she had grown in two years. He had not been involved when Catherine went through her menses; once again the army had had other duties for him to attend to. He had returned to find his daughter had matured, and had to make do with Kit's explanations. Kisses from Catherine became different. She would close doors on him and became more exclusive and bossier. He could not tickle her like he used to—she would turn on him. "No, Dad. I'm a big girl now." How would this event change Charlyyk?

Helen watched the reactions cross Bryn's face. "Let's wait and see how she changes. Let's take it one day at a time." She spoke quietly in an assured way. Helen had sat down with Charlyyk and talked about her own experience when she began her periods. She had been at boarding school at the time. The nurse of the college had been informed and had explained the process to her.

Bryn's memory wandered back to the day when Catherine had been chosen to play for England. She had clasped his face in her hands and kissed him on the lips. "Love you, Daddy." He had not lost his daughter. She was still there, just bigger.

With this thought, a smile crossed his face, which in turn brought smiles to Helen's and Charlyyk's faces. The sun was shining inside the cottage with a warmth of happiness.

At Carpenters' cottage for Sunday dinner, the conversation was mainly about Charlyyk. Michel had got in touch with Professor Taylor and agreed to share the study with him. Helen and Charlyyk were labelling the used pads with date and time.

When Charlyyk arrived, Gwen gave her a big hug, congratulated her on becoming a woman, and presented her with a small gift. The pleased look she gave Gwen as she carefully unwrapped the neat package turned into a whimsical smile. Her eyes sparkled, for Gwen had given her a Pandora bracelet with a charm indicating she was female.

The bracelet was lovely, it felt nice, and it looked good on her wrist. She knew Gwen would not give her something like this unless there was a meaning attached to it. Charlyyk's brain did not take long to register the meaning of the charm. "It's lovely, Auntie Gwen. Love the charm."

Later in the afternoon, Charlyyk told Michel about her homework. Michel explained the difference between 15-year-old boys and girls. "When girls go through what you are experiencing, they need more iron in their diet than boys do. Boys require more protein and calcium. Though we talk about the average age of this and that, the fact is that some teenagers develop early and some later. You could say we go through a seven-year cycle of life. From birth to age 7 the growth rate is fast. Around age 14, some teenagers develop a lot of spots. This could be down to how the blood changes or to poor diet. From there to 21, we grow to our full height and fill out. We get stronger. From 28 to 35 years old, we are, as the saying is, in our prime. By age 42, we should be more aware of our health. That's when our immunities start breaking down, and poor diet or an unhealthy lifestyle could catch you out. After that, it's potluck."

Charlyyk looked at him. "And me?"

Michel smiled apologetically. "We don't know. That's why we study you—to find out." He took a sip from a teacup and placed it back on the saucer. "We humans are aware that we experience a lot of hereditary disorders. Cancer is one of them. We ask people to keep a check on themselves and inform their doctors early when any symptoms develop. We have more chance to act and reduce unnecessary deaths that way. With you, we need to be proactive to obtain as much information as we can, so we can give you the best care we can."

Helen gave Charlyyk's arm a little squeeze. "As you can tell, sweetheart. As we find out more about you, you find out more about us. We are all different from one another in our chemical make-up. Where one person has more of one thing, another person may have less. Each one different. Each person has to find out about themselves and their own personal needs, exploring what suits them best so they can lead a healthy lifestyle."

Charlyyk thought through her own experience of how her friends had different problems with themselves. She began to understand why Mr Waverly had given them the homework—to make them more aware of themselves.

Janet was staying at the cottage. She had ten assignments to finish. As usual, Bryn had given her his study to use.

Charlyyk had to catch the school bus. This was a different Charlyyk. She was more assertive and more in control of herself. It could be seen in her walk and the way her hips moved. Sarah saw it. Her expression said, "Wow."

Helen whispered to Bryn, "Has she hitched her skirt up?"

"I don't know whether she has or not, but bloody hell, she has done something."

As Charlyyk boarded the bus, she turned, put two fingers to her lips, and blew them a kiss. Bryn, returning the gesture, said to Helen, "Where does this two-finger kiss come from? She used to use her whole hand."

They waved the bus off and head indoors. Bryn was utterly perplexed as to what had just occurred, and went in search of a task to take his mind off it. He opened the garage doors and started to grease the rollers. Kit's voice was in his head, complaining about Catherine's attitude. "It's OK for you," she had said to him. "You don't have to live with a girl of 14 who bloody well thinks she 18!"

No, he had not seen it. All he had seen was his sweet little girl growing bigger. A week later, he had been in some dirt pit of a country, blowing up a secret launch pad which was a threat to world peace. Could he see the wrong in his little girl? Did he *want* to see something wrong?

He shook his head. He had missed so much of his children growing up. What did Catherine say? "Still playing toy soldiers, Dad."

His thoughts kept going around and around; he was feeling very uncomfortable about it all. *Was I really that selfish, living a* Boy's Own Storybook *life, like the one my father read to me at bedtime? If that was the case, no wonder the kids of today grow up with the attitude of* Grand Theft Auto.

Helen's call took him away from his thoughts. "Bryn! I've made lunch, love." The cheery way she said it calmed him. He wiped his hands with an old cloth and was soon in the cottage. The heating making the cottage homely.

He sat down with Helen and Janet. The conversation was soon about Charlyyk. Bryn told them of the thoughts he'd had—how he felt he had been selfish and had missed the best part of his children's growing up because of it.

Helen took his hand in hers. "Oh, come on, sweetheart. You are too hard on yourself."

Janet looked startled. "Most men would not be so honest with themselves. They would say nothing, for fear of looking weak. My father in particular would have made up something to justify himself. An out-and-out coward, that's my dad ... but I still love him."

Helen knew what army life was all about. One was given a number, and when they said jump, one jumped. But she also knew that some men's names were always put on the top, time after time. They knew what to expect from them and demanded just that. It was not a written law, just the rule of the jungle—the pecking order of army life.

Sarah could not get over the change in Charlyyk. At lunchtime, she said to Sandra and Julia, "Come on! The way she's walking, and even the way she talks, it's so … you know, different! I'm not saying it's bad. It's just not her usual self."

Julia stared at Charlyyk. "I think you are right. There is a different air about her. Look how she is talking to Peter and Mike."

Sandra leaned back in her chair. "I'm not looking at Charlyyk but at Peter. He's mesmerised by her. He's gone all gooey-eyed. Look at the way Charlyyk is using her hands. She's got Peter in a trance." Mike was no different. When Charlyyk's hand moved, Mike's and Peter's heads moved in the same direction. The three girls could not help laughing.

Charlyyk, hearing the laughter, looked at them with a smile so big, that anyone seeing her would have smiled with her. She waved her hand with an exaggerated flutter, and the three girls knew that she had been listening to them all the time.

Getting up, Charlyyk joined the other girls. "Yes, a lot happened this weekend. I had my first period. After my morning run on Saturday, I took a bath, and when I dried myself, I found blood on the towel." She went on to discuss the advice Michel had given her. Sandra was quick to gather the rest of the class and inform them of that advice. The posse did not just look after Charlyyk, but the rest of the class as well.

Janet worked hard all morning and achieved a great deal. So, when the producer of *The Sky at Night* phoned, she was not upset about being disturbed. She walked to the lounge, talking to the producer. Janet got Bryn's attention. He picked up the other phone and joined in on the call. They all agreed to do an interview at the next weekend. The producer would send a team down to do a survey on Wednesday.

Janet looked very pleased with herself. "Thank you, Bryn. The exposure I'm getting from this is enormous. It is all down to you giving me your trust. But do you know, the bit I love the most is the way you have brought me in as one of the family. Charlyyk has made me her friend. I feel at home here just as I do in my parents' home."

Charlyyk bounded in from school. Bryn met her off the bus, and the buoyant Charlyyk could not have been happier to see him. She flung her arms around him and hugged him tightly. As they walked into the cottage, she bubbled with excitement, telling him what her friends were saying about the changes in her. "A lot of what they said was good. I had been so worried about how I was going to change. More so into what. Now I understand when you said about giving me space to be the person I want to be. I realise that the change is in my perspective of life, not of other people's views. It's a mental attitude, not all about the physical changes. When I talked about it to Julia and Sandra, they said I've got girl power. I'm still not sure in what that means, but it sounds good!"

Helen and Janet could not help overhearing what Charlyyk had said. Her excitement made her speak loudly. Janet slid her arm through Charlyyk's arm. "For so many decades, men have controlled women for their own satisfaction. Now women have emerged from men's shackles and taken control of themselves. That's girl power."

Charlyyk's face changed. The smile had gone. "But Dad has never shackled me. He has always asked me what I would like to do, not demanded."

Helen answered, "Janet is right, but 'shackled' is a metaphor for male behaviour as a whole—something in general, not individual."

Janet squeezed Charlyyk's arm. "I like your dad too. He is something special."

Helen gave Janet a playful tap. "You concentrate on James. Bryn is mine."

Bryn could only admire his two women. Not only had Charlyyk changed; so too had Helen. When they had first met, he had seen the girl in Helen. She had needed someone to allow her to come out of her shell. Now that she was out, she would never return to her old self.

CHAPTER 2

THE SKY AT NIGHT

Bryn and Helen made sure the house was clean and tidy. The team from *The Sky at Night* were expected at two. Janet stayed in Bryn's study, going over various materials to assist the survey team if needed.

The team arrived at ten minutes to two. Introductions and general talk occupied the time until three. Then they measured the lounge, set up a camera, and made various notes about how the shooting could be done. They were still there when Charlyyk arrived home.

The cameramen showed Charlyyk how the camera worked and demonstrated it through a monitor. They set up another camera in the garden so it could tell them if the sky was clear enough and there was no light damage. They left at six, completely satisfied with what they could achieve on Saturday.

After dinner, Janet produced material that could be used for the interview on Saturday. Helen's interest was growing stronger the more she learned about the early days when Charlyyk first arrived. Harold had made three monthly assessments of her changes. Gwen had kept a diary. With her photos and Michel's notes, Helen got the full picture of Charlyyk's progression.

Listening to Janet, Helen understood why Charlyyk had responded in the way she did. She had been copying Harold and Bryn in the careful way she listened, then weighed up and valued what had been said. She did not offend anyone but gained their trust. Her hard-working, matter-of-fact manner had been learned from Gwen and Catherine. "Charlyyk is a survivor," Janet said. "She adapts to survive."

"Her motto seems to be 'don't make enemies but friends'. Charlyyk is a very clever girl," Helen agreed.

On Friday, after Charlyyk had left for school, Helen and Bryn checked to see what shopping was required, as there would be no chance to get shopping on Saturday. The trip to the supermarket went without a hitch. Bryn was becoming used to Helen being with him. He liked how she got on with everyday tasks without continually asking him what he thought. She accepted responsibilities as if she had been there for years.

During the afternoon, Janet was showing them some of the articles she had finished, and the phone rang. Helen picked it up. "Hello? Rachel, how are you? Let me call Bryn."

Bryn took the phone. "Hi, sweetheart. Wednesday, 19.00 p.m., Heathrow, Terminal 5. OK, love, see you then." He beamed.

Helen slipped her arm into his. "I'm going to meet them at last. I'm so looking forward to it."

Janet looked pleased as well, remembering how well she had got on with them in Houston, especially Rachel.

When Charlyyk arrived home, Helen told her that Thomas, Rachel, and Rachel's mother were coming on Wednesday. The pleasure they both took in the prospect pleased Bryn. He saw a bond building between them. What also pleased him was the way Janet had helped Helen with the housework.

He knew Janet was keen to meet Maggie Aderin-Pocock, an exciting Nigerian-British space scientist. "She should be called Peacock, not Pocock, for she is so colourful," Janet had said to him.

That night, Charlyyk was restless and could not sleep. She went down into the lounge at three and read a book on post-war Britain. When Bryn found her there, he made her a cup of tea and sat down to talk her through what was troubling her. "Over these last few months, so much has happened. I've missed Catherine. I know I have Janet and Helen and new friends at school, but with school and the trip to America, my head has been full of lots of things going around and around. They're not frightening things, they're nice things, Cinderella things. It's like a fairy godmother has not just waved her magic wand, but tipped a whole sacksful of magic dust over me."

He held her in his arms like any dad would do, and gave her a gentle squeeze.

Charlyyk loved the emotional thing these earthlings did. "Come on, Dad. Let's go for a run. Then I'll have a kip in the bath."

She was in the bath for about an hour. Bryn and Helen started to worry about her getting cold and went to hurry her along. They found her fast asleep. Bryn lifted her out, and they dried her and put her to bed.

The television crew arrived while Charlyyk was in the bath. They had set up and were testing by twelve, when Charlyyk came down. She was wearing the Laura Ashley dress that Gwen liked. She knew it would portray her as a young girl, which she felt was the right image, as this programme would probably be shown in many countries.

The floor manager was a little worried; they were short a make-up artist. Bryn suggested Liza Martin and gave him the phone number. The presenters arrived at two. The Martins arrived ten minutes later. Charlyyk was pleased to see Sarah had come as well. "My mum was so excited when they called her!" Sarah exclaimed. "She kept turning around in circles, Dad had to get her things together. Otherwise we would still be waiting for her."

Chris Lintott, Maggie Aderin-Pocock, and Pete Lawrence sat down with Bryn, Charlyyk, and Janet to work out what they wanted to discuss. Pete Lawrence had some great images of the Draco constellation, where Charlyyk's home planet was thought to be situated. He had been at the Johnson Space Center as one of the astronomers, and had brought back much of the material they had produced there.

With Bryn's and Janet's help, Maggie eased Charlyyk's overexcited enthusiasm. She had Charlyyk laughing when they did a test in front of the cameras. Chris Lintott did a test run with Bryn and Janet. Liza Martin was kept very busy, but did not falter in the face of the demanding challenges. Sarah was very proud of her mum. She sat with her dad and the Hobarts and Helen, well out of the way. The camera set up in the garden promised a clear sky.

Then the shoot began. Pete Lawrence explained to the TV audience where they believed Charlyyk originated from. "The Draco constellation circles the northern hemisphere. The Pole Star is situated within it. All the abductions by the light beam occurred in the northern hemisphere. This fact gives credence to the hypothesis that Charlyyk's planet must look to our northern hemisphere. A sun like our own is also situated in the Draco constellation, with the similar levels of lithium depletion. This points to the presence of planets, including the possibility of small Earth-like planets in its orbit. But this twin sun is 210 light years from Earth."

He pointed to a graph that showed how long it would take to reach Mars and the distance differential of where Charlyyk's planet was presumed to be. The notion that Bryn and Charlyyk had experienced six months of travelling time at the speed of light had to be thrown right out of the window. It was just not logical.

Charlyyk's views of her life, how she had survived, and the reality of other planets with different life forms made the programme fascinating. The presenters gave every known detail they had gained through Charlyyk's and Bryn's observations of their experiences.

During the show, Maggie was keen to talk to Janet about encouraging girls to take up science as a career. She named some of the female scientists who had inspired her. "So many good women have taken up the challenge of space. Did you get the chance to meet Amy Ross at NASA? She helped to design the Z-series spacesuit. One of the biggest challenges in space is mobility, and she led her team to achieve that in the Z-series. There are many avenues girls can take up that are connected with space—it does not mean only one thing."

Charlyyk was careful to portray herself in an open manner, encouraging the questions asked of her. When asked what, she ate on her planet, she purposely did not mention eating small animals, only vegetation, fruit, nuts, and insects. She did not want to upset even most timid of viewers.

Janet spent Sunday at the Parsons' farm. There were only three on the early morning jog. Their conversation was mainly about the eagerly awaited arrival of Thomas, Rachel, and Rachel's mother. Helen was keen to find out as much as she could about them—what their needs were, if anything, and what she should be wary of.

Charlyyk kept quiet to allow Bryn to comment. When he finished, she corrected him where she had thought he had made mistakes. She reminded him that Helen wanted to make a good impression, and it would be good for him to help her the best way he could. "I am trying!" he blurted.

The glare Charlyyk gave him made him think again. "OK, I might have been a little flippant about Rachel's mother."

Charlyyk again looked sternly at him. "We will be sharing our home with them for over a year. Let us try and get it right from the first day, if that is not too much to ask?"

Later, when Bryn and Helen were showering together, Helen asked him to explain Charlyyk's attitude. He did not want to talk about it at first, but he did not like getting yet another stern look from Helen.

"OK. When Thomas was here before, I wanted him to stay longer. But he said he had to go; he had commitments in America. I accused him of slinking back because of Rachel's overpowering mother. Don't forget, I was not in a good place at that time. So, when I mentioned that Rachel's mum could be a little bit overpowering, Charlyyk was remembering that conversation. That's why Charlyyk was so curt towards me."

They dried each other with large, warm bath towels. Helen had been thinking about what Bryn said. "I've not heard Charlyyk speak so angrily before. But it was a controlled anger which did not have any malice to it." She started to get dressed. "Has she ever spoken like that before?"

Bryn shook his head. "No, not like that."

Helen was quiet. She finished dressing, then put things away in their appropriate places. "Then she is changing?"

Bryn sat on the end of the bed, looking out the window. His mind drifted back to something Harold had mentioned. Harold had been reading one of Dickens' novels, *Oliver Twist*, to Charlyyk. In it, the orphan Oliver asked for more. Charlyyk wondered, "Why should he ask for more? Was he not satisfied with what he had?" When Harold tried to explain, she had looked angry. "He should have tried to live how I had to. He would have not complained about an orphanage then." Bryn related this to Helen.

Helen nodded. "She senses some forms of injustice. There are other sides of Charlyyk we've yet to discover. Interesting."

At breakfast, Charlyyk did not mention anything relating to the morning run. She laughed about Gwen and her experience in the church. "I waited for something to happen, but nothing happened. Then everyone got up and left. I looked around to see if I had missed something, but no. The place was empty. It was no different to when we found it!"

Helen said, "Gwen has always believed in God. Her belief gives her a form of inner strength and helps her to accept the injustice that man does to man, like the violence that exists today."

Charlyyk looked into her empty cereal bowl. "So Gwen believes that praying will solve the problem?"

Helen sensed that she was being set up. "Well, yes!"

Charlyyk cocked her head to one side, a smirk on her face. "So if a big Fuung is attacking me, I should kneel down and pray that it will not eat me?"

Helen had fallen into the hole. Charlyyk's face now had a smile. "It would eat me—maybe because it doesn't believe in God!" Charlyyk burst into laughter. "I am joking. I know Gwen is very serious about her faith, and I do respect her for it."

Helen shook her head. "You little bugger!" They laughed with each other.

Bryn already knew this side of Charlyyk. She only joked with those she loved. She would not get upset easily, and especially not with Gwen. Charlyyk had already upset Gwen once and did not want to make her cry again.

———

At the Carpenters' cottage, Michel explained to Charlyyk the reason for the test he and Professor Taylor were doing. "When a woman has a period, it flushed away her old eggs. But in other living beings on this planet, a process like a period has other functions. We are trying to find out the function your period is for. And there may be other things we can evaluate by doing these tests. We are not looking for problems, just trying to get an understanding of how you will respond."

To Charlyyk's surprise, Michel pulled up his shirt to reveal his stomach. "As you can see, I have a navel, whereas you do not. But there are life forms on this planet that don't have navels either. One is a Duck-bill Platypus which lays eggs and excretes milk. That only goes to show we have much to learn. These tests may satisfy our curiosity and provide us with a chance to give you the best health care we can."

Charlyyk accepted Michel's explanation without fuss or concern. She had come to trust Michel implicitly. Whenever he examined her, he always explained why and wherefore.

CHAPTER 3

THE ARRIVAL

Charlyyk had already left for school. Bryn had a few repairs to do. Helen sorted the laundry. Then Toby arrived and, as usual, walked straight into the kitchen and put the kettle on. "I must have a cup of coffee. I've a throat as dry as the bottom of a birdcage."

Helen laid out mugs and a jar of instant coffee. "Are you in need of feeding?"

The look he gave her did not need a reply, and she soon rustled up bacon and eggs and a large round of toast.

Bryn entered the kitchen. "Cor, that smells good." Helen did not hesitate. Egg and bacon between slices of toast was placed in Bryn's hands.

"To what do we owe the pleasure of your company, Toby?" Helen asked. She knew Toby would not be there unless he had a problem.

"There are no problems. But when you are ready to wipe your records from the databank, type in your password followed with the words 'final exit' in all caps. Then you will be free to marry Bryn."

The smile on Helen's face relayed to Bryn that she was ready to relinquish her past and start her new life with him. She kissed Bryn and then leaned back with the look of a cat that had licked the cream. "Well, that's found the four corners of the jigsaw. Now we just have to fill it in."

Toby said, "Your military records are intact. We have placed a military history for a Sergeant Helena Baker, so you have cover from any fall out from Interlagen. We have given you a stellar civil service record, which allows the government room to honour you if they wish to do so. That leaves me to suggest the new year for your resignation. I've already taken up the reins. You may press the button when you are ready."

Janet's red Mini pulled up in the driveway. Helen went out to help her unload it. Their comings and goings between car and Charlyyk's room lasted ten minutes. After, Janet showed Helen her latest articles, ready for publication. One was destined for *The Sky at Night Magazine*. But it was the one for a girls' magazine that caught Helen's eye. It was mainly about Charlyyk going to school. It was witty and showed the funny side of Charlyyk. The in-depth comments from her fellow students gave younger readers a real vision of a girl facing the same difficulties every young girl had to go through in growing up.

When Charlyyk came home and read the article, she looked at Janet with wonder. "Did they really say that about me?" Janet showed her the notes she had taken. "'Like a comfort blanket'?" Then, reading a bit more, "'Like a big, all-knowing sister'?" Charlyyk was not upset. She looked humbled.

Helen placed her arms around her. "Well, what do you think?"

Charlyyk reread the notes. "I like what they have said. It shows that they respect me as a friend."

Bryn came up to them. Helen gave him what Janet had written. He read it and then reread it. "Janet, this is so Charlyyk." He put his arm around Charlyyk's shoulders. "What do you think about it, sweetheart?"

Her shoulders rose and her head dropped to one side. "I cannot but like it. It is what Janet has seen. I remember being there, and those things have actually happened. But I did not expect what they have said about me!"

She showed Bryn the pictures she had painted. "They are not as good as the paintings Jan and Sarah have painted, but I like them."

"So do I, sweetheart. I know what you have painted and how you used the colours. With time and practise, everyone can improve. But the main thing is you enjoyed doing them!"

Excitement built in the Collier family for the arrival of Thomas, Rachel, and Rachel's mother. Helen pulled out cupboards, washed them, and placed back their contents in an orderly manner. Bryn was called upon to agree to what could be thrown away. Janet took the books from the bookshelves, cleaned them, and rearranged them back on the shelves. Furniture was moved to allow vacuuming in areas that generally were inaccessible. Black plastic bags were filled up with things deemed rubbish.

When Charlyyk arrived home, she walked around the cottage, inspecting the enormous effort the three adults had achieved. Janet was still cleaning out an old cupboard under the stairs. She found an old wooden box which had been hidden in the darkness. All heads turned when she called Bryn's name. "There is a large wooden chest in here."

Bryn pulled it out. It was an old blanket chest. The catch was stiff with age. Bryn soon had it open. Inside were cotton sheets and curtains. Among them lay an ancient leather-bound Bible, wrapped in a waxed linen cloth.

Janet opened it very carefully. On the inside of the cover was written *This is the Allcott Family Bible, 1557.* The first entry was *John Edward Allcott, Born 29th May 1557, To Edward James and Mary Anne Allcott, née Parsons.*

The Bible became the talking point of the evening. Many entries had been written about the history of the Allcott family. The text was a Coverdale Bible, printed in English. Janet explained to Charlyyk that the Roman Catholic Church had ordered the death sentence on those who tried to translate the Bible into the English language prior to Coverdale's version.

Charlyyk cocked her head to one side, her impish look saying *I told you so.* Helen looked at her sternly, her own expression saying *Don't you dare.* Bryn nodded. "Charlyyk, Gwen has strong feelings. Don't upset her."

Charlyyk said aloud, "I would not do that. Gwen means a lot to me. But when she is not here, well, my feelings are my feelings."

Janet seemed a bit upset. "Why do you feel that way?"

"Gwen's belief is not logical. It is a form of brainwashing. It's telling people to believe that prayer is going to solve all their problems. But it does not. Only action solves problems. Gwen's belief tells people not to face reality, but to roll over, cover their heads, and hope the problem will go away. Religious leaders should be encouraging people to face reality and work through problems with logical thinking and rugged endeavour."

Charlyyk's succinct way of talking made Janet realise she had strong feelings about how she saw certain forms of injustice. To Charlyyk, faith was an injustice.

Janet had spoken to Gwen how Charlyyk handled Bryn's going to Switzerland for the meeting and leaving her with Gwen and Harold. Gwen had replied, "Charlyyk did not want Bryn to go. But once he had left, she just accepted it. At first it concerned me, so I asked her how she felt. Charlyyk said she would miss him while he was away, but she knew he would return. Then she carried on as if Bryn had not gone away.'

On Wednesday, for once, Charlyyk did not want to go to school. Bryn and Helen had to work hard to push her onto the bus. Sarah could tell Charlyyk wanted to be somewhere else. "You did not want to stay at home. The time would just drag."

Charlyyk said dejectedly, "I know, right? I don't want to miss meeting Thomas and Rachel. It's going to a different place, and seeing something different."

"But you went to Heathrow to see Catherine off."

"Yes, but that was Terminal 2. This will be Terminal 5."

Once Charlyyk had met up with the rest of the posse, however, she quieted down and forgot her anxiety.

Helen and Janet had made a list of needs and headed for town in the Discovery. It was going to be a long day. As the hours drifted by, the tempo quickened. Then, all at once, Charlyyk was home. It was as if there were an electrical storm brewing. Everyone got ready to head for Terminal 5, Heathrow Airport.

Bryn had hired a mini bus taxi with enough room for the luggage. Charlyyk was the first one in the taxi, urging them all to hurry. Helen and Janet sat with her to settle her down.

Standing in the arrivals lounge, Charlyyk paced about. She could not keep still. Bryn had to take a grip on her to slow her down; she was oblivious to what was happening around her. Charlyyk kept anxious watch as people strolled through the arrival gates. The minutes seemed like hours to her. Then came the first sight of Rachel, with Thomas, struggling with an overloaded trolley, trailing close behind.

Charlyyk slipped Bryn's clutches, diving under the barrier and into Rachel's arms. Thomas had expected that to happen and urged Rachel to go ahead of them. Rachel's mother grabbed Thomas's arm, afraid she might get knocked over.

Bryn helped to get them to a place where they could greet one another without obstructing the other passengers. The introductions were warm and sincere. Bryn collected another trolley, as the one Thomas was pushing was well overloaded.

Rachel's mother was at first very wary of Charlyyk and kept a slight distance from her. Charlyyk did not seem to concern herself. Other passengers and their relatives looked upon Charlyyk with amusement at her excitement. As at Disney World, Charlyyk was in no way able to control her emotions when she became excited. Janet, as usual, took video footage for her own advantage. She would be able to use this material for teen girl audiences.

Helen soon had Rachel's mother, Margret, settled. She walked her arm in arm to the waiting taxi. Thomas and Rachel took control of Charlyyk, with Bryn and Janet close behind

Then something was thrown at Charlyyk, which missed. Bryn quickly directed Rachel towards Helen. Thomas closed ranks with Bryn to shield Charlyyk. Airport security was soon in attendance. A man was escorted from the area. Two armed officers stood by to protect Charlyyk, but Charlyyk did not agree with that. "Please, no one was hurt. I would like to speak with the man if I may."

Helen stepped forward and spoke with the two officers, who agreed to Charlyyk's wishes. A meeting in the detention room was set up.

The man looked angry when Charlyyk entered the room She sat down opposite him. Charlyyk said, "I did not ask to come here or have any say about living with you. I can only hope to live in peace with you. I promise that I will respect all your customs and traditions and behave as you would want me to behave as citizen. So please, if you have any grudges against me, this is your chance to voice them."

The man just glared at Charlyyk. Then slowly, he relaxed. "You are not one us. You could bring us trouble if your people invade."

Charlyyk smiled warmly. "I lived in fear every day of my life. Where I come from, my people were the food for many beasts. My new father rescued me from that. Now I am here and find my life among you so nice. My friends treat me with respect. I would like to treat you with respect and not press charges. Could we leave as friends? When my friends agree on something, they like to shake hands. Will you shake hands with me?"

Slowly, the man's expression changed. He nodded and offered his hand to Charlyyk. "Sorry. I should have controlled myself better. It was a rash moment. Accept my apologies."

Charlyyk accepted his hand and gently shook it. "Thank you. I appreciate your friendship and wish you well."

The drive back to the cottage was noisy. Charlyyk was back to her old self. Margret, not being sure of Charlyyk, continued to distance herself from her. Helen assured Margret that Charlyyk would settle down.

At the cottage, Thomas took charge and showed Margret where everything was. Helen had a surprise for them. While they were at the airport, Helen had asked Harold to hang one of the drawings Thomas had done of Kitty and Catherine. Helen had had it framed. Harold and Gwen had collected it in the morning.

Helen admired the looks of satisfaction on everyone's faces. "I thought it was fitting that Kitty should take pride of place. She was so much the driving force and an influential part of this family." Bryn was taken aback by the gesture. He gave Helen an appreciative hug. She received the same from Thomas and Rachel. By this, Helen was saying she was not competing with Kitty.

Gwen confided in Thomas. "When Helen asked Harold to collect a package from Taylors Shop and hang it here on the wall, I did not realise it would be a picture of Kitty. Harold unwrapped it, and I must admit, I became a little emotional about it. I think it is such a lovely gesture. Harold knew that Helen was telling us that we should not forget your mother."

Rachel was nearest to Helen when Gwen was speaking. Rachel placed her hand on Helen's hand and congratulated her.

Thomas put his arm around his father's shoulders. "Where did you find it, Dad?"

Bryn described clearing Thomas's old room, and how they had come across it at the back of the wardrobe.

Rachel and her mother examined the pen-and-ink drawing very carefully. "How old were you when you did this?" Margret asked.

Thomas stepped forward and looked at the picture. "I was 18. It was one of the drawings I submitted for my first year at the art college."

Harold cooked dinner. As they enjoyed the fruits of his labour, Margret saw a different Charlyyk. The girl was subdued and coherent. A conversation sprang up between them, with Rachel prompting Charlyyk to talk about her art. Janet provoked laughter by telling them about Charlyyk's behaviour in art class. Charlyyk said, "My duel of brush against the paper can be a messy ordeal and leave many victims splashed with colourful mementoes of those encounters." She waved a spoon about. "En garde, or I will cover you in paint!"

After the evening meal, Charlyyk showed them her artwork. Margret perused the pictures as she would do professionally. "Your use of colour is splendid."

"I get a little carried away with the amount of paint I load my brushes with. I'm much too enthusiastic to get the paint onto the paper. I end up with runs."

Margret smiled. "That's not what matters. What matters is the vibrant way you administer the brush strokes. That shows how you enjoy your art. Those who look upon your work will feel the same way. With many famous artists, you must not stand too close to their work, but at a distance only. Otherwise you will not see what they were trying to achieve. But looking at what you have painted, I can see open spaces, trees, and the sun's rays shining through the branches. The butterfly is larger than normal, because that is how you saw it. With time and practise you will challenge yourself and become more aware of perspective and technique. Thomas will no doubt give you a few tips."

Rachel tugged on Thomas's arm and whispered in his ear, "Mum's warming to her. Look how she has moved closer to her."

Torrential rain made a morning run difficult but did not deter them. Soaking wet and muddy, they returned in high spirits. This was Janet's last day. She had two interviews booked before the Christmas break. She had cleared with the Colliers her latest articles. She gave Charlyyk a cuddle. "I'm staying with the Parsons for Christmas, so I will see you then."

Rachel, Janet, and Helen waved goodbye to Charlyyk as she left for school. Inside the cottage, Bryn was sorting out a couple of issues that Margret had spoken of. "The mattress is too soft, and the pillows are too firm. I struggled all night to get a good night sleep."

Bryn nodded. "I will sort it immediately. We will go to the store today, and you can choose whatever mattress suits you."

Thomas felt a little awkward, but his father just smiled at him. His father's casual manner allowed him to relax. But Thomas knew what his mother-in-law really wanted was a new mattress. She was not prepared to sleep on a mattress that others had slept on before.

They met the girls in the kitchen. Bryn said that a trip to the furniture store was the first item of business for the day, then a stop to see Bill Symonds. "I spoke to Bill the other day about a runabout for Thomas. He has a choice of three. You won't have to feel that you must rely on us. You'll have the freedom to come and go as you please."

At the academy, Mr Pearson raised his voice to get his charges' full attention. "Come on, let's calm it! OK, we touched on the elements of the social changes that Britain has gone through. Can anyone add anything more towards it?"

Charlyyk put her hand up. "Mr Pearson, you did not want us to bring politics into this, but politics created some of the changes."

Tim Pearson looked at Charlyyk. He had thought she would be the last person to bring this up. "Have you any views about this that you think relevant?"

Charlyyk sat forward in her chair. "Women were given a bit of a raw deal in the law courts. They were treated differently to men in the workplace. Even if they did the same work as men, they received only half the wages. This could only have changed through politics."

"Yes, I must concede you are right." Turning to the smart board, he entered onto it what Charlyyk had mentioned. "Right. We can see here the fundamental changes that have happened to Britain, and the time span in which these changes took place. Are there any other changes you see here, and why?" Peter Elliott's hand shot up. "Yes, Peter?"

"The National Health, sir. My gran and granddad said it once cost ten shillings a week to stay in the hospital, and out of my granddad's wages of four pounds and seventeen shillings a week, they found it quite hard to pay."

Julia made the next move. "New medicines have made the most of changes to the NHS. This has made it a job to keep up with the changes and with the rising population. Unless new hospitals are built, the old, out-of-date hospitals will struggle to keep up."

Paul Gunn gave out a chuckle. "A bit like my hamster in its wheel—the faster it goes, the faster the wheel goes. Then the hamster stops with fatigue, and the wheel spins it around as though it is in a tumble dryer. It has no control."

Jan said, "My nanny Scott reckons the NHS is like a furnace. Whatever government is in; they have to stoke the furnace with more and more money."

Tim Pearson was annoyed with the comments about the NHS. "The National Health Service was set up to give every person good medical care at the point of need, not only if you could afford it. Although there was a cross-party acceptance that this country was in need of nationalised health care, it was Aneurin Bevan who eventually got it through Parliament. In 1948, the first NHS hospital opened in Manchester." He entered more detail on the smart board. "Right. Make some notes on where we are and try not to be too political. What are we trying to achieve here? In the Scottish referendum, the voting age was lowered to age 16. You may one day be given that opportunity. How would you know what to take into consideration when casting your vote? I as a teacher should not politically influence you in any way. You must evaluate what you see as best for you and the country. That's why this is a debate—so you can voice your opinion and to listen to others' opinions. The changes made could make a big difference in all our lives."

During the lunch break, Charlyyk felt the low vibes Sandra was giving out. She knew that Sandra's father was not well, and sat down beside Sandra to give her comfort.

Mrs Landon was keeping a close eye on Sandra. She made her way to where the girls were sitting and joined them.

Sandra started to talk about her father. "The trouble with chemotherapy is that it affects the patient's immune system, and the patient is prone to infection. My father was rushed to hospital last night in a very critical condition. I was all right this morning coming to school, but then I started to think about him, and it just became unbearable."

Mrs Landon asked if she should call for her mother. Sandra, with a worried look on her face, said, "Please don't. Mum is suffering inside, and I don't want to be another worry for her. She should be with my dad, helping him."

Charlyyk put an arm around her shoulders. "As your mother needs to give your dad strength at this moment, you also need someone to give you strength, I have a spare bed at home. If you ever think it would help, please don't hesitate to use it."

Mrs Landon phoned Sandra's mother. After, she spoke to Sandra. "Your mother is at the hospital and agreed that if you would like to stay with Charlyyk tonight, you could. She also said that your father is in a stable condition, but not out of danger. She intends to stay by his side."

Charlyyk phoned home. Margret answered. "They are all out at this moment, Charlyyk. I will relay your message to them."

At Bill Symonds' garage, Thomas received the call from Margret. Passing his phone to Helen, he left it to her to resolve the situation.

Bryn was sitting in a silver 2012 Citroen Picasso C3 MPV 1.4 VTi. "It's not what I like, Bill. But it's not for me."

Ted lifted the bonnet. "As you can see, it's spotless. I have cleared the service record with the Citroen service department—it is genuine."

Rachel had fallen in love with the car the moment she saw it. When she came back from the test drive, she had not changed her mind. Bryn saw that Rachel was set on this car. "OK, Bill, let's do the figures." Bryn headed for Bill's office.

Helen helped Thomas to sort out the road tax and insurance. "There. You have wheels."

When Bryn returned, he gave Thomas the documents to the car. "It's all yours, son."

"Thanks, Dad."

Thomas and Rachel waved as they drove off the forecourt. Bryn shook Bill's and Ted's hands and thanked them, then headed to the academy to pick up Charlyyk and Sandra.

At the school, Mrs Landon welcomed Bryn and Helen and told them what Sandra's mother had said. Helen was soon comforting Sandra. "Come, let's take you to your house and pick up a few things you will need."

When they arrived at Oakleaves, Charlyyk showed Sandra around the cottage. The tour ended in Charlyyk's bedroom. Helen put fresh linen on the bed. "Any likes or dislikes, Sandra?"

"May I have a hot water bottle? I hate a cold bed." Then with a sheepish look, she added, "May I also have some warm milk when I come to bed, please?"

Helen placed a hand on her shoulder. "Of course you can, Dinner will be ready in about twenty minutes." She smiled at Sandra. "Don't forget to phone your mother. She will be concerned, and will want to know that you are OK."

Charlyyk looked at Helen with great respect. She had seen the sweet side of Helen but sensed that Helen could be very strict if need be. It was evident in the efficient way she handled situations with cool, calm control. She did not fluster, nor did she shirk responsibility.

But what had Charlyyk most interested was Helen's understanding of the medical conditions Sandra had referred to when talking about her father. How had Helen gained this knowledge? Michel had talked to Charlyyk about Bryn and the infections that he had suffered upon his return. She had understood the implications and the threat of infection to him.

After dinner, in Charlyyk's bedroom, the two girls busied themselves with homework. Charlyyk encouraged Sandra to keep busy as a diversion from her troubles.

Rachel entered with a hot water bottle and warm milk. She stayed for a while, discussing their homework. Then she tucked them up in bed. Sandra's traumatic day had taken a lot out of her, and she was soon fast asleep.

CHAPTER 4

CHARLYYK'S HOUSE GUEST

On Friday morning when Sandra woke, Charlyyk's bed was empty. Sandra tossed the duvet to one side, slipped out of bed, and went to the window. It was dark outside, but she saw the fields, and the three runners heading for Parsons' farm.

She stayed at the window, looking out. The view was new to her. Sandra's bedroom window looked out onto more houses. The gardens were small where so many houses were built close together. She felt that if she spread her arms out, she could touch the house next door at the same time as her own. But at least she had a home to live in. Many families struggled to afford housing, renting tiny flats in the middle of town. She would not like to live there.

She thought of how lucky Charlyyk had become. But she realised that Charlyyk had suffered also. Sandra wondered how she would have coped with the constant threat of a beast wanting to tear her to bits. She shuddered at the thought.

Moving away from the window, she saw a folder lying on a side table. Written on the front of it was *Charlyyk's fears*. The writing was distinctively Charlyyk's. Picking the folder up, Sandra sat on the bed and began to read.

The writing at first was hard to read. It dated from the period when Charlyyk had first learned to write.

> *I am putting down in writing my fears so that I can appreciate what I have and accept it as normal. My biggest fear is to wake up and find it was all a dream, and I will have to find food and water again. My second fear is to lose Bryn, my saviour and my security. Gwen and Harold are my teachers, but most of all my comfort. They make me calm. To lose them would really upset my balance.*

Once she learned the crabbed script, Sandra went back to the start and read it over again. She saw the influences that had changed Charlyyk's perceptions of life. The folder held a jumble of writings. Little notes appeared in the margins—these were Charlyyk trying to understand herself. She did not write about other people, only about herself. Sandra closed up the folder when she had read its contents and replaced it as she had found it.

The sound of Charlyyk's voice took her away from her thoughts. Charlyyk came bounding into the room. "Hi! You are awake. Good morning. Do you need anything?"

Charlyyk stripped off her clothes and headed for the shower. Sandra was amused at the way Charlyyk's little tail flicked about. It did not wag, but now and again gave a little swish. Sandra followed her into the bathroom and sat on the toilet, watching Charlyyk shower. She saw Charlyyk's body was similar to her own, apart from aspects of her bone structure.

When Charlyyk stepped out from the shower, she grabbed a towel to dry herself. Sandra gazed at Charlyyk's female physiology. Her breasts were developing, and she had no pubic hair.

Charlyyk sensed Sandra's curiosity. "Do you find me different?"

Sandra gave an awkward smile. "I think you're fascinating, I was looking to see how different you are to me."

Charlyyk stopped drying herself. She led Sandra back into the bedroom. Charlyyk took Sandra's nightie off and then beckoned her to stand side by side in front of the long mirrors. "Well, what do you think?"

Sandra admired the comparison. "Apart from your height, facial features, hands, and feet, there's not a lot of difference."

Charlyyk laughed. "I'm almost human?"

Sandra laughed with her, and they gave each other a hug. "Come on," Charlyyk said. "Let's get ready for school."

At breakfast, they could not stop talking. Helen reminded Sandra to speak to her mother before the bus arrived. Sandra made the call right there and then.

Charlyyk looked on nervously, hoping for good news. Sandra's approach was calm: holding the phone like a delicate flower, the tip of her tongue just showing through her lips as she listened. A smile broke across her face. "Yes, Mum. That's great. Love, you too." She put the phone down, still smiling as tears streamed down her face. "Dad has pulled through. Mum sat there all night, holding his hand."

"That's great news, Sandra," Charlyyk said.

Helen was on hand with plenty of tissues.

When the bus arrived, Sarah and Mace stepped off. The hope for good news was written all over their faces. Mace picked up Sandra's bags as the girls ushered Sandra onto the bus.

Helen had phoned Mrs Landon and informed her that Sandra. She promised that she and Bryn would be on hand if there was any need. Mrs Landon waited at the school gate with Mrs Butler. They watched as the bus arrived.

The posse was in attendance. Julia could not wait for Sandra to get off the bus. She rushed to greet her friend. Mrs Landon nodded to Mrs Butler with a pleased look. "She is in good company, but let's keep an eye on her, just in case."

Bryn and Thomas made a few adjustments to the guest room for Margret. She had mentioned that a mark on the wall opposite the window was giving her cause for concern. "I'm sorry to bring this matter up, Rachel, but the shape of it looks similar to a skull. I have had a sleepless night over it."

Thomas felt a little guilty, and offered his help to ease his conscience. But his dad just said to him, "These are teething problems. Let's not make an issue out of them, but try to resolve them. We have to remember if she were not here, nor would you and Rachel be here. To me, it is well worth keeping Margret happy."

The smile on his dad's face eased Thomas's worries. The delivery of the new mattress would also alleviate his concerns about his mother-in-law.

At the back of the garage, Bryn found a tin of paint that had *Guest Room* written on it. There was sufficient paint to complete the task. With a small brush, he applied a strip of paint to test the colour. He joined Helen and the others for coffee in the lounge while the paint dried. The conversation was about Charlyyk and Sandra.

Rachel was talking as Bryn entered. "I must admit, comparing the Charlyyk I saw in Houston to the one I see now, she has changed dramatically. She is much more mature. But still, there remains a part of her that has not changed. The way she mothered Sandra was very touching. Then she herself wanted the loving touch of Helen. She seemed to like Helen's direction—or should I say trusted Helen's direction?"

Bryn sat down next to Helen. "Don't be fooled. Charlyyk has learned to survive the best way she can. She uses everything to keep her balance. Charlyyk has worked out that without us, she has nothing She bends, like a tall blade of grass, with the wind, so as not to break."

Thomas looked at his father quizzically. "Do you mean she's using us to gain her own advantage?"

Bryn smiled at his son. "Don't we all use each other to our own advantage?"

Margret looked at Bryn and pursed her lips. "You know this and allow her to use you?"

Helen left them and headed for Charlyyk's room. When she returned, she held the folder that Sandra had read that morning. Helen passed it to Thomas. Rachel moved closer to Thomas so she could also read it.

After a while, Rachel said, "I see what you mean. This is her way of understanding our way of living and moulding herself to it so she can live. She's a very talented girl."

Thomas passed the folder to Margret. She put her reading glasses on. Sitting back in the armchair, she began to read. Now and again, she stopped and went back a page or two. After a long while, she said with a lump in her throat, "Poor girl. It must have been a very worrying time for her. I can feel the anxiety in her writing. She is telling herself what she must do to earn your trust. But there are no nasty words about anyone, just discussion of how she must adapt if she is to survive." Margret removed her glasses and wiped her eyes with a tissue.

Thomas said, "Should we not put this back where she hides it?"

Helen glanced at him. "She does not hide anything. It is left out in the open. Charlyyk will talk to you openly about it. She feels that the more she knows about us, the fewer mistakes she will make."

Twenty minutes later, when Harold and Gwen arrived, Margret mentioned Charlyyk's folder. Harold said, "Charlyyk knew that Bryn needed help when he found himself stranded on a planet that was way beyond his knowledge. She smelled his uncertainty. She knew it was not fear, but a strong determination to find a way out of his predicament. This is the example she had taken to help her survive. When she learned to write, these were her scribbles, to keep herself in line with those who live on this planet. It's like the old saying: 'When in Rome, do like the Romans.' Charlyyk and I used to debate what she had written. Charlyyk would ask if I agreed with her understanding of the way we live. She needed to be sure she had not misinterpreted any of her findings."

During lunchtime, Mrs Landon had spoken with Sandra's mother. Now she sat with Sandra. "Your father is responding very well, but it still needs time. Charlyyk's parents have assured me that you may stay with them as long as you want to. They also said they would take you to the hospital to see your parents." Sandra thanked her for her care. Louise Landon gave her a gentle squeeze and a warm smile.

Bryn and Helen arrived at the school after lessons to pick the girls up. They waited patiently as the posse said their goodbyes. When Charlyyk and Sandra got into the car, Helen gave Sandra a carrier bag with a few items inside. "I've spoken to your mother. She needed some bits, which I've placed in the bag. We can go to the hospital now so you can see her."

SPENCER CARVIL

When Bryn had dropped Helen and Sandra at the hospital entrance, he drove to a parking space close at hand. Once he had parked properly, he turned to face Charlyyk. "How did it go at school today?"

Charlyyk climbed into the front seat next to him. "Sarah and Jan gathered the class together and organised us so Sandra always has someone to talk to. She did not mope about or get despondent. Mrs Landon spoke to her at lunchtime. The teachers did not bother her, though they made sure she got involved in the lessons. My classmates asked that I should just be myself. At first I did not understand. Mike explained that in moments like these, some people will overthink what is happening. That can easily lead to making thing worse. He is so nice when you get to know him."

Bryn gave her a smile. "You said he does not look after himself properly, and he smelt of yesterday's dinner!"

Charlyyk laughed. "I did, didn't I? But that's because he is always inside his own head, not outside it. He is thinking all the time, like daydreaming. It turns out he is trying to solve different problems." Then she laughed. "Mostly the ones he causes himself!"

Sandra, upon meeting her mother, ran into her arms and buried her head in her mother's breast. Her mother allowed her to let her emotion out before she said anything to her. Outside the ward, some bucket chairs were situated, and her mother took Sandra to them. Sandra sat on her mother's lap. Helen sat beside them as they discussed the condition of Sandra's father.

"He is frail but has responded well to the treatment. I will stay tonight with him. The doctor said that if he is OK by the morning, he should be able to come home on Sunday." This perked up Sandra. She and her mother left Helen sitting there and went to see Sandra's father.

When Bryn saw, them coming through the entrance, he started the car and cruised gently towards them. When he pulled up, Charlyyk hopped out of the vehicle and allowed Helen to sit up front with Bryn.

It was a frosty Saturday morning. It gave a silvery glow to the countryside, so that although it was dark, it was still easy to see where one was going. Thomas joined them on the morning jog. He was a regular jogger around New York's Central Park. He took the lead with his dad. As they passed the cow sheds, the familiar figures of James and his father Edward could be seen bringing out the cows that had been milked. James, seeing Thomas, shouted, "Come up for a coffee! Bring Rachel!" Thomas replied that he would.

Charlyyk told Helen about Sandra. Although Sandra had slept, she had tossed and turned all night. "I stroked her head and settled her for a little while. But eventually she went back to tossing and turning."

When they returned back to the cottage, Rachel had already started getting breakfast. Sandra was watching and talking to Rachel. Sandra looked happy.

While everyone ate breakfast, Sandra sat next to Helen and Rachel. "It's nice here. I love the atmosphere. It makes me feel warm inside—you know that cosy feeling you get when you are contented? It makes me feel like my cat Bonny after he has had his favourite meal. He curls up and purrs. That's how I'm feeling at this moment."

Rachel put an arm around her and gave her a gentle squeeze. "I know what you mean. I feel it when I come here. It feels … this is home."

Margret gave Rachel a frosty look. "Your apartment is so lovely—the modern furniture, the stylish paintings. You reckon it is not homely?"

Thomas could not allow Margret to dominate Rachel. "The apartment is for show. It is there for our clients. We will be changing it to bring up our family. Rachel will tell me where and how she thinks the changes should be made."

Rachel smiled. She often said to her friends that although Thomas resembled his mother, he had inherited his father's hidden strengths.

Helen, seeing Margret's hurt expression, decided to change the conversation. "What are your plans, Margret?"

Margret's face brightened up. "We have a delivery of paintings arriving in early January. We have yet to finalise Manchester and Liverpool, so I have to go there to confirm the arrangements we made over the phone. All the artists have confirmed the dates they can attend. Janet has asked to write an article, and we will take her up on her offer."

Helen turned her attention to Thomas. She was keen to take the friction out of the situation. "So when will I be able to see some of your work?"

He looked up at the picture hanging on the wall. "That's an early drawing of mine. My latest works have all been sold, but I promised Charlyyk I would give her lessons. I will do a couple more paintings then."

The sun was warm in shaded areas away from the cold breeze that persisted in blowing. Bryn was washing the Discovery. Helen sorted the dirty laundry with Rachel. The morning drifted by.

At twelve thirty, a text message came. Sandra could not contain herself. "Dad will be coming home. Mum is going home now to make things ready for him." The girls rushed to Helen to relay the news.

Helen had Sandra's mother's phone number just in case of an emergency. She dialled it. "Hi, Rebecca, it's Helen. Do you need any help?" They agreed that Sandra would stay till four, and then she could go home.

Charlyyk, watching how Helen handled the situation, arranged her thoughts in her mind. Would she need this way of handling situations as she grew older?

At four thirty they arrived at Sandra's house. The reunion between mother and daughter was very touching. Rebecca thanked them warmly for looking after Sandra. As Helen and Charlyyk drove off, they stood at their front door, still cuddling each other and waving their goodbyes.

CHAPTER 5

CHRISTMAS INVITE

The sun had just started to make an entrance to the day as the four runners returned to the cottage. Thomas asked Charlyyk if she would go with them to church that morning. She looked hesitant. "I know Auntie Gwen goes every Sunday, but Uncle Harold only sometimes."

Thomas put on a "please please me" face.

"I don't know" was her reply. She rushed off to shower.

Thomas looked up at his father, who was smiling at him. Bryn put his arm around his son's shoulders. "She just cannot see what other people think they see, like you and Gwen."

Thomas sank down into the nearest chair. "Well, at least I tried."

Rachel and Margret walked into the room. "What were you trying to do?"

Thomas shook his head. "I asked Charlyyk if she would go to church this morning."

Rachel sniggered. Her mother gave her a quizzical look. "Why are you sniggering?"

Rachel did not back down. "I spoke to Harold. He said she can't be brainwashed. She has been to church once. She informed him that nothing happened. A man with the dress on bored everyone and expected people to pay him."

Helen and Bryn quietly left the room, trying hard not to laugh. "Come, sweetheart. I need your personal attention in the shower," Bryn said as he gave her arse a slap.

"Oh, Sir Jasper, do not harm me!" Helen took hold of his hand and dragged him towards their bedroom.

At breakfast, Margret intended to raise the issue of church again with Charlyyk. Given what Rachel had said, she was puzzled to pick the right words to say. "How was the run this morning, Charlyyk?"

Charlyyk finished eating her muesli. "It was nice. It refreshes you for the day."

Margret could now open her gambit. "I go to church to refresh my inner self!"

Charlyyk did not respond. Helen and Bryn looked down, making sure that no one could see their silly smirks.

"Oh yes, the tranquillity it gives me is so rewarding," Margret continued.

"That must be nice for you." Charlyyk took a sip of water. "You must go with Auntie Gwen. She gets the same feeling you do. She will appreciate your company, as Uncle Harold does not always go to church."

Helen collected the dirty dishes and took them to the dishwasher. If she had not, she would not have been able to control herself.

"So would you like to come to church with us today?" Margret persisted.

Charlyyk made no attempt to fudge her. "No, but thank you for asking."

Margret was not someone who gave up easily. "I think it will please Gwen if you give it a try."

Charlyyk finished her water. "I have been to church. I found it so cold that it made me shiver. Whatever the effect it had on Auntie Gwen, I missed it. And looking at everyone afterwards, it seemed they missed it too."

Rachel had been watching Helen. Though she could only see her back, the tell-tale signs of the trembling of her body said Helen was either crying or laughing. Rachel accepted the latter.

Thomas, Rachel, and Margret left for church. Bryn, Helen, and Charlyyk left later for Carpenters' cottage. Harold was in the kitchen when they arrived, He was in fine form. Michel was in the chair which sat in the kitchen corner. Charlyyk kissed Harold, then jumped on Michel's lap. He liked the way she cuddled into him. "Hello, how are we?"

Charlyyk threw her head back. "I'm fine, Michel."

He put his arms right around her and gave her a squeeze. "The test we've been doing on your menstrual cycle has not shown anything different or anything to worry about, but we are still going ahead. Your occasional insomnia we can put down to you losing iron during your menstrual period, which you soon replaced. We will no doubt understand more about it when you have your next period."

Helen asked, "Could we give her something to counteract the loss of iron?"

"I don't like to give her chemicals unless I really have to." He paused. "We could do a menu test—work out a month's food according to one diet, then a second month according to another. I can compare their effects with blood samples."

Harold whisked the batter for Yorkshire puddings. "We should feed her on beef. That would put some mettle into her."

Charlyyk looked sternly at him. "Uncle Harold, you know I cannot eat red meat like beef. My stomach cannot digest it. Even turkey I find hard to digest."

The sound of Gwen's voice was Harold's cue to put the Yorkshires in the oven. Harold kept to his mother's way of putting the batter in the roasting tin with the beef cooking over it. He made onion gravy, which was always a favourite of Thomas's. Bryn and Helen had laid the table. Gwen showed Margret some of her magazines. Thomas and Rachel drifted into the kitchen, lured by the intoxicating aromas that Harold had conjured up.

"Uncle Harold, you haven't?" Thomas's eyes closed. His nose sniffed the memories of his youth—those wonderful days when Harold would reward him for achieving good marks in his exams with the gift of thick onion gravy poured onto a Yorkshire pudding.

Harold carved the roast beef. The first slices were for Gwen and Margret; they did not want pink meat. Charlyyk and Rachel ate fish pie. During dinner, Thomas recalled memories of other family coming together. He suddenly remembered that Helen had not been there. "I'm so sorry, Helen."

Helen just smiled. "Don't be. Those memories should never be forgotten. They should be remembered and retold over and over again. From what I have been told about Kitty, she was an exceptional woman and should always be remembered."

Gwen took Helen's hand in hers. "Thank you. You don't know how much we appreciate what you have just said."

Thomas agreed. "Not only does Charlyyk gives you her blessings, so do the rest of the family."

Michel raised his glass. "Here's to Helen: you are staying whether you like it or not!"

Helen buried her chin in her chest. "Oh yes, I like it. I like it a lot."

Charlyyk picked up Michel's glass, held it aloft, and said, "To my new mum, Helen." She took a sip. Her face screwed up, her eyes closed, and her body trembled. "*Yuck*! How can you drink that? It is horrible!" Charlyyk's first taste of red wine looked to be her last. It gave the rest of them something to laugh about.

Margret was seeing Charlyyk as a person. She realised that this alien was not what Margret had thought at first—a family pet—but someone who thought things through and showed feelings. Margret had started to think of Charlyyk as any other young girl.

Rachel touched her mother's hand. "You OK, Mum?"

Margret smiled at her daughter. "Yes, I'm all right. I now see what you have been telling me all this time about Charlyyk. It is true—she is just a little girl growing up."

Margret sighed. "She may look different, but she is no different to any other girl."

Gwen overheard this. "I was no different than you at first. But when you come to know Charlyyk as we do, you can't help but love her. What she has given Bryn has been remarkable. He was a lost soul after Kitty died. Yes, he had Catherine and Thomas, but no Kitty. Charlyyk has been his salvation. Just look at him."

Margret watched Bryn and Helen, who were lost in each other's company. "Without Charlyyk, they would never have met."

Charlyyk listened as they spoke about her. She was pleased to be able to judge each person's eyes for false feelings. Margret was Charlyyk's main concern. The remarks Thomas and Rachel were making to Margret were becoming more and more harsh. Thomas was home, and he was being influenced by its presence.

Harold asked, "What plans for Christmas have you, Michel?"

Michel responded, "Ah yes, have you not spoken to the Parsons? They want us all there for Christmas. I will let them talk to you first."

<hr>

Monday, with Charlyyk at school, Helen sorted out what was required to be ready for Christmas. She was so involved in what she was doing, she did not know she was being watched. "Well, what a busy bee we have here."

Helen spun around. Jane Parsons was standing there. "Jane, you frightened the life out of me." With her hand on her chest, Helen took a deep breath. "Coffee?"

"Why not?" They walked into the kitchen. Jane picked up the kettle and filled it with fresh water.

Soon they sat down with mugs of coffee, "This is nice," Helen said.

Jane smiled. "We are having a big do on Christmas Day for the farmworkers and their families We wondered if you all would like to come. We have come through a tight financial period, and we would not have been able to without the help of everyone. This is our big thank-you. We have cleared out the old barn and made an area to park."

"Can we help in any way?"

Jane paused. "You know, Kit and I were very close. When she died, a bit of me died with her. I must admit, at first I was wary of you. I thought that you would not live up to her. But I was wrong. In your own way, you are much like her—not in looks, but in the same type of character. I would love it if we could be friends."

Helen gave her squeeze. "I would love to have you as a friend. It would please me no end." After a moment, she said, "We found an old Bible belonging to the Allcott family, dated 1557." Helen delved into the cupboard and retrieved the Bible. Sitting next to Jane, Helen unwrapped it, turning the cover to open it. She placed it in front of Jane.

Jane's finger followed the text. "Wow, Edward is going to love this. This answers a lot of questions. May I take this to show him?"

"Of course you can. We have seen mentions of Parsons marrying Allcotts."

Jane turned a few more pages, then turned the book over to see the back page. "Oh my, this is getting better all the time."

Helen strained to see what Jane was reading. "Come on, put me out of my misery. What do you see?"

Jane pointed to writing in red ink. *"On this day, August the 10th, 1898, a boy is born out of wedlock to Alice Allcott. The father, Edward Parsons, may he rot in Hell."*

Helen looked at Jane. "Oh, such scandal."

"It would have been enough for pistols at dawn in those days," Jane said with a little twinkle in her eye. "There was a rumour in the family that the Allcotts ended up as head herdsmen after being the real owners of the farm. That was why Ned Parsons rebuilt this cottage for them. They were as good as family. The dates tally up. Arthur Allcott was Ned's elder half-brother!"

There were no more entries of births in the Bible, only the marriage of Arthur to Christine Bishop in 1913. She died in childbirth in 1915; the child was stillborn. That was end of the Allcott family.

Bryn was in a happy mood. A nippy little tune he had heard on the car radio was playing in his head, and he whistled it as he entered. "Hi, Jane. Hello, sweetheart." Then he saw the Bible laid out on the table. "Ah, you've seen it. What do you reckon, Jane?"

Jane said, "Some interesting bedtime reading, probably."

Bryn sat down with them. "We noticed the Parsons name cropping up now and again." Jane showed him the last page. "That should keep Edward interested."

Jane closed the Bible and wrapped it in its cloth. "I've come to invite you all to have Christmas Day with us."

He kissed her on the cheek. "Thank you, that sounds great. We accept wholeheartedly."

Jane left twenty minutes later, holding the Bible very close to her.

Bryn helped Helen to finish cleaning up while he discussed how they should do the Christmas shopping. "Rachel and your good self should take Charlyyk one day. Thomas and I will take her another day. I have been to the bank and drawn some money out for her to spend. I have also opened an account in her name and ordered a debit card for her."

Helen gave him a stern look. "But you give her pocket money. Is this a wise move?"

"I did the same for Catherine and Thomas when they were this age. I gave them an allowance to teach them how to handle their own finances."

Bryn took some of the boxes to be stored into the garage. Helen dumped the rubbish in the wheeled bins. Back in the kitchen, Bryn went on, "I give Charlyyk pocket money so she has something to spend at school, but I want to teach her how to manage buying her own clothes and entertainment on a set allowance."

The day had gone quicker than they expected, and Charlyyk returned home. Removing her coat, she soon was asking Helen about Christmas. "Everyone at school is talking about what they are getting their parents. I was at a loss to say anything. I did not know what was expected of me."

Helen guided her to the sofa and sat down with her. "Your father said today that you should go shopping with Rachel and me one day, and with him and Thomas another day. He has drawn out some money for you to spend." The look of excitement on Charlyyk's face and the hug she gave Helen left no doubt that this was what she wanted to hear.

When Bryn entered the lounge, she threw herself at him and kept kissing him.

"OK, enough!" He laughed. "I gather you heard about the shopping."

"Yes, and with my own money." She hugged him once more.

"I get the picture. You just want me for my money."

Helen came up from behind and tickled her. "You old gold-digger."

Charlyyk exclaimed amid shrieks of laughter, "Less of the old! If you haven't noticed, I'm quite young."

Helen tickled her some more. "OK, you young gold-digger."

Over orange juice and biscuits, Bryn explained his intentions. Charlyyk gave him a wide-eyed look. "So I can buy my own clothes?"

"Remember when Michel said that there was going to be a change in you? Well, this is a part of that change. Growing up means taking on responsibility for yourself. We should not think it is going to happen overnight. We must allow time for adjustments and learning what to do. The important thing is to get it right in the end."

Charlyyk now had a serious face on. "Thank you both for having trust in me. I promise not to let you down."

Thomas, Rachel, and Margret arrived later. They had been to an art gallery in London to finalise a shipment of paintings. Over dinner, Bryn explained his idea for shopping. Rachel was the first to say it was a great idea. She loved the thought of taking Charlyyk to the stores. "It will be like Houston all over again." Charlyyk's face was full of excitement.

At school the next day, Charlyyk talked excitedly to the posse about going Christmas shopping. "I've never had a lot of money before, but then I never needed it. I'm going to have an allowance to buy my own clothes and other things I need."

Sandra touched her bottom lip with one finger. "My parents could not afford that for me. Since my dad has been ill, money has been very tight."

Charlyyk looked very solemn. "I mustn't allow this to go to my head or take things for granted. I feel so awful."

Julia touched Charlyyk's hand. "Don't be silly. Sandra is not trying to put you down. Everyone here has a different family situation. I get an allowance and have to budget how I use it." Julia had never mentioned this to anyone before. "It's a modest contribution, but it makes me understand the cost of things. Dad would say that to obtain the price of those shoes, he would have to work hard for three hours. Sometimes the cost is not just about money."

Peter sighed. "I have to do a Saturday job if I want anything. I give my mum some of it. She doesn't ask, but I know she appreciates it."

At home in Oakleaves, Charlyyk talked with Helen, Rachel, and Margret about what the posse had discussed.

"Gwen has told me about the different circumstances that families find themselves in, and that I should not think everyone else lives the way we live. But I forgot. I felt so bad. It made me feel I had been gloating."

Margret asked her why she'd had that impression.

"Julia said her dad had to work three hours to get the money for her shoes. I have never seen Dad go out to work. I did not understand that value of money. I knew things cost money, but the value—that's different."

Margret said, "My father used to say that no matter what the inflation is, a day's money buys a pair of shoes and a week's money buys a suit."

"Peter told us that he works all day on Saturdays and gives his mother some of it. That made me feel guilty."

Helen gave a little laugh. "But sweetheart, you do give something. When you help with the housework, you are giving something back."

Charlyyk perked up. "Do I? Oh, yes, I see what you mean. Peter does not help indoors, so giving his mother some of his wages compensates her for his not doing housework."

Helen nodded. "Yes, sort of. He might still do a few things for his mother, though."

Charlyyk became quiet. She was going through what had been said in her mind. "Yes. As Harold, would say, when help is needed, we must roll up our sleeves and put our noses to the grindstone."

"That's right," Rachel said. "In the hour of need, one must do one's duty."

Charlyyk looked around, then bit her bottom lip. "This is telling me that it is not what I spend, but what I can save."

Margret smiled at her. "You could look at it differently. Ask yourself, 'Do I really need it?' If you do, then buy it."

Charlyyk beamed. "I could give myself many reasons to spend money."

Helen chuckled. "Saving is a virtue we should all adopt, but saving for the sake of saving and not acquiring the essentials of life is downright silly. Moderation is what's required."

"I was only kidding. I do understand. Dad has put his trust in me, and I should repay it by treating it with respect."

Helen gave her a hug and a kiss. "That's my girl."

On Wednesday, sitting down at the kitchen table for a mid-morning coffee, Margret remarked on the previous day's debate. Bryn listened intently. "I'm sure that in a year's time, you will see a different Charlyyk. She has changed so much just in these last three months."

"Taking into account the length of the intervals between the three times I have seen her, the changes have been immense," Thomas observed. "She has grown so much, especially since Houston. She has so matured, she's almost a different girl."

Rachel did not agree. "She is the same girl. What I have noticed is how she imitates the people around her whom she admires."

Helen said, "Oh, definitely. She certainly does that."

Margret seemed more relaxed talking about Charlyyk. "Is this how she handles adapting to living with us?"

Bryn said, "I think if I were in her shoes, I'd probably do the same."

"I'm with you on that," Margret replied. "She certainly is a remarkably adaptable young girl."

Thomas dunked a digestive biscuit in his coffee. "I just love her. She is so refreshing. You always get an honest reply from her."

"At Disney World, she was so excited," Rachel mused. "She knew she was making a fool of herself, but it did not embarrass her. She just accepted it and laughed at herself. It was so funny. I wish I were able to be like that, make a mistake and not be concerned about it. Not worry what others think of me."

Margret had not listened to Rachel. Her mind had been elsewhere. "The TV show you all did, I just loved it. I watched it with my neighbours, Bill and Brenda O'Brien. Bill thought Charlyyk was sweet. Brenda liked the brightly coloured clothes Charlyyk wore. Why were you not there, Helen?"

"Work, I'm afraid. Could not get away from it."

Margret had a quizzical look. "You're not working now, I see?"

"No. I've retired. It was what I was doing at that time—making way for my successor so I could spend my time here." She looked at Bryn with a soft, loving smile. "And I just love it. It's been like living in another world. I know how Charlyyk feels."

Rachel looked between them. She saw their chemistry. "Good for you. Enjoy every minute of it. You both deserve what you've got here. Thomas and I think the same—we can't wait for the wedding."

Margret chirped, "Well, you haven't, have you?"

The laughter took a little time to subdue. Margret took the longest time to settle once she realised what she had said. Helen's smirk did not hide how she felt. "That's the beauty of being the age we are, Margret. We can live the rest of our lives without any regrets. You could say we can go for it big time. We have nothing to lose."

<hr />

When Charlyyk arrived home, she spoke with Helen about Sandra. "She is struggling to cope with her father's illness. Her mother is working hard, trying to put a brave face on. But Sandra knows her mother is struggling too, and that is upsetting her."

Helen picked the phone up and dialled Sandra's mother. "Hello, Rebecca. It's Helen. How's it going?" The sigh Helen heard held more relief than stress. "Is there anything I can do for you?"

There was a slight pause. "I could do with a little company if you could spare me your time?"

Helen said she could, and they agreed they would see each other at ten the next morning.

On Thursday morning, Helen arrived at Sandra's house. She needed an umbrella for the drizzling rain. At the door, Rebecca was already waiting. Helen gave her some flowers; she had stopped at Marks and Spencer, which was close by. They kissed each other's cheeks and went inside.

Rebecca's husband Len was sitting in an armchair by the window. A duvet covered him. Helen placed a hand on his shoulder. "You are looking a lot better than when I last saw you, Len."

He said with a weak smile, "Thank you, I'm feeling much better."

"That's good to hear." Helen placed a box of mixed pastries on the table. "I thought these would go down nicely with tea or coffee."

Rebecca started to relax. Having someone different to talk to was like having a weight taken off her shoulders. Helen kept the conversation light and cheerful, trying to distract Rebecca's mind from the constant strain she found herself in. Helen left at one so that Len could rest.

At the door, Rebecca gave Helen a big hug. "You don't know how much I enjoyed your company. Thank you."

Helen promised they would do it again. "If you need me, just call."

CHAPTER 6

GETTING READY FOR CHRISTMAS

Friday was the last day of school. The Christmas break had come. The posse gave each other cards and keepsakes. The school tingled with expectation.

Peter had brought in a twig of mistletoe, and had eyes on one person to try it out on. Mace suspected that Peter's intention was to get a kiss off of Sandra, and he warned her. Most of the posse knew that Peter had a crush on Sandra, but as yet he had not made a move. Could today be the day?

Charlyyk had spoken to Julia about Peter before, telling her how she had sensed the vibes both he and Sandra gave out. But Julia had dismissed the idea. Sandra had never mentioned Peter in that way. Now Julia was not so sure, seeing Peter building his courage up. Mike was a little nonplussed about it. He could not understand why Peter was behaving the way he was.

As Sandra collected her things from her locker, Peter made his move. The posse had positioned themselves for the clearest view they could obtain without giving the game away. Peter made his way towards her, the mistletoe in his hand behind him. "Sandra, can I wish you a Merry Christmas?"

Sandra looked at him and smiled. "Of course you can."

He held the mistletoe above her head and leaned forward. She reached up and, cupping his face in her hands, kissed him on the lips. "Merry Christmas, Peter."

Julia's look of disbelief was aimed at Charlyyk. "How did you know?"

Charlyyk smiled. "When they got close to each other, their smells changed—not one of them, but both of them. My nose does not lie. It tells me everything."

The posse started clapping, then burst into song. "We wish you a Merry Christmas, and to seal it with a kiss." They converged, congratulating Peter and Sandra.

Julia still could not see how Charlyyk could have known about them. "Are there any other surprises that you know about?"

Charlyyk stepped back. "Yes, but I must not tell you."

"Why?"

Charlyyk took a good look at her. "It is much too early to reveal who likes whom. When the vibes grow strong enough, I might tell you."

Julia tugged on her arm. "Oh, come, Charlyyk. You can't leave me in suspense. It is not fair."

Charlyyk took her arm in hers. "You are not ready to know." She kissed Julia's cheek.

Sandra eyed her two friends and was soon by their side. "I've been waiting for Peter to make the first move. If he was big enough to do it, it meant it was the right time to accept him."

Julia looked at Sandra with annoyance at not being let in on Sandra's secret. "You're saying you knew all along how he felt, and you felt the same way, yet you did nothing to push it forward? Why not?"

Sandra smiled. "It was too soon. I did not want to unsettle him or make him feel too big and important. He has to come to me on my terms, but thinking they were his terms. If I had confided in you and you had let it slip out, that might have scuppered my control of the situation."

Sandra pulled Charlyyk closer. "I have so much to thank you for, Charlyyk. Your mum visited my mum and dad yesterday. My mum was so happy when I got home, and it picked my dad's spirit up no end. The smile on Dad's face when he heard Mum whistling as she cleared up after dinner—that was the best Christmas present I could ever have wished for."

Julia joined in the cuddle, and together they wished each other Merry Christmas. Julia casually asked what Charlyyk was doing up to Christmas. "Christmas shopping in London with the girls on Saturday. Monday, I shop with the boys in Winchester."

Julia gave Charlyyk a playful punch. "For someone who doesn't believe in God, you certainly like the trappings of Christmas."

Charlyyk did not need to time to think; she had fielded the same comment before. "You bet! We know that Jesus lived. The Bible tells us many confusing stories about his miracles, but the Romans wrote clearly in their records that Jesus lived. Are you not celebrating the birth of Jesus? That's not to say that praying to your so-called God will change a thing."

Charlyyk walked with Mace and Sarah to catch the bus home. They stopped to watch Peter walking arm in arm with Sandra. He held out his other arm for Julia to join them. That day, Peter grew extra inches. As they walked out of the school gates, Sandra turned and blew the others a kiss.

On the school bus, Sarah sat with Charlyyk. "Mace said you've known about Peter and Sandra for some time. We knew about Peter—that was so obvious—but Sandra never gave a hint she liked Peter."

"There are others who, at this moment, don't know their true feelings. And there are those who have feelings for someone, but the other person doesn't reciprocate. Time can change matters."

Sarah looked long at Charlyyk. "Well?"

Charlyyk pulled her closer. "Do you have feelings about someone?"

Sarah said, "I thought you could tell me?"

Charlyyk gave a chuckle. "What's this? Wishful thinking? No, it doesn't work like that. You get feelings for someone, and your body responds to those feeling by giving out signals. My nose then picks up on those signals. I can't pick up anything from you; you are safe."

Sarah looked disappointed. Charlyyk put her arms around her. "Look, it is early days. You have time on your side." Sarah's look did not change. "Look at it from my side. I've no chance. If I liked somebody, people would say it was wrong. Friends yes, relationships no."

Sarah's face changed then. She had not considered that situation. She had always looked at Charlyyk as one of the girls. She returned Charlyyk's hug. "Sorry. I was acting selfishly."

The colour of Charlyyk's eyes changed to a soft blue. "No, don't say that. You will meet someone. Your body will respond to them. At this moment, it has not happened, but that doesn't mean it won't happen. Take Mace. When he gets near Julia, his body responds, but Julia's doesn't. Eventually, though, hers may."

Sarah looked at Mace. "He likes Julia?"

Charlyyk chuckled. "His body is reacting, but his mind does not know it. If Julia's body responds to his vibes, his vibes will accelerate. Mace will sense those vibes, and that will tell him he likes Julia."

Sarah mused, "That makes sense, so if Julia's body doesn't respond, they won't want each other. He could meet someone else, and their vibes could respond to one another, and he would never think of Julia?" Charlyyk nodded. "Gotcha."

Charlyyk sensed Sarah's despondency. Her love for Mace was a sister's love. But Sarah could not distinguish between types of love and did not want to lose him to someone else.

When Charlyyk arrived home, she gave Helen an extra hug. "What was that for?" Helen asked.

"That was from Sandra for what you achieved with her mum and dad. She said her mum was whistling while she cleared up, and it made her dad so happy."

Helen returned the hug. "That makes me happy too. Find out if we can see them over the Christmas."

Charlyyk could not have been happier herself. "We could get something nice they could share."

At dinner, the discussion was about the shopping trip to London. "We will go by train, then Underground," said Helen.

Charlyyk looked at her hands.

Rachel laughed. "No, we have not to dig our way into London. The Underground is another train that travels underground."

Helen carried on. "I booked a table at La Brasserie for one thirty. You'll love it, Margret. Also, you will meet my parents. I've invited them to lunch."

Bryn put his arm around Charlyyk. "And its baked beans for me."

Charlyyk cuddled up to him. "I'll tell you what the meal tasted like when I get home—but hey, what's wrong with baked beans?"

Bryn tickled her. "Thanks for nothing." And tickled her some more.

Saturday, Christmas shopping day, Charlyyk could not have got dressed any quicker than she did. Rachel came to the rescue. "There's a saying, 'more haste less speed'. Now slow down. Deep breaths. Relax."

Charlyyk settled the febrile excitement that had built up inside her. With Rachel's help, she felt much better. By the time they were ready to leave, Charlyyk was looking resplendent. Helen had brought her a Burberry camel coat, which she wore over the Laura Ashley dress. She also wore cherry-red tights and brown leather court shoes. Helen had put foam padding inside them to fit Charlyyk's narrow feet. Not only did she look good, but more importantly, she felt good.

Bryn took many photos of them. He was proud of how they looked. Then he drove them to the station.

Standing openly on the platform was another first. Charlyyk found herself thinking about her home planet and all the terrors that came with it. *Now look at me.* She saw everyone was watching her. She nodded to them, acknowledging them with a warm smile,

Margret watched her. She could tell that the more Charlyyk met people, the more she looked in control.

The train pulled into the station. As the doors opened, Helen stopped Charlyyk from getting too near to the train. The surge of passengers getting off could have knocked her flying. As they boarded the train, the other passengers strained to see Charlyyk, trying to get photos of her. Margret felt the stress of it and wondered how Charlyyk coped with that constant pressure.

Helen had it all under control. Even when the train pulled into Paddington Station, although the platform was crowded, they seemed free to walk along. But Margret put her foot down when she saw the crowds heading for the Underground. "No, we don't. Taxi."

They walked outside. Many taxis were waiting outside. Soon they were heading for Regent Street's shops.

Charlyyk could not believe how many people there were in London, all rushing about with their own agendas. Then she was amazed when she saw what was waiting for her. The shops were decked out for Christmas. A mass of twinkling lights was strung across the streets and shop window displays. Charlyyk found herself looking at the decorations more than the items for sale. Other people found themselves looking at Charlyyk.

In the end, however, she was carrying many bags. Her amazement had not stopped her buying. Rachel watched Helen take control of Charlyyk. Helen's hand would gently put Charlyyk on course in the direction they were heading for. Helen kept the conversation going smoothly all the while. She knew that Charlyyk's mind could go floating on a sea of clouds, eyes and ears moving about in every direction like a ship's radar scanner. Charlyyk's mind was bamboozled by everything that was happening. She tried to make sure she had not missed a single thing.

At La Brasserie, the staff were soon fussing around her, making her comfortable. Helen's mother was already seated. When she saw Charlyyk, she was up, her arms stretched out. "Sweetheart, come here. Let me see you. My, you do look grand."

Edward was soon with them. "Come, Charlyyk, give this old man a big kiss."

Helen introduced Margret and Rachel to her parents. Elizabeth was quick to drop the "Lord" and "Lady" tags that Margret eagerly wanted to use. Elizabeth urged, "Please, it gives us credence in our work, but we are going to be family. Let's drop the pomp and ceremony. It gives me indigestion."

Charlyyk sat between Elizabeth and Edward. Their constant banter amused her.

The maître d' was soon at their beck and call. Waiters served the drinks, hurrying about to make sure their needs were met. A young Chinese waitress looked after Charlyyk and stood close behind her. She was under strict orders to be on hand at all times. Anna arrived late. Elizabeth had pre-ordered for her. Much was spoken about how Charlyyk liked the decorations, and how she was finding spending her own money. The lunch took an hour and a half. An extra half hour was required for saying goodbyes.

Helen had a few favourite stores. Margret wanted to go to Liberty's and Harrods. Rachel wanted to visit Harvey Nichols. By the time they had finished, poor Charlyyk was finished too. She flopped into a seat on the train, her legs spread and her arms dragged down to her sides. Helen and Rachel took lots of shots of her on their phones. Helen sent her photos to Bryn.

Rachel used an emptied bag as a fan. Margret magically pulled a water bottle from another bag and gave it to Charlyyk. "This might make you feel better."

"Thanks, Margret. You are a lifesaver."

"My dear girl, it was a pleasure."

Helen smiled a victory smile. The trip had been a roaring success. Margret had entered the human race at last.

Rachel grasped Helen's hand and gave it a squeeze. "Thanks for a fabulous day."

"Yes, a great day," Margret agreed. "My appreciation also."

Charlyyk raised a hand and flopped it down again. "I'm shattered."

Bryn met them at the station. Rachel tried hard to help Charlyyk, whose legs were sagging, but could not move her. Bryn scooped her up and carried her to the car. "I just want to go to bed," Charlyyk groaned.

Bryn was busy in the kitchen when Charlyyk arrived, dragging her feet. Her eyes were like slits, her mouth ajar, and her little purple tongue tried hard to moisten her lips. "Fluid. Any type of fluid."

Bryn filled a glass with water. With his arm, gently around her shoulders, he guided her to a seat. "Morning, sweetheart." He watched Charlyyk's shoulders sag and her feeble attempt to get the glass to her lips. "I do believe you should go back to bed."

She looked at him and gave a deep sigh. "Yes, you are right."

Bryn took the glass of water from her and helped her back to bed. He went back to the kitchen and collected a tea tray.

Helen looked at the tea, not at Bryn, as he entered the bedroom. "Oh, yes, there is a God."

He placed a teacup and saucer on the nightstand while Helen got herself sorted. He took the tray to Thomas and Rachel's room, tapping on their door. "Are you decent? I have some tea."

Thomas answered, "Come in!"

Bryn placed the tray on their side table. "I have not poured it. There's a cup there for Margret. It's pouring with rain outside, but the forecast said it will be dry later."

"Cheers, Dad."

Bryn made his way back to Helen. She pulled back the duvet so he could get into bed. "Charlyyk looked like a walking zombie," he said.

"London can be quite tiring for non-city folk."

The bedroom door opened and Charlyyk's head appeared. "Can I?"

Helen and Bryn opened their arms. Charlyyk soon nestled between them.

Helen would have given anything to have been allowed this when she was a little girl. She wished she could have been a real mother and given birth to her own little girl. Looking at Charlyyk, Helen thought, *you will do.* She gave Charlyyk a big hug.

Charlyyk returned the hug. "Helen, when can I call you Mum?"

This unexpected question brought tears welling up in Helen's eyes. For a moment, she found it hard to answer. "When you think I've deserved it." Helen's bottom lip quivered and a single tear trickled down her cheek. She pulled Charlyyk towards her and hugged her. She had been wanting this to happen. This sealed the affection among them, the making of a family.

Bryn grabbed some tissues and joined in with the bonding, wiping Helen's eyes. Charlyyk said, "I've got the best mum and dad in the world."

Breakfast was a lazy, unhurried affair, with much talk of London over many cups of tea. They shared photos of themselves in the shops, the restaurant, and the train. Helen cleared away and they moved to the lounge.

At eleven Janet and James arrived. They behaved like an old married couple, loving but controlled. Upon hearing of the exploits in London, Janet tickled Charlyyk. "You did that without me—how dare you?"

Rachel showed Janet some video of the trip that she had not shown the others. In it, Charlyyk turned around and around, amazed at the colourful illuminations. The look of wonderment on her face was a treat to watch.

"Rachel, this is fantastic!" Janet exclaimed. She said to James, "Work, hon. Keep yourself amused." And they trooped off to Bryn's study.

Janet soon had downloaded the video and the photos. With the help of a voice recorder, she took statements on how the shopping expedition had gone. She gave Charlyyk little nudges, their friendship blossoming. "Are you coming to the party at the farm on Christmas Day, Charlyyk?"

"Will there be a lot of people there?"

"About the same number as you have in your year in school. There will probably be some of your school friends there, and of course I will be there."

"That's true, and of course James as well."

When they returned to the lounge, Janet said, "Bryn, a men's magazine wants me to do an article on you. Could that present a problem for you?"

Helen's head shot up. "It could. I will get on it tomorrow."

Janet collected her possessions, including James, and with kisses all round, they left.

Margret gave Helen a bemused look. Rachel saw it. "Is there a problem, Mum?"

Margret hesitated. "Why would Helen sort that for Bryn?"

Helen responded, "I met Bryn through my capacity as the intelligence officer in charge of Charlyyk's protection. Although I have resigned from the position, my successor has not yet formally taken over. I'm still technically in charge."

"But everyone knows who Bryn is?"

Thomas sat next to his mother-in-law. "You asked me once why I did not talk about my father very much. The reason is that Dad's military commitments prevent him from talking about his involvement in the operations he has served on."

Margret still looked puzzled. "But Bryn doesn't look that type of person?"

"My father did some very dangerous things connected to our homeland security," Thomas said. "Those operations need to be kept secret, not known to the whole world, so any publication must be cleared first by those in a higher position."

At Carpenters' cottage for dinner, Margret asked Gwen about her brother. Gwen showed her the family photo album. "All the pictures in this album make me feel good. It has Bryn and Kit's wedding, the baby photos, the children growing up, and their wedding photos. These make me happy."

Then she went to the sideboard and collected a black-covered album. "This is my sad album. It contains photos of Bryn's battle injuries and his condition when he returned from the abduction. During the many trips, he did, I sat here shaking in fear, wondering how he would return or if he would return. I tried to give strength to Kit and the children, all the time fearing the worst. I feel for all the service families when their loved ones march off to war. I really do know what they are going through."

Harold took the black album from Margret. "Bryn has retired from that life. We won't need to get this out any more. Now we can relax and enjoy life."

Margret looked at Gwen's anguished face. She was still living those moments. Her shoulders trembled as she sought to control the feelings that the black album provoked. Margret understood why Harold did not want Gwen to open it again.

Bryn, Helen, and Thomas were in the kitchen, talking with Michel. Charlyyk sat on his knee. She loved the way they talked about so many things, each with their own take on the stories. They laughed at silly mistakes without getting angry or sulking, as she had seen students at school do.

She liked to observe those around her. How else could she survive living among them? And what fun they were— all so different from one another, yet their vulnerabilities were similar. They all thought about wanting or not wanting. They thought about being big or small, pretty or ugly, rich or poor, good or bad.

Charlyyk looked at herself. *I can't hide from who I am, even if I wear make-up. I'm different, and it is obvious. I must just make the best of it.*

She realised Michel was talking to her. "Charlyyk, I'm going to turn you into a guinea pig. I'm setting up a programme of diets, so we learn what is right for you. Auntie Gwen feels the stodgy food you've been eating may be bad for your long-term health. I'm asking the family to list your favourite foods and the order in which you eat them. I will look at their nutritional benefits, as we see them, and balance them up to suit your needs and taste.

This will mean more blood tests to assess how the diets are working."

"Not right on Christmas, please. That's when the nice food is put on show."

Thomas laughed out loud.

"It's OK for you, Thomas," Charlyyk retorted. "You will be able to eat all the goodies while I can only stand there in envy."

"Sorry for laughing, but what an image! You standing there, looking at the food, licking your lips, saliva running down your chin …"

Charlyyk's body went stiff. "Go on, rub it in."

Michel cuddled her. "I love you too much to do that to you, Charlyyk."

"So when?"

"Mid-January. Let's get Christmas over and then sort out a routine to suit you."

She liked what she ate and did not like the idea of changing. But Michel always looked after her. He would not suggest something unless it meant her best welfare was at stake. "Thank you."

Helen said, "Come, let's go to the table."

Charlyyk sat between Gwen and Helen at the table. A large dish of roast potatoes, cooked in duck's fat with sprigs of rosemary and sprinkles of sea salt, sat majestically right in front of her. Helen whispered in her ear, "You've got till mid-January, so enjoy."

"I have, haven't I?" Charlyyk's shoulders scrunched up, her fists clenched, and the wickedest look appeared on her face. A voice in her head said. *You bet I will.*

CHAPTER 7

WINCHESTER

On Monday morning, Charlyyk was feeling impatient. "Come on, Thomas. You are losing me shopping time."

Charlyyk was heading for Winchester. Bryn had promised Thomas that that was where they would do their Christmas shopping. As a boy, Thomas had loved the atmosphere of the antiquated cathedral city, especially at Christmastime, when it offered a German-style Christmas market. Thomas liked to sit in the café opposite the cathedral and imagine gentleman in tricorne hats and ladies in crinoline dresses walking those same cobbled streets in bygone days. Some of the current shops dated from that era, which added to the nostalgia of the world-famous Hampshire city.

Bryn gave Helen a nice cuddle and caressed her face with his hands as they waited for Rachel and Thomas by the car. Thomas no doubt was being given his instructions—or other things, as Bryn thought when he saw Thomas's red face appear. Charlyyk sniffed him and gave him a knowing look. This made Thomas feel even more awkward.

Charlyyk had set her budget for buying presents. If she was diligent, she might have money left to buy a new dress for the party. With this thought in her head, she was not keen on Thomas keeping her waiting.

Finally, however, Winchester loomed in front of them. She had not expected the enormous effect its presence would have on her. She knew the cathedral was a religious building, but had not expected it to be so gigantic compared to the little church in her village. Once again, her eyes could not take in all she was seeing. The cathedral tower rose to a height of over forty-five metres, and the building had the greatest overall length of any Gothic cathedral.

Bryn parked the car and they walked to the shops. "Well, Charlyyk, what do you say about this, then?"

She looked around and around at the decorations, the shop windows, and the displays. Then she saw it—as a magnet to metal, it was a girl to dress. Charlyyk was drawn to that shop window like a moth to lamplight.

Bryn took her hand. "Come, let's walk around and make notes. Then we will eat lunch and plan how to spend the afternoon."

Helen had been in touch with Toby. He was soon in contact with Thames House and the Ministry of Defence departmental offices. He promised to contact Helen as soon as he had an understanding of the matter of a possible publication about Bryn's life. "The ministry has been expecting this since Bryn introduced Charlyyk to the world. They have had many meetings to sort out what could be exposed. They will inform you."

Margret and Rachel went off to the town together, leaving Helen on her own. At one, Gwen and Harold arrived. They wanted Helen's advice on their choice of present for Margret. "We were not quite sure. She can run hot or cold at any time."

Helen agreed with them. "Sometimes, I do believe she has a dislike of men. Maybe she still hasn't got over her husband's infidelity, or just won't?"

They made cheese on toast with some baked beans and large mugs of tea. Then they sat at the kitchen table, talking.

At Thomas's favourite café, they ordered a light meal. Charlyyk ate a baguette with a creamy Brie cheese, salad, and cranberry sauce.

She had made her list and the order to buy the gifts in. If everything went to plan, that should leave her standing outside the dress shop with money in her purse to fulfil her dreams. But what was making her more pleased was that hardly anyone had taken much notice of her. The waitress in the café had said, "Yes, madam, what can I get you today?" When waitress had placed her plate in front of her, she'd said, "And the baguette is for Charlyyk." It was said simply, with no fuss, as though the waitress had known Charlyyk all of her life.

When they were ready to leave, Bryn said he wanted to go in one direction. Thomas and Charlyyk wanted to go in the opposite direction. "See you both at WH

Smith's," Bryn said. And off they went in their different directions. Charlyyk was arm in arm with Thomas. She was in heaven. She had never felt so in control of herself.

After they finished shopping for presents, she stood outside the boutique. "Well, are you or are you not?" Thomas enquired.

"Thomas, this is something you have to savour. You must not rush it. You must realise that this is the very first time I have bought a dress of my very own. This moment is special, and you are sharing it with me." She admired the dress from outside of the shop.

The door opened. The shop girl was standing there. "You will have to try it on. We have fitting rooms."

Charlyyk bounded into the shop and was soon being given the full treatment. Two girls fussed around her. They showed her many dresses they had in her size. She felt dizzy for choice, but kept going back to the original dress in the window. The girls pampered and fussed to make sure she was happy. Even the shop owner got needle and cotton to make a slight adjustment to the dress so that it would fit her slight frame. Charlyyk spun around. In her head, she was Elsa in *Frozen*. When the girls asked if she was happy, all she could do was nod her head. She was speechless.

Thomas took video of the whole thing and streamed it to Rachel as it was happening. Rachel had urged him to do just that. He had needed buttering up to comply, of course, but what man didn't?

Bryn had tired of waiting at WH Smith's and went in search of them. It wasn't hard to find them; he remembered the look on her face when they first arrived. When he walked into the shop, Charlyyk still had the dress on. She swirled around in it, showing it off. It had a light green, blue, and pink floral print, a tight bodice, three-quarter-length sleeves, and a knee-length full skirt. Bryn nodded his approval. The two shop girls went with Charlyyk into the fitting room to change. Bryn heard laughter.

One of the girls came back with the dress to be wrapped. When Charlyyk appeared, she seemed to have grown taller. Another big step had been taken. She felt important, like she was becoming her own woman, just as her dad had said she would.

Bryn did not expect the amount of love in the kiss she gave him, but he sure appreciated it. How proud she looked, leaving the shop and carrying her prized purchase. How proud he felt, seeing how she was handling her new life. But he knew that he was going to need Helen's help and guidance with Charlyyk all the same.

At Oakleaves, Margret and Rachel had returned. Rachel could not wait to show Helen and Gwen the video that Thomas had sent her. Gwen wanted to see it again, but her phone did not receive videos. "If I changed my phone, could you send it to me?"

Rachel gave Gwen a big hug. "Of course I will."

Helen loved it. "Just look at her face! If she tried to smile any more, her face would simply explode."

Harold melted to see this girl growing into a woman. A little waif of a thing two years ago had not known where she was and could not speak. Now she was turning people's heads, turning into a woman. The emotions inside him took over. He found he had to sit down.

Gwen sat down beside him. "Can you believe this is happening?" he said to her.

Gwen took hold of his hand. "It was always going to happen one day. She was bound to grow up. They never stay the same. Think of all the students we have nurtured over the years. They have grown, and now some of them have children of their own."

Helen watched these two help each other to grasp the reality of life. Charlyyk was not simply another student. It was like bringing a little ball of fluff home, be it a puppy or a kitten, and living with it constantly. No matter how it looked or what it became, it grew to be a big part of you. Charlyyk was no pet, though to many she might have appeared to be one. To Harold and Gwen, she was so much more.

Suddenly the door opened and Charlyyk stormed into the cottage. All heads turned towards her. Who would she run to first? She didn't run. She put a package on the table, dove inside of it, and gently took out a dress. Slipping her coat off, she undid the button on the dress she was wearing and dropped it to the floor.

Gwen was startled. "Charlyyk, a lady does not disrobe in front of everyone."

Charlyyk totally ignored her. Her new dress was soon hanging on her.

Rachel said, "It's lovely! The gentle colours and the style really suit you. It fits your complexion beautifully."

"Thank you. I fell in love the moment I saw it."

Charlyyk looked at Helen. Helen raised her hands, and Charlyyk rushed into them. Helen beamed with pride. Charlyyk buried her head in Helen's breast. For a few moments, they cuddled each other. "Do you like it, Mum?"

Helen could not hold back the tears. All she could do was to kiss Charlyyk on the top of her head. "I love it, sweetheart, and you too."

Gwen was not envious but pleased. She had been hoping that Charlyyk and Helen would bond as a mother and daughter. She waited for them to ease the emotions down. When she thought, the time was right, she intended to say something.

Charlyyk turned towards her. "Auntie Gwen." No further words were needed. The love oozed from them both. Charlyyk sat on Gwen's lap. Harold leaned over and joined in the embrace.

Margret felt out of the equation. Helen sidled up to her and placed her arm on hers. "Give it a little time. You have only been here a couple of days. Rachel has known Charlyyk for some time. I was the outsider once. You will see—she will pull you in, but only if you want to go. Once you show her you want to, she will do the rest."

<hr />

After the morning run and breakfast, Charlyyk locked herself away in her room. After an hour, she made a phone call. Twenty minutes later, Sarah was there with a large carrier bag. She walked straight in. "Hi, everyone. The cavalry is here." She disappeared to Charlyyk's room.

Within the hour, the music was loud and the singing was melodious—or maybe more like a meltdown, but they were enjoying themselves. Everyone was relieved when Sarah went home. Across Charlyyk's bedroom were the most decorative parcels you could imagine.

Rachel could not help but stick her head into Charlyyk's bedroom. "Wow. That was not the cavalry—that was a fairy godmother."

Charlyyk could not hide from the reality that parcel wrapping was not her thing. "I tried, but it did not happen, so I phoned Sarah. I showed her my attempts on my phone, and she said, 'Hold on, tiger. I'll be there in a tick.' She is so … so vibrant."

Rachel smiled. "And loud." Rachel sat on the bed. "Have you anything to do this afternoon?"

"Yes. Helen is taking me to Sandra's. We have bought them a hamper. Why don't you come?"

When they arrived at Sandra's, the Fortnum and Mason hamper that Helen and Charlyyk had brought was most welcome. "We were going to buy you flowers," said Helen. "But we thought that Christmas was for spreading good cheer, and not everyone enjoys flower. Each of you will certainly find something in the hamper to brighten your Christmas."

Rebecca looked a little wistful. "I could not afford to buy you anything in return."

Charlyyk said, "But you already have. You have given us the trust of your friendship, and that's worth more than money can buy. So please accept this with our thanks."

Sandra could not help but give Charlyyk a hug. "We as a family accept. This is a pleasant surprise that is most appreciated. Even Dad will find something to like from that Aladdin's box. Thank you. Thank you very much."

Helen gave them hugs and wished them a Merry Christmas. "After you get on your feet, we must have a get-together and celebrate your husband's recovery."

When the three returned to Oakleaves, the cottage felt lovely and warm. A flickering log fire was burning in the grate. Gwen and Margret were looking at some of Thomas's old sketches. He had done them as a lad, depicting the family as he and his sister had grown—the different styles of clothes, and best of all, the hairstyles. There was a rough drawing of Bryn after a tour in an African jungle conflict, his hair long. Margret commented, "All he needed was a bandanna tied around his forehead, and he would have made a fine Rambo."

Rachel saw how Thomas had honed his early drawing skills and was soon asking questions. Thomas could not keep out of the debate that was directed at him. "Man, before he could talk, used drawings to teach his children what to hunt. The more you draw, the better you can express yourself. Charcoal, the earliest writing tool, rubbed off easily, so man learned to use water and then egg white to mix with the charcoal and make it more permanent. That was discovered in some of the early cave drawings—the start of art as prehistoric man knew it."

Charlyyk sat between Bryn and Harold. One of her ears had turned towards Gwen and the other was directed at Thomas. Harold gave her a gentle nudge. "You are earwigging, Charlyyk!"

Charlyyk's mouth dropped open. "Who, me?"

Harold gave Charlyyk a stern look. "Yes, you, and it's rude."

Her head bent, but her eyes looked up. "How am I to learn if I don't keep my eyes and ears open?"

Harold's look was still stern. "Then join in the discussion. That way you are not being rude."

Helen brandished the local paper. "Anyone interested in going to midnight Mass at the cathedral?"

Margret's head shot up. "That sounds good, Helen. I would love to go." Gwen and Rachel nodded in concurrence. Margret asked, "How about you, Charlyyk? Would you come and give me moral support?"

Charlyyk looked concerned. "Why, Margret? Does a bigger god lurk there?"

Gwen thought. *That's how Charlyyk would see it: small church, little god; big church, big god. If the little god concerns her, what might a big god do?* Aloud, she said, "No, Charlyyk. Same God, just more singing."

Harold touched Charlyyk's hand. "Give Margret a chance. She wants to make friends but doesn't know how."

Bryn had been silent but was listening to what was being said. "You don't have to, but it would be a nice gesture."

His quiet, controlled voice and gentle manner softened her. "OK. I will go with you, Margret."

Margret smiled at her. "Would you wear your new dress? You looked so lovely in it earlier."

A smile shot across Charlyyk's face upon the realisation that she had a reason to wear her new dress. "Margret, that gives me an excellent reason why I should go."

Gwen, Helen, and Rachel started to prepare dinner. Charlyyk could not resist the temptation to join them. She loved the banter among the women as they were cooking. Margret noticed how Charlyyk joined in with the chores, always willing. The effort she gave was full-on; she never held back.

Margret remained in the lounge with the men. She asked more about Charlyyk. Harold explained the rudiments of their first encounters and her efforts to adapt to human ways. "It was never going to be easy, even for us, let alone her. But as Bryn recovered from his injuries, Gwen and I took over her upbringing. We had retired from teaching, as we did not like the direction the education system was heading. It meant we could put our whole effort into bringing her up, trying to find a system she could understand and follow. Between us, it started to flow. She had to make changes to adapt. That girl gave us 100 per cent effort; we could only try and return it. The nightmares she had took some getting over. She was just a slip of a girl. Now we see her growing into a lady. It makes us want to cry—that is how proud we are of her."

Bryn sat in a semi-prone position that made him comfortable. "What happened on that planet frightened me. What it did to her, I don't think anyone could fathom. Without her help, I would have surely died that night from loss of blood and freezing cold. I love that girl so much. She is as much to me as Catherine and Thomas are."

Margret now understood Charlyyk's position in the family circle. She remembered Thomas saying, "That girl is Dad's saviour."

Harold smiled. "Wait until you hear her singing. That is something else."

Margret thought back to the morning, when Sarah had been there. "Was that Charlyyk this morning?"

Bryn laughed. "Oh, yes. Did you like it?"

Margret's hand went to her mouth.

Harold nudged her. "You will be all right tonight. She will be more worried about Gwen's God appearing than trying to sing."

Margret let out a loud laugh. She imagined Charlyyk peering around the cathedral, looking for anything resembling a god.

When dinner was ready, Margret sat opposite Charlyyk. "How was your friend today?"

Charlyyk gave Margret her serious look. She felt for Sandra at this time of concern. Sandra had said that, although her father's improvement was encouraging, it didn't mean he was out of the woods.

Rachel explained to her mother about the hamper. "It was a lovely gesture for the whole family. Each one could find something to enjoy."

"I wanted to buy some flowers," Charlyyk said. "Helen suggested the hamper when we were on the train going to London. When we went to Fortnum and Mason's for mid-afternoon tea, we selected what would be in it, and had delivered here for today."

Helen smiled and nodded her approval. "I advised Charlyyk to give them something that was useful and would cheer them all up. After many suggestions, this proved the best idea. The input Charlyyk put into it led to the final result."

Gwen winked at Charlyyk. "I would have loved to have gone with you, but I hate London. The pollution in the air and the constant noise are not for me."

The ride to Winchester Cathedral took two cars. They managed to find parking places in Colebrook Street, then joined the congregation in the cathedral.

Charlyyk had not prepared herself for the interior of the massive structure. It had looked huge from the outside, but inside it seemed overwhelming. She was still uncertain what was going to happen. Using Bryn and Helen as shields, she felt protected. As she sat down, pushing herself closer to Bryn and pulling Helen closer to her, she was ready for anything to happen.

The service started with singing. It was so different than the church in the village. The service flowed at a gentle pace, and Charlyyk settled into the relaxed rhythm. She did not look worried at what could happen but found herself more interested in the cathedral itself. Her thoughts started to drift. She thought of the holes in the ground she had once lived in. Her thoughts had revolved around what she would find to eat during the next light period, and what could be waiting for her when she left the tunnel. A cold shiver shook her. Taking a tight grip on Bryn's arm, she buried her head against him.

Helen, seeing her struggling, put her arm around her. "We are here, sweetheart. You are not alone." When the service was over, Charlyyk settled down and was more herself.

As they were leaving their seats, an elderly couple, came to them. The woman held out her hand to Charlyyk. "May we wish you a Merry Christmas? It gives us so much pleasure to see you have joined us tonight. It must be bizarre for you, but the fact you have made such a big effort to be here warms our hearts. May God look over you and protect you from harm."

Charlyyk responded, "Thank you for your kind words. My new family and I return your compliments and wish you and your family a very Merry Christmas."

Sandra and Julia had emphasised the importance of returning compliments. Julia had said, "Saying the wrong thing leads to many problems for celebrities. The press and Twitters love to make more of it than it usually deserves."

A small group of worshippers had lingered outside the cathedral just to get an extra glimpse of Charlyyk. She acknowledged them, pausing long enough to allow them to take photos of her.

Margret walked with Gwen. "Charlyyk certainly knows how to handle the situation."

"We did not teach her how to behave, because we did not know what would be required. It seems she has grown into it."

They collected the cars. Margret went in Gwen's car and continued asking about Charlyyk. "How did she adapt to school life?"

"Like a duck to water."

Harold said with a smug look, "She had two years of education from us. It was like moving on to the next year for her."

Margret saw that a gradual progression had allowed Charlyyk to adjust in stages. "You make it sound like it was a walk in the park. Hearing the whole story, I can only marvel at what you have achieved with her."

Gwen quickly responded, "We were only allowed to achieve what we did because Charlyyk wanted that for herself."

Harold added, "You can lead a horse to water, but you can't make it drink."

CHAPTER 8

CHRISTMAS DAY

Bryn and Charlyyk were the only ones who ventured out to run on Christmas morning. It was dark. Only the gradual rise of red looming up in the east indicated it was morning. Side by side they strode. As they reached the top of Bishops Lane and looked over the surrounding countryside, the sun had risen just enough to anoint the tops of the trees with a golden crown of glory.

Charlyyk held her head up high, her eyes closed, feeling the sun on her face. It gave little warmth, but still it felt lovely. Janet had asked them to take as many pictures as they could whenever opportunities arose. Bryn put the camera into burst mode and just clicked. The trees still held the remnants of autumn, and a drifting wisp of mist among them looked magical.

The women were getting breakfast and singing Christmas carols when Bryn and Charlyyk returned to the cottage. That special Christmas morning feeling radiated among them. Helen grabbed Charlyyk and smothered her with kisses. "Our very first Christmas, Charlyyk! Merry Christmas."

Charlyyk responded, "With many more to come."

Rachel, Thomas, and Margret joined in the well-wishing. Bryn also received many kisses. After the runners took a quick shower and got dressed, they were at breakfast. Margret had made waffles smothered with maple syrup, and Charlyyk could not get enough of them. Helen had to stop her. "You will not have room for Christmas dinner."

After clearing the table, Helen and Bryn handed out their present to Charlyyk. The little parcel was lovingly wrapped. For a moment, Charlyyk did not want to harm it. She gently used her long fingers to unpick it, removing each piece carefully to reveal a small leather-bound case. A gold wristwatch sparkled within. Helen had especially had it made to fit Charlyyk's wrist. Bryn helped her to put it on. The kisses she smothered them in told them she loved it. She shot off to collect her presents to give them all.

Helen and Bryn opened a silver picture frame, embossed with flowers. "It's for your wedding photo," Charlyyk explained. The look of pleasure on her face told them how she felt about them getting married.

Rachel gave Charlyyk her and Thomas's present. The beautiful wrapping and ribbons excited Charlyyk. She did not know where to start to unwrap it. Finally, with a flourish, she pulled the ribbon. Lifting the lid of the box, she discovered soft silk lingerie. She let it slide through her fingers, then held it gently to her face. She thanked Rachel with hugs and kisses, then smothered Thomas equally.

Margret waited till she had settled before she gave Charlyyk her present. When opened, it revealed a rose-pink, leather-bound diary with a clasp that could be locked. Down the spine, a pen nestled, ready to be used at any time. Charlyyk held it in her hands gently. "Thank you, Margret. It's so me. I love it." She carefully placed her arms around Margret's neck and kissed her sweetly.

Margret responded by putting her arms around Charlyyk's waist. "My dear child, getting to know you, the real you, is a pleasure. You are many surprises all wrapped up in one big, beautiful person. Merry Christmas."

After the giving of presents, Helen set up the computer for the video link to Auckland. The Leany family were ready. Little Amy waved the doll that Charlyyk had sent her for Christmas. Lots of laughing and gaiety were shown all around.

Then Catherine held up a present. "Dad, can you give this to my sister?" Bryn leaned forward. Through a well-rehearsed sleight of hand, it looked as though he had pulled it out of the screen. An identical present was in his hands. Even Margret was taken in by the trick. Bryn turned and offered the gift to Charlyyk, whose mouth was gaping.

Catherine and Brent watched intently as Charlyyk opened it. A new set of silk bed sheets and pillowcases were inside. "Sweet Christmas dreams, little sister." Catherine and Brent blew her kisses, and Charlyyk returned them. The feel of silk was Charlyyk's most treasured luxury. She could not explain why it felt so right to her.

The drive to Parsons' farm for dinner did not take long. Harold and Gwen greeted them alongside Janet and James. Inside the old timbered barn were two long rows of tables decked out with Christmas fare. A giant Christmas tree stood proudly at one side of the entrance. Decorations adorned the interior.

Edward and Jane Parsons were overseeing the arrangements. The atmosphere was chaotic, as many of the farm employees and their families were enjoying the get-together. A group of musicians were tuning their instruments, and catering staff were setting out the tables. Some of the farm children went to Charlyyk's school and were soon surrounding her, wishing her Merry Christmas.

Janet and James organised games for the younger ones and soon had Thomas and Rachel roped in. More employees arrived. Margret looked on with amazement at such an enormous undertaking. Bryn and Helen lent a hand with the proceedings. Harold and Gwen talked to some of the older children and their parents. Comfortable chairs were laid on for some the elderly people. A form of order was gradually being reached, considering how many were there.

The sound of sleigh bells outside were heard. The children flocked to the barn's entrance to welcome Father Christmas. A horse-drawn carriage appeared, and a sizeable, jolly man with an authentic white beard gave a guttural "Ho, ho, ho!" The children ran around him in glee. He gave out presents all around and spent much time with the younger children.

By the time he left, guests were starting to sit down for the meal. Centre tables had been set up, where there was a choice of meats for carving. Vegetarians were also catered for. Barrels of real ale and bottles of red and white wines were situated for easy access. After a big thank-you from the Parsons family, the feasting began.

An area was cleared after dinner, and entertainment was laid on. Buffet tables were set out later, and barn dancing was the order of the evening. By ten that night, Bryn had an exhausted Charlyyk cuddled up on his lap. She had joined in with everything. The younger children followed her around as if she were the Pied Piper.

Janet thought this was a good time to ask Charlyyk about her recollection of previous Christmases. "At my first Christmas, we had just finished being in quarantine. There was a living Christmas tree from a previous year that Thomas had planted in the garden. Bryn decorated it while Gwen and Harold decked out the lounge. There were no presents. The games we played were silly but much fun.

"When the next year came around, I had a more robust idea what Christmas was about. I contributed much more towards it, giving it all my enthusiasm. I learned the meaning of being a party girl."

Janet was careful with the next question she asked, knowing Charlyyk's view of religion. "So you know what Christmas represents?"

"The followers of Jesus Christ celebrating his birth." Charlyyk too was being careful. The times she had upset Gwen were still vivid in her mind. "The banqueting has more to do with the approach of winter. Food that would soon degrade needed to be consumed and not wasted."

Their morning run on Boxing Day was meant to clear the previous day's excesses from their bodies and the cobwebs from their minds. Their pace was a steady jog, allowing them the chance to talk.

Thomas, Rachel, and Margret headed for the Forest of Dean to catch up with an old college chum of Thomas's. Thomas had promised to visit next time he was in England. They would return on Wednesday.

A phone call from Helen's father gave her a chance to set a date to see her parents over the Christmas period. "Yes, we would love to see you on Monday. It will be just us three. Love, you all. See you Monday. Bye."

Charlyyk at the same time was speaking to Sandra, who informed her that Julia was spending the day with her. She loved the hamper idea, saying what a great gift it was. Her father had perked up, and the doctor was pleased with his progress. Her mother had managed to relax, and she was looking a lot better for it. This made Charlyyk happy. She could not wait to tell Helen the excellent news.

Helen and Charlyyk spent most of the day together. They talked, looked at photos, and just ambled through the day. They loved being together and talking about girl things. Charlyyk was not the only one adjusting to a new way of life—so was Helen.

Bryn spent the day catching up on paperwork. He went through some issues that Janet had touched on that needed answers. A bottle of single malt whisky helped him get into the right mood for it.

Three of them enjoyed a brisk jog on Saturday morning. Their chit-chat made the run seem quicker than usual. Over breakfast, a shopping trip was discussed. Bryn suggested Southampton for a change of scenery. Any new destination suited Charlyyk. She had previously said to Helen that on her home planet, they strictly kept close to places they knew were safe. All she got to know about her world were the confines where they lived.

Now with a purse full of Christmas gift vouchers and money people had given her, Charlyyk was keen for some retail therapy. One of the girls she had met at Christmas dinner had shown her skinny jeans that she had been given for Christmas. These were the top of Charlyyk's list of must-buys.

The drive to Southampton was on congested roads. Many other people had the same intentions as themselves. Finding a parking place was frustrating. Charlyyk was jostled on the streets for the first time and did not find it pleasant. Helen became more and more concerned. Bryn agreed to call it a day and return home. But Helen still needed a couple of things. They called into a Tesco supermarket to pick up some essentials.

In the same shopping centre, Charlyyk saw the store where the girl had said the jeans could be purchased. She dragged Helen into the store. She was determined to salvage at least something from the day. Helen and Bryn sat back and let Charlyyk fend for herself. She left the store a happy girl, with many items of clothing she had purchased for herself.

Home at Oakleaves, she immediately tried the garments on again. She matched them with her other clothes, explaining to Helen her reasoning behind each purchase. Most reasons had to do with how the clothes would change her appearance and lift her mood. "I sometimes feel down on myself and need to lift myself up. I know that really, I should not be here. I should be with the group, helping them to survive. Sometimes the guilt of it makes me sad."

Helen placed her arms around her. "Sweetheart, if you had not come here, you would have died on that terrible planet."

Charlyyk wrapped her arms around Helen and squeezed her tight.

"And I would not have met you and your dad, now would I?"

Charlyyk looked up into Helen's face. Her wistful expression made Helen kiss her. "We have to thank each other for the position we find ourselves in," Charlyyk said. "Without one, there would be no other."

Helen gave her an extra hug. "Without your dad, where would either of us be?"

Charlyyk's morale had lifted. "Not here, definitely. But I still wake up in the night, worried that it is all a dream. I have to tell myself that if I were not living through it, I would not have known about this sort of life, so it cannot be a dream. But it still feels too good to be true."

Helen nodded. "What does that make us?"

Charlyyk's eyes sparkled. "The lucky girls."

Helen gave her a hug and big kiss. "Here's to the lucky girls. How about a takeaway?"

"You bet. Michel hasn't set my new diet as yet, so I'm free to indulge in any fancy I like."

Bryn found them discussing a menu that was laid out in front of them. "Don't forget my spring rolls and dumplings. What were you plotting in your room?" He dug his finger into Charlyyk's ribs.

With a squeal, she turned and wrapped her arms around his neck. "How we were going to get you to pay for the meal, Dad?"

Bryn gave her another dig. "So you *are* a little gold-digger!"

"You bet."

On Sunday at Carpenters' cottage, Charlyyk explained to Gwen the events of Saturday. "It was so crowded! I was being pushed around like a rag doll. But it had a plus to it—we stopped at a retail centre, and the store that Charlotte's jeans had come from was there."

Gwen had admired what Charlyyk was wearing: grey skinny jeans, black ankle boots with pointed toes and three-inch heels, a white long-sleeved blouse, and a black cashmere jumper with a deep V-neck. Her rose-gold hair matched her new gold wristwatch, which just showed under the cuff of the blouse. The outfit was simple but stylish. Helen was as proud as punch. She admired the way Charlyyk was associating with Gwen. The little girl was definitely growing up.

Michel teased Charlyyk during dinner. He had finalised diet sheets for her, but had not as yet shown them to her. He hinted but would not confirm. "You are rotten!" Charlyyk exclaimed. "Don't torment me. Otherwise I will ignore you."

After dinner, Harold prompted Gwen, "Shall we?"

Gwen walked to the sideboard and collected an ornamental case, sitting back with Charlyyk. She opened the case. "This necklace belonged to my grandmother." She allowed the necklace to fall between her fingers. It was a beautiful gold pendant on a square chain. It sparkled as the light hit it. "It is made from the same gold the Queen's wedding ring is made from, mined in the same gold mine in Wales." The pendant was oval in shape and depicted a mother and child.

Charlyyk reached for it and let it dangle between her fingers. "It's lovely, Auntie Gwen."

Gwen placed it around Charlyyk's neck. "I spoke with Catherine, and she wanted you to share our family history, both you and Helen." Gwen's hand delved back into the case and removed a little leather pouch. Opening it, she took out a wide, plain gold wedding ring. "This was also my grandmother's," she said as she passed it to Helen.

The ring slipped onto her finger. Helen showed Bryn how it looked. "It fits you well and looks very elegant. Are you sure, Gwen?"

Gwen retrieved one more item—an old, tattered photo. "This was my granny, Gwyneth, on her wedding day. I am named after her." The resemblance was noticeable. The pendant could be seen hanging around the neck of the young bride. "She was just 16 when she married my grandfather."

Gwen picked up some papers. "These papers are the history of her family. She ended up being an orphan at the age of 12. Her ageing aunt looked after her till the aunt died. My grandfather married her to stop her from going to the poorhouse or the convent." The handwriting on the papers had faded a bit but could still be read. "They were together sixty-five wonderful years."

Bryn said, "She was pretty to the day she died. Granddad doted on her; she only had to smile at him and he would melt."

Charlyyk looked at Bryn quizzically. "He would melt?"

Harold laughed. "Not like that. He would give in to her, do as she bade him."

Charlyyk thought for a moment. "Yeah. Julia said she has her father wrapped around her finger. She only has to say 'Daddy ...' and he gives in to her." She glanced down, then flashed her eyes towards Bryn. "Daddy ..." she said.

Michel lay back in his chair. "Careful, Bryn, she's learning fast."

Helen slipped the ring off her finger and handed it back to Gwen. "It is a lovely gesture, Gwen, and I would love for Bryn to put it back on my finger when that day arrives."

Charlyyk looked at Gwen, her eyes full of doubt.

"The pendant is for you to keep, Charlyyk."

Charlyyk smiled as she fingered the necklace.

Michel touched her on the shoulder. "Now you are worth knocking off with all that wealth on you."

"Don't scare her, Michel," Helen chided.

Charlyyk said, "I'm not going to wear the necklace to school."

The drive to London fascinated Charlyyk. She gazed with wonder at the crowded streets. There were so many cars and buildings, let alone people. Outside Helen's parents' residence, Anna was there to park their car. Edward welcomed them onto the property. "How was the drive up?"

Bryn cocked his head to one side. "Fair till we hit London."

Elizabeth had made a beeline to Charlyyk and Helen. "Hello, my girls, at last." She gave them both a hug. "Come, let's get a drink."

Sitting in the kitchen, Helen was surprised her mother knew where things were kept, let alone how to boil a kettle. Anna strolled in and within a few seconds was in charge. She started up a conversation with Charlyyk. "How was Christmas?"

Helen and her mother left them to talk and went to the drawing room to meet up with Edward and Bryn. When Anna carried in the tea things, Charlyyk was helping her.

Over tea, Anna recounted her version of Charlyyk's visit to Winchester Cathedral for midnight Mass. "Charlyyk was concerned that, because it was a cathedral, it might contain a bigger god."

Edward laughed. Elizabeth was not happy with him. "No, Ed. It was a serious worry for the poor dear, not understanding the meaning of our complicated religious fervour. She was waiting for some sort of sign of what we were praying for. When nothing materialised, it must have been very confusing for her."

Edward gave a sideways glance at Charlyyk. "Forgive my rude behaviour, Charlyyk. I saw you in the church, hiding behind your father, waiting for a second coming of the Lord."

Anna stifled a laugh. Elizabeth gave her a stern look.

Helen tried to change the conversation. "Shall we go for a walk later?"

Anna announced, "I've arranged a special lunch for today—something light, not too heavy. It will be better to have a walk after that than after something heavy."

Charlyyk was curious about the way the room was laid out. It was a mixed bag of odds and sods. None of the furniture matched. The coffee table, or whatever it was, was covered in reams of paper in disarray. Some of the piles had paperweights on them. Anna touched her arm. "Ongoing paperwork, Charlyyk. The piles with paperweights are waiting for confirmation. The ones without are being read at this moment."

Charlyyk was amazed. "They have read all that?"

Elizabeth said, "Most of it is about points of law, mostly international. The government needs advising on some of it, and some of it is for companies that need advice on particular parts of EU law."

Edward made a gesture with his hand. "I'm looking into reforming the House of Lords. It needs change. Some want it more democratic; some want it reduced in size. What I must do is to look at all the possibilities, so that it meets our democratic constitutional duties and what's best for the UK. Not like political parties, who only have set agendas, set tendentious objectives, and forget about the chaos they cause implementing them."

Anna set the lunch: savoury pancakes, filled with asparagus and a light cream cheese and ham sauce, with a mixed bean salad. Bryn and Edward picked at it at first but ultimately cleared their plates.

After lunch, they took a stroll around the area. The pavements were busy, but not like Southampton. As people recognised Charlyyk, little pockets congregated near her. Charlyyk walked between Helen's parents with Bryn behind her, between Helen and Anna. She felt comfortable and acknowledged anyone who showed interest in her.

When Elizabeth met some old friends, she could not wait to introduce Charlyyk as their future granddaughter. Anna commented, "She sure is strutting the strut." Helen noticed that her father had grown an inch or two; he too was milking the occasion. They waved to all and sundry, no matter who they were. It really did not matter. He was as proud as any grandfather with a new grandchild.

On Tuesday, the unexpected arrival of Toby at breakfast was greeted with suspicion. "Hello, what are you doing here?" Bryn demanded.

Toby pulled a chair up. "I've come to see the New Year in with you, if that's OK?"

Helen poured some coffee for him. "Breakfast?"

A broad grin flashed across his face. "Yeah, I'm famished. Full English would be nice."

Bryn asked suspiciously, "So?"

Toby could not hide behind a false smile. "That's always been the trouble with you, Bryn—you don't trust me."

Bryn took a sip of coffee. "No, I trust you to try anything you can to get your own way. Why are you here?"

"You've made up your mind that it's time to take over?" Helen asked.

He pulled a paper from his inside pocket. "This came to me late last night." He placed it in front of Bryn. When Bryn had finished reading it, he took it to Helen. She was cooking. He assumed her spot at the stove so she could read. It was a request for the Collier family to visit Russia and China. The dates coincided with Charlyyk's summer holidays.

Helen looked at Toby. "You could have shown us this at any time. Spit it out—why now?"

Toby gave her a sheepish look. "OK. I was lonely, and I thought of you two."

Bryn touched Charlyyk's hand. "He has upset Wendy."

Helen placed breakfast in front of Toby and picked her phone up. She texted, *"What has Toby done?"*

Toby was an old childhood friend of Wendy and Brian Bailey, from Manchester. He had been trading on his friendship to stay with them while protecting Charlyyk.

Helen received a reply ten minutes later. *"That freeloader! He walks in, expects to be fed, then sits there waiting for everyone to fan him. He goes off without a by-your-leave, then drifts back in as though he never left. Bloody sponger."*

Helen placed her phone in front of him. "You earn good money, Toby, so why?"

Charlyyk left the table. "He is lazy, not lonely."

Toby's mouth dropped open. "How can you say that?"

Charlyyk put her dirty crockery in the dishwasher. "When the truth smacks you in the face, how can you ignore it? You don't need a wife; you need another mother." She closed the door to the dishwasher. "Or a slave."

Bryn could not help but nod. "Looks like you have got to sort your life out before you get thrown out of all your friends' houses."

Toby asked, "How did you cope with living on your own, Helen?"

She filled the kettle and put it on the hob. "I bought my apartment. It was not too close to anybody or anything. It had parking under, and a janitor who looked after the flat when I was not there. An excellent restaurant was around one corner, and a great fish and chip shop around the other. And the pub was a real godsend. Many times, I found a quiet corner there with a pint of ale, pie, and mash. Very fattening, but a lifesaver."

Toby reflected. "Is it still for sale?"

Helen left the kitchen. When she returned, she gave him an estate agent's brochure. Toby read through it. Helen pointed out some of the additions; the built-in safe was a big plus. He was soon on the phone, setting up an appointment for a view.

CHAPTER 9

RINGING IN A NEW YEAR

Thomas and his charges arrived at one fifteen. Rachel was first to enter, followed by her mother. Bryn, after saying his hellos, went to help Thomas with the bags.

Helen and Charlyyk sat down with cups of tea. Rachel told them how the trip had gone. "Mum loved Thomas's friend Jim. She wants to show some of his paintings at the exhibition. They will complement some of the other exhibits."

Margret opened a portfolio case, revealing five paintings of scenes from around the Cotswolds. Charlyyk was amazed. "These are paintings?" she exclaimed, thinking of her own attempts. "Wow!"

Margret smiled at her. "These are the results of many years of studying art, the same as Thomas has had to do. Through much practice, Jim has achieved this very high standard of workmanship."

Charlyyk greeted Gwen and Harold when they arrived at two. Charlyyk could not stop talking to Janet when

112

she arrived shortly after. There was much to talk about concerning Charlyyk's trip to London. As the two girls laid the table, the laughter and gossip did not stop.

While Helen, Gwen, and Jane prepared the meal. Bryn, Edward, and James Parsons talked about the family Bible that Janet had uncovered. Michel and Harold soon were involved in the story of the Allcott family. Edward relayed that the Parsons had been the head herdsmen to the Allcotts and not the other way around. Then a John Parsons had left farm life and become a mercenary soldier. On his return home, he found the farm in neglect and bought it from the contemporary Allcott, reversing their roles. Over the years, the Parsons and the Allcotts had intermarried, and the last Allcott had been Ned Parsons' half-brother.

Michel had a response to the story. "As you walk into the Fords' farmhouse, there is a family tree hanging on the wall. It was compiled by Burke's Heritage in 1965. It goes right back to 1678 with the marriage of a Ford to an Allcott."

The conversation carried on through dinner. Janet admitted that she and James had researched the family on the internet. James laughed. "We stopped when we got to 1774. There we found an Agnes Parsons, who gave birth to seven children and never married. None of the fathers were named. Janet took the first names of the children and compared them to the names of all the local males living at that time. It was speculative but came up with some interesting results."

Gwen could not resist saying, "That's what a good journalist does—speculate, hoping that if they turn over a few rocks, a snake might appear."

Janet smiled at her. "Sometimes bones rattle about. With a little digging, you can find a trace of flesh, and when you dig some more, blood may flow. That's what my first editor told me: 'All you've got to do is keep digging.'"

Helen quipped, "Remember Watergate?"

"Exactly. Isn't the truth worth digging for?"

They all helped to clear up. Gwen put the television on. "BBC 1, the fireworks display at the London Eye. I don't want to miss it."

Bryn said to Charlyyk, "Did you text Catherine?"

Charlyyk showed him the texts. Catherine had written, *"Happy New Year, sis. How's your resolution going?"*

Charlyyk had replied, *"Failed. I'm getting bigger."*

Bryn opened a couple of bottles of champagne, ready to greet the New Year. Upon the chimes of Big Ben, the cheers and celebrations were in full swing. The fireworks looked spectacular. Charlyyk was getting to like all the funny things Earth people did to party. These pleasures made her more aware of the two different lives she had lived.

At three o'clock the following afternoon, Janet returned with a few articles she had been working on. She had spoken to Bryn the night before about them. Bryn went through with her a number of photos they had taken of Charlyyk. Janet was as pleased as punch about the information he gave her. Bryn had also shot some video footage, which she downloaded to her computer. The shopping expeditions to London and Winchester gave her much material to work with.

"The feedback I'm getting has been very encouraging," she said. "I want to set up a trust for her. Charlyyk should get something out of all this. I've spoken to my accountant, who will arrange the legal set-up. He will be in touch with the HMIR to make sure it's straight and above board. My accountant recommended setting a percentage of my revenues on these assignments, to be agreed by all parties. I hope you will be happy with what I'm trying to achieve."

Janet searched in her big shoulder bag and retrieved an envelope. "This is a letter you will need to pass to your accountant."

Bryn looked a bit concerned. "Janet, we are not doing this to make money."

Janet smiled. "I did not know where this would go when it all started. But now the cheques are coming in. If some money goes to Charlyyk, it will offset the tax I have to pay, and Charlyyk will have something to fall back on later. A trust would be the best way forward for her."

Helen knocked on the door and entered with two mugs of tea. "I thought you might like these?" Bryn was quick to involve Helen in the conversation. "That sounds like a good idea. I like it, Janet."

Janet gave a breakdown of how she operated. "I have a virtual assistant. She is disabled but can work a computer, and she works from home. Since this project has taken off, she now employs two other girls. The press gets in touch with her, and she sorts out what my schedule will be. All my paycheques go to my accountant, who settles payments. All I have to do is the fun side—write about my friend Charlyyk. Life could not be sweeter."

Helen put her arm around Janet's shoulders and gave her a squeeze. "You make it sound like a life of Riley."

Janet laughed. "James reckons it sounds as easy as rolling in pig shit." Then Janet got serious. "Now how about your story, Bryn?"

Helen responded, "Many operations that Bryn was involved in are still classified and cannot be discussed. But Bryn has outlined information he can disclose. We feel if you read through it, you might be able to form some sort of story that will fit the type of publication you write for."

"Yes. I can aim my questions in the right directions. That could work."

Bryn opened his filing cabinet and pulled out a folder. "This is it, my life story—the good, the bad, and the downright ugly."

She quickly shuffled through it. "This will make some good night reading. Thank you, Bryn."

Later, at Parsons' farm, the Parsons discussed Bryn with Janet. Jane went to the shelf of an antique Welsh dresser and removed a large biscuit tin. She showed Janet letters she'd had from Kitty, Bryn's late wife. The letters spoke of the empty anguish Kitty went through when Bryn went on what he called 'one of his jollies'. The dates tied up to the years in Bryn's document. Janet picked up on the times he returned home. She made many notes about those times. Jane related the occasions when he came back in none-too-good condition. The children would rally around Kit, pulling him through the pain he tried not to show, but that they knew he was suffering.

Edward showed Janet photos of Bryn in those days. "It's when you see the scars that you realise what he has endured for Queen and country. On one occasion, the team he was leading got caught in a mortar attack. With much shrapnel damage to himself, he dragged two of his men to safety, saving their lives. Bryn is a born leader. When he first arrived in the village, Kit and the children had already lived here for six months. Kit rented the Taylors' old cottage. He was so quiet, nobody realised who he was. They thought he was just Gwen's brother."

Sitting up in bed, cuddled together, Janet and James read Bryn's account of his life. Parts of it were in brackets between blanked-out pieces, with *Classified* written in the brackets. There were many such brackets.

Janet already had a profile of Bryn in her head. It did not change. She knew this quiet man had inner strength that had been born in him. He had not needed to work on it, just let it mature, like the scotch whisky he drank.

On Friday, Janet spent more time going over and over Bryn's story and how he would like it to be told. She knew this type of man did not like bringing attention to himself. He would instead want the focus to go to others. But this spotlight was something he could not hide from. It was Janet's duty to portray him in the right light—not try to hold him too high, so others might knock him down, but rather to describe him as the loving dad he was.

Bryn had already seen that he could not hide from it. The detail he had given her was intense—in a way, he had given her too much. She broke each section down bit by bit, intent not to lose the full meaning of why she was doing this in first the place.

By the afternoon, she had three stories, that related to the man, yet did not make him an alpha male—well, not quite. From the first day, the Collier family introduced Charlyyk to the world, the media had delved into Bryn's past. The researchers soon found evidence of his military life, and much interest had been shown in the snippets published already. The scars Bryn had shown to prove he had been in conflict with a strange beast had revealed other scars as well.

Janet phoned Harold and Gwen and soon was in her Mini, heading for Carpenters' cottage. When the Hobarts read, what Janet had written, Harold could not say very much. He saw the Bryn he knew in each profile, but which one he preferred was hard to say.

Gwen was different. She took a couple of things from one and added them to another. "That is my brother."

Harold read Gwen's changes. "I agree. That puts it in perspective."

Gwen and Harold would not let Janet go quickly. They discussed how long Janet felt she would be following Charlyyk's story. "That depends on the interest of the general public. No interest, no story."

"Then what would you do?" asked Gwen.

"I would carry on doing what I'm doing here, but about other people. This project has given me such a huge profile, I do not envisage ever being out of work, unless I get too cocky and blow it. Then, I suppose, James could make me an honest woman and turn me into a mother. That would change my life and how!"

A light, drizzly rain swept over the county. The weather front had slowly moved up the English Channel from the Atlantic and affected the southern coastal regions. That did not deter the effort being shown by the four runners. They skipped over the slippery ground and the many puddles. Their chatter was lively.

Helen's Pilates was paying off; she was more light-footed. Age limited her, but she felt better for her efforts. Thomas only ran when he thought he needed to, but these runs made him feel he should try harder.

Bryn's initial idea behind the runs had been to decrease the amount of studying Charlyyk was doing. The brainstorm had turned out better than he first thought. When Kitty became ill, Bryn had stopped training to look after her. After Kitty's death, he just imploded. He could not find the incentive to do anything. When he was abducted, he realized he still needed to be fit to survive. He now was determined to be ready for what might come next, for he knew this had not finished. There were too many unexplained issues.

He had a talk with Michel about the effects on Charlyyk of eating food she had not eaten before. Could it change the way she grew? He had Michel's full attention. Michel had noticed the effect of the different food. Also, exercise was increasing Charlyyk's physical size. Harold had mentioned it at Houston. The height detail that Lynda Bryant had put into her illustrations of the aliens had given Michel concerns. If Charlyyk achieved such height, it could make people wary of her.

The cottage was warm and welcoming when they returned. Rachel was in a loving mood and snuggled up to

Thomas. This made him feel good inside. Soon they were heading for their bedroom under the stern eye of Margret.

After breakfast, Thomas planned to take his charges to Portsmouth to visit the Mary Rose exhibition.

Janet arrived at ten. "I've come to see you, Helen." They headed for the study. "I've gone over the information Bryn gave me. This is what I've come up with. I could not show Bryn until I had spoken with the special people very close to him."

Helen sat down and read what Janet placed in front of her. When she had finished reading, she said, "Just a minute." And she left the study.

She returned with Charlyyk. Janet explained what the meeting was about, then allowed Charlyyk to read what she had written. It was the original version, without the changes Gwen had suggested.

When Charlyyk had finished reading, she laid out the pages and bracketed individual sentences in pencil. "Move that to there, and that to there." She sat back.

Helen said, "Yes, you are right, darling."

Janet then put what Gwen had edited next to the other papers. Charlyyk read Gwen's version. "Yes, that's my dad." There was pride in her voice. Helen could only put her hand on her shoulder and squeeze. Janet explained what Gwen had said.

Charlyyk looked straight into Janet's eyes. "You have to have lived with a person like my dad to really believe that people like him exist. He's not the only one, but there aren't many. How does a girl like me deserve a man like him as a father?"

Janet wrote down what she had said. "That's the ending I was looking for."

Helen cuddled Charlyyk. "I could not have said anything that summed up the true feelings of us all better than what you just stated."

Janet proofread the main article, then pressed print and watched as paper unfolded from the printer. Janet asked Helen to get Bryn. "Let's see what he thinks."

Bryn came into the study. He sat down and started to read what Janet handed him. When he finished, he said, "That's three ways of seeing me, but do we really see ourselves as others do?"

Then Janet showed him the finished article. He was not sure. "That's not how you saw me, surely?" Janet asked him to explain. "The first three depict how you saw me. In the last one, you have asked those close to me to comment." Janet related what she had done these last three days. Bryn then agreed to the publication of the final article.

"I want a particular photo to go with it. Could you dress in something casual but classy?" Janet asked. "You help him to choose, Helen. Charlyyk, I need you to wear something similar."

The photo shoot was set up. A white sheet was draped on one wall, with folds to give it some features. A wing chair was set out for them to sit in. Lamps and reflectors were set up to prevent shadows. The shoot lasted about an hour. Janet used three cameras for different effects.

When she checked the results on the computer, the picture that stood out the most was of Bryn with Charlyyk sitting on his right leg. His right arm was behind her, his right hand cradling her right elbow. Her right hand was draped over the arm of the wing chair. Their left hands were together. They looked into each other's eyes, pride radiating from them.

Charlyyk put A4 photo paper into her printer, and they printed out four copies. On the back of one of the photographs, Janet wrote the number of the photo, to save time when she needed copies. "This will be in next month's issue. I will get the mag to send you a copy," Janet informed him as they cleared away the equipment.

Helen had prepared lunch, and they sat around talking about how Christmas had gone. Janet was full of herself, as James had mentioned casually that they were to marry. The tingling excitement she expressed was palpable. Helen could tell by her body language that the idea of marrying James excited her.

Charlyyk's nose twitched. Bryn could tell she was seeking the smell of Janet. Then she stopped. Bryn raised his eyebrows. Charlyyk shook her head with a look of disappointment.

Helen could not help but follow the unspoken conversation. More and more, she understood how Charlyyk responded to situations. Ear movement was first. Her ears moved in specific patterns and twitched when she became excited. Her eyes changed colour. Mix observation of the ears and the eyes, and that told her when Charlyyk was happy, agitated, or threatened. The movement of Charlyyk's nostrils was harder to detect, but Helen was learning. She had time on her side.

When Janet had left the cottage, the photos still lay on the table. Bryn put two more pictures of Charlyyk with them—one from when she first arrived on earth, the second from a year later. Even Charlyyk saw the changes. She had filled out and was six inches taller. She stood more upright, straighter in the back. Her face was softer and her hair no longer straw-like. She saw the confidence she now projected. She was different, just as Michel had predicted. But she still felt the same.

Charlyyk looked at Helen, then at Bryn. She felt secure, like a lion cub lying next to its parents, enjoying the warmth of the sun. She was without a care in the world. What was for dinner was the only thing she had to think about. That summed up what her life had become with Bryn her dad. He always supplied her needs on this planet.

Bryn had been watching her. "What are you thinking, sweetheart?"

She sidled up and nestled into him as though he were a duvet. She slipped an arm around him to get even closer, looking up into his eyes to show the affection that only a daughter could demonstrate. "Love you, Daddy."

Helen saw Bryn melt before her eyes. He could say no words, but his gooey smile and shining eyes spoke volumes. Even she felt emotional watching them.

When Thomas, Rachel, and Margret returned from their visit to the Mary Rose, their smiles said that the day had gone well. Margret was taken aback by the history of it all. "Placing the history with the artefact gave the exhibit so much meaning," she said, sitting down with Charlyyk to describe the day.

Rachel helped Helen with the evening meal. She said her mother had not moaned or criticised once—well, only when she was tired and wanted to leave. It had made for a lovely day.

Over dinner, Helen told Thomas about Janet's visit and the photo shoot. Thomas read the article and perused the photos. "She is such a talented person. She certainly has a way of showing the best in people."

Margret wished she had been there. "We must go and see her and set up a time for an interview. Rachel, we need to get the advertising sorted."

Rachel stopped eating. "Can't we use the catalogue from the exhibition in Chicago? It would fit the artists who are exhibiting their works."

Thomas looked at Margret. "Just change the cover and the introduction. It could work."

Margret went silent, but all saw her brain cells working. Then she spoke. "I hate to admit it, but I think you are right." Rachel had a smug look. She looked down at what she was eating so her mother could not see her, but her eyes flashed up to see Thomas doing the same. The little nods they gave each other said that a plan had worked.

Helen observed that what Bryn had said about Margret bore a lot of truth. Margret was very domineering, but Thomas and Rachel could control her to a point. Helen wished she could be a fly on their bedroom wall, to see how they managed their plots. They seemed able to do so subtly.

Some idle chatter was bandied around for a little while. Helen sensed it was meant to take the conversation away from the catalogue. They had furthered their course, and it was wise not to rub Margret's nose in it. She was capable of changing her mind deliberately.

Sunday saw a light flurry of snow, but it was wet, so it would not last long. Charlyyk did not like the damp cold. Her home planet was arid, with few clouds. There was hardly any rain. The moist atmosphere of England made the cold feel colder, but the run warmed her. The pleasant feeling it gave her made the effort well worthwhile.

During breakfast at the Parsons' farm, Janet's phone started to vibrate. The editor of a men's magazine wanted a photo of Bryn in a different pose, without Charlyyk.

Janet turned up at Oakleaves around about ten. She was with James, who drove Edward's Discovery, towing a trailer. They came in through the rear garden. Charlyyk was soon there. She knew James would rough her up, but she liked it from him. His large hands were rough but could be so gentle.

"Well, how are we going to proceed with this?" Bryn asked.

James slapped him on the back "It's OK. We will be gentle with you. We have been talking. I've brought the props."

James walked into the garden, and Bryn followed him. On the back of the trailer were logs and a large axe. James asked, "Have you got something to wear that would look rugged?"

Bryn went to his bedroom and pulled out a case from behind the wardrobe. The torn T-shirt and cargo trousers were within, wrapped in plastic bags—just as he had stored them, still stained with his own blood. He donned the cargo trousers but not the T-shirt, instead taking another old T-shirt from a bureau drawer. As he passed his study, he retrieved the hacking blade he had brought back from that hellhole of a planet. Carrying the blade and the torn T-shirt, he returned to the garden.

Janet, with help from Charlyyk, had set up the lights and reflector screens. Janet wanted to bring in one of the trees as a backdrop. She used James as a model to set up the cameras.

When Charlyyk saw Bryn's trousers, she stood still, rooted to the spot, her ears and eyes twitching. She was not comfortable. James saw it and scooped her up. Helen was soon there.

The smell from the trousers perturbed Charlyyk even more. When Bryn slew the Feeng, its blood had splashed them, and she could still smell it—faint, but it was there. Charlyyk's built-in fears were playing games in her head, warning her of danger. But as James tried to take her away, she would not go. Struggling, she wriggled free from his hold. "I must face it. I must conquer my fears. The Feeng is dead. It should not upset me. I am here; it is not." She went to Bryn and wrapped her arms around him.

Helen made tea to help settle Charlyyk. She sat with her as Charlyyk drank it, talking her through her anxiety. Helen could tell she needed this to give her confidence in herself. Once again this was for Charlyyk and nobody else but her. Charlyyk conveyed how those beasts haunted her dreams. To end her nightmares, she had to find a way to banish her fear.

Meanwhile, Bryn tried many poses and wielded the axe, cutting several logs to achieve the right effects. James suggested that Bryn take the T-shirt off. Steam rose from him.

James dove into Janet's shoulder bag and found a bottle of baby oil. James handed it to Helen. "I think you would enjoy doing the honours more than I!" Helen applied the oil to Bryn's body. The glistening sheen gave him a hot and sweaty look. Though Bryn had thickened around the waist and did not have a great six-pack, the oil showed that his physique was still good for a man his age.

Rachel, watching with her mother at the door to the cottage, saw the possibility of another angle. "Thomas! Those pyjamas I love to wear and you don't like—could you fetch them, please?" He came back with them. Rachel took Charlyyk's outer garments off. The simple shift in a pale lime green blended with Charlyyk's complexion.

"Right, Dad," she said. "Put the axe down and wear the torn T-shirt." Bryn put the T-shirt on. "Now stand with your feet apart."

Rachel guided Charlyyk to Bryn. "Pass that weapon to me, James." She put the blade in Bryn's hands. "Charlyyk, kneel between Bryn's legs. Yes, bend your right leg in front of Dad's left leg. Put your hand around and above his knee. Bend your left leg so your weight is resting on it. Now peer around Dad, looking at me. Dad, place the weapon between your legs. That's it." She turned to Janet. "How about that?"

Janet took a burst of shots. She saw what Rachel had done and imagined other directions for the shoot. "Charlyyk, grip your dad's ankle with your left hand. Put your right hand above his knee." The camera whirred. Then Janet asked Charlyyk to look around as if searching for a beast.

Janet downloaded the photos to her computer, and they gathered around to see the results. Each shot was examined. Four photos were selected and printed, and the print images were re-examined. Janet sent digital versions to the men's magazine editor, and they waited. The reply came back: *"Great shots, thanks. That's a wrap."*

The relief on Janet's face showed how much this meant to her. The editor led a best-selling magazine for men that was sold all around the world. Publishing there was another coup for Janet.

Bryn and Charlyyk changed clothes in their respective rooms. As they came back, Margret was setting dates with Janet for an interview. Janet had already made inroads with various magazines. "The biggest one is *The Art of Watercolour*, based in Naintré, France. It will run the spread. I suggest we concentrate on that as the main article. I will use some of that material to send to other magazines. *The Art of Watercolour* also wants in-depth interviews with some of the artists and would like one of their own writers to conduct those interviews. They will be in touch with us this week."

Janet thanked them. James had already cleared the equipment and props away. With hugs and kisses, they were gone.

Carpenters' cottage was a hive of activity. Rachel and her mother had folders in front of them and were discussing the upcoming schedule. Michel held Charlyyk on his lap, chewing the cud with Harold and Bryn. Gwen, Helen, and Thomas were talking about the Mary Rose.

Over dinner, the photo shoot was widely debated. Gwen gave Charlyyk a comforting hug. "You poor thing. It must have been terrifying for you."

"Auntie Gwen, they don't live on this planet, so I must dispel the fear I have of them. Then I might not have bad dreams about them, waking up in a state of worry that they are chasing me."

Gwen understood her anxiety. She had spent many early mornings cuddling Charlyyk to settle her down. Gwen had felt the tremors in her body and had unwrapped the sheets tangled around her legs. The claws on her toes dug in when she was dreaming of running away from the beast.

Margret kept looking at the far wall. "Gwen, that painting, the one where the little girl is holding the rabbit …"

Gwen gestured towards Thomas. "Thomas gave that to me. It's from a photo he took which I liked. As you can tell, I still love it."

Charlyyk left the table and took a closer look. "That resembles the sketchbook we found in the back of the wardrobe, Dad."

Bryn agreed. "You are right. Your auntie Gwen will no doubt show you the original photo. She has it hanging in her bedroom."

Gwen turned to Helen somewhat awkwardly. "The original includes Bryn and Kitty in an intimate position. Every time Bryn saw it, he needed time to get over the pain it gave him, so I have hung it away from Bryn's gaze. I think he will be all right with it now though."

"I want Bryn to still be in love with Kitty," Helen said. "She was the love of his life. He should not turn his back on such a wonderful woman." Helen's look was sincere. Gwen knew she was not trying to push Kitty out of their lives. "Remember, she is the mother of his children. And what a fantastic job she did bringing them up. I am prepared to share Bryn with you all. The memories of Kitty are something you should all cherish."

Margret was concerned that asking about the painting had caused a problem. Thomas explained, "The painting is based on a photo that Uncle Harold took."

Harold nodded. "When Bryn came home on leave one summer, we all went to Dippers Meadow on a picnic. I had been taking photos of the children, as you can tell from the painting. But in one photo, Bryn and Kit were in the background. Only when we had the photos developed did we realise the tender moment they were sharing."

Thomas said, "My art teacher was showing us how to paint a picture from a photo. You can leave the irrelevant bits out to improve the composition. I took no notice of what Mum and Dad were up to. I was focused on improving the composition with my sister at the centre. Only later, when my hormones started to be active, did I notice what I had overlooked before—a rather sensuous, emotional photo."

Rachel winked at Gwen. "So that's why it hangs in the bedroom, eh, Gwen?"

Gwen's face flushed. "Go on, make it sound worse than it is." But the words had joviality in them, not malice.

Margret, listening to this family, sensed the honesty they had with one another. There were never hard feelings or ill thoughts. They were a "pull your sleeves up and get on with it" family. At first, she had not been sure how Michel fitted in. Now she saw he was a member of the family, not just a friend. He also pulled his sleeves up.

She looked at herself and realised the position she was in. *I'm going to be here for a year. I feel that Bryn is tolerating me for Thomas's sake, but why? Am I that bad?*

Her thoughts were cut short by the sound of laughter. They were reacting to Charlyyk's remark, "It cannot be a painting. It has no runs in it."

CHAPTER 10

HOME TRUTHS

On Monday morning, Charlyyk checked that she had everything ready for school before sitting for breakfast. Helen was busy cooking breakfast and packing her lunch at the same time. Rachel, coming into the kitchen and seeing Helen rushing about, stepped in to help.

The school bus was spot on time, and they waved Charlyyk goodbye. Margret had been very quiet. Nobody had said anything about how quiet she was. Instead, they talked about how quickly the holiday had gone. Then, out of the blue, Margret asked, "What is it that people have about me? I don't think I am a bad person. Or am I?"

Rachel changed seats and sat next to her. "No, Mum, but you must loosen up a bit. Dad was a bastard to you, the way he cheated on you. But not everyone is like Dad. You must try to climb down off that high horse that you sit on and meet the ones you like halfway."

Margret's face dropped. "You are my daughter. I'm not like that to you, am I?"

Rachel placed her arm around her mother's shoulders. "Yes, you are. And if you are like that to me, how about

Thomas? If he were not like his mum and dad, he would have run away screaming by now. I warn you now—if ever that happens, I will be with him."

Margret looked distraught. "I don't mean to be like that!"

Thomas came and sat the other side of Margret. "You are Rachel's mother, and I must respect that. But my real duty is to Rachel, even more now she is carrying our first child and your grandchild. I have told Rachel that if your manner does not change, after the birth we will move away from you, because our child is not going to live a life of worrying what he or she says to you. I have family who would love to have us permanently."

Margret, her face ashen, looked at Rachel. "Yes, Mum. I will follow Thomas to the other end of the world and leave you behind, if you put me in a position that I would have to choose between you."

Margret stood up and left the room, tears streaming down her face. Rachel made an attempt to follow, but Thomas stopped her. "Give her time to think it through. She has to understand that we mean what we have said. Give in to her now, and you will always have to give in."

Rachel did not have tears in her eyes, which told Helen they meant what they had said.

Bryn looked at Helen, who nodded to him, then rose and left the table.

Helen tapped on Margret's door and walked in. Margret lay sobbing on the bed. Sitting beside her, Helen stroked her back. "Come. Life is not easy, but to ease the pain, let's talk about it. Maybe we can come to an understanding that will allow you to keep your family together. We could start by thinking about your new grandchild. My parents never thought that they would have any. The fact that they now have Charlyyk has given them a whole new purpose in life."

Margret stopped crying and turned over to face Helen. A wisp of a smile appeared on her face. "Yes." She raised herself and sat next to Helen. "Thank you."

"Sort yourself out, and I'll go and make a pot of tea."

Ten minutes later, she returned, carrying a tray. "I've brought some of Charlyyk's favourite Kit Kats."

Margret had done some thinking while Helen made the tea. "Was I that bad?"

Helen looked at her sympathetically. "No, not that bad. It was a constant nag, nag like a dripping tap. It becomes a nightmare in the end."

Margret winced at that thought. "It doesn't sound good, does it?"

Helen took a bite of a Kit Kat. "You could look at it differently. Think of all the pain and grief that Bryn has suffered. Does he take it out on everyone around him?" Helen smiled a gentle smile. "You are still going to need some help to get you through this. I think if you ask Rachel and Thomas to help, they will."

Margret found herself scoffing a Kit Kat. Helen offered her another. "How do you think they could help me?" Margret asked.

"How about asking them?"

"But what should I ask them?"

"Ask them to tell you when you act inappropriately, if only by a hand signal."

Thomas and Rachel were in the lounge. Bryn had spoken to them when they were in the kitchen. "You have to hit hard sometimes to get the message through. Your mother can be nice, and for all your sakes, I hope a solution can be found. I would love to be with Amy all the time. But it would mean a strain on Cat and Brent's relationship. I must respect that you have chosen to make a life for yourself, just like I did with your mother. With plane travel, we're never too far away for a visit." Bryn then went to his study.

Helen entered the lounge with Margret. "Where's Bryn?" Thomas replied that he had gone to the study. Helen left them and went in search of Bryn.

Margret sat down with Thomas and Rachel. "Helen has been very kind to me. We have looked at the ways you might be able to help when I forget myself. You have not to grin and bear it, but let me know. Helen described my silly ways as a dripping tap—nag, nag, so I'm reaching out to you both. Please give this silly old woman a second chance to redeem herself."

Rachel kissed her mother. "Mum, I love you, and so does Thomas, but you must want to do this. If you don't, get on a plane and go home now. Take into account you won't just lose me, but also a grandchild. This is not Thomas talking. This is me."

Margret saw her daughter meant every word she was saying. "Yes, darling. I do want to change. I want what they have here—a happy family. I want to be a loving grandmother."

"Then let's give it a go, Mum. Look, when we told Thomas's dad we were coming to stay for a year, his first words were 'How about your mum? She will want to be with you at the birth.' His first thoughts were for you. That is how Thomas thinks—more about others than himself. That's why I love him. He doesn't look over his shoulder to see what I'm doing. He looks to see if I'm all right."

Bryn was sorting out the paperwork for his accounts. Helen brought up her bank details and checked them against her statements. A letter from the accounts office notified her of the way her pension would be paid. A cheque would be put in the post as a one-off payment in recognition of her service. She passed the letter to Bryn. "My dowry, kind sir. I do not come empty-handed."

At lunchtime, Helen asked Margret if she would like to go shopping. Margret jumped at the idea and could not wait to go. Rachel helped Helen to finish the chores so her mother could go.

Thomas went through his art equipment. It had arrived in a large container: easels, brushes, and most of all, paper, handmade in different grades.

At the bottom, right-hand corner of the garden, very overgrown, was Thomas's old studio. It was a large summer house with lots of windows for natural light. Since he moved to America, the trees and shrubs had overgrown and covered it.

Bryn collected the hedge trimmer from the garage, and, like a man on a jungle mission, attacked the overgrown bushes. Thomas pulled the debris away as Bryn chopped. Once a path was cleared, Thomas took a key fob from his pocket, found the key, and opened the door. Releasing the bolts that held them, Bryn opened the shutters up.

Thomas looked around the inside of the studio. Rachel joined him there. Old works were scattered about the walls. Two old chairs stood together. Catherine had been an avid model from an early age. Even Kit had taken her turn. Their help had allowed him to mature as an artist. Many props for still life's were scattered about. Thomas noted, "We've a lot of work to do here. It is so dusty."

Bryn, in the meantime, had found the fuse in the consumer unit. He switched it on, checking that the RCD unit worked. When he returned to the studio, Rachel had started cleaning. Thomas was removing items to allow clear access.

Helen and Margret returned from their shopping, laughing, and the kettle was soon on. Bryn told them that Thomas had opened the studio. Helen looked surprised. "What studio?"

Bryn walked to the window. "That one."

The two women looked out of the window. Margret, watching Rachel and Thomas working together, saw they were a team. The way they bounced off each other was heart-warming to watch. Margret poured two teas and took them out to the studio.

Helen had a satisfied smile on her face. Bryn put his arm around her waist. "Did it work?"

"Oh yes. I got her to talk. Then she could not stop. It all came out. She was so demanding, her husband, Mark, could not live up to the constant nagging. As an artist, unless you are famous, you struggle. And with Margret as a wife, he struggled even more. He had already left her before he knew she was pregnant."

"So she knew what she was doing and still could do nothing about it?"

Helen walking away from the window. "Knowing and doing are two different things."

Charlyyk breezed in, aiming for the fridge. Bryn's voice was stern. "Don't you dare touch that fridge door, young lady."

Charlyyk touched a laminated A4 sheet on top of the fridge. It had her diet on it. "I can have a drink of milk when I come home from school. Look, it's here."

Helen added, "We have it all under control. We've had a serious talk, and Charlyyk agrees that this diet is for her long-term health."

Charlyyk changed her clothes. She soon had the scent of Rachel and headed for her. She stood there wondered how a large studio had materialised at the far end of the garden. Rachel showed her the inside. "Thomas wanted to get this sorted because he promised to give you some lessons."

Thomas had to settle her down. "Painting is about control, Charlyyk."

When he felt, she was ready, he wet some paper and stretched it, laying it flat on the workbench. He sponged some more water on it and showed her the technique of wet on wet. He gave her strong, vibrant colours: Prussian blue, Venetian red, and cadmium yellow. He put a little of each into separate bowls. Adding some water, he gave her a mop. "Dunk it in the bowl, then drop some from thirty centimetres above the paper."

The paint hit the wet paper and exploded out. She yelped with glee at the results. She dropped different colours in massive bursts. He made her stand back and view what she had achieved using only three primary colours. Before the paint dried, he dabbed a tissue in the centre of each colour burst. Then Charlyyk dropped other colours into the burst for more effect.

While she painted, Thomas stretched another piece of paper. "Right. We will let that dry. Here is what art is all about." He created a rainbow, brushing a yellow strip straight across the paper, then blue to form the bottom. She saw how, when the blue touched the yellow, green appeared. "Water is like a mirror. It reflects. So, if the sky is blue, the sea is blue, using nature's own colour system."

Then Thomas applied the red to the top part of the rainbow. Where the red touched the yellow, orange emerged, creating a complete image. Charlyyk nodded. She saw how, when the sun hit drops of rain, the drops reflected natural colours to create the rainbow.

Rachel came in to let them know dinner would soon be ready. "That's pretty, Charlyyk," she said encouragingly. Charlyyk's wide eyes and pursed lips spoke for her. She kept touching a corner of the paper to see if it was dry.

At dinner, Charlyyk could not stop asking questions about how Thomas had started in art and what he found difficult to grasp. Thomas and Margret had different answers to the same questions. This did not confuse Charlyyk. She had noticed matters were the same with the posse, each one experiencing a different difficulty than the others.

On Wednesday, Thomas and Rachel spent the day in the studio. Helen kept them supplied with beverages and snacks. Helen enjoyed sneaking quick looks, watching Thomas at work. He had three pieces on the go at the same time. He was using previous drawings and photos as references for the theme of autumn in New England. Another was an image of Dippers Meadow, meant for Charlyyk's bedroom.

Margret spent the morning in Bryn's study, going over the details for the layout of the first exhibits. She was delighted that the gallery had offered her some of their best watercolour paintings. She was keeping her fingers crossed for the Brighton and Hove City Council to allow *The Chain Pier, Brighton*, painted by Turner, to be shown.

Janet's request for an interview with Bryn had stirred more interest from the military chiefs about Bryn's exploits. The phone call he received from Major Carter came as no surprise to Bryn. "Hello, Major. What can I help you with?"

The major was quite apologetic. "Sorry, Captain, but the big chiefs want to talk with you and Charlyyk."

Bryn did not answer straight away, but gave himself time to think it over. "When?"

"I told them you would not like Charlyyk to lose more schooling, and it would have to fit in with her schedule."

"Where?"

"I suggested the Chelsea pensioners' home at the Royal Hospital Chelsea."

This tickled Bryn. "Why? Are the big chiefs that old?"

The major chuckled. "This Saturday at ten. Will Helen join you?"

Bryn beckoned Helen and explained the request. Helen took the phone. "Alan, will this be a full weekend?"

"It could be. Would this create a problem?"

Helen said to Bryn, "No later than Sunday midday. Charlyyk will need some rest."

She gave the phone back to Bryn, who asked, "Did you hear that, Major? No later than noon Sunday."

"I will convey your decision to them. Thank you, Captain."

Charlyyk burst into the cottage, grabbed a glass of milk, and headed straight out to the studio. Helen did not have a chance to say hello but followed her.

"Well, what you think?" Thomas was asking. He pulled up a chair for Charlyyk. "I've about four hours' more work to complete it." Charlyyk just stared at it.

Helen stood behind her. "Isn't it lovely?"

"No bulrushes, there in that area where the tree hangs down," Charlyyk said. She knew every bit, every blade of grass. Dippers Meadow was her domain. This was where she drifted in her mind when she needed to shut the rest of the world away. It was where she went as a refuge—lying in the grass, listening to the strange, beautiful sounds of birds and insects. Her planet had been quiet compared to the vibrant noises of this world.

At dinner, Bryn informed them of their forthcoming visit to the Royal Hospital Chelsea. Helen told Charlyyk about the

Chelsea pensioners and the charitable work they did. To be eligible to be a Chelsea pensioner, a veteran must have served twenty-two years in the services to the rank of warrant officer. Charlyyk noted, "So, Dad, you could qualify to be one."

Margret confirmed she would be away for four days, as the shipment of paintings was due to arrive tomorrow. She had booked herself into a hotel close by the gallery. Thomas and Rachel smiled their approval.

By Thursday, winter had arrived. It was freezing. Under Charlyyk's tracksuit was another layer of clothes. Jane Parsons had knitted Charlyyk some gloves and a pom-pom hat in pink wool for Christmas. This was the day to wear them with pride. She was keen to show James that she had them on as she waved to him, passing by the cow sheds.

At breakfast, with Helen's guidance, Charlyyk checked her homework for Mrs Butler. She could not thank Helen enough for the help she had given her—and what Helen had put in her lunch box. Rachel could only smile at their interaction. She joined Helen to wave goodbye to Charlyyk as she left on the school bus.

Rachel said, walking back indoors, "I just love the way you and Charlyyk have with each other. If that is motherhood, I can't wait to have it."

Thomas and Rachel went to the studio. Bryn and Helen went to the study to catch up on the evidence they might need at the weekend.

At the academy, Mr Pearson pointed at the smart board. "We have many indications of how Britain has changed. Would anyone like to add to them?"

Charlyyk was the only one to respond. "It appears that progress in electronics has led the way: fridges, freezers, television, and computers. It was fridges that allowed people to make food last longer. Washing machines and vacuum cleaners made household chores easier and gave women more free time. Some women started to go out to work to supplement the family budget. This allowed ordinary families to afford cars and go abroad on holiday. With joint incomes, buying a house became possible." Charlyyk had spent many hours on the internet, looking at all the changes that could have been the reasons for such a dramatic change to the British way of life.

This pleased Mr Pearson. This was what he really wanted to hear. "Anyone else?"

Mike raised his hand. "My nan said that the first luxury item they got was wall-to-wall fitted carpets. They were made with a synthetic material and not wool."

Mr Pearson entered on the smart board what Charlyyk had said. "Yes. It is not always politics that changes people's lives, but new inventions and industry that can have the biggest impact." He made a few notes. "Well done, Charlyyk."

At the cottage over some lunch. Thomas showed his father and Helen the finished paintings. "It was Rachel's idea to paint Dippers Meadow. It will give Charlyyk a settling effect when she is reminded of her own planet.

She sometimes feels guilty that she is safe and the group were not."

Margret admired the two other paintings. "I remember when we went there and saw you sketching those scenes. They are lovely. I understand what you mean about how a painting might help to calm Charlyyk. I'm getting the same effect from these paintings."

Thomas and Rachel had already been to town and purchased a picture frame for the painting of Dippers Meadow. They hung the completed picture in Charlyyk's bedroom. When she arrived home from school, Rachel was excited to see the expression on her face as Charlyyk admired the painting.

Rachel was not disappointed. Charlyyk almost flipped as she had done at Disney World when meeting Olaf. She sat on her bed, just gazing at the image. Her hands were clasped between her knees. Her body leaned forward. There was a longing look on her face. She was there in the painting, lying in the grass, listening to the birds and the insects.

On Friday, Margret said her goodbyes. Thomas and Rachel were driving her to the hotel. She would oversee the opening of the container that the artwork had been transported in, and check that they were in good health. Thomas and Rachel would drive on to Liverpool to set up the next exhibition.

CHAPTER 11

CHELSEA PENSIONERS

On Saturday, the drive to the Royal Hospital Chelsea did not take long. For Charlyyk it was another new adventure. It was just as exciting for the pensioners, who stood to attention and saluted when the Colliers entered the building from the Chelsea Gate entrance. It had been commissioned by King Charles II and designed and built by Sir Christophe Wren three hundred years before.

Major Carter welcomed them in and showed them to the room where the interview would take place. Many officers were already known to Bryn and Helen, and many warm handshakes were exchanged. Bryn knew it was going to be an informal interview because of the way the seating had been arranged in a circle.

Major Alan Carter opened the proceedings by requesting they all drop rank. "Bryn would like matters to remain informal, for the sake of Charlyyk. As this is the first meeting among all of us about the abduction, Bryn, we would like emphasise that the active military members here have had many other meetings prior to today. Your detailed report showed us that you had not lost your understanding of how important this could be. The meeting in Interlaken was only about you. Today we would like to hear from you both."

Bryn did not hesitate to tell his side of the story and show the evidence he had brought with him.

A rather young brigadier, Alex Hutton, spoke to Charlyyk. "The battleground can be frightening to hardened soldiers, let alone a young girl like yourself. How did you see it, my dear?"

Charlyyk had thought about what questions would be asked and had considered her responses. "At the time my group was trapped, we were gathering the fruit from the *cruul* tree. Maarlyyk was keeping watch while Taarlyyk and I collected the fruit. We knew we had little time, as the beast was aware that the fruit was our favourite food. Maarlyyk gave out a warning that she could smell the Feeng approaching. We made our move towards our home burrows. Suddenly a net fell on us. We were scooped up by many bear-like beasts. As the net tightened around us, we could not move. From the little that I could see, we were carried for some way. We were placed on-board the craft that transported us to the place where I met Dad."

Charlyyk took a moment to compose herself as the memories flooded back to her. "I was so frightened—frozen to the spot, unable to move in the holding pen. One by one, we were pulled out to be eaten by those beasts. I had given up thinking about survival. I just wondered when death was going to happen.

"One of the beasts plucked me up as though I were an apple. But another beast wanted me too. The one that had lifted me took me away from the pen. I was stressed out with the expectation of being ripped apart. Remembering the screams the others had made, I knew the outlook was not good for me."

Charlyyk's body was trembling. Bryn squeezed her hand.

"It started to pull at my arm. Then all at once, a body flew over us and grabbed at the head of the beast. I heard a crack. The beast had not stood a chance. It let go of me, and I dropped to the floor. I saw the reason for it letting me go—the strange thing that had saved me was struggling to get to its feet. I just lay there, not daring to move, waiting to see what this strange being was going to do. It took no interest in me but looked closely at the weapon the beast had. I looked around to see if I could flee, but I was not able to do so.

"I saw the stranger was hurt. I made my mind up that if I could help it, it could help me."

Helen poured her a glass of water, and she sipped from it.

"I could tell the strange thing was struggling." Charlyyk took another sip of water and carried on telling the story of how she had struggled to sew Bryn up. "When I had done the best I could, this stranger fell asleep. It was cold, so I took the garment the dead beast was wearing and covered us with it. I cuddled the stranger that had saved me, to keep us both as warm as possible. Later, I heard the other beasts crowding in, looking at their dead comrade. I woke the stranger to warn it of the danger we were in."

Alex was more interested in what she had seen in the arena. "Did you see anything different to what Bryn saw?"

Charlyyk thought for a moment and looked at Bryn. "Dad had lost a lot of blood and was struggling to maintain his strength. I kept an eye on the near and present dangers that were mounting. The beam of light kept dropping more and more severe problems on him. The furry alligators did not come from the beam of light, but from a cage that was dropped from a place near where my dad saw the other alien. How he found the strength to hurl a furry alligator at it, I do not know." Charlyyk looked at her dad with a lot of pride. She knew what he had done for her. "But it was the Feeng that caught him with a terrible hit to his chest. I was already clinging to his legs when the beam of light engulfed us. And then we were somewhere else."

Alex looked at a sheet of paper. "About the holding pen—can you tell us what you can recall of what went on there?"

Charlyyk paused for thought. "When we were herded off the craft that took us there, we were pushed into a large crate. It smelt of other creatures." She stopped and closed her eyes. Bryn knew the trembling in her body was a reaction to the nightmare. Charlyyk's hand reached out for his. Her grasp was tight. "We were lowered into the hellhole before the crate was opened. I smelt something that I had smelt before. I could not see it, but the scent was in my nose."

Alex went to say something, but Major Carter stopped him. "Be patient. Charlyyk is delving into her memory banks. Give her time."

Helen could tell by the way Charlyyk's ears and eyes were twitching that she was in a different place. Then her eyes opened. "It was at the place where the group lived. It was there." She looked terrified.

Helen took her hand. Charlyyk's eyes had changed to a mauve colour. This worried Helen, and she got Bryn's attention. He too became concerned, but he did not want to disrupt her thinking.

"We found strange footprints around the opening to our living burrow."

Alex could tell by the way Charlyyk was behaving that these footprints were different than what they had seen before. "How strange were they?"

Charlyyk held her hands up. "All beings on our planet have four digits. These footprints had only two, wide as a cow's." She took a deep breath. "Knowing how Fuung and Feeng smell, I knew it could not be either of them."

Alex could not understand why she was so frightened. "What is it that troubles you?"

She looked at him. "It had killed a Fuung and dragged it off."

Bryn's head shot around to look at her. "No wonder you were frightened."

Alex still could not grasp what they were talking about. Helen showed him drawings of a Fuung and a Feeng. These made clear the difference in their size and what they could be related to. Then he realised why Charlyyk was concerned.

Bryn thought about what Charlyyk had told them. He had a flash of memory of when he first found himself in the arena. It had not been light he had seen out of the corner of his eye, but a large, dark form moving away. Hard as he tried, he could not tell what it was. What was happening at that same time with the Feeng concerned him more.

Major Carter had given the military chiefs a breakdown of what had been disclosed already and copies of the pictures of the aliens. The story that Charlyyk had told was new. Her statement brought in the likelihood of another alien. But with no description, it did not really give the military anything to work with. If the new alien had only two digits, how could it kill? And drag a Fuung away? It did not make sense unless this new alien was a mode of transport for something else. "Charlyyk, did you smell anything else at the time when the Fuung was killed?"

Charlyyk's eyes closed. Her ears were twitching. Her eyes moved under the lids. For a time, she held Bryn's hands. He felt the tension coming from her. When she opened her eyes, she turned and looked at him. "The alien on the craft—not the pilot, but the second one—was also there."

Lieutenant Colonel Jim Murthy was an old friend of Bryn's. "What are you thinking, Alan?"

The major nodded with a knowing look. "Like we would use a horse." He turned to Charlyyk. "How big were those footprints?"

She thought for a moment. Taking a sheet of newspaper, she folded it to the size she remembered.

Alan took a good look at it. "That's a lot bigger than a carthorse's hoof." It was not much to go on, but each little nudge brought something new to the table.

Time had passed. A Chelsea pensioner approached and announced that dinner was ready. He escorted them to the dining hall.

Charlyyk sat among the pensioners, enjoying the old stories from these veteran soldiers. When Bryn was asked to retell a story, he described leading his squad into their first mission in Kuwait during the Gulf War. He explained how nervous they were. Sergeant Brodie asked him to give the soldiers words of encouragement. Bryn obliged with a story. "We were on the beach. The wind swept in from the sea, blowing the sand into our faces. A lone piper could be heard in the distance, and shots were going off all around us. Bannerman pointed to the top of a large sand dune. The time was ten past eleven. 'We must be there by twelve!' he demanded. The sand was soft and made the going very hard. We formed a caterpillar and pushed ourselves up the sand dune. Shots could still be heard all around us. Men were falling. They were left where they fell. We achieved our objective and reached the top by twelve, just in time to see Nick Faldo and Seve Ballesteros tee off on the ninth at the Old Royal Troon Open."

Major Carter could not stop laughing. He had heard it before, but he knew the calming effect it had had on those young soldiers going into battle for the first time. It had settled their nerves, so when they hit the front line, they worked as a unit. Many army training instructors used Captain Collier's training techniques because of the success they had with them.

Brigadier Alex Hutton had heard of the deeds of Captain Collier. His men never questioned him because they knew he always had their welfare at heart. He never asked them to do something he would not do himself. Charlyyk and Helen revelled in the way the old soldiers showed their man so much respect.

Charlyyk and Helen were separated by a robust pensioner with a large white moustache and wire-framed glasses. He spoke to Charlyyk. "What do you think about your new dad?"

She said with a soft smile, "My auntie Gwen has a lot of faith in her god. I have the same faith in my dad."

During the meal, some of the pensioners asked questions of Charlyyk. She would leave the table, walk to those who asked a question, and give her answers directly. Helen admired the time and patience she gave them all. Charlyyk had realised that some of the pensioners were hard of hearing, and she did not like shouting. It gave the other pensioners a chance to see her close up, and they appreciated her efforts.

When dinner was finished, they carried on talking. The brigadier asked Charlyyk about her planet. She was quick to point out that she never travelled far from the place where she lived, due to the danger of being eaten. Lieutenant Colonel Jim Murthy then asked, "You have lived among us for two years. Do you question how you have been able to adapt to our ways?"

She looked slightly annoyed. "I have to adapt. I have no choice but to adapt. If you mean have I found it hard, no. Guidance from the family has made it as easy as possible."

"Then what sort of question do you ask yourself?"

She looked down into her lap, her hands clasped on her knees. "Why there were no older ones in the group and no babies. Why there were only females, all of the same age. Living among you, I see family units. We did not have that, but I must have come from someone. You don't just appear like magic, do you?"

Bryn and Helen looked at each other. They had not heard this before, and they wondered how they had missed asking about her family.

Alex Hutton wrote down what had been said. "What made you think along those lines, Charlyyk?"

She shifted to make her tail feel more comfortable. "Going to school and seeing the same age group, but with mixed sexes. In my group on my home planet, there were only *lyyks*. At that time, we were trying to survive, so we had no reason to give it any thought. Now it does not make sense. No matter how I try, I cannot resolve it."

Major Carter sat down next to Bryn. "The more we uncover, the more we add to the confusion."

Helen looked around. The questions had dried up. "I think we should call time on this. We are not getting anywhere, and we need to give ourselves time to reflect on what has been said."

Alex Hutton spoke with Jim Murthy, then said, "Yes, we agree. If we need to talk again, I suggest that we meet you at your house. Thank you for assistance."

Alex wanted to dissect the information that had been given before asking any more questions. He felt they needed a clear objective as to where the next questioning should be directed. "We can tell the circumstances of the meeting of Bryn and Charlyyk were hit or miss. To make anything from what we have heard will need careful consideration."

On Sunday morning, a cold, biting wind blew. It made the three of them push harder. The wind was holding back the chance of rain. Charlyyk covered her head with the hood to protect her ears, just in case. The trumpet shape of her ears could fill with rainwater, making it uncomfortable for her. Gwen had made her plastic covers for her ears so she could shower easily. But she felt self-conscious about wearing them in public.

The shower, when she could feel the water flowing over her without worrying about her ears, was a sheer delight. Shampooing her hair was something else she delighted in. Michel had noted how her body had changed due to Earth's custom of bathroom pampering. Her skin had been leathery when she first arrived. Now it was soft, and her hair glowed smooth and silky.

Standing in front of the mirror, she loved feeling herself. She could not help herself from running her hands over her own body, exploring the changes. She dressed in her new silk lingerie and the dress she had bought at Christmas. She felt she had won the lottery.

Helen wondered where she was and came to see if she was all right. "Hi, there, are you OK? I was getting worried."

Charlyyk was sitting at her dressing table. Helen stood behind her, took up the hairbrush, and gently brushed her hair. "Thanks, Mum."

Helen smiled at her, bent down, and kissed the top of her head. "Pleasure, darling."

At Carpenters' cottage, Bryn explained what had occurred at the meeting the day before. Harold and Gwen listened intently. Harold mulled over the information. "So at no time did you see any older persons in your group?"

Charlyyk pondered the question. "No. I have asked myself the same question many times." But another thought keeps entering my head—the thing that killed the Fuung, was it protecting us?"

Helen said, "That could mean all this could have been orchestrated by them?"

Bryn's face showed he agreed that the possibilities were there. "It is feasible. It was set up very nicely. Anyone could have been chosen at random, but this was not random."

Helen saw Charlyyk was getting concerned. She placed her arm around Charlyyk. "I'm so glad it was you, sweetheart."

"I was worried you might have got angry," Charlyyk said. She gave a little gulp. "Thinking you were set up."

Harold made a motion with his hand. "But what could they be doing this for? There must be a reason."

Gwen stepped into the conversation. "Let's think about it. We have to be logical with the information we have to go on. A snap decision could lead us astray." Gwen felt Charlyyk was thinking too hard. Gwen had spent most time getting to understand Charlyyk and her special ways. She had seen this change in Charlyyk's demeanour before, and it had led to problems. Helen and Gwen took Charlyyk into the lounge to settle her down.

Bryn and Harold filled their glasses and quietly went over much of what had been talked about. Harold collected some paper and started to put things in order of events—sequences that Bryn had described. It did not change anything. The matter still did not make any sense at all. He screwed the paper up and tossed it into the bin.

The next morning followed the usual routine: a run, breakfast and then onto the school bus. Charlyyk was quiet. The thoughts of the weekend would not go away. Mace tried to talk to her, but Charlyyk could not engage.

At school, the posse allowed her a little space. After the first lesson with Mrs Butler, Mike spoke to Charlyyk. At first, she did not want to talk, but he would not let her carry on taking her problems on her own. During Mr Waverly's lesson, Mike made a plea to Charlyyk to speak to the class. She had helped many of them when they needed help, and he argued it was her duty to allow them to help her. Mr Waverly was keen to help persuade Charlyyk to talk.

There were tears in Charlyyk's eyes. Mike took her hand and supported her. "A trouble shared is a trouble halved," he said.

Julia was the next one to give her encouragement. She took hold of Charlyyk's other hand, not saying anything, just giving her a squeeze.

Charlyyk saw the concern on all their faces. She took a deep breath and told them a little about what had happened at the weekend and revelations that had been discussed.

Mr Waverly pulled a chair up and sat in front of her. "Charlyyk, you have done nothing wrong. You were just a pawn in some other people's game."

Mace and Sandra could not stand back and allow their friend to take the guilt solely on her own shoulders. They approached her in a caring manner.

Mike said, "We all love you. You have given us great pleasure with your friendship. In your own way, you have helped us all to look at ourselves more closely. You never expected anything in return. This is our chance to support you. If you can't say more to us now, talk to your new family. They won't blame you but love you, just like us."

At lunchtime, the posse was in full support mode. They gave Charlyyk space and tried hard to keep off the subject of the morning.

Mr Waverly informed Mrs Landon about what had happened. She was soon on the phone to the Colliers. Helen answered the phone and assured Mrs Landon that they had allowed Charlyyk time to think through what had taken place on that faraway planet. Her unique way of looking at problems usually resulted in a solution. Helen thanked Louise and confirmed her intention to discuss the matter with Charlyyk's father.

The school bus trundled down the lane and stopped at the cottage. Charlyyk stepped down from the bus to see Bryn and Helen standing together with warm smiles on their faces. As she walked towards them, they raised their hands to greet her. She rushed into their arms and buried herself in them. They could feel her body trembling with total emotion.

Bryn knelt in front of her. "Sweetheart we both love you very much, and that will never change. We are a family. Whatever happens, we will stick together."

Inside the cottage, Charlyyk relayed what her classmates had said to her. Helen picked up on her admiration of Mike. He had orchestrated the class to rally around her.

After dinner, Bryn made an effort to sit with Charlyyk, giving her plenty of cuddles.

Later when Charlyyk was in her bedroom, she texted Janet, explaining what had happened. Janet did not text back but phoned her instead on the landline. Their conversation lasted for an hour. Charlyyk conveyed her fear that she had been used to in some way. She could not work out logically why the aliens had done what they had done. Janet promised she would return on Wednesday.

At breakfast, Helen spoke with Charlyyk. Bryn watched on, pleased with how Helen was handling the situation. Helen walked with Charlyyk to meet the school bus. Charlyyk put her arms around Helen and gave her a big, loving hug. The bus door opened. Mace and Sarah were soon surrounding her. The warm smile Charlyyk gave Helen from the bus gave Bryn satisfaction that his two girls were as one again.

At school, the posse was soon in attendance, checking to see if Charlyyk was OK. She thanked them all for helping her. To Mike's surprise, Charlyyk gave him an extra big hug and a kiss on the cheek. "You persisted in helping me, and I am so grateful. I was so down on myself,

I could not see the truth—that when you have friends who care, you should listen to them."

The school bell rang, and they attended their lessons. Mrs Landon called for Charlyyk to see her in her office. "Charlyyk, Mr Waverly and Mrs Butler informed me how upset you were yesterday, and how it affected the whole class. How are you today?"

Charlyyk tried to smile but struggled. "I've spoken with my parents. I now see I should have been more open with them, and not bottled up my emotions. I thought I had let them down, that I would have been to blame if my dad had died on that planet. But my mum said I could not blame myself if I did not know why what was happening."

Charlyyk went on to explain the story in full. She described how Mike had persisted in urging her to talk to the whole class. Mrs Landon stood up and took Charlyyk's hand. "Come, let's take a walk."

Leaving the office, they walked around the school. Louise Landon showed Charlyyk the importance of school life. They looked in on classes and observed the involvement between teacher and students.

"When you see your aunt and uncle, look at the photos on their walls. The photos show you how we as teachers get involved and try hard to get the best from you. Any problem that you may have can upset school life. We need the students to confide in us so we can help. You are fortunate to have such good friends. Friends bring out the best in each other, as you brought out the best in Mike. Mr Waverly remarked on how he handled the situation. Mr Waverly said he was the most unlikely person to have done what he did yesterday. Such friendship you could not buy for all the money in the world, so value it with pride."

At lunch the posse asked Charlyyk about her morning. They had observed her walking with the headmistress and were inquisitive. Jan especially pushed for details, but Charlyyk only gave them a brief summary of what was said.

Back home at Oakleaves. Charlyyk was more forthcoming about what had occurred that morning. Helen did not tell her about the phone call she had made to Louise Landon, informing her of the weekend revelations. Getting Charlyyk to talk about it settled her.

During dinner, Charlyyk remembered that Janet was returning on Wednesday and informed her parents. Bryn agreed with Helen that a visit would be good for Charlyyk.

When they returned to Oakleaves after their morning run, the laughter and playful mood carried on through breakfast. Charlyyk was back to her usual self.

She ran to the bus, eager to be with her friends. She hugged Sarah and Mace. Bryn and Helen waved her off. Life at the cottage was normal again. The playful way Bryn grabbed Helen's hand left no doubts in Helen's mind that the good life had returned to Oakleaves.

Meanwhile, Tim Pearson's class were studying the smart board. "These are the points you have made about the changing face of Britain. I want you to write a speech about it. You should write only four paragraphs to explain your point of view. May I suggest that when you write, you allow time to read your work and check your use of language? Plan your format. How will you open your speech? First paragraph: a direct statement of how you feel and why. Second paragraph: seeing other points of view. Third paragraph: the evidence for your point of view. Fourth paragraph: the effect of what you propose. And how will you close your speech?"

At lunchtime, the posse gathered to discuss the homework Mr Pearson had given them. Sandra and Peter, now an item, sat with Julia and Charlyyk. Mike was now a major player. The rest of the posse were in close order. The debate was orderly, each making notes on what was discussed. Keeping a close eye on them was Mrs Butler. She looked pleased with what she saw. Her report to Mrs Landon was that all was well.

Janet was at Oakleaves when Charlyyk came home from school. She stood in the driveway, waiting for the bus to arrive. Charlyyk had missed her badly, and the embrace they gave each other showed Janet had missed Charlyyk too.

After dinner, Charlyyk explained to Janet the confusion she had got herself into. "I felt that it was me who was at fault. I needed to put it right, but could not see how. The more I thought about it, the worst it became."

Janet gave her a cuddle. "Now you see what real friends are about. We are here to help when time get hard. Those who stay and help are your true friends."

CHAPTER 12

ANALYSING CHARLYYK

Bryn trailed the women on the morning run. The three were talking girl talk, and it was probably not for Bryn's ears. He did not mind. Seeing them all happy gave him satisfaction. It was a nice family unit they were becoming.

Helen was at ease when Janet was there. She found herself confiding in Janet the things she found hard to talk about with Gwen. Although Gwen was no problem to talk to, she was still Bryn's sister, and Helen had felt twinges of awkwardness.

After Charlyyk had gone to school, the adults went to Carpenters' cottage. Over coffee, they discussed the situation that the weekend had thrown up.

Harold seemed surprised by how Charlyyk had reacted, but Gwen was not. "Any thought that could have jeopardised Bryn would have concerned her. Because she could not see the truth of it, the problem compounded. The more she thought about how to solve the problem, the bigger the problem became. We have a lot to thank young Mike for. He grasped the situation before Charlyyk had a total meltdown."

Harold could not understand Gwen's theory. "But Charlyyk's logic has always served her well. She usually finds what she is looking for. And if she can't find the solution, she keeps trying. The tension in her increases till it creates a ticking time-bomb. If allowed to go on, it would have led to a meltdown."

Gwen glanced at Harold with raised eyebrows.

Janet said, "I totally agree with you, Gwen. It's the way she handles most things, with logical solutions. The problem was that she could not be logical with the evidence she had, for it was all conjecture and no facts."

Helen asked Janet if she was going to use this knowledge in one of her articles. "Definitely not," Janet said. "I am now Charlyyk's friend, and that brings responsibility to act as a friend. I told you all from the beginning that I was not here to dig the dirt. She has vulnerabilities I will not discuss. Charlyyk really isn't any different than us. She has a brain; she just uses it differently."

Helen reached over and touched her hand. "You are right. She really isn't any different. She is a young girl growing up on a different planet."

Bryn had been quiet up till then. "We are not condemning her. We need to understand her. We know from past experiences that she is sensitive, as most people can be. She has feelings very similar to ours."

Janet selected a biscuit from the plate in front of her. "When James talks about Charlyyk, he has a great deal of respect for her. He acts like a big brother towards her, and it has rubbed off on me. When I think about her, it's like I'm her sister. We all want the best for her."

Gwen nodded. "I feel like a mother duck towards her, always trying to shelter her under my wing."

Helen gave a big sigh. "Charlyyk calling me mum makes me go weak at the knees. And when she cuddles up to me, I could just melt. I never in my wildest dreams thought this would happen to me, so when she was so troubled on Monday, I felt it too. It really hurt. But as Bryn has said, we need to understand her so that we can help her."

<hr>

Bryn and Helen waited for the school bus the next day under the shelter of a large golfing umbrella. Helen stepped toward the bus to meet Charlyyk and give her cover. The laughing face of Charlyyk brought out a laugh in Helen. "What's the laugh for, sweetheart?"

Charlyyk stood as close to Helen as possible because of the rain. "Fred the bus driver said you looked like a mushroom standing there."

As they entered the cottage, to Charlyyk's surprise, James appeared. "Hi, twinkle." She rushed into his arms and kissed him with as many kisses as she could. Janet poked her with her finger. "Get off, he's mine." Then Janet tickled her.

Helen took Charlyyk's coat. She sat with James and Janet while Bryn and Helen prepared the evening meal.

When James returned home, Janet and Helen sat with Charlyyk, discussing her homework for Mr Pearson. Bryn watched the interaction between them. It confirmed his theory that they were a good family unit.

The men's magazine for which Bryn had posed in the photo shoot had sent him a mock-up to peruse before general release. It was spread out in front of him. He was not sure he liked it. The article that was printed before his featured a scantily clad girl who looked younger than Charlyyk. But Janet had confirmed she was of legal age.

The editor had not made significant changes to Bryn's story; it was as Janet had written it.

Another article caught Bryn's attention, and he read with interest about prostate problems in middle-aged men. He was not struggling with that issue himself, but he thought it was good to keep an eye on it, just in case.

On Friday, the weather was damp. The trek up the lane leading to the farm was very slippery. James had kept an eye out for them and came over to the gate to collect kisses from Janet and Charlyyk. Bryn could not help laughing at the little heel click James gave as he turned away. Then James slipped as he landed and found himself flat on the ground. The two women rushed back to check he was all right.

Janet had collected enough material to write about the visit to the Royal Chelsea Hospital. She was also finishing an article for a teen magazine, based on the fashion side of Charlyyk. She was expecting to take some fashion shots of her at the weekend.

Mike had asked Charlyyk to help him with his homework. He had completely messed up. Charlyyk went through it with him, supported by Julia. Afterwards, Julia said to Charlyyk, "It wasn't that bad." She had noticed Mike was more assertive than he used to be. "What do you reckon—do you think Mike is changing?"

Charlyyk thought about it. "I believe we are all changing. We have all started to look at life differently. Take Peter and Sandra for example. They are not stupid with their relationship. It is nice to see how they respect each other." Charlyyk sensed that the vibes Julia was giving out about Mike had become stronger than before.

Sarah overheard what they were saying. "Do you sense something, Charlyyk?"

"Well, my nose is picking up something." Sarah and Julia leaned closer so Charlyyk could whisper, "Jan is giving out vibes."

Their eyes widened and they closed in tighter. "Who with?"

Charlyyk lowered her voice further. "No one in our year. It happens every time Mace's brother is around."

Sarah asked breathlessly, "Is he responding?"

Charlyyk smiled. "Oh yes. It is still early days, but there is a reaction from him."

There was glee in their eyes, knowing something no one else knew. Charlyyk was quick to remind them, "Now don't say anything. Otherwise, you could spoil it." She looked at them both very sternly. "Promise me you will not say anything to anyone. If you do, I will never confide in you again."

They both promised her that the matter would stay between them.

Charlyyk did not want Julia to know how and who she was responding to—well, not yet.

Thomas, Rachel, and Margret arrived at Oakleaves at three. There was a jovial atmosphere among them as they entered the cottage. Bryn greeted them. Helen was already making tea. As usual, they congregated in the kitchen.

Margret was most pleased with what Janet had written for them. When Janet entered the kitchen, Margret spread her arms out to greet her. "Thank you, Janet! Thank you so very much! The articles are fantastic."

Bryn still could not believe the changes that had happened in his life since his return to Earth with Charlyyk. He had gone from obscure loneliness to living in a beehive. Helen touched his hand. "Come on, sweetheart. The bus will be here soon." He looked into her eyes, slipped his arm around her waist, pulled her towards him, and kissed her. Helen sighed and leaned back. "I will give you twenty-four hours to stop doing that, kind sir." Then she kissed him back. "The bus?"

With that, they went to meet Charlyyk, cuddling under the golfing brolly. Charlyyk stepped off the bus with an enormous smile spread across her face. She had already spotted the Picasso parked in front of the garage.

Her jaunty walk towards the cottage left Bryn and Helen in no doubt that they had their daughter back.

Inside the cottage, everyone was waiting for Charlyyk with lots of hugs and kisses. To all their surprise, Margret produced a large shopping bag. "Charlyyk, I saw this and I thought of you, so with all my love, this is yours." Charlyyk peered into the bag and took out an emerald-green dress of fine wool knit. It was V-necked and had three-quarter-length sleeves, with a half collar that rose up at the back.

Janet looked at how Charlyyk received this gift, taking mental notes, trying to understand the emotions she was experiencing. "Come, let's try it on."

They collected up the bits and went to the bedroom. Charlyyk was a little taken aback by this surprise from Margret, and it showed on her face. Janet helped her to put the dress on. Opening the wardrobe doors, she allowed Charlyyk to see how it looked on her. Charlyyk admitted that the dress looked better on than it did off. "It looked a bit old-fashioned when I took it out of the bag, but now—wow. It reminds me of Audrey Hepburn in *Breakfast at Tiffany's*."

She turned this way and that. She thrust her hands in the side pockets pulling the skirt out and letting it go. She looked at herself from the back to see how her tail behaved in the dress. "Let's show Margret what a great dress she has brought me."

The family was amazed at how the dress transformed her. It put a few years on her; she did not look at all a little girl. Margret asked her to turn around. Then she gave Charlyyk a hug. "This is just as I imagined it in the shop. I am so pleased I bought it. You look fantastic."

CHARLYYK

Charlyyk hugged Margret. "Thank you so very much. It was such a lovely gesture, and I really do appreciate it."

Janet was already considering the photo shoot options for Charlyyk. "Black shoes, a little heel, patent. Yes, tomorrow morning we are going to a little shoe shop I know." Janet pressed buttons on her phone. "Tina, Janet Stokes. Listen. Narrow fitting, size six, black patent, a little heel, anything?" Janet waited for the reply. "Good girl. See you early tomorrow."

Rachel sidled up to Janet. "Can I come?"

Janet took her arm in hers. "Of course you can. Love to have you on board." Then she turned to Bryn and Helen with a guilty look on her face. "Sorry, I hope you don't mind?"

Bryn looked at Helen. They both nodded. "Of course not. Charlyyk must be able to do these things."

For the rest of the day, the cottage was a hive of activity. Margret went over the details of the exhibition. Thomas and Rachel explained how the trip to Liverpool had gone. Janet took Bryn and Helen through the details of what she wanted to achieve.

Charlyyk was in her bedroom on the computer. Julia was on the other end, telling her of the emails she was getting from Mike. "He needs to react to someone, so I told him to speak with Mace. Did I do right, Charlyyk?"

Charlyyk agreed with her and signed off. Mike needed help, and Mace fit the bill perfectly. Charlyyk had watched the changes in Mike, and she knew these were not intentional. They were just happening. Mace's quiet manner was what Mike needed.

Janet was at the wheel of her red Mini, with One Direction beating out of her car stereo system. The girls sang along— well, the two women sang and Charlyyk howled. They were making good headway towards Bourne End and the shoe shop.

At the cottage, Bryn was in conversation with Major Carter. Bryn had told him of their theory, and he had dropped in to go over the details with Bryn. "It definitely makes sense, but it throws open a lot of other questions the top brass have been looking at." They discussed a few angles. Helen had made a detailed report for Major Carter to pass along to the various armed forces. In it, Helen mentioned that Charlyyk had remarked on the point that her group were all females of a certain age. Major Carter pursed his lips. "It's been a constant drip, drip of information, Bryn."

"Yes, but that's usually what happens in these circumstances. You cannot remember anything. Then you're given some little nudge and you do remember, or see it in a clearer light." Bryn stopped and looked towards the floor. He closed his eyes, then looked at Alan. "I saw a large shape move out of the corner of my eye when I was trying to survive, but can I see it now? No. One day something will trigger that image, and it will be back to the drawing board."

Janet parked the car in a pub's car park just down a side street from Tina's shoe shop. Tina found Charlyyk's feet a little troublesome. "My, they are narrow." Janet knew she would not give up on Charlyyk.

Tina's assistant came back with four boxes. In the second box was a lovely pair of black, kitten-heel, multi-strap court shoes. Then the Cinderella moment when the foot fitted the shoe arrived. As Charlyyk walked up and down, stopping and turning, she looked the happy bunny.

Also in the box was a little clutch bag made of the bookbinder leather to match the shoes. Rachel and Janet just loved them together. Tina could not find a price for the shoes as they had been in the shop for many years. Janet worked out an offer that Tina could not refuse. Neither Janet nor Rachel could resist picking up a couple of pairs of shoes themselves.

The drive back to Oakleaves was much the same as the drive to town, complete with a full-throttle sing-along to One Direction.

Major Carter completed his talk with Bryn and warned him that more meetings would be required.

Margret was with Thomas in the study, finalising the set-up for the exhibition. Bryn and Helen came in, and they all enjoyed a cup of coffee. The trio arrived, still in fine voice. Helen took an interest in Charlyyk's new shoes, but it was the little clutch bag that stole the limelight. Helen remarked, "It's the feel of the leather. It's so soft."

After the coffees, Janet, with the help of everyone, set up the photo shoot: the lighting, the white linen drapes, a few props here and there. Charlyyk came in wearing the clothes she normally wore—tight jeans, a casual top, and her favourite white tennis shoes. She posed like the models in the fashion magazines. The white drapes could be altered by colour filters to create a different ambience.

Then Charlyyk changed into the Laura Ashley dress and cherry-red tights. She also put on the Burberry camel coat. Rachel and Helen did her make-up and hair between shots.

Next to be worn was the dress she had brought at Christmas and the dress Margret had brought, with the black shoes and clutch bag. Then Charlyyk surprised them by posing in her silk underwear and nightwear. Helen kept a close eye on these proceedings.

Time had flown by. They were all a little tired and hungry. Everyone was pleased to hear that Bryn had ordered a table at an Italian restaurant.

Clearing up did not take long. They were all keen for dinner. The conversation was mainly about how the day had gone. Harold and Gwen were already at the Restaurant Milan, an authentic Italian eating place, with long tables to accommodate families. This was a favourite of Harold and Gwen's, and the head waiter, Gino, was already buzzing around, making them feel at home. Gino's younger brother Alberto took the rest of the party's coats and seated them.

Helen liked her new life. She recalled lonely nights eating on her own. What a change had occurred. She loved family life. Yes, sometimes it was hard work, but God, it was worth it. The family's cheery banter confirmed her reasons for marrying Bryn.

Charlyyk was involved with everyone. Her laughter was infectious. This was the party girl having fun. A smile broke over Helen's face. She was gratified to find herself in this inestimable position at this time of her life.

⁂

On Sunday morning, Rachel lay in a nice warm bed. She felt contented, and she pulled the covers up and re-settled herself.

Ten minutes later, the door opened. Her mother entered bearing a tray with two large mugs of tea. "Move over, sweetheart and let your mother in."

Rachel could not refuse. It had been a long time since this had happened. The morning of her wedding had been the last time, and it had felt special then. "I have never stopped loving you, Mum, nor shall I ever stop loving you. But I love Thomas more, and now I'm with child, you stand a close third. You are not out of my daily thoughts. It's not for me to give you a chance, but for you to earn it."

Margret realised what Rachel was telling her. It would come down to what she did, not what Thomas and Rachel did. The onus was on her.

Rachel placed her empty mug on the bedside cabinet. "When you see Thomas, his dad, Harold, and Michel, you see in them what most girls' mothers would love their daughter's husbands to be like. But it does not mean that's what they will end up with. I am blessed with Thomas, and I intend to keep him, whatever it takes. When Thomas's mum came to our wedding. I saw how she handled Bryn. I vowed to carry on using her method with Thomas. Yes, Mum, it suits me fine. Thomas gets what he wants and I get what I want. I'm as proud as punch with that."

Margret saw herself in Rachel—the same determination, the same drive. But Rachel's endgame was very different to her own.

Rachel cuddled her mother. "Join us in our adventure. Don't walk away to be on your own."

The door opened and Thomas walked in. Seeing the two of them in bed together made him smile. "Hi. This looks cosy. Can I refill your mugs?"

The two passed their mugs to him with cheeky grins. "Yes, please."

When Thomas had left. Rachel looked at her mother. "See, Mum? I've caught the biggest fish in the sea, and I mean to keep him."

Margret stroked Rachel's tummy. "That's one special keep net, darling."

Rachel's wry smile and little snigger implied she knew the meaning of what her mother had said.

Breakfast was loud and buoyant, with much flippancy. They bantered about the way Charlyyk had performed the day before, comparing her to top fashion models and arguing over who she had tried to impersonate. Thomas remarked, "It definitely isn't Elle Macpherson, the Body." Everyone named a different model. Each one was subjected to scrutiny. Thomas brought the loudest laugh when, with a haughty flick of the wrist, he pronounced, "Of course it could only have been Julian Clary."

The phone rang, taking Bryn to his study. Thomas, Janet, and Charlyyk went to the lounge to go over photos of Charlyyk. Margret, Rachel, and Helen cleared the breakfast table.

Bryn was surprised to hear Brigadier Su Shi on the other end of the line. "Bryn—may I call you Bryn, not Brian?"

"Yes, Bryn will be OK."

"Bryn, I have a report in front of me from Major Carter, describing your theories. They leave us with many questions still to be answered."

Bryn picked up a folder. He had predicted that calls would come as soon as Alan Carter released the report Helen had written. "I have the report in front of me now. Are there any points I can help you with?"

"Yes. How was it that we did not pick this up earlier? It puts an entirely new meaning on events, even a different route to go down."

"We were casually talking when Charlyyk was asked if she had had any worries on her planet. She spoke about the group she was living with. She could not understand why they were all of a set age, with no one elderly or very young. It was like being in her year at school. That started a discussion between my brother-in-law and myself."

"I see. We were only looking one way at this. I will speak with Yuri, and Chad. Probably I'll get back to you. Bye."

Bryn let Helen know what had been said. Helen wondered if Su Shi was annoyed by the report. Bryn replied, "No, he was his usual self-inquisitive to get at the exact meaning of what was said."

Seeing Rachel's baby bump had made Janet broody. Her desire for James was becoming stronger. She felt a need to hurry back to Parsons' farm. Janet phoned James to brace himself for her return; he was quick to instruct her to meet him in the barn. This excited her even more. The roar of her poor Mini as her pedal hit the metal ended with the back end of the car skidding as it left the drive.

Rachel nudged Thomas. They had seen how impatient Janet was getting as she hurried to finish what she had started that morning. The roar of her Mini brought out an urge to rub baby oil on Rachel's bump. Their rush to the bedroom brought smiles to everyone else's faces.

Margret looked at Helen. "And it's not even spring,"

Later, at Carpenters' cottage, the men were in the kitchen and the women were in the lounge, each talking about their own favourite subjects. Bryn relayed the conversation he'd had with Su Shi.

Michel, stroking his chin, had the look of someone who had been asking himself the same question more than a few times. But now he was sure. "Would you bring Charlyyk to my surgery one evening?"

Bryn asked, "Why?"

"Look at it this way—if there was an intentional reason for Charlyyk to be here, could those aliens have planted something in her to monitor her?"

Bryn and Harold stared straight at Michel, not in shock but in realisation.

Harold said slowly, "It could be a possibility."

Michel was still stroking his chin. "The tests I have carried out on Charlyyk indicate that an X-ray would not have any detrimental effect on her, so let's give that a go."

Thomas asked, "Are you sure it won't harm her or set off a chain reaction in her?"

Michel nodded. "Better we do it than the government. At least we would know when to stop, but would they?"

Harold said, "I'm with you. Better us than them."

Bryn nodded. "When, Michel?"

Michel sounded more eager. "Tomorrow night. I will set up the surgery. I will tell her that it is essential we carry out these tests tomorrow night."

Over dinner, Michel slipped the matter of the X-ray into the conversation as though it were a matter-of-fact thing. Charlyyk had complete faith in Michel and did not query his request. Gwen and Helen looked first at Michel, then at Bryn and Harold. Their concern faded as the men looked satisfied with Michel's suggestion.

On Monday, the school bus dropped the students at the school gates. Friends mingled, talking about their weekend activities. Charlyyk, Sarah, and Mace strolled towards the area where the posse always congregated, exchanging hugs, high-fives, and kisses as they met.

Charlyyk was impressing them with photos of her fashion shoot when the school bell sounded. There was a surge to get into the warmth of the school.

At lunch, Charlyyk enjoyed what Helen had put in her lunch box. Helen always made sure each day's lunch was different.

Bryn and Helen for their part were having lunch with Margret. Thomas had taken Rachel shopping, and they would not be home until late. The phone rang. Helen answered, but soon gave it to Bryn.

"Hi, Bryn, Chad. I've spoken with Su Shi about the report your Helen gave us. I agree with him—this opens a new can of worms. I do believe another chat is in order. I am in touch with your Home Secretary and Defence Department to come to you this time, if you don't mind?"

"No, we don't mind. We welcome it. Charlyyk has had enough of evils, and we have just settled her over this, so please come to us."

Chad paused. "The computer guy from the Johnson Space Center wants to come and discuss some of his findings with Charlyyk. Is there somewhere we could put him up?"

"Bring him. I remember him well, and Charlyyk would love to see him again. We will sort him out."

Helen was listening in on the conversation. "Harold liked him. Let's ask him."

In Miss Vasey's class, the students watched Charlyyk apply wet on wet, just as Thomas had shown her. She switched brushes to add strokes of paint, turning the splotches into flowers. There were no drips of paint. She looked relaxed as she worked. She was enjoying the experience no end. Learning technique had given new meaning to art. She realised there were many ways to do art.

Alice Vasey showed her how to use sea salt and cotton buds to soak up wet paint, and how to use the blunt end of the brush to make white strikes and give a different aspect to the painting. Charlyyk saw more clearly what Margret and Thomas meant about learning different techniques to gain different results.

That evening, on the drive to Michel's surgery, Bryn allowed Charlyyk to sit in the front so she could choose the music she liked. He did this to make sure Charlyyk was settled. He even tried to show an interest in what she wanted to play, again to relax her.

Michel welcomed them to the surgery. He had a Labrador dog on the table. "Come in. Let me show you how it works." Clare, Michel's protégée, took an X-ray of the Labrador. They waited a little wait for the result and put the X-ray image up on the screen. "As you can see, he has swallowed his owner's car keys. Look where they are." Clare pointed to the tell-tale white outline on the X-ray. "Notice that you can see the whole bone structure of Bruno. Now, too many X-rays can be harmful, so we must put in place a few safeguards. I will guide you through the procedure."

Charlyyk removed all her clothes and jewellery. She put on a gown and got on the table. Clare showed her what position she wanted her in. Then Clare set the procedure in motion. Clare moved her occasionally to achieve a different view. When she was done, they waited while Charlyyk dressed.

The X-ray results were just as Michel had thought. A plate was visible, the size of an old-fashioned razor blade. The X-ray plates allowed them to see how the aliens had attached it to the base of Charlyyk's skull by two pins.

Charlyyk was not upset but took a keen interest in it. "Can you remove it, Michel?" she asked.

"No. The pins could do you damage if we remove them. I would rather we get a specialist team to attempt that. We love you too much to jump in as amateurs and do you harm."

Helen put an arm around her. "We will find the best people to do the right thing for you, sweetheart. That's a promise."

Clare said, "I will enlarge the X-ray plates so we get a clearer idea of what is involved. It will give us some indication why that thing was planted there in the first place."

Charlyyk's thoughts were like those anybody else would have: "Why?"

Charlyyk with Helen, being cuddled. Helen felt Charlyyk's insecurity and vulnerability. They were like a small child's weakness as it held on to its mother for safety. Helen kissed the top of Charlyyk's head and heard herself saying, "Now, now, little one. Mummy's here." Tears welling in her eyes, Helen pulled the girl closer. She remembered what Gwen had said about feeling like a mother duck. Helen felt just like that.

On Tuesday, Charlyyk woke to find Helen in bed with her, wrapped in her arms. Charlyyk lay unmoving, recalling how she had asked Helen to stay with her. When Helen made a promise, she saw it through. She indeed was a good mum, and it settled Charlyyk to know she was so loved.

Bryn peered into the bedroom. Charlyyk lay in Helen's arms with the most contented smile on her face, looking back at him. She winked and blew him a kiss. He shaped his hands into the letter *T*. She nodded.

Bryn headed for the kitchen. When he returned, Helen was awake and sitting up in bed with Charlyyk. He placed the tray on the bedside cabinet and gave them each a kiss, then handed them their teas. "How are you, sweetheart?" he asked Charlyyk.

"I could not feel better than I do right now. I am humbled to have you two as my parents. I promise you both I will make you proud of me, as I am proud of you." Charlyyk had thought about all the possibilities and had come to accept the plate in her head. It had not troubled her. She had lived without any side effects. She was fine. She had come to this conclusion during the night. But it raised other issues—why did her memory only begin from the period of her group life in the burrows? She had no recollection of her earlier childhood, such as Sarah, Sandra, and Julia could recall.

There was no run that morning. It was a time to reflect on being a family unit and relating to each other as one. They talked for some time, reflecting on what had happened since they had met and how they found themselves enjoying each other. Time flew by quickly, and it was a rush to meet the bus.

Harold and Gwen had already spoken with Michel when Bryn and Helen arrived at Carpenters' cottage. They immediately enquired about how Charlyyk was taking it. Bryn strolled off with Harold, telling him of the evening's events. Helen sat with Gwen, doing the same thing. The conversation had not changed as they sat around the dining table over coffees. Bryn informed them that Chad and Su Shi had spoken with him and planned to visit him. Helen told them of the computer expert who had asked to come. Harold agreed that they would put him up at Carpenters' cottage.

Charlyyk did not divulge any information to the posse about her visit to Michel's surgery. Still, Mike commented, "You look particularly happy with yourself. Is there any reason for this?"

Charlyyk gave him a kiss on the cheek. "Yes, and it's thanks to you."

Mike looked really pleased with himself. "Because of me?"

She gave him a big smile. "You made me realise the value of friendship, and I cannot thank you enough."

Julia witnessed what was said. She put her arm on Charlyyk's arm and watched Mike turn and walk away. "I don't know which one of you benefited more out of that situation." They agreed that yes, he had certainly changed for the better.

Later at dinner, Charlyyk talked to Helen about Mike. "He has become cleaner. There are no stains of previous dinners on him. His hair is washed, and he smells nice. I'm hoping he and Julia get it together."

Rachel picked up on how Charlyyk hesitated before mentioning smell. "Do you get vibes from him?"

Charlyyk looked concerned. "No, he must not. I could hurt him. He will be better off with Julia." With that, Charlyyk left the table and hurried to her bedroom.

After helping Helen to clean up, Rachel knocked on Charlyyk's door and entered. "Sorry, Charlyyk. I should not have said anything." She sat beside her on the bed. "If you feel it's wrong, then make sure you don't encourage him. Keep his friendship."

Charlyyk held Rachel's hand. She felt the same loving warmth from Rachel as she felt from Catherine.

Rachel went on to tell her about the boys she'd had friendships with at school and at college. "At first, each one seemed to be the only one in my life. Then a new boy would come along, and so on, and so on. If you get the drift?" Rachel laughed. "It is all a learning curve to understand what kind of feller we will one day want to marry."

Charlyyk had understood Rachel. "But that is not going to happen with me. Would it not upset the people? I need people to like me, not see me as threat."

Rachel stood up. "I was not thinking about that, Charlyyk. I see you as one of us—a girl like every other girl." Rachel walked to the door. "Night-night. Sleep well."

On Wednesday, the girls strode out front on their run. Charlyyk told Helen what Rachel had said to her. When they reached the cowsheds, James called out to Charlyyk. He made a hand signal of thumb and little finger to ear and mouth. That meant only one thing. She called back, "Yes, I will", and carried on running,

At breakfast, Charlyyk phoned Janet. "Hi, kid," Janet said. "You OK?"

Janet's croaky voice told Charlyyk she was not well. She coughed. "I fell ill with the flu on Monday. Seen the doctor. Working in bed ... best as I can." Charlyyk wished her well and promised to phone again.

Harold and Gwen arrived at midday for lunch and remarked on the anxiety Charlyyk had endured these last few weeks. Helen was quick to ask them whether this was normal for a teenage girl. "Is this what you were telling us about some time ago when this first started?"

Gwen nodded. "Yes, you are right, we did."

"We know Charlyyk can be sensitive," Bryn said. "Her feelings are based on her fears, on what she could lose."

Margret could not resist the temptation of voicing her opinion. "She is so young, yet so old. Her unique way of looking at problems can be her strength or her downfall. Much like your Margaret Thatcher—this woman is not for turning, so she could not amend her mistake."

Harold thought through what Margret had said. "You are implying that her thinking is set in stone. Generally, she can work out the right answer in a logical format. But when she can't find the answer, she can't stop thinking about it, and then it can only end in a meltdown."

Margret nodded her agreement.

Helen said, "The way we use our grey matter is not the way she uses hers. When I help her with her homework, she has it all mapped out in her brain, like it is indented with bullets and numbers."

"When are you going to London, Margret?" Bryn wanting to change the subject.

"Friday, for four weeks, with Rachel and Thomas. I was hoping that Charlyyk could be there for the opening on Sunday."

Helen raised her eyes. "You had better ask her tonight."

Gwen asked with a pleading smile, "Can we come, Margret?"

Thomas walked over to his aunt. "We have already printed your VIP tags." He gave Gwen a big hug.

Dinner was busy. Charlyyk was in full voice. An intense debate had been going on in school, and she was giving her account of it. "Mr Pearson had to step in. Mike called Jan a social snob, and Mace called Peter a red in the bed. I thought Peter had cut himself while he was in bed. Julia started laughing. Jan thought she was laughing at her. Peter stood up to Mace. It was utter chaos, but fun to watch."

After a while, when everything seemed settled, Thomas asked Charlyyk if she would like to go to the opening of the exhibition on Sunday. "Many famous people will be there—including, rumour has it, a famous boy band member who is a keen artist."

Charlyyk immediately made her mind up. She said regretfully, "I don't know, Thomas. I have other engagements to attend to."

Looking at Margret's and Thomas's faces, she could not keep up with the pretence. She burst out laughing. "Of course I'm coming!" She gave Rachel a high five— well, in Charlyyk's case, a high four.

On Thursday morning, Helen nudged Charlyyk as they ran down Bishops Lane. They headed along the left path to Dippers Meadow on the return run. "I have lost ten pounds since I've been jogging and doing the Pilates. That equals three inches off my waist," Helen said.

Charlyyk laughed. "So it's your bum you need to work on next, then, is it?"

Charlyyk had become used to the noises that came from her mum and dad's bedroom. Catherine had shown her books on childbirth. She knew what they were doing. It was perfectly reasonable of them, although some nights she wondered what would have been expected of her if she had not come to this planet, but remained on her own world. All she had ever seen were *lyyks*. She had never seen or smelt a *haagh*, the male of her species. This thought sometimes troubled her. How did she know her native language? Who had taught her? What was the purpose of the metal plate? These and many more things she could not explain.

Charlyyk looked into her lunch box. Helen kept to the diet that Michel had set up for her. The array of fruit, nuts, veggie wedges, and hummus dip were strictly routine, but not the Kit Kat bar neatly concealed under the vegetable wedges. "Thank you, Mum."

Charlyyk watched the posse. Mike was talking to Jan. Peter was talking to Mace, so no problems there. Julia slid in beside her and looked into Charlyyk's lunch box. "Swop you a quarter of egg sandwich for a celery stick and a dunk in your hummus." The swop was made, and two happy souls enjoyed lunchtime.

Charlyyk liked Julia a lot. The large red birthmark that covered one side of Julia's face had made Julia insecure. The posse did not take any notice of the birthmark. With them she could be herself, as she was at home. But away from them, the insecurities flooded back big time.

Being around Charlyyk and seeing how she handled constant attention had made Julia's problem seem small. She was gradually finding it easier not to worry about her birthmark. Sandra's relationship with Peter had altered their friendship a little, but that was what Julia expected. They made adjustments and carried on being friends. Julia's confidence had grown stronger. She pushed herself forward in school more. Her parents were happy. Julia's smiles were bigger and warmer. Their little rosebud was blooming into a flower.

In the teachers' study, Mrs Butler gave her assessment of the improvements Charlyyk's class has made since she arrived. "It's above normal. Their grades have gone up."

Tim Pearson said, "Definitely, I agree. The results are a grade higher. Even their homework is much improved."

Richard Waverly shrugged. "What can I say? She has had an effect on the whole class just by being here. They have matured so much. Even Mike, who I thought was a hopeless case, has changed. I'm at a loss for words for it. Am I happy? Oh, yes, indeed I am. Bring it on."

Louise Landon cast her attention to Alice Vasey, who was reading a letter. "Alice, are you with us?"

Alice's head shot up. A broad grin smothered her face. "Yes, I have been listening. It's not about what Charlyyk does. It's the role the rest of the class have taken on. It's like they have become her guardians, and that has made them mature as they have."

Alice looked down at the letter Charlyyk had given her that morning. "This letter invites me to go with Charlyyk on Sunday to a watercolour exhibition in London as a VIP guest. I've never been given anything like this before." She read the letter over again, as though she could not believe what was written.

Louise Landon showed interest. Could this be a good thing for the school? The board of governors' meetings always produced something good for the school if the school get a positive mention in the local media.

At Oakleaves, Margret, Thomas, and Rachel were hard at it, getting confirmations established and ticking off each one. Bryn and Helen made teas and coffees to keep the troops happy.

When Charlyyk arrived home, all was calm. Charlyyk went straight to the fridge and poured a glass of milk under the stern eye of Bryn. Charlyyk knew he was watching her and raised the glass so he could see it. Helen hovering close, asked her about her day at school. "It was good, Mum." She kissed Helen's cheek and whispered, "Thanks for the Kit Kat."

Helen returned the kiss. "My pleasure."

Charlyyk then went to her room to change and to talk with Janet, to see how she was coping with her flu symptoms.

On Friday, Alice Vasey found Charlyyk sitting with Julia, swopping lunches. "Charlyyk, thank you for thinking of me. I will be there. I'm so excited to meet so many prominent artists. I'm tingling all over with excitement. I will definitely see you on Sunday."

Julia looked at Alice as she walked away, or rather skipped away. "Well done, Charlyyk. You have made the most-liked teacher in the school very happy. Well done."

Charlyyk felt humble. She had thought about Miss Vasey when Janet, who had held that slot on the VIP list, became ill. Margret had asked her which friends she would like to take Janet's place. Charlyyk did not want to favour one of her peers over another and thought of Miss Vasey instead. Now it looks like she had been smart, but she had not been thinking like that when she made her decision.

Margret, Thomas, and Rachel had already left for London when Charlyyk came home from school. Harold and Gwen were there to greet her. After Charlyyk had changed and spoken with Janet, she was happy to share herself with the family. Gwen mentioned that it was going to be a cold, wet weekend. "What will you be wearing, Charlyyk? These places can be draughty."

Charlyyk thought through her wardrobe. The dress she had bought at Christmas seemed too young for this occasion. The green dress that Margret had bought had sleeves too short and would make her look too mature. Her Laura Ashley dress would not be warm enough.

Helen opened her laptop and looked online. They scrolled through page after page, discussing all the possibilities. A tailored jacket and skirt were Charlyyk's choice, but in what colour? The outlet was a tailoring firm in Basingstoke. Helen phoned them and agreed to meet them tomorrow morning.

CHAPTER 13

THE SCENT OF AN ALIEN

On Saturday morning, the shopfront sign said *Little and Large Tailoring*. The traditional bell rang when they entered, amusing Charlyyk. She wanted to hear it again, but Gwen stopped her. The middle-aged lady who greeted them was charming. "Hello, I spoke to you yesterday," Helen said as she held her hand out.

"Oh yes, the tailored suit," the lady said, looking at Charlyyk. "Yes, we can help. We cater for large companies normally—airlines and others who need to dress their staff in good-quality uniforms of all shapes and sizes."

This was not like any shop they had been into before. They stood in a reception room. Fashion posters were on the walls. The middle-aged lady opened a door and asked for assistance. A girl took her place and invited Helen, Gwen, and Charlyyk to follow her.

They entered a large warehouse filled with racks and racks of clothes. At a table, full of tailoring bits and pieces, the girl measured Charlyyk, then showed her suits in black, white, blue, greens, and more. Charlyyk took a fancy to a light maroon suit. The girl checked sizes and selected one. "Slip this on."

Charlyyk slipped on the jacket and looked in a long mirror. The colour was right, but the jacket was a bit baggy. She was disappointed. "It's too big."

The girl did not seem concerned. "Is the colour right and the material to your satisfaction?" Gwen stepped forward, felt the material, and nodded. "Right. Next stage." She took the jacket off Charlyyk and selected another one. Charlyyk noticed this one was not finished. The seams were open, and she started to worry.

The girl took out some pins and started to fit the jacket to her. When she had finished pinning the garment together, Charlyyk's smile told everyone that she liked the look of the finished article. The girl called out, and an elderly gentleman came and took the jacket away. "Now the skirt. Any particular style" She showed them a style book. The women agreed to a two-pleated skirt. The girl selected a garment for Charlyyk to try on. The skirt fitted her hips, but the waist was not finished and the skirt was too long. Out came the pins, and it was soon adjusted. Charlyyk liked what she saw. Once again, the skirt was taken away.

After a lengthy wait, the suit was ready. On the way home, they stopped at Liza Martin's and asked her advice on make-up for Charlyyk. She was going to be in the spotlight, and they were making sure she would stand out from the crowd without looking too old. Gwen had told Helen that Margret would milk Charlyyk's presence. The press coverage would be much higher than normal, since the press was usually restricted from access to Charlyyk.

On Sunday, Alice Vasey was like a cat on a hot tin roof. This was the third outfit she had put on, and she was still not sure if it was right. Her flat was in disarray, and time was running out. "This will have to do." She headed for the door to meet the Colliers at Oakleaves.

It was going to be a tight fit to get everyone in the car, so they took the Discovery. Charlyyk sat in the fold-down seat at the rear. When they arrived at the exhibition, Rachel was pleased to see them. A steward parked the car. Thomas whisked Charlyyk and Alice off for a quick tour and to meet some of the artists. Margret took the rest of the family on a more selective tour.

Alice, who was in awe of Thomas, kept close to Charlyyk. She wanted to learn as much as she could with so many great artists on hand. Alice made the most of the opportunities afforded her.

Now and again there was a camera pointed towards them. Alice notice that Charlyyk did not let the press attention get to her. She gave them ample chances to take pictures. "Don't you mind all this intrusion, Charlyyk?"

"No, miss. Janet agreed with what was to happen. I will have to do a press interview later. That has been given a time limit so it does not get into a media scrum."

As the guests and VIPs arrived, Charlyyk was kept away so Margret would get the best effect when she was introduced. Charlyyk was not nervous. Her nods and hand waves were all given with gentle smiles. Gwen had written an opening speech with help from Janet. The press coverage was intense, but Charlyyk knew if she tried to hide, the press would give her a hard time.

The first reporter asked his question. "Charlyyk, you seem to like art. What is the type of painting you prefer?"

"With so many styles, it will be a few years before I am able to answer that question. It takes much dedication and time to attain a high standard. Only then will I be able to truly understand how they make watercolours look like photographs."

"Miss Vasey, you teach art to Charlyyk. What can you tell us about Charlyyk's artistic approach?"

Before Alice Vasey could reply, Charlyyk waved her hand as if she had a paintbrush in it and was attacking an easel like a sword fencer.

Alice said with a laugh, "Yes, just like that. We are lucky we can wash the paint sploshes off quite quickly." This brought a few chuckles from the press.

Charlyyk gave an inner smile, knowing she had got the right response—laughter. She had watched a film on the television about a robot that understood a joke, and that made him human. Jokes could be the way to get people on her side. By the reaction from the press, it looked good.

When they returned to the cottage, Helen invited Alice to stay awhile, which she accepted without hesitation. Charlyyk showed Alice Thomas's studio and some of his early works. She stayed late into the evening.

Gwen saw why the students liked her. She had a natural way about her. She listened intently to what was being said and did not try to put anyone down, Alice remarked that she reckoned each student had a talent trying to break out. "Art is a good tool to judge social problems in students. From the subjects, they paint and the way they apply the brush strokes, we can detect all manner of mental attitudes. I use all my knowledge to get the best from each student. Mrs Landon knows this can help her discover which students might be in need of specialist help. But don't misinterpret that I'm a spy of some sort—I only inform her when it is necessary."

On Monday in the teachers' meeting room, Alice Vasey was in full flow. Louise Landon could not have been prouder. Her school had been mentioned on the news, and a teacher from her school had been shown as a VIP at an important exhibition in London. This would sit well at the next governors' meeting.

"What do you think we could get out of this, Louise?" asked Wendy Butler at her side.

Louise's brain was working overtime. "I have a week before the meeting to sort something out." She had learned not to get too ambitious, lest she end up with nothing. Running a school needed teaching and management. Too many heads were teachers, not managers, and many schools failed because of it.

Charlyyk told the posse about the weekend and showed them the pictures that the family had managed to take.

Sarah was keen to find out how the make-up went. "Send me that one, Charlyyk. Mum would love to see that one."

Then Julia spotted Miss Vasey in the photo. "She looks so different." The posse gathered around to give their opinions.

Bryn was cleaning the car when Helen called him in. "Phone, sweetheart. Chad."

Bryn entered the cottage and picked the receiver up. "Hi, Chad, what's up?"

Chad did not stand on ceremony. "First of February. Yuri, Su Shi, Arn, and of course myself. Bruce Foster still intends to come. We will keep it simple."

Bryn was not surprised. "That's fine. We will see you then."

Helen heard everything. "Saturday, then."

Bryn returned to cleaning the car.

Later in the evening, BBC Channel 4 showed an hour-long programme about the exhibition, and footage of Charlyyk was shown in full. Charlyyk took mental notes on what she had done and the visual look she gave out. When the programme finished, Helen asked her how she felt.

"My hands need improving. They sometimes look a bit ungainly. My walk has improved. The make-up gave me better complexion. I will tell Sarah tomorrow. Julia and Sandra are going to tell me what they think. Overall I see much improvement on last time. I'm pleased."

Helen liked what she had said. Bryn could only smile. He knew Charlyyk rehearsed her moves with Julia and Sandra, her personal coaches.

And so, it was. On Tuesday, Sandra was walking up and down in the locker area. "See what I mean? Not too much on swinging the hips; you are not a fashion model. What if Kate Middleton did that? The press would make her life a living hell. Keep the walk natural."

Julia said, "I picked up on your hands. You are right. If you have your sleeves longer, they may make your hands look shorter."

Charlyyk thought for a moment. "In the warmer weather, I don't think it would work."

Sarah looked at her own hands, opening and closing them. "What if you half closed your hands in this manner?"

The other members of the posse were listening in. Mike stepped up. "Like holding an imaginary tennis ball."

Charlyyk opened and closed her hands. Peter took a recording on his phone, then showed it to her. "Yes, that could work. I will practise it in the mirror.

Helen and Bryn started the task of getting ready for the weekend. Just before Charlyyk was due home, the phone rang. Helen saw the surprised look on Bryn's face. He had not expected this call. She moved towards him. He turned the sound up on his phone. "Bryn, may I stay at your house?" It was Su Shi. "My wife would like to come with me. We will be there Friday, if that is OK."

Helen nodded. Bryn said, "Yes, we will be ready for you." He rang off.

Helen placed her arm around his waist and nestled her head against him. "Thomas's room?" Bryn gave her an unmistakeable look. She punched him playfully. "Oh, come on—for Su Shi and his wife to stay!" He tickled her till she wrapped her arms around his neck and kissed him.

On Wednesday, the frost was hard due to a high weather system. The sky was clear of clouds. In the east, the sun was beginning to rise, and a tint of red could be seen. The family group of three were in close formation, discussing Janet's extended recuperation from the flu and the advent of Friday, when Su Shi and his wife were coming.

As they turned left at the bottom of Bishops Lane, Charlyyk suddenly stopped. Her nose twitched. Her head moved from side to side. She stepped forward, her nose taking in as much as it could.

Bryn and Helen likewise stopped. Bryn held Helen back, the commander giving his scout a chance to evaluate the danger signs. Then Charlyyk stopped sniffing. Whatever it was had gone.

"What do you think it was?" Bryn asked. His military training had kicked in. He knew from experience that Charlyyk had smelt danger. The threat of it was written all over Charlyyk's face.

"I've smelt that scent before on that planet we were on, Dad." Charlyyk looked at the ground. "It was not here yesterday morning. Whatever it was, it was here last night, before the frost settled. There are no signs of prints on the ground." Then she was up and running, with Bryn and Helen in hot pursuit.

Breakfast was quiet. Charlyyk was scanning her memory cells and did not want to talk. She took her dirty dishes to place them in the dishwasher, then paused. She put her plates in the dishwasher, closed the door, and headed to the door. She paused again, longer, and then she was gone.

Helen had been holding Bryn's hand and watching his face for any acknowledgement. Bryn's eyes had been on Charlyyk all the time. Now that she had gone to her room, he turned and spoke to Helen. "The aliens have been here."

CHAPTER 14

THEY LEAVE THEIR CALLING CARD

Her startled, worried expression showed that Helen wanted to know more. "How do you know that?"

"If it had been a beast, there would have been a footprint of some sort. But there was nothing, so if she has smelt it before but can't recognise it, it has to be an alien."

Bryn got up and made himself a coffee. Helen knew he was thinking. Otherwise, he would have made her one as well. As she started to clear up, Charlyyk came back in, dressed for school. Bryn and Charlyyk looked at each other and said at the same time, "It was an alien." With that Charlyyk kissed them both and went to meet the school bus. Helen now was the one thinking.

Bryn took her hand. "What is it?"

The puzzled look on Helen's face was still there. "When I first came here, this would have frightened Charlyyk to death. Now she has just dismissed it as though this type of thing happens every day." She looked directly into Bryn's eyes. "This is scaring the shit out of me, and I'm not afraid to say it."

Helen picked up the phone and punched in some numbers. "Wendy, Helen. Early last night, at the bottom of Bishops Lane, was there any activity?"

Helen waited for the reply while Sergeant Wendy Bailey read through the reports.

"Yes. At five past seven, a blip showed on the monitor for ten minutes. A car was dispatched, but nothing was there. They covered the area but found nothing."

Helen had the speaker volume up to full so Bryn could hear. "Thanks, Wendy. It was something that Charlyyk smelt. We were not sure, but you have confirmed it. She picked up the scent of something. It could be an animal she has not come across before." Helen put the phone down. "I trust Charlyyk's nose," she said to Bryn, concern still in her voice. "And once again it shows how good her sense of smell is." She looked at the garden door. "Now no arguments. New bolts for the doors. Today, Bryn!"

It was lunchtime at the academy, and Julia was on the scrounge for goodies. Charlyyk was in a pensive mood. "What's up, kid" Julia asked. "You're never this quiet unless something is worrying you. Cough it up. What is it?"

Charlyyk looked around to see if anyone was within earshot. She whispered, "Do not look alarmed or say a word." She paused to await Julia' nod. "Last night, an alien was at the bottom of Bishops Lane. It was not there for long, but it had been there. I smelt it."

Julia's head spun around. "You're not kidding, are you?"

Looking into her lunch box, she selected a stick of carrot, then dunked it in the hummus. "No."

Julia sat looking at her lunch box, but it was not for a tasty morsel.

After dinner, the three of them sat down to discuss the weekend. Helen wanted to lay some ground rules down. But Bryn said. "No. Just be yourselves. It should cause no problems." Bryn was more concerned about what Charlyyk might have said at school.

"Julia won't say anything. She has been trustworthy since I met her, and she won't change. We made a pact to be honest with each other. I've told her things before about other students, and she has always kept her side of the bargain."

On Thursday, the three runners arrived at the bottom of Bishops Lane. Bryn and Helen stayed back. Charlyyk checked with her nose, but smelt nothing odd. They relaxed and carried on.

Gwen and Harold arrived later and were soon helping to make ready for Friday. At three Michel turned up. He was there to sort out Charlyyk's diet and to collect a blood sample. Talking to Bryn in Kit's clinic, he showed Bryn a scanner. "We use this to check the chips we put in animals. Some chips give out more data than others.

This might pick up something that the plate in Charlyyk's head is sending out."

When Charlyyk returned home, she was pleased to see Michel. "OK, which goodies am I allowed to sniff and which ones am I allowed to eat?" She showed a lot of interest when Michel showed her the scanner. "Let's do it." But it resulted in nothing, not a blip.

They sat around the kitchen table, drinking teas. "It's possible that it's a different type of science, or maybe it controls Charlyyk." Michel was not sure what the plate could be. He used electrical gadgets to assist him, but that's as far as it went. Chemicals he knew about, pressing buttons he was all right with, but that was that.

Helen looked at Charlyyk and saw she was deep in thought. "It does not matter, sweetheart. We will be stronger together, facing it, head-on." Charlyyk was not worried about that. Her mind was on whose scent she had picked up. The trace of memory bank was muddled with other scents.

On Friday, the garden door burst open. Charlyyk had tried not to be boisterous; she had started to realise her strength was increasing. "Sorry, Dad. I must do better." She rushed to her room.

The school bus arrived right on cue. Charlyyk got a hug and a kiss from each parent. Then they watched as the bus disappeared from view. Helen had settled into this idyllic lifestyle. She would kill to keep it.

Time drifted by. After tidying up and a little dusting, she was ready. She gazed at the picture of Kitty on the wall. "Thank you. It was your love that made this family. Let me do you justice and keep this house as happy as you intended it."

At two thirty, a large limousine pulled into the drive. The doorbell rang. Helen checked how she looked. Bryn nodded his approval, and they opened the door.

Su Shi and his wife were standing there, wrapped up against the English weather. Bryn welcomed them in. "Lovely to see you again!" Inside the lounge, Bryn took their coats. They were dressed in Western clothes. Su Shi's wife was slim and five feet six inches tall.

"Su Shi, this is my wife-to-be, Helen."

Su Shi bowed and shook her hand. He said with great charm, "My darling wife, Liu."

Bryn shook her hand. Helen stepped forward, and by instinct, the women kissed each other's cheeks. "Can I get you something to drink?"

Liu took Helen's arm. "Come, let's talk in the kitchen while the men talk here."

Liu's English was excellent, and soon they were talking freely. "I met Su Shi in Oxford. My parents owned a restaurant in London. I was studying economics. On hearing of the love, I had for Su Shi, my parents were not happy and refused me permission to marry. When Su Shi went home, I felt terrible, so I bought an air ticket and never returned to England until yesterday. I went to my parents' house. My mother just stood at the door and stared at me. I turned and walked away. Twenty-three years have passed, and she still felt the same."

Taking the tea tray into the lounge, the women continued the conversation with the men. "I was taking a big gamble marrying Liu" Su Shi observed. "If she would disobey her parents, she was bound to disobey me."

Liu was charming. "Our two sons are at Oxford. We will go to them after we leave here."

Helen checked the time. The smile on her face got bigger. Su Shi was quickly on his feet, and helped his wife to hers. "Where have we to go?"

"Just to the front door," Bryn said.

The bus was stopping at the drive. The bus door opened and Charlyyk stepped down. She saw them and rushed to greet them. Su Shi greeted her as a much-loved uncle would do.

Inside the cottage, Charlyyk was introduced to Liu. When Charlyyk mentioned she needed a drink, all the women headed for the kitchen. Liu was making herself at home, and Helen was getting to like Liu more and more. Liu said, "I cook Western food at home, so don't be nervous. Su Shi has not stopped talking about Charlyyk since he met her in Houston. He has been on tender feet, thinking of coming here. But don't think I've been dragged here. I really wanted to come. Su Shi's description of Charlyyk fascinated me too. I threatened him with divorce if he did not bring me, so no pressure."

Charlyyk drank her milk. "But I'm not that special. I'm no different than any of the girls at school."

Liu looked at her. "That's right, you are no different, but you are also one of a kind. That's what makes you so important. When our friends heard that Su Shi had met you, we were inundated with questions from everyone. The picture he took of you and him is his card to anywhere in China, and my God, doesn't he use it. He is treated like Britain's great Queen." Liu's all-knowing look told Charlyyk she enjoyed the benefits as well.

"So I guess you want your own photo of me?" Charlyyk asked.

Liu's eyes opened wide in a look of "Please".

"OK, when I change out of my school clothes." Charlyyk went to leave, then looked at Liu. "Do you want to come?"

Liu did not need a second invitation. Helen watched as they left the kitchen together.

Gwen and Harold arrived ten minutes later. Harold joined Bryn and Su Shi. Gwen went to the kitchen with Helen.

Liu sat on the bed, talking to Charlyyk. She asked about the life Charlyyk now lived. Charlyyk found Liu easy to talk to, just as Su Shi was.

The ringtone on Liu phone, started to play. Her son was calling her. Charlyyk, now dressed, sat by Liu's side. Liu showed her son the image of her and Charlyyk side by side. He was impressed with his mother's newfound stardom. "Mum! You're now as big as Dad."

Charlyyk listened to Liu's carefully worded questions about how she had adapted to life on Earth. "Liu, I wanted to adapt. I needed to adapt. Bryn gave me a chance to survive, and I took it. Did I know what was going to happen? No. I did not know, but given what has happened and how it has happened, I cannot have any regrets. Hearing all the different ways my school friend's lives have played out, I now know how privileged my life has turned out to be. Yet now and again I feel I have taken it for granted."

Charlyyk paused for a moment, contemplating her thoughts. "It is so easy to let yourself get too accustomed to a way of living. It becomes how you believe everyone behaves. When you hear the problems of others, you have to re-assess your own advantages. Yes, you can say I've been spoilt, and you would be right to say so. Michel tells me to not concern myself, but to join in with the family and help to make their lives as easy as possible. At first, I could not understand his meaning, but now I'm beginning to."

Dinner time was busy with conversation. Liu proved she was no shrinking violet and held her own. Helen observed her. She had a unique personal style that worked for her. Her hand movements had an elegant flourish. Su Shi gave her the room to talk, never once interrupting her. It was a good pairing. His views on life were a mixture of Eastern and Western cultures. Liu gave Helen the impression that she had been a hands-on mum—no nannies for her. The little things she and Su Shi did for one another, Helen saw were done out of love.

Helen reflected on herself. Before she had met Bryn, she would only look for faults in people. Now she found she was looking at the real part of people. She knew she had changed and liked the new person she was becoming.

Gwen and Harold had much to say, as most of the questions were associated with the very early days of Charlyyk being on Earth. They talked about the problems they had faced, trying to keep her concealed yet still trying to educate her.

After dinner, Liu insisted on helping Helen. A friendship had started to take shape. Charlyyk took notice of them. Her ears were moving in many directions. Su Shi noticed how Charlyyk could keep one eye and ear in focus on whomever she was talking with, while the other ear and eye were on walkabouts.

Bryn as usual said nothing unless someone spoke to him. Gwen had brought her happy photo album, and when Liu sat down, it came out. To Gwen's surprise, Liu had brought her own album. Her iPad was full of beautiful pictures depicting where they had lived and the children growing up.

Harold and Gwen left when Charlyyk went to bed. That left four of them to carry on with the conversation. Bryn brought out a bottle of Balvenie Caribbean. This was his favourite single malt. Wally Blyth had introduced him to it. Su Shi smiled as Bryn poured out a shot of whisky for him. Liu pushed her glass forward. "I hope it is not just for the boys?"

Su Shi was quick to explain. "Liu's flatmate at university came from Glasgow. In three years, together, something had to rub off."

Liu gave a little chuckle. "The secret of whisky drinking is how much water. You take a drop of whisky on the tongue and count in seconds the tingling sensation your tongue feels. The number of seconds is equal to the number of drops of water you should add."

Bryn smiled at her. "What is your favourite?"

But it was Su Shi who answered. "Any full bottle."

Liu's chuckle was getting more like a laugh. "Su Shi looks at cars and asks, 'How many miles to the gallon?' About me, he asks, 'How many bottles to the year?'" She gave an impish smile. "At four bottles a year, I am still cheaper than his cars."

On Saturday, Helen was surprised to see Su Shi and Liu fully kitted out in tracksuits as they entered the garden. After stretching, they were off at a settled pace. The light was starting to show, and as usual, the girls were in front. Arriving at the top of the hill, Liu saw the sheer splendour of the sun hitting the tops of trees. Many colours were laid out around them. "I have missed England so many times. It has a beauty all its own."

Liu paced on the spot, then looked down into the other valley, where Dippers Meadow lay. "I can see why you love it here, Helen. It's not spring, yet the landscape looks so lovely."

At the bottom of Bishops Lane, Charlyyk pushed forward, sniffing the air. Helen's tension was noticed by Liu. Charlyyk shook her head and carried on running.

The first to arrive for the meeting was Brigadier Alex Hutton and Major Carter, then Yuri with Arn, and finally Chad. Alan Carter had requested the men wear lounge suits. It would not impose on Charlyyk. It would help her to relax and talk freely.

When all the introductions had been done. Helen took Liu to Gwen's. Charlyyk played mother and soon brought out drinks for them all. Helen had placed water bottles at appropriate places before leaving.

Alex made the first move. "Charlyyk, something was said at our meeting to trigger this theory of yours. Could you explain, please?"

Charlyyk took a sip from her cup. "Listening to my friends' stories about their families, I realised I did not have that where I came from. When the question was asked, it triggered those nagging thoughts in my head. Why were we sent here, back to Dad's house?"

Charlyyk saw that they all had recorders working but were still making notes. Alan Carter was making a video recording. When they were ready, she proceeded. "That night, other things started to niggle at me. On Sunday, the next day, we went to Gwen and Harold's for dinner. We got talking about what had come up at the meeting. I mentioned about the Fuung that had been killed and dragged away from where my group lived. Could the thing that had killed the Fuung be protecting us, and if so, why?"

Again, Charlyyk waited while they noted this information and chatted a bit. She collected the X-ray images and sat down again.

"The conversation on Sunday led us to believe that this whole thing had been orchestrated," she continued. "Michel, the vet who keeps me well, suggested that I might have been projecting messages to whomever, so he took these X-rays of me to see if I was being monitored."

The men examined the X-rays. Bryn explained that pins secured the plate to her skull. "We have used a scanner on the plate, but it sends out no signals we can detect."

Chad punched some numbers into his phone. "Bruce, when can you get here?"

Bruce Foster was dropping his bag at Gwen's when the phone rang. The taxi he had arrived in had already left. Helen offered him a lift and told Chad they would be back in ten minutes.

Bryn showed the military chiefs an enlarged X-ray of the plate. A strange formation of fibres seemed to flow from the ends of the pins that attached the plate to Charlyyk's skull.

When Bruce arrived, Charlyyk was the first to greet him. Chad asked Bruce to look at the X-rays. As he did so, Chad went over the details of their theories. "Can you detect if that plate is sending out any messages? That's what we need a direct answer to."

Bruce opened his tool case and selected a meter. He placed some probes into it, then asked Charlyyk to turn around. He took bearings from the X-ray and then sank the fine needle ends of the probes into the back of her head. She did not flinch. He turned the meter on, and the dial flickered. Chad, eager to find something, looked pleased. Bruce changed the setting on the meter. Nothing. He changed the settings three more times. Still nothing. Bruce confirmed that he could not detect a signal.

Su Shi sighed. Alex looked at him. He saw that Su Shi was happy. "This means Charlyyk is no threat to us, and I am relieved." Alex again shot a look at him. Su Shi said, "Why I am pleased? If you thought she was a threat, you would send her to be terminated. That's the last thing I want to happen to her. She has shown us only that she too would like answers. She has put herself out to cooperate with us in every way possible. Is this not proof of her innocence in all of this?" Su Shi meant every word he had said.

Next, he asked, "Bruce, that meter—what do you use it for?"

Bruce replied, "Microelectronics. The sort we use in spy bugs." He showed them how it worked and the range it covered. "No minute amount of electricity could escape its sensitivity." He took the probes from Charlyyk's neck and without hesitation stuck them into his hand. He showed them the meter reading. "We all have electricity running through us. As you can see, Charlyyk's reading is much lower than mine. The first reading was to calculate her base level of electrical impulse, so I could tell whether she carried enough electricity to send out a message. There was not enough to send anything at all."

The military chiefs sat around and debated what had been discussed. While the chiefs talked, Charlyyk took Bruce to the kitchen, gave him refreshments, and chatted with him. Bruce said, "The Kepler telescope has discovered many more planets. In the corner of one of the pictures, I discovered this." From a side pocket, he took out a photo of a formation of planets. Nestled among them was a planet that Charlyyk thought she recognised. "It was nowhere near the other planets, but feeding the right information into the computer, it fitted to a T what you told me."

Charlyyk studied the picture. "So where is this one situated on the solar map?"

Bruce took out a solar map. Unfolding it, he laid it out on the worktop. He pointed to where the planet was situated, millions of miles away from where they had first thought.

"What did you tell them, Bruce?"

He looked at her. "I haven't disclosed too much information, just in case it was wrong. I will have to spend much more time on it to be sure. Talking to you personally was the best option open to me. Helen said you go to your aunt and uncles for dinner tomorrow. Let's meet there. I have some better footage on my computer to show you."

Bryn entered the kitchen. "They are leaving, Charlyyk."

Charlyyk left Bruce in the kitchen ad said goodbye to those who were going. She walked back to the lounge. Su Shi was asking a question of Bruce. Bryn was listening in. "No, Su Shi, all electricity is the same. These meters were designed for a special type of micro readings. Any strong current could burn this type of meter out, as it is so delicate. The plate looks like a circuit board, but for what purpose I do not know."

Each country's military attaché wanted to relay the X-ray evidence back to their scientists to evaluate, and bade farewell to Su Shi.

Charlyyk put on her coat. "Dad, I need some fresh air. Would you like to walk to the village with me, Bruce?" Charlyyk was keen to find out what Bruce needed to know to find the right answers to his questions.

The walk to the village gave Bruce freedom to speak to Charlyyk. "Every planet has a different colour. It is one of those unique fingerprints we have to identify them. The minerals on each planet reflect light differently. Even gases can reflect light in different ways. We use those as identity tags. These fit in with what you spoke to me about. The colour fits the minerals, and the smells fit the gases, if you get my drift."

Charlyyk left Bruce with Gwen and Harold and returned to Oakleaves. Liu had persuaded Helen that she and Su Shi would order a Chinese dinner for them tonight. But the person she phoned was a cousin, not a takeaway restaurant, and he was coming to them himself. "This is the traditional way we dine," Liu said. "The chef cooks a large bowl of rice, and we sit around the table. Each course he cooks, we eat there and then. It is a great way of eating."

When the doorbell rang, there were three people standing there: Chi, Liu's cousin, and his twin daughters Pia and Liu. Chi's wife had stayed behind, looking after the family's restaurant. Chi had not seen Liu since she left England to marry Su Shi. He wanted to know as much about her life as he could, and what a lot of talking they did.

Harold, Gwen, and Bruce arrived later. Harold brought the wine. Bryn only had reds, which could be much too heavy for Chinese food. Charlyyk explained to Chi what she could eat and what she could not. A whole, boned chicken stuffed with all types of delicate things had Charlyyk drooling.

Traditional Chinese meals like this one were long affairs, but most enjoyable.

On Sunday morning, Charlyyk felt she really needed a run, but at a slow pace. She had woken early to put down in writing what she had remembered in her sleep. Whichever way this panned out, she wanted to know the truth.

Still, the evening meal had to be worked off. It had been delicious. She had found herself stuffing the last morsels down her throat with her fingers. Her mouth watered at the memory of the chicken, prawns, and noodles.

As the run reached the top of Bishops Lane, she was feeling better for it. She stopped. Among the smells of the farm, she detected that strange scent. Helen and Bryn picked up on it. Again, it was eleven hours old, but something had been there. Charlyyk started to look around. Just a couple of feet away from the highest point was what she had been looking for.

She removed a shoe and placed her foot by the side of a large print. Bryn came and knelt down by the side of her. The print was four inches longer than her shoe. "It's big," said Bryn.

Helen peered over his shoulder. "It's definitely the same shape as your foot, Charlyyk."

Su Shi looked at it. The footprint was just like Charlyyk's, but larger. Liu asked what it meant. Su Shi worked it out precisely and described it to her in full detail. "What time was it here, Charlyyk?"

Charlyyk made a quick calculation and gave a little intake of breath. "About seven last night." Helen sensed how Charlyyk was feeling and placed her arm around her.

Bryn weighed up the two times. "So about the same time each night." Helen took photos of the print, and they resumed the run.

At breakfast, Su Shi spoke freely. He felt that this was just the start of the aliens making contact. "If they were going to invade. I think they would have done that already."

Bryn drank his coffee. "I believe it could be Wednesday night at seven."

Everyone went quiet.

Charlyyk looked at Bryn. "Dad, what should we do?"

Bryn could not ease her fears. "Nothing, sweetheart. We will just have to wait to find out."

Liu spoke with Su Shi in Chinese. He said to the group, "My wife said I should be here."

Bryn could not agree. "The fewer people, the better. We must set up some recording device so everyone knows how it went, good or bad."

When Bryn looked at Helen, her intelligence training had kicked in. She was already on her phone. She nodded at Bryn. "Sorted. They will be here tomorrow."

"Right. Now we must wait."

Liu was not happy. "You are taking on too much on your own. Can we not help?"

Bryn gave Charlyyk's hand a squeeze. "Charlyyk and I were thrown into this unwillingly. They had their reasons for what they have done, and I feel the aliens need to explain to us what they are trying to achieve."

"I understand what my father is saying," Charlyyk added. "They need me to be the intermediary in this, to play a part as a translator. They sent me here to learn your language and your ways, to grow up among you, and to be trusted."

Su Shi stroked his chin. "A clever scheme, so the plan is not to invade, but what?"

Helen sat next to Liu. "The plate in Charlyyk's head, could that have something to do with it? Will the aliens connect to it in some way?"

Liu's face showed signs of confusion. "How have you come to this conclusion, Bryn?"

Bryn closed his eyes tightly, then opened them. "They must be observing us somehow to know our movements—the precise time and places they have left their scent, knowing full well Charlyyk would pick it up. The footprint is their calling card to us all, and the days between, that's letting us know when."

The knowing look on Su Shi's face showed he was up with Bryn's thinking. "Whatever you need, I will back you wholeheartedly. Please let us be comrades in body and soul. I am coming to believe we could be like family, and I will give you my complete trust." He offered Bryn his hand, and they wrapped their other arms around each other in a manly hug.

Later at Carpenters' cottage, they went over Bryn's theory. Gwen started to worry again. Harold put his arm around her. "This has to be played out, darling. If Bryn is right, this could be a blessing for us all. It could well be our chance to get on with our lives and be able to plan for the future."

Gwen was not taken with what he had said. "I cannot see it that way at all. I see it far differently than you do, and it really concerns me. We have no idea what these aliens are capable of doing."

Michel said, "Bryn, you could be right. According to your theory, the plate was meant to programme Charlyyk to play a part they had orchestrated for her, blanking out the bits they did not want her to remember, to allow her to adapt here."

Bruce had been quiet. He felt like he was an interloper, but he knew what was going on. "Can I help in any way with my computer skills?"

Su Shi looked at Bruce, then at Bryn. "Could you set up a computer link between the two cottages?"

Bruce smiled. "Like riding a bike."

Bruce produced one of Apple's new wrist phones. "I can connect this so we could have complete communication with Bryn at all times." Then he opened his laptop and waited for it to warm up. He was soon punching data into it, then the map of where they were. "OK, Charlyyk, put this on and go anywhere, but keep talking."

Charlyyk left the cottage and walked to Sarah's house. Inside with the Martins, she spoke with them, thanking Liza for the make-up she had given her to wear at the art exhibition.

Back at Carpenters' cottage, Bruce showed them what was happening on the laptop screen. They could hear everything that was being said.

When Charlyyk returned to the cottage, Bryn nodded at her. "It worked a treat."

Bruce opened another programme. "This is that group of planets. As you can see, it is nowhere near that other grouping of planets. I believe you were transported from some distance. These aliens are quite advanced."

Su Shi looked over Bruce Foster's shoulders. "Who else knows of this?"

Bruce took a deep breath. "No one wants to listen. They want to take what was said before as fact, and not confuse it with what I have told them."

Su Shi thought for the moment. "We'll let them." Helen looked surprised. Su Shi continued to explain. "We are at a very delicate stage. This could keep them quiet for the moment. I believe that Bryn is correct in his analysis of what is going to happen. This is not an invasion. The aliens could need our assistance in some way. At this moment, the fewer people who know, the better. We'll give them a chance to make contact. We need electronic surveillance so if this should go wrong, we all have evidence of what happened."

Helen accepted what Su Shi had said. "I must find an explanation for the surveillance equipment that is coming tomorrow."

Su Shi looked at Liu. "We will extend our holiday to see how this unfolds."

Liu did not look upset. "I should say so. We are not leaving here until we know they are OK."

Charlyyk went to Liu. "That is such a nice gesture, Liu. Thank you."

On Monday, a large black van pulled into the drive. Helen went to meet them. Three men were soon opening doors and removing equipment. Helen explained what was required to the leader, a large black man. His family had originally come from Ghana. He quickly grasped Helen's instructions, and Helen left them to do what was required.

Su Shi told his sons that he and Liu were having such a good time, they would stay at Oakleaves to the end of the week. Liu promised to phone them with updates.

At four, the van left. Bruce arrived and checked the equipment. "That's good." He attached some hardware of his own, little toggles here and there. Then he set his computer up. He could see all the rooms, covering different angles.

Su Shi was happy. "We can see all this at the cottage too, Bruce?"

"Yes. Tonight, I will check it through with Harold and Gwen. I will record what we see and play it back tomorrow to make sure it works."

The camera set up on Thomas's studio in the garden would tell them of the alien's arrival. Bruce checked that it played on Charlyyk's iPad. Everything was set, with some time for adjustment if required.

Charlyyk looked apprehensive. "What's the problem?" Helen asked.

"What if it wants to take me back?"

Bryn took her in his arms. "That would be up to you. You are growing up and have started to make your own decisions, so it will be your choice." Charlyyk still looked worried. Bryn reassured her, "I would not let them drag you away."

Her face brightened, and Charlyyk hugged Bryn. "I love my life here, Dad. I won't give it up."

Later at Carpenters' cottage, Bruce set up his computer. Harold and Gwen watched intently. He scribbled notes and adjusted a few settings. "All looking good and working well."

On Tuesday, the run was as usual. Bryn tried to keep the appearance of normality. If the aliens were watching, he wanted to make them cognisant of his life. He needed to get this right at all cost.

At school, Charlyyk too kept up the appearance of normality. She joined in with everything as if nothing odd were happening. When she arrived home, the pressure of it definitely showed. Her movements were stiff with tension.

Helen took her in her arms. "Come, sweetheart, let's go and relax in a nice bath." Charlyyk liked the idea of that. Lying in the warm bath, she began to relax and drift into a dream, thinking of all the lovely things that had happened to her.

She woke in a panic, having dreamed she was being chased by a Feeng. She looked around the bathroom to see where it had gone. The realisation that it had been a dream brought her sweet relief. In her bedroom, getting dressed, she returned to her musings about the plate attached to her skull. If it had programmed her to remember only certain things in her life, could the alien change it back? If so, would the new memories be even more painful? She shuddered at this thought. "I cannot go back. I have a mum and dad here."

Charlyyk was in a state of confusion. She did not know what was going to be asked of her. And there was not enough evidence to base any theory on or to ease her concerns. She sat on the bed, trembling. When Helen came in, Charlyyk rushed to her, gripping her in desperation. "Hey, what's the matter?" Helen asked.

Charlyyk's hold just got tighter. "Don't let them take me away. I love you too much. I can't go back. I love it here with you." Her tears wetted Helen's blouse.

Helen cuddled her in both arms with a little rocking movement. "There, there, little one." Helen's maternal instincts set in. She kissed Charlyyk on the top of her head. "There, there, little one. Mummy loves you." Again, the realisation of what she had said brought tears to her eyes. She really did feel a mother's love for her daughter.

In the lounge, plans were being drawn up. Su Shi, Liu, and Helen would go to Carpenters' cottage at five, leaving Bryn and Charlyyk alone in Oakleaves. Bryn would leave the garden door open. He would block the entrance to the drive by closing and securing the gates, so no unexpected visitor could disrupt them. He had to check the gates, because it had been a few years since they were last closed.

Liu was enjoying the drama; it was entirely new. To be involved with her husband in this way was exciting her. She watched Helen's reactions. Helen was calm underneath all this pressure. Liu admired her. There was more to Helen than the records of the Chinese government had on her.

CHAPTER 15

A CHANGE OF MIND

On Wednesday, nervous tension could be felt throughout Oakleaves like an electrical storm brewing. Charlyyk did not want to go to school but knew she must. She clung to Helen that little bit longer, and kissed her with feeling. Bryn watched them and noted the love they had for one another. The cuddle he gave Helen as the school bus disappeared from view showed how he appreciated her.

Helen did not want to look Bryn in the eye. Her tears were flowing. She tried to appear strong, but it was all too much for her. She buried her head in his chest.

Su Shi and Liu were at the entrance door. Liu felt for Helen. Being a mother, she knew the pain mothers shared with their children. When Helen and Bryn reached them, Liu put her arms around Helen and shepherded her indoors.

Su Shi had already put the kettle on. "Tea has a calming effect at these moments," he said. It had just that effect on Helen.

Bryn cleared around the gates, and with some WD-40 he eased the rusty hinges. Soon the gates were lockable.

He then went to his study and retrieved the weapon that was in the case.

Helen looked at it. "What do you expect?"

"This is for show. I will place it in the centre of the table. If I am right, the alien will ignore it. Then we can take matters slowly. I believe it will show the alien I mean business if it tries to act with any form of aggression."

Liu had not seen the weapon before. She only knew what Su Shi had told her about it. It looked just as Su Shi had described it. She felt the edge. "It's not very sharp, Bryn."

"No. I don't think it was a true weapon."

Su Shi asked, "What makes you say that?"

"The hands of the beast that carried it were too large for the hilt. The weapon would not have sat well in its grip. I sometimes wake up at night with little things nagging at me, and this is one of them. Real soldiers carry weapons that sit comfortably. They check the balance. The feel is the most important thing on any weapon. This was a prop."

At the academy, Charlyyk kept up the pretence that all was well, but inside she felt the nerves getting to her. She tried to laugh them off, but that almost backfired on her, because her humour made no sense to the posse. Mace sat and talked with her. He sensed that something was amiss. "What is troubling you?"

Charlyyk knew she could not lie to Mace, so she skirted around the issue with half-truths. "I've been worried that the aliens will come back and take me away from you all.

And it has been a cause of concern to me, for I would not be able to stop them."

Mace put his arm around her shoulders. "That would worry us. You have been the making of us. We have grown stronger as a team, and that includes you. We would hate for that to happen, so let's pray it does not."

Charlyyk touched Mace's hand. The look she gave him told him she appreciated his kind words.

When Charlyyk returned home, Helen fussed around her. She had made dinner for them early and tidied up. At five thirty, after an affectionate goodbye to Charlyyk, she left with Su Shi and Liu for Carpenters' cottage.

Bryn closed the gates and locked them. Charlyyk showered and changed into the Laura Ashley dress. When she came down, she looked really nice. Bryn cuddled her. Charlyyk had thought that if she dressed in something really nice, the aliens would leave without her. This was her biggest fear, for she knew she would be unable to stop them. They had the means to beam her back to wherever she had been taken from. These thoughts spun around inside her mind. She clutched at any flotsam for survival.

Bryn set the scene. He was a warrior, and he wanted to portray that image. He wore a tight T-shirt and army combat trousers.

At five to seven, Charlyyk's iPad showed a blurred image appearing. The garden door was open, ready to receive it.

The golden mane of its hair was the first they saw of it. It stood seven feet tall. It had the same features as Charlyyk. Its long hands again were the same as

Charlyyk's. Its flowing robes were a creamy white that draped to the floor.

The nods the tall alien conveyed to Charlyyk, she returned, knowing what they meant. Bryn keeping a watchful eye on what was being played out between them.

The alien looked at Charlyyk and spoke in Charlyyk's native tongue. She spoke back and bowed. The alien looked at the weapon on the table. It bent and picked the weapon up by the centre of the blade. It put the weapon in front of Bryn. Bryn nodded and allowed it to talk with Charlyyk.

Charlyyk turned to Bryn. "Dad, this is Drenghaagh. He is the leader of his group. He wants to put a headpiece on me. Is that OK?"

Bryn nodded. He knew that this was an act that had to be played out. They had to find a level where they could discuss the meaning of this whole saga.

Drenghaagh. took two metal headpieces from his robe. He put one on his own head, then gently put the other on Charlyyk's head. With a slight awkwardness, he sat in the chair opposite Charlyyk. He nodded to her, and then he spoke. This time he spoke in English, and Bryn could understand him.

"My name is Drenghaagh. I have much to tell you. I knew eventually we would find the right paring, but it came at a terrible cost. On my home planet, our genes have eroded. Our civilisation has been around a million years longer than your civilisation. We have evolved so much that it is causing our downfall. We have tried to keep everyone alive through good living and medical care, but that no longer holds the faulty genes at bay. No one

CHARLYYK

wants to do anything about it. Now we must begin again. We have found a suitable planet, but we need to establish the right system, so we do not make the same mistakes again. We see the same problems exist on this planet, and you too will self-destruct in time."

Bryn was troubled by what he heard. "So why have you let Charlyyk live among us?"

"The new planet we have chosen has the same bacteria that exist on your planet. We have lost four colonies due to them. Charlyyk is an orphan of those past mistakes. We have placed a plate in Charlyyk. It has a few functions. First, it stopped Charlyyk's memory of the first stages of her life. Second it gave her some immunity to your bacteria. She has been here for two orbits of your sun, and Charlyyk has survived. It has increased our belief that we can solve one of the problems of colonisation of our new home planet."

Drenghaagh reached across the table and gently stroked Charlyyk's face. "You have changed so much, Charlyyk." He nodded to her. She nodded back. Drenghaagh turned back to Bryn. "The plate also allows us to communicate through these headpieces."

"We thought at first that that was how you monitored her."

"No. We have a place on your moon, and we use your satellites."

Bryn noticed how similar Drenghaagh and Charlyyk were. There was no mocking, just a matter-of-fact, straight-to-the-point manner.

Drenghaagh looked carefully at her. "You have settled here. Your new family treat you well?"

"Yes. I love my life here." Again, there was nodding between them.

Charlyyk rose from her chair and put the kettle on. Drenghaagh watched her carefully. She made a mint tea and a coffee. She gave Drenghaagh the tea and Bryn the coffee. Charlyyk explained to Drenghaagh, "The heating of the water kills the bacteria." Then she made herself a mint tea.

Bryn observed every movement. He was not worried. He knew Drenghaagh was not here to do harm. Drenghaagh was a graceful creature. Charlyyk's brain was picking up the wavelengths Drenghaagh was sending out and naturally responding to them.

Drenghaagh turned to Bryn. "Have you any questions?"

Bryn answered, "Yes, many, but where do I start?"

Charlyyk asked, "The planet I was placed on, was it my home planet?"

"No. The planet was too arid. It was only a short-term solution. The planet you found yourself on when you met Bryn was also too arid to sustain life in the long term."

"And those beasts that killed my group?"

"Placed there to serve the purpose of pairing. Any one of your group could have been paired with the chosen male specimen who now is your guardian."

Charlyyk placed her hands together on the table and stared at them. Memories of her group flooded back. The screams that haunted her were there again. Bryn reached out, and she went to him, sitting on his knee for protection. It was Drenghaagh's turn to observe. He saw the way the two of them connected. His eyes turned a different colour, his body moved, and he stood up. "I must leave," he said, and was gone.

Bryn comforted Charlyyk, whose sobs had started to subside. They heard voices. Helen was the first one in, and soon was cuddling Charlyyk. Su Shi checked on Bryn.

Liu went to Helen, also to check on Charlyyk. The iPad was giving out noises. Bryn saw Harold's face appear on it. He asked if everything was OK. Bryn's mind went through what had occurred. He had not been in control, and it was bugging him. What made the alien Drenghaagh leave? Bryn racked his brain. Su Shi was talking to him, but he was not listening.

"Why did it leave in that manner?" Su Shi asked for the third time. "We saw Charlyyk go to you. We waited. It rose from the chair, and then it was gone."

Helen had Charlyyk settled and sat down by the side of Bryn. "There was a sudden change. Its head twitched and its eyes went a different colour just before it left."

Harold, Gwen, and Bruce entered the kitchen. Bruce was carrying his computer. Harold walking to Bryn. "Why did it just get up and go?" he asked.

Bryn could not answer him. He did not know the answer for himself.

Bruce set up his computer in front of Bryn, He watched the video from start to finish. "Bruce, can you get a closer look at those eyes?" Bruce zoomed in on them. Bryn shook his head. "Don't know, it shows nothing." Charlyyk asked Bruce to show her the recording.

Helen, Gwen, and Liu made coffees and talked among themselves, trying to find answers. They sat around the kitchen table but could not find no solution. They decided to sleep on it.

On Thursday morning, Bryn and Helen sneaked a look into Charlyyk's room. The bed was empty. A feeling of misgiving crept through Helen. She feared the worst. But Bryn's reaction was different. He just walked to the kitchen. There was Charlyyk, drinking water. Seeing them, a smile spread across her face. "I needed to clear my head from last night." She was already dressed for her early morning run.

Liu was next to arrive, ready for the run as well. She greeted Helen with a kiss. She had a hug for Charlyyk. "How did you sleep?"

"Not a lot. I need the run to put me in the right frame of mind for school."

Once Su Shi arrived, they were soon limbering up. They set off at a steady pace across the field. The chill air caught at the backs of their throats. As they reached the top of Bishops Lane, the sun was peeping over the horizon. Su Shi was ready to talk with Bryn. "Have you thought more about last night?"

Bryn was quiet for a moment. "I could not sleep, so I lay with my eyes shut. That colour change in the eyes—I've seen it on Charlyyk. I am racking my brain to remember when and why it occurred."

Liu ran with Charlyyk. "What was it that frightened you last night?"

Charlyyk said, "I was not frightened. The memories of my friends dying are terrible. The alien—and let us not forget he is of my people—let it happen on purpose. That was why I was so upset. I have an inbuilt detestation of violence that is similar to Gwen's. I sensed the same from Drenghaagh. So how could they have done what they did to my group?"

During breakfast, they allowed Charlyyk to talk. Su Shi slipped in a question: "Why did the eyes change colour like that?"

Charlyyk picked up her dirty things and said, "A sudden change of thinking." She placed the dishes into the dishwasher and closed the door. "Must rush, school!" Kissing them all, she grabbed her bag. With Helen in hot pursuit, she went to meet the bus, leaving the two men looking at each other.

Liu was quick to pick up on it. "A change of mind—so it was not scared?"

Bryn smiled. "That's it. A dramatic change of thinking—that's what it was with Charlyyk."

Su Shi now had a smile. "It's not over. This is just the beginning."

Helen, returning, saw the smiles on their faces. "What have I missed?"

Liu took her hand. "The alien was not scared. He just had a change of mind."

Helen called Harold. "Has Bruce gone?"

"No, why?"

"Don't let him go. We need to talk."

"What has happened?" Helen told him what had transpired that morning.

Later, Harold, Gwen, and Bruce arrived. Su Shi spoke to Chad on the phone, with Bruce confirming the action from the night before and sending Chad a download from his computer. Su Shi said he would drop on Chad en route to China. Then he phoned his sons to say he would see them tomorrow and to book a table with their cousin Chi for a family meal.

Bruce set up Helen's laptop so she could use the surveillance equipment. He also installed a guide on how to use it. "I have to return to Houston tomorrow to report on this, but Charlyyk has given me enough information to resume my own search for her planet."

Julia was keen to find out what had happened the previous night. At lunchtime, they found a secluded place where they could talk without being heard. Charlyyk explained, giving Julia a detailed vision of Drenghaagh. Julia's mouth dropped at what Charlyyk told her. "Well, were you not frightened?"

Charlyyk did not lie. She told of her fear of being taken away. Julia saw tears well up in her eyes. She cuddled Charlyyk when she heard about Charlyyk's feelings regarding what the alien said had been done to Charlyyk's group.

Julie's calm approach communicated to Charlyyk that what was done was done and could not be reversed. It helped Charlyyk to settle before going to her next lesson.

After school and back home at the cottage, Charlyyk was pleased to see Bruce had not yet gone. She was quickly in conversation with him. They were all sitting in the lounge. The question was asked, "What does *dreng* mean?"

"Leader, lord, chief. *Haagh* means male," Charlyyk replied. "It is deemed an honour if one is called

Haarhhaagh, a man of men. It is like a British soldier being awarded a Victoria Cross."

Then Charlyyk stopped. Bryn, saw she was thinking and put his hand up to tell them all to wait. A moment later, Charlyyk said, "The headpiece—it has given me more information than I knew before." Bryn continued to signal them to wait. "Some memories are returning that had only been a mist at the back of my mind. I must not push too hard but give my brain time to adjust."

On Friday, Su Shi and Liu packed and were ready to leave. Their farewell to Charlyyk was warm and moving. Charlyyk had come to like them very much and was genuinely sorry to see them go. She was pleased to see them wave goodbye to her as the bus drove off.

Liu was happy to have many pictures on her phone to show her friends. She had more bragging rights to get her into all the right places.

At ten o'clock they said their goodbyes to the rest of the family. A chauffeured car was taking them to Oxford, to the student house they had rented for their sons' university stay.

Later, Harold sat with Bryn in his study. "Do you think the alien will return?"

Bryn was confident it had only just begun. "If it has only had a change of mind, yes. But how and when is a different story. We have to wait and find out how the situation will unravel."

At the academy, the posse had gathered together for lunch. The main topic was Charlyyk's new diet. The salad looked nice. The avocado dip Charlyyk thought needed improvement. Michel did not want her eating salt, and she missed it. Under the rye crisps, the tell-tale signs of a Kit Kat brought a little comfort to her. Julia managed to find a friendly soul who had some salad cream in a sachet, and lunchtime took on another meaning for Charlyyk.

This normality was helping Charlyyk to keep a stable hold on how her brain was reacting to all that had happened. The new memories were confusing to her—like a dream, a mixed bag of jumbled nonsense.

CHAPTER 16

THE LIGHT CONSUMED THEM

On Saturday, the three runners passed the cowsheds. James exchanged his customary blown kiss with Charlyyk. They carried on till they reached the top of Bishops Lane, then began the return home. The light consumed them. In a flash, they were gone, as if nothing had been there.

In a safe position on the dark side of the moon, a spacecraft sat concealed. Charlyyk saw Drenghaagh's hand reaching down. She reached up, and he helped her to her feet. He noticed her worried expression. "I have not brought you here to take you away, so don't be alarmed."

Two more aliens were helping Bryn and Helen to their feet. "Welcome. Please make yourselves comfortable. You are our guests," Drenghaagh said. He pointed to some seats. "Let me explain myself." Bryn saw that all the aliens were wearing headpieces. "When I was with you, I saw the bond that you share with one another. The thoughts I was receiving showed that Charlyyk had made many friends. It would be wrong of us to take her away from you."

Helen's face changed. The anxiety had gone.

Drenghaagh said with a reassuring look, "But it has its problems, as you can tell. Charlyyk is growing. She has a healthy appetite. If we allow her to grow, she will tower over every human and indeed pose a threat to them. To help Charlyyk, we need to adjust the plate in her head to stop this growth from happening."

Bryn saw more aliens assembling. "Come, Charlyyk, let us proceed." Drenghaagh showed her to a table. A female alien, a *lyyk* with a light blue tint to her skin, helped Charlyyk onto the table. Charlyyk lay face down. The *lyyk* gently lifted Charlyyk's hair back. A large overhanging machine was lowered and positioned.

Helen gripped Bryn's hand. She felt helpless. There were more aliens than humans.

Drenghaagh stood beside her and placed his hand on her back. "She will feel no pain. A tingling sensation will travel through her body. The operation will do her no harm. We are going to alter the genes that we have gained knowledge of. This will restrict Charlyyk's height and allow her to grow fingernails, not claws. Some of us will also benefit from this."

A *lyyk* came to them. "It is nearly completed. We will have to give her chance to gather herself." Then she went back to the table.

Charlyyk sat up and looked at them. She gave a big sigh, then smiled. Two of the *lyyks* helped her to a seat. Her legs were a little wobbly from the procedure. A *haagh* brought her something to drink and offered Bryn and Helen refreshments. Helen was a bit hesitant to accept the offer, but Bryn agreed and took a sip to show Helen it was fine.

Drenghaagh started to speak again. "This will allow her to live normally with you. We have an armband to place at the top of her arm. This has a way of giving us an idea of how she is health-wise. The person who looks after her will need this."

He gave Bryn a square object with rounded corners, about the size of a cigarette packet. One of the *lyyks* stepped forward and lifted her sleeve to reveal a band on her arm. Drenghaagh showed Bryn how the square object worked, then placed the gadget against the band. It flickered briefly with blue and green lights. "That is all that has to be done. The body's own immunities will do the rest"

The *lyyk* then fitted the band to Charlyyk's arm. She used the gadget, watching it flicker. It stopped. She gave the device back to Bryn and left.

Drenghaagh explained the necessity of waiting two years to make contact. "We did not know if the immunity we had placed in Charlyyk worked. Two full solar cycles were necessary to determine if it had."

Bryn was most impressed with the way the aliens treated his family. He felt he had to say something about the way the military was looking at the threat of an alien invasion. Drenghaagh summoned his aides, and for a moment they talked among themselves. Bryn noticed it was not a heated discussion.

One of the aides left, and when he returned, he gave Bryn a small metal disc. "Place that on your communicator.

That will allow us to be seen and to talk with them. Charlyyk will be able to activate it when required."

Helen now felt relaxed and went to see how Charlyyk was. The other aliens watched the interaction between them.

One of the aliens came and sat with Drenghaagh. "I'm Strenghaagh. My role is as an analyst. We have studied your people and find they are unstable, excitable, and act on impulse. They are highly likely to react at the slightest provocation. We would like very much to dispel their concerns and remove any sense of threat of them that might make them retaliate with force."

Bryn picked out the nods they gave to each other. Drenghaagh smiled at Bryn's observations. Before Bryn could ask, Charlyyk answered him. "It is a sign of friendship, like when you shake hands." Drenghaagh asked Charlyyk in their language if she felt good. She assured him she was fine, then spoke to Bryn and Helen. "Mum, Dad, I am good."

One of the *lyyks* came in and gave them a ring each. "This will help you with your return to your planet," Drenghaagh said. There was a little interaction between Charlyyk and the *lyyk*. Helen remembered Charlyyk responding to Sandra the same way at Christmas, like a thank-you gesture.

Drenghaagh showed them to the area where they had landed on the craft. They positioned themselves. He nodded to them. "We will meet again." A flash, and they found themselves in their garden. This time they experienced no problems as they materialised.

There were two anxious people inside the cottage. "Do you know what time it is?" asked Gwen, wringing her hands. "I've been worried *sick* wondering what happened to you all."

Helen looking at her watch. It read 2.20 p.m. "Wow, it did not seem like that length of time."

They sat down around the kitchen table and explained in full detail what had happened aboard the spacecraft. Charlyyk showed the band on her arm, and Bryn the disc and the gadget that went with the armband. All of them showed the rings on their fingers. Harold wanted to see how the disc worked. But Charlyyk said, "No, too early,"

Bryn called Su Shi, and explained that they had had a meeting with the aliens, whom they now knew were called the Laights. Su Shi said he and Lui would return to the cottage on Monday. Bryn knew it was better to report than to keep quiet.

The Sunday morning run had a different feel to it. Helen checked her weight and was pleased—another three pounds lost. She liked what she saw in the mirror, and so did Bryn. "A wedding dress would look nice draped over those breasts," he said. She reached over and kissed him.

Life was feeling good for Helen. This weight loss was not for Bryn; this was for her and her self-esteem. She felt like a butterfly and not a moth. She was matching strides with Charlyyk and Bryn. This was definitely the girl in her, not the old lady.

Breakfast was taken casually, at a slow pace. Charlyyk showed no effects from Saturday and was in good spirits. *Monday morning with Julia is going to be awesome,* she thought.

Bryn carried on as if life were normal. He was completely unfazed by the latest developments.

Later at Carpenters' cottage, they talked with Michel about what had happened on board the Laights' spacecraft. He was very interested in what the Laights had said about fingernails. When Bryn showed him the gadget for the armband, he remarked. "Now that is what we all want—something to kick-start our immunity into action." When Helen told him what the plate in Charlyyk's head could do, he sighed a big sigh. "Lucky we did not try to remove it."

Bryn's updates to Catherine and Thomas, made over the Skype connection, met with mixed reactions. Both were concerned that if it had gone wrong, what then?

Charlyyk was quick to reply. "My people are a passive society. They will not upset the balance of life by doing harm."

On Monday, there was a rush to the bus. Charlyyk could not wait to tell Julia all that had taken place and the changes that the Laights planned for her.

Su Shi and Liu arrived at Oakleaves at ten. The conversation about all the latest developments lasted till twelve. A phone call to Chad was next, via a Skype connection. Bruce could be seen with Mrs Lomax, studying his video recording of the first meeting with the aliens. Chad felt a bit miffed that he had not been there. "We must meet up again, and soon."

Lunchtime found Julia and Charlyyk huddled together. Julia's mouth gaped when she heard what had happened to Charlyyk. The armband and ring on her finger sealed the story. "How tall was he?"

"See the door over there? Well, six inches taller, almost up to the clock."

Julia gave a wide-eyed look towards the clock, then back at Charlyyk. "To that height! And they promised they could keep your height at what is a more normal height for us. Wow, that's clever." Julia's face lit up. "And you will get fingernail like ours!" To Julia, the fingernails sounded more important.

Yuri welcomed Bryn's phone call and kept him on the line for some time, asking many questions. "I will speak with Chad. I expect that we will all catch up on these new developments. Look forward to seeing you then."

Bryn put the phone down, a soft smile on his face. He liked this larger-than-life Russian who took life at a moderate pace. He was much like Bryn in many ways— saying nothing until he had thought things through, weighing everything up, judging actual value. It could also be said he was making sure the English he was speaking was correct, but Bryn was sure Yuri indeed was a good man. He did not complicate issues, and he usually made sound comments.

Bryn had left Helen to speak to Major Alan Carter, who needed the same updates. The detailed reports that Helen gave the major, he did not need to question.

The arrival of Charlyyk at Oakleaves brought them all together. Sitting with drinks in hands, they started to look how their lives would be from now on. Charlyyk made the first suggestion. "My diet should change—this one sucks!" Bryn and Helen burst into laughter. Charlyyk had brought the unexpected events back to normal.

After dinner, Charlyyk helped Helen to tidy up, then went to her room. She needed to talk with Janet. "Hi, kid, how do you feel?"

"Much better, thanks, Charlyyk." Janet sounded better than the last time they had spoken. "Mum and Dad are here. Edward and Jane invited them to stay for the week. Dr Patel has said when people have a full-blown virus, it can really bring them down and weaken their immunities. Edward has brought a couple of crates of Guinness. I am getting used to them, and look forward to when he has poured another one for me." Janet gave Charlyyk a little chuckle. It was not what she would have thought she would like to drink.

"Janet, much has happened, and we need to talk about it. Will it be OK if we come to you?"

There was a pause. Then James answered, "What's up, Charlyyk?"

Charlyyk took a deep breath. "James, we have had developments here. I do believe we should tell you all about them, as you are like family to us."

James felt concerned. "Whatever could it be?"

Charlyyk felt a little awkward. "Promise you will not tell anyone!"

He was getting confused. "Why? What's up?"

Charlyyk's voice became firmer. "Promise me?"

"OK, I promise. Now what is it?"

"We have had a visit from my people."

James did not answer straight away, but when he did, it was slow and precise. "From your people?"

"Yes, from my people."

James took in a large breath. "Bloody hell."

Charlyyk hear mumbling between him and Janet. Janet's voice upped a pitch. "Is that true, Charlyyk?"

"Yes, Janet, with video proof."

Janet sounded a bit gurgled over the phone, and then the line went dead. As Charlyyk tried to redial, the landline phone rang. Helen answered. Charlyyk went into the lounge. "Yes, Jane, what a great idea," Helen said. Charlyyk beckoned her. "Yes, Jane, she is by my side now." Helen passed the phone to Charlyyk.

"Sorry for the confusion, Charlyyk. Janet dropped the phone, and they bumped heads trying to retrieve it. We will see you tomorrow."

As Charlyyk replaced the phone, Helen put her arm around her.

On Tuesday evening, the drive up to Parsons' farm did not take long. James was at the front door, waiting. Charlyyk was first out of the car and into his arms. "Hi, twinkle." The manly way he greeted her brought out a couple of squeals from Charlyyk. Bryn and Helen followed.

Charlyyk went through to the kitchen to greet Jane, then went on to the back, where Janet was sitting with her parents and Edward in the large conservatory.

Janet was very pale. The flu virus had really taken its toll on her. "Don't come too close, Charlyyk. I don't want to pass this to you."

Charlyyk just smiled and pulled her sleeve up, showing the armband. It was a thin strip of metal in a zigzag pattern that allowed it to expand with the movement of her biceps. "They gave me this to protect me." Then she bent down and kissed her.

Janet touched it. "How does it do that?"

"It gives my immunities a kick-start."

James was standing right behind her. "May I see?" He touched it. "Wow, it actually came from outer space?"

Charlyyk said with a wry smile, "Yes, James, just like me."

Janet introduced her to her parents. They both were hesitant at first, but Charlyyk pushed herself forward, not allowing them any choice but to shake her hand.

Helen came in and showed them the recording of the first encounter. Bryn was soon filling in the story. When the others heard that the Colliers had been taken on Saturday morning from the top of Bishops Lane, they were gobsmacked. So near to the farm, yet they had seen nothing! Helen gave them the rest of the details. Poor Janet tried to get enthusiastic but found it hard.

Charlyyk was more concerned about Janet than about telling her what had happened to herself. Then Charlyyk changed. Her expression was deep and meaningful. "All of you are like family to us. We must keep this in the family until it is allowed to be broadcast to the world. This will no doubt be look at by all the nations' governing bodies before it is released. So please—just us."

Edward remarked about the plate in Charlyyk's head. "And that really can alter the way Charlyyk grows? Bloody marvellous."

After dinner, Jane asked Bryn about Thomas and Rachel. "When will they be back?"

Bryn looked at Helen.

Helen answered, "They will return in two weeks, stay for two weeks, then go to Liverpool for six weeks. We will have a lot of material for Janet, but we will have to hold on to it until Janet is feeling better."

Edward laughed with Bryn about the feature in the men's magazine. "I was taken aback by the girl in the article before yours. She looked younger than Charlyyk."

Jane quipped, "You sure you were looking at her age, Bryn?"

Charlyyk added, "Helen would have blacked his eyes if it were anything different."

Charlyyk sensed that Janet's parents were apprehensive of her. They had been quiet all evening. She managed to get James on his own. "So when are you going to ask them? Although you are both old enough to not have to ask."

James looked at her forlornly. "I keep plucking up the courage, and then it goes. The cat catches my tongue."

When they were back with the others in the conservatory. Bryn asked James how life was treating him. Charlyyk gate-crashed. "Edward, when are you going to shoot the farm cat?"

Edward looked at her. he knew Charlyyk would not say such a thing unless there was a reason behind it. "Why have I to shoot the farm cat, Charlyyk?"

"James is trying to pluck up the courage to pop the question, but that bloody farm cat keeps catching his tongue. At this rate, he will never ask."

Jane took hold of Helen's hand. Both had closed their eyes. Bryn shot a look at Charlyyk. Edward looked at James. Janet took hold of her mother's hand. Her father placed his hands on his own knees. But nobody said anything.

Then Charlyyk said, still looking at James, "Well, that's good. No one's objected, so it's a yes, then." She walked to the kitchen and poured a glass of water.

Charlyyk knew what she had done, but wondered if it would have the right results. She could have handled the matter in a much more sensitive way. A smile broke out on her face as she remembered James's expression. She collected herself so she could go back to the conservatory.

On her return, they were all congratulating themselves. Janet, seeing Charlyyk, struggled over and hugged her. "Thanks, sweetheart. You are a treasure." Jane and Mary Stokes, Janet's mother, were smiling. So was Helen. Charlyyk saw it and gave her a wink.

The drive home was lively. Bryn made faces at Charlyyk in the rear-view mirror. Helen reminded him to keep his eyes on the road. She asked, "What made you say that, Charlyyk?"

"It was Dad's fault. He asked James what was happening, and the answer was nothing. James needed a kick."

On Wednesday, when Charlyyk came home from school, she spoke to Helen about what the girls were discussing at school. "Valentine's cards, Mum?"

Helen looked at Charlyyk with a "do we need to go down this path" expression on her face. "When a girl or boy fancies someone, they can send a valentine card anonymously, giving them clues as to who sent it and hoping the other person will respond likewise. Usually it's meant to get a romance started. But many just want to brag about how many cards they've received. It is what's known as bragging rights."

Charlyyk thought it through. "So I could send someone a card, without saying it was me." Then she stopped. "That won't work, will it? As soon as I write something, they will recognize my hand." She went quiet for a moment. "That would cause more problems. I think it would be wiser not to send any cards."

"Have you someone in mind?"

Charlyyk's face did not change. "No, no one." Charlyyk started peeling the potatoes. Her thoughts were still on what they had been discussing. "So what would one write on a card?"

Helen put chicken pieces in a roasting tin and added a little stock to keep them moist. "Most people write poems or some type of verse, like an ode, which I believe is normally meant to be sung."

Charlyyk laughed. "Well, that will be no good for me, with the voice I've got."

Helen sensed that she had an issue. "What's bugging you, Charlyyk?" She covered the chicken with foil and placed it in the oven.

Charlyyk put the potatoes on to parboil. "I feel the meaning of love, the love for all the people who have given me a chance to live here, and especially those who are closest to me … Well, that love gives me a warm inner glow that Gwen says her god gives her. But when I see you and Dad enjoy each other, or Janet and James's rampant love for each other, I wonder, will I miss that type of love? I don't know and may never know. Yes, I'm different. I don't know what would be expected from me if I returned to my own kind. I just don't know what would be expected from me, full stop."

Helen for a moment said nothing. She noticed that Charlyyk's eyes had stayed the same colour, so it was just casual talk. "I was brought up by nannies. It left me cold in my feelings. I never looked at the other sex for pleasure. I only cared that they were efficient at their job. But your dad, well, the more I saw him, the more I wanted him. I could not stop thinking of him. I would do anything for him. If I never had met your dad, I would have carried on being a nun."

Charlyyk strained the potatoes and twirled them in the colander. She emptied them into the roasting tin and replaced it in the oven. Then she placed the dirty dishes in the sink. "What are nuns?"

"They are women who give their lives to God. They give up material things, and they go through a ceremony of marrying God, accepting his ring."

Charlyyk's face did not show any change. "Are there many of them?"

"Yes, thousands."

Charlyyk checked the potatoes. "That many wives should keep him busy. No wonder he doesn't turn up to church on Sundays."

Helen took a grip on the table, trying hard to stifle her laughter.

At Thursday lunch at the academy, Charlyyk met Julia. They had started to form a pattern. They positioned themselves so that they could see all the posse. They could talk without being overheard. The posse thought they were simply sharing their lunchboxes. But their primary interest was gossip about the interactions among them all—who was getting on with who.

Peter and Sandra were getting closer, and Sandra had the control. George was getting closer to Jan. Mace and Sarah had a brother-sister relationship. Charlyyk could sense Mike's vibes for Julia were still showing, but very faint. Julia's vibes were the same, but Julia spent more time with Charlyyk. She was keeping Mike at bay for the moment. Spotty Paul, who was self-conscious, sat on the periphery, prepared to be used. Stella, who lived close to Jan, was like Paul. Charlyyk felt sorry for them and sought where she could alter their prospects and bring them forward into the group.

On Friday, they had returned from their run and were enjoying a glass of water in the kitchen. Charlyyk was giving her idea for the weekend. "Let's take it easy. After what happened last weekend, we could do with a bit of laziness."

Helen liked that idea. "How about a movie? There must be something we could see."

Bryn nodded. "Catch a bite to eat, then cinema sounds good."

The doorbell rang, and Bryn made his way to find out the reason why. The post lady was standing there. "Hi, Bryn. This bag of mail is all for you. Happy reading." He thanked her, returned to the kitchen, and emptied the bag over the kitchen table. He picked up a handful of letters and looked at them. Helen did the same.

Charlyyk could see they were all addressed to her, opened a couple and laughed at their contents. Then she went to get ready for school.

Helen and Bryn sorted the piles into order: the good, the bad, and the downright unreadable. Charlyyk took a handful to show the posse at lunchtime. All the girls read the cards.

One of Charlyyk's eyes was watching Stella. She looked so forlorn, it concerned her. Charlyyk got up and sat with her. "Aye, you don't look happy."

Stella tried to smile. "I'm OK."

But Charlyyk sensed a lump in the throat. "Come on. You are one of the posse, so if there is a problem, it's my problem too. Talk to me."

Sandra, who was nearest to them, sat on the other side of Stella. "What Charlyyk just said goes for all of us. If you have a problem, you can talk to us all."

Stella looked down at her hands. "I feel that nobody likes me. I feel different from all of you."

Sandra placed her arm on Stella's and gave her a hug. "Charlyyk is different from all of us, yet she talks to us. To make friends, you must meet people. Take that big step forward and say hi, and you will hear them say hi back to you. It's as easy as that, just as we are doing now."

Charlyyk took Stella's hand in hers. "Happy Valentine's Day, Stella."

The rest of the posse was soon there, checking what was going on and joining in. This gave Stella moral support. Her smile showed just that.

As the bell sounded for lessons, Charlyyk spoke to Paul. "That goes for you too, Paul. Don't stay on the side-lines. Come into the middle or you will fall out of the group."

Paul's pasty face smiled at her. "Thanks, Charlyyk."

Sarah gave Charlyyk a hug. "Good on yer, kid. Well done."

Charlyyk started to think what she had said was due to her changing. *Careful. Don't look too mature. Remember to act your age.*

CHAPTER 17

THE SILENT VISITOR

On Friday evening, Michel and his protégée Clare were
writing their reports and discussing their schedules for
the next day. Clare had been with Michel since leaving
university. She loved his natural, relaxed manner. He never
panicked. When she suggested changes to the clinic, he
would just smile. "So when are you going to implement
these changes, then, Clare?" He gave her the freedom to
express herself. She had told her parents that Michel gave
her the feeling it was her clinic she was working in, not
his. Michel had been open with her when Charlyyk first
arrived. He let Clare know what was happening, and why
it must be kept secret at all times.

The sense of a presence in the room with them made
them look up. The very distinguished, tall figure was
the *lyyk* that had put the armband on Charlyyk. She was
wearing clothes similar to Drenghaagh's but in a soft shade
of blue. She gave the friendship nod of her head, then sat
in a chair opposite Michel. "Please do not be afraid. I have
come to explain the procedure of the armband we have
placed on Charlyyk's arm."

252

Clare did not look concerned about this tall, elegant alien. She pulled her chair closer to Michel and cleared the screen of his computer. She was ready to take down what was going to be told them.

˙The *lyyk*'s passive nature was why Clare had not panicked. The alien was so relaxed that Clare just went with flow of the moment. "My name is Klyklyyk. The armband we have placed on Charlyyk will respond to electronic signals from Charlyyk's brain or any sign given by her nervous system. The meter that goes with the armband has two functions. The first is to tell you that the band is working properly, blue to green. Straight green means it is fighting a virus at that moment. A yellow light tells you that the band has a conflict with the plate in her head. Take the ring from her finger and place it on the next finger, then check the band for a straight green. If it is still yellow, keep moving the ring to another finger till the meter reads green." Klyklyyk looked at Clare to see if she had taken notes. "Charlyyk will experience a slight tingling. Then her claws will drop off. Her fingernails will have already started to come through. It will take a few light moments to complete the procedure. The slowing down of her growth should cause no problems at first, but in two solar cycles, she will feel some side effects. We will be on hand when that happens." Klyklyyk rose from the chair. "Thank you for looking after Charlyyk." She turned and was gone.

Clare printed off two copies. "I will laminate these. We will need to place one in Kitty's clinic." Michel took notice of the laid-back way Clare had behaved to this tall stranger. He had not felt so calm at first. It was how Clare had reacted that settled him.

On Saturday at the breakfast table, the Collier family were still reading the mail. Some of the letters were from teenagers struggling to find their identity. Some asked how Charlyyk had coped, adjusting to life on their world.

Helen tried to explain the strained relationship some families found themselves in. "It's not always the teenagers who are at fault. Some parents are lazy parents, not expecting to contribute to bringing up their children. They blame the government for their own failings."

Charlyyk was keen to find out more. "When looking at some student attitudes at school—surly, aggressive, obstructive—I wonder how they could behave in that manner."

Bryn said, "We call that having a chip on the shoulder. Sometimes it is a way of trying to influence others to give in to their way of thinking or their wants. Weak parents are to blame. The parents are unable to say no to their children at an early age. Some parents are like that themselves, and it brushes off onto their children."

Charlyyk listened carefully. "It sounds like all parents are at fault one way or another."

Helen put down a letter she was reading. "No, that's not quite true. The nanny state has some part to play in it. Education used to be about teaching children the basics of life and allowing their natural aptitudes to come forward. Those who were good at set subjects went on to study them at university. Now the government wants to put all children into the same box. Those natural abilities are being lost."

She did not finish what she wanted to say. A knock came on the door, and they heard Michel's distinctive voice. "Anyone at home?" He walked in, Clare close behind him. "Had a visitor last night. Klyklyyk?"

Charlyyk smiled. "She is nice."

Clare asked what the name meant.

"Silent girl or quiet girl. It's a name given to someone who tends to listen, not to speak."

It was Michel's turn to smile. "Well, she spoke to us. She explained the workings of the armband and the meter. Clare took it all down, and we need to leave a copy in Kit's clinic."

He passed it to Bryn. He read it, with Helen reading over his shoulder at the same time. "That's detailed."

Clare stepped forward. "Can we test it?"

Helen headed to the clinic. "Come, let's get it."

They returned with the gadget in their hands. Charlyyk had soon rolled her sleeve up. Clare placed the gadget on the band. It flashed blue to green. Then she took Charlyyk's hand with the ring on a finger and placed the meter on the ring. Again, it flashed blue to green.

She noticed that Helen and Bryn were wearing similar rings. "May I?" She beckoned.

Helen lifted her hand and the gadget flashed blue to green. Bryn was intrigued and offered his hand. Blue to green. "Interesting," he said. "I wonder what they do?"

Charlyyk offered them refreshment.

"Coffee would be lovely," Michel said, placing his hand on Charlyyk's back as they all headed for the kitchen.

Clare was pleased that Michel had insisted she come. She had never seen Oakleaves, but felt, she knew all about it from Michel's descriptions. Michel explained to the Colliers why he had brought Clare. "I'm not getting any younger, and Clare has been like a daughter to me. If anything, undue happens, I want to know that Charlyyk will be taken care of."

Clare kissed him on the cheek. "More like you treating me like a daughter."

Later that day, the Colliers met Harold and Gwen at a fish restaurant. Charlyyk liked it there. She enjoyed the relaxed manner of the staff and the freshness of the food. It was situated on the outskirts of the town, so there was easy parking. Its basic furniture was comfortable too Harold reckoned the best part was the chips. Their conversation focused the visit from Michel and Clare.

At the cinema, Charlyyk wanted to see *Guardians of the Galaxy*. With popcorn and orange juice, she was ready. They all enjoyed the film, and each had a favourite part. Gwen had not liked the choice of the film at first, but she admitted she loved it at the end—although Groot was hard to get her head around. A moving tree took some believing for her, but then so did Rocket the racoon. When Charlyyk mentioned that she too was different, Gwen just nodded with closed eyes.

On Monday morning, Charlyyk sat down to breakfast with a pile of the sealed letters she had written. Helen looked at the distance some were to travel. "They will cost a bit to send."

Charlyyk counted twenty letters, half going overseas. "Those are the ones that had no email addresses on them." She felt that she should justify why she was sending them.

Helen said she would post them for her. "How many did you answer, then, sweetheart?"

Charlyyk checked her diary. "One hundred and fifteen. Some had no reply addresses, so I could not reply." Charlyyk then left for school.

Helen, though retiring from her role in intelligence, had not stopped acting on behalf of Toby Scalon. She had sent in her reports. After lunch the first replies from the military came in, all saying the same—that they would convey the report to their superiors and would be in touch. They relied on Bryn and Helen for first-hand knowledge of what was happening.

Helen called Rebecca, Sandra's mother, to check on Len's condition. It gave Rebecca a good feeling. It was a distraction from what else was happening. Len had put on weight, and his strength was returning. They agreed to meet again the next Wednesday.

On Tuesday, the crisp, chill air showed the vapour from their mouths as they hit the top of the hill. Charlyyk ran in place and looked around. She marvelled at the way the sun caught the top of the trees and the mist hung in the branches. Helen and Bryn had smiles on their faces. This was a family enjoying life.

Julia Peters, awakened by her dad, was someone else whose life felt good. She reached for her father's hand, and he turned and sat on the edge of the bed. He was a teddy bear of a father, big and cuddly, and always had a warm, loving smile for his daughter. He helped her onto his lap, his big arms wrapped around her. "I've to go to work, sweetheart. See you tonight. Have a lovely day at school?"

She slid off his lap and kissed him goodbye. He may not have been the most intelligent dad in the world, but to Julia, he was the most loving dad in the world. She stood with her mum at the door and waved him off.

Iris Peters, Julia's mother, was as thin as her husband was big. The pain they both felt when they saw the large birthmark down the right side of their new-born daughter's face only made them love her more. As Charlyyk's first years on Earth were spent hidden, so were Julia's. She met Sandra at primary school. Sandra did not worry about the birthmark. Now with Charlyyk as a friend, life was good.

Over breakfast, her thoughts drifted back to when she first went to the academy. Sarah, Mace, and Peter soon became friends, but when Jan joined them, she had made fun of Julia. Sandra turned on Jan, so much so that Sarah made Jan apologise to Julia. Now they were all friends, and it felt good.

At school, Julia asked, "Where's Charlyyk, Mace?"

Mace looked around. "I don't know. She was with us when we left the bus."

Charlyyk met them at the lockers. "At lunchtime, we have a meeting with the teachers." They all looked quizzically at her. "Don't look so worried! I have something to tell you that I think you should all know."

At lunchtime, Charlyyk led the posse to the teachers' meeting room. Mrs Landon welcomed them in and beckoned Charlyyk to speak. "In these last few days, much has happened." Charlyyk went on to tell them about the visits she had had. She showed them the armband, but stressed the importance of secrecy until it had been disclosed formally. "I appreciate the way you have all protected me since my arrival. This is me, putting my trust in you. Please show me that my trust in you is vindicated."

Julia felt at ease. Keeping the secret from the rest of the posse had been hard. Now they all knew the truth. But she still knew that the secret must be kept. Charlyyk was displaying her respect for them and was making them aware of the trust she had in them.

The nods, hugs, and kisses she received meant so much to Charlyyk.

On Wednesday, Bryn went with Helen to see Rebecca and Len. Bryn soon set up a conversation with Len, while Helen gave Rebecca her full attention. The pastries they had brought went well with the coffees. Helen and Bryn left at one.

Rebecca cuddled up to Len. They were in bed by two. Rebecca made all the play as Len was still not up to full strength. When Sandra returned from school, her mother was still on a high. Her dad looked like the cat that had licked the cream. He could not help passing winks at Rebecca. After dinner, Sandra texted Charlyyk, thanking her for what her parents had achieved.

Charlyyk showed Helen the text. Helen could not help but show Charlyyk the text that Rebecca had sent her: *Helen, we are husband and wife again. Thank you, X.*, Charlyyk knew what the text meant. The cuddle she gave Helen left no doubt at all that she knew. Helen was showing Charlyyk her trust in her.

Bryn had received notice from Number 10 to join the prime minister at the United Nation's meeting in New York. A car would pick them up at eight on Friday evening, Bryn relayed the news to Helen and Charlyyk.

Charlyyk immediately set up her computer. Bryn gave her the disc. She placed it on the laptop, then turned the disc till it changed to a blue colour. She put the ring on her finger against the disc. The image of Drenghaagh emerged. Charlyyk spoke in her native tongue with him. He nodded and was gone. "All set up and ready to go, Dad." Charlyyk gave the disc back to Bryn for safekeeping.

On Thursday, the posse crowded together, listening to Charlyyk explain the latest developments. Mrs Landon and Mrs Butler joined in. "Will you do the school proud and wear your uniform, Charlyyk?" Mrs Landon asked.

Charlyyk gave the request some thought. "Yes. I think it would be good to wear it."

Louise Landon was in seventh heaven. *This will go all around the world. The next governors' meeting will be a doddle.* The two teachers walked away, looked as though they had won the lottery.

When Charlyyk arrived home, she spoke with Helen about the uniform. Helen thought it was a good idea. "It will give the people around the world the perspective that you are just a teenage girl."

Bryn agreed. Suddenly Helen's look of understanding turned to panic. Charlyyk asked, "What's wrong?"

Helen threw her hands down her sides. "Look at me! I've lost so much weight, I've nothing to wear!"

Bryn laughed. "Then tomorrow morning we must visit Little and Large." Bryn had been impressed with how they had supplied Charlyyk with a suit at short notice, and the way they had accomplished such high-quality tailoring at the drop of a hat.

The plane that waited for them was one of the new aircraft with sleeping capacity. The prime minister was pleased to see Helen and welcomed her with a kiss on the cheek. Bryn's introduction to the PM was warm. The PM asked him to sit with him during the flight, as he had so many questions to ask of Bryn.

Then it was Charlyyk's turn. The PM knew a great deal about her and was soon laughing and joking with her. By ten, Helen and Charlyyk had settled down to sleep.

Bryn answered more questions from the PM. By twelve, they too had settled down to sleep.

The Colliers had been booked into a hotel ten minutes away from the UN Building. There was an icy chill blowing down from the north, and Charlyyk preferred to stay in the hotel until called for. Major Carter was at hand with four security personnel.

Charlyyk liked the limo drive to the meeting. They were ushered into the building. More security covered every entrance, Lieutenant Colonel Chad Smitt had done his homework and had given Captain Hanne the role of honour looking after the Colliers. When the time came to enter the general meeting chamber, Charlyyk strode in flanked by Helen and Bryn. Helen, in a black two-piece suit, stood up to address the contingent of heads of state.

When the mumblings subsided, Helen spoke. "I hope you have all read the dossier that we have circulated, giving you the details of what has occurred so far. What you are about to see is our first meeting with the leader of the Laights, Drenghaagh." Bryn pressed the key to start the video clip, and an image appeared on the giant screen. The meeting hall was hushed. Helen waited for the video clip to finish, then paused for a few moments more to allow the interpreters to finish their work.

The hum in the hall rose and subsided. Helen then carried on. "After that meeting, a few days later, we were taken on board their spacecraft for further instruction. They wanted to make it clear that they were there to help Charlyyk so she will be able to live among us." Helen gave precise details as to how this was to be achieved. She played another video clip showing the armband and the X-ray pictures of the plate in Charlyyk's head. "During our meeting aboard their spacecraft, Brian Collier mentioned the threat they might pose to our world."

Sensing calm, Helen carried on. "The Laights' leader, Drenghaagh, took Brian Collier's comments very seriously. He wanted to give you all assurances that their presence here is for peaceful reasons only." She looked around the hall to make sure she had their full attention. "Drenghaagh wishes to speak to you directly." She nodded to Bryn.

Bryn placed the disc onto the computer. Soon an image was projected on the large screens. Charlyyk was ready to set the wheels in motion. Helen carried on. "Ladies and gentlemen, Drenghaagh."

Charlyyk touched the disc with her ring, and Drenghaagh appeared. He looked majestic in his flowing robes and golden locks. "Please don't be afraid. We are at peace with you. We have been monitoring your planet for many solar cycles. We wish you no harm. You have given us so much valuable insight with which to colonise our new home planet, which has many features that you have here. We have placed a monitor station on your moon. This will have a minimum of our people to observe that Charlyyk is well. We would like, when she has grown, for her to be our ambassador, showing our good intentions towards you."

Drenghaagh knew that he had to protect Charlyyk. "Charlyyk has been innocent of what we placed upon her. Our intention to have her return to her own people had to be reconsidered, as Charlyyk has a strong love for those she has lived with and wants to remain here with them. We understand the bond that ties her to them and respect her wishes. We hope you too respect her choice to stay with you on your planet. Thank you for listening."

The nod he gave was to Charlyyk. Helen noted a particular change of eye colour and ear twitching between them. There was a final nod, and the transmission was terminated.

The Collier family waited for comments. The activity around the meeting hall was not an uproar, more like the sound of bees in a beehive.

France was first to ask a question. "How long have they been monitoring us?"

Charlyyk stood. "Give or take a decade, about two hundred years."

The mumbling became a little louder. Canada was next to speak. "That fits in with the sightings recorded by a First Nation tribe on a deerskin dating back to 1840."

Much discussions were in progress all around the hall, but no more questions were asked of the Collier family. After many minutes, a UN aide asked if they would like to leave. "This could go on for some time." They quietly got up and left.

Drinks were arranged for them. Helen asked Charlyyk about the eye contact she had made with Drenghaagh. "We are expected to make contact with him when things are quiet."

Bryn looked at her. "You saw that in his eyes?"

"In a lot of countries, hand gestures go with the language. It is the same with us. Eye and ear signals can mean more than words."

As they waited, an elderly lady approached them. "I'm an aide to the secretary-general. Will the aliens be making contact with you again?"

Charlyyk did not flinch. "Yes, of course."

The lady turned and re-entered the hall.

Waiting time always seems longer than it really is. Bryn hated this part—the hanging about, waiting for something to happen. Charlyyk reached over and took his hand. He smiled at her, but she could feel the twitch in his hands.

The lady re-emerged and headed towards them. "Could you come this way?" Instead of leading them to the main hall, she headed towards some other doors and along a corridor to an elevator. They went three floors up, and she showed them to an office. "Please make yourselves comfortable."

The secretary-general came in after ten minutes and introduced himself. "I am pleased how this has turned out. At first, I was most concerned that an alien invasion was about to happen. I have never known a more peaceful conclusion to a United Nations assembly like this one." He made himself comfortable in his chair. "I, like so many of us, have followed your story with great interest. But it did have a very serious side to it. Major Arn Sigurdsson has assured me that I should put faith in you for the way you have conducted yourselves. You have told us everything you can about what has happened."

He smiled at Charlyyk. "Looking at you in your school uniform makes us realise that you are a young girl and not a threat. Whoever suggested your outfit I must thank, for it was the best way to stabilise the delegates here today."

He gave Bryn a sheet of paper. "These are my personal telephone numbers. You can reach me any time you think it necessary to do so."

The meeting continued on a personal note. He asked Charlyyk her views of living on this planet. He slipped in a more direct question now and again, just to make sure he knew all there was to know.

Later at the hotel, the family made ready to have dinner with the UK delegation. Helen dressed in a black dress. Charlyyk wore the green dress that Margret had bought her. Bryn wore a light-blue serge suit.

The large round dining table was set out majestically. Charlyyk stood by the side, just staring at it. The centre decoration of flowers looked good enough to eat, never mind their decorative effect. A waiter seated them at the table. If the PM was at twelve o'clock, Helen sat at three, Charlyyk at six, and Bryn at nine. The delegation was interspersed between. No politics were discussed, but there were many more personal questions for the family to answer.

Sunday, on the drive back to the cottage, Helen found herself cuddling a very tired Charlyyk. The whole weekend had really caught up with her. Helen was concerned about school the next day. Bryn had to carry her into the cottage and straight to bed.

Earlier Charlyyk had mentioned a funny sensation in her fingers and toes. Helen undressed her and checked her toes. The redness around the claws were signs of the changes Drenghaagh had promised.

On Monday, Charlyyk awoke to feel the strange sensation of losing her claws. She headed for Bryn's bedroom. At first she had to hold on to furniture for balance, but gradually she managed to adjust.

Helen, seeing her, was quickly out of bed. Assisted, Charlyyk sat on the bed and showed Helen what was happening to her. "Does it hurt?" Helen saw the tips of fingernail just appearing.

Charlyyk smiled. "No, it just feels strange."

Bryn leaned over to look. "They look tender, sweetheart." Bryn gave her a gentle cuddle. "Come, let's get into bed and have a late morning."

Charlyyk loved this side of human life. Before she met Bryn, she had cuddled for warmth and protection, but this was different. The more Charlyyk did it, the more she liked it. As she watched, Helen smoothed her hands over Bryn. Charlyyk saw how he enjoyed it, and when he applied the same to her, how Helen enjoyed it. She understood the meaning of endearment, love, and affection now. That was what humanity was all about— the desire for the love of one another.

Breakfast was laughter all round as Charlyyk tried to hold a spoon. Helen phoned Michel, but he was out. Clare said she would come instead. Twenty minutes later, Clare was holding Charlyyk's hand and checking her fingertips. "And they are not painful?"

SPENCER CARVIL

Charlyyk showed interest in how Clare was treating her. "No, not at all."

Clare then looked at her toes. "Same again, no pain?"

Charlyyk shook her head. "No."

Clare reached into her bag. A tube of antiseptic cream was her answer. "This will just soothe the area." She asked Helen if she had some cotton pop socks. Helen fetched them. "The toes need more protection, and the pop sock will help."

As Clare tidied up, Charlyyk walked up and down. "Yes, that feels better already. Thank you, Clare."

Clare asked Helen for the gadget. Helen fetched it and gave it to her. Clare rolled up Charlyyk's sleeve and checked: blue to green. "Great. That shows it's all working well."

Helen gave Charlyyk a pencil and a piece of paper. "Write your name, sweetheart." Charlyyk found it tricky at first, but soon had adapted to the changes.

Bryn came in. "I've informed the bus driver we will take her to school later."

Clare finished her cup of tea. "I'm going that way. Can I drop her off?"

On the drive to school. Clare talked about many things, mainly of herself. Charlyyk found this a nice change. People were always asking her questions.

At lunchtime, the posse and Mrs Butler found Charlyyk's weekend adventure fascinating. But losing her claws, that was different. There were lots of oohs and aahs from them all.

Mrs Butler was quick to inform Mrs Landon about the success of the school uniform. The photo in the New

York newspaper that Charlyyk had brought back even mentioned the school. Twitter had also covered the story. Mrs Landon smiled as she read the paper over and over again. "Now let's see what the governors say to this."

Harold and Gwen had been waiting for the school bus to arrive. "Hello, darling,"

Charlyyk accepted Gwen's kiss. "Auntie Gwen, look. My claws have gone."

Harold gave her a squeeze. "How're your toes?"

She gave them a turn on the balls of her feet. "Perfect. It's so much nicer already."

Janet and James arrived after dinner. Janet, looking more herself, grabbed Charlyyk in a bear hug, and smothered her with kisses. Then she showed her the ring that James had given her. "Charlyyk, I love you." She could not hide her feelings. She was ecstatic with joy. "I cannot begin to tell you what this means to me, and it's all down to you."

James stood close by. With the look of a big, loving brother, he gathered Charlyyk up in his arms and gave her a kiss. "Twinkle, we both love you. Just wait till my mum gets hold of you. Make sure you take a deep breath. You sure will need to with the kiss she is going to give you." The big cuddle all three gave left Charlyyk speechless but proud.

Helen gave Janet the report she had written about the weekend, plus photos and a video clip. Janet checked it through with Gwen. "I can get much from this. The photos and video clip tell me everything I need to know.

I've checked the tweets on Twitter. Some of the delegates have put their views online, so I can cross-reference."

Bryn and Harold were watching. "Remember when Janet first arrived? Now look at her. She's family."

Harold looked up at the picture of Kitty on the wall. "Do you know, Bryn, if that picture could talk, it would say Kit approves of what is happening here." The two men looked at each other. Harold gave Bryn a hug. "Don't wait too long. Marry Helen—the sooner, the better."

Later in Charlyyk's bedroom, Helen knelt in front of Charlyyk, applying cream to her toes. Bryn, sitting beside her, saw how much the toenails had grown. "This morning, we could just see them. They must have grown an eighth of an inch!"

Helen saw that the holes where the claws had dropped out were closing. The pulpous ends of Charlyyk's fingers were also changing shape. "We should soon be able to apply nail varnish to them."

The smile on Charlyyk's face reflected the girly feeling she was experiencing.

CHAPTER 18

SETTING THE DATE

On Tuesday, Charlyyk was ready for her morning run. The three runners were in a line. The talk was about how the changes could give Charlyyk a much better way of life. Not that she had ever complained. Overnight the nails had grown another eighth of an inch. Charlyyk was feeling the excitement of being able to do her nails like all the other girls. She had always listened to Gwen, Catherine, Rachel, and Helen discussing their nails, their shape, how long they should be, and what colour they should be painted. Now she could join in with them.

During lunchtime at the academy the posse gathered around Charlyyk, admiring the changes. The girls inspected their own nails and made comparisons. As they started to attend their next lesson, Julia slipped her arm into Charlyyk's. "How do you feel?"

Charlyyk tossed her head back and said with a satisfied chuckle, "Human."

At the Parsons' farm, Bryn and Helen were sitting in the large conservatory with the Parsons and Janet. "Have you set a date, Janet?" Bryn was keen to know.

Jane reached across and placed her hand on his knee. "Interested in a double wedding, Bryn?"

Helen took a sharp look at him. Her expression read, "Well, are you?"

Bryn smiled back at her. "We have yet to set a date. I would rather have it sooner than later."

The two women looked at each other. Then Janet looked at James for confirmation. "We want to wait for a year, so we can plan our future together properly."

Edward held Jane's hand. "We agree with them. When planning a future, you need a little time to get it right." He added with a stern look at Bryn, "But you two, come on. Get your arses in gear and make it happen."

Helen gave Bryn a hug and a girlish smile, "I'm ready when you are."

Bryn and Helen returned to Oakleaves in time for the school bus and were waiting as Charlyyk stepped down. Charlyyk could tell that there was a new air about them. Her nose was picking up different vibes, but they were good vibes. The sweat-with-sweat smell was not fresh, so it was not that. She looked into their faces, a searching look. "You've made your minds up? You have a date?"

Bryn stared at her. "How can you tell that? Not your nose again?"

Charlyyk high-fived Helen. Holding hands, they did a ring of roses. Bryn could not have been happier. He had spoken with Catherine earlier. She had blown lots and lots of kisses at him through the Skype connection.

Preparing the dinner, Helen told Charlyyk what they must do to be able to marry. "We must get a licence, call the banns, send out the invitations, and choose a wedding dress and flowers." Helen spun around and around. She was in heaven. Charlyyk watched on with a big, silly grin on her face. Helen took Charlyyk in her arms and lovingly looked into her eyes.

Charlyyk, softly said, "My mum."

Helen replied with tears of joy, "My daughter."

Bryn watched this affectionate bonding. He had started the ball rolling, but it was now entirely out of his control. The wedding witches would gather in their covens and hatch their spells, plotting their magic to make it an extraordinary day. He would be placed in a trance to agree to everything they boiled up in their cauldron. Yes, he had witnessed this before his own wedding to Kitty, as well as for Catherine's and Rachel's weddings. Though the women called themselves fairy godmothers, the results were still the same.

On Wednesday, the fingernails were halfway out. Charlyyk kept looking at them. "They won't grow any faster, sweetheart." Bryn placed his arm around her shoulders.

"I know, Dad, but don't they look good? And to think they will be fully grown in time for the wedding."

Helen moved closer to her. "The timing is perfect. We will have time to shape them and make them ladylike." They rubbed noses, two women on the same mission.

The posse had already brought in samples of colours. Sarah had each finger painted in a different tone to show

Charlyyk how it worked. Liza, her mother, had done them especially for her the night before. But when Charlyyk let it slip that they would be fully grown for the wedding, it all took off: bridesmaids dresses, how to do her hair, who would be invited. Charlyyk threw her hands in the air and screamed, "YES, BRING IT ON!"

Helen, Gwen, and Charlyyk were talking with Catherine. "Now the plotting begins," Bryn remarked with a heavy sigh.

Harold pulled out his wallet and took out a ten-pound note. "A pound for every major change from now to the wedding."

Bryn laughed. "You don't think that will cover it, do you?"

On Thursday, the first thing that Charlyyk did when she opened her eyes was to look at her fingernails. They were three quarters of the way up. She lay back in bed and waved her hands in front of her. The claws were history. Her hands were still long, but that did not matter, not at this moment in time. Hearing Bryn moving about, she made a move to get up. She felt like dancing and skipped across the bedroom.

With her tracksuit on, she tied the laces on her tennis shoes and met Bryn and Helen in the garden. Did she notice the cold? Not at all. She was off, with Helen and Bryn in her wake. The skip in her stride showed this was one happy girl. Her little tail wagged. Helen and Bryn could only smile at how her tracky bottoms were behaving.

At breakfast, the jungle drums were beating in the form of the telephone ringing. Helen's ecstatic talk made Charlyyk and Bryn head for cover. When the school bus arrived, Charlyyk kissed Helen goodbye and Helen did not even notice her. So much was going on in her head.

Bryn kept in his study, out of the way. The wedding witches were cackling their spells, and he did not want to be caught up in them. But it soon became apparent that he had to play his part. His mobile pinged with a text message: "*Wedding car? Bill Symonds?*"

Bryn texted back, "*When?*"

The reply was instant. "*Now. I'm outside.*"

Bryn settled next to Harold in the passenger seat. Harold took off. "Just had to get away, Bryn. Gwen has got every issue of *Vogue* with anything about brides and weddings. Jane, Janet, even Elizabeth—the phone has not stopped. Gwen has even pulled poor Liza Martin into it." Harold looked stressed. "We went to bed with the magazines and woke with the magazines."

Bryn nodded. "You pushed me to name a date. You must have realised what was going to happen."

Harold's distressed look acknowledged what he had started, but there was no way of ending it. They were going to have to see it out to the very end.

Bill Symonds, seeing them drive in, stood there with his hands on his hips, smiling as they walked up to him. "What have you done, Bryn?" Bryn just looked at him. "Tina has not stopped talking about the new outfit she will need, hairdo, the works." Bill turned and walked towards his office. "Come, we will need a stiff drink."

Bill called out, "Ted, you had better come too."

Louise Landon and Alice Vasey headed towards the posse. "Hello, girls, can we sit with you?"

Louise sat next to Charlyyk. "We know how excited you must be, Charlyyk. Your auntie Gwen has informed me of the upcoming wedding."

Alice looked as excited as Charlyyk. "How do you feel, your first time being a bridesmaid?"

Charlyyk stopped and thought for a moment. "When I was asked that question in Houston, I could not understand the meaning of it. It sounded illogical—all that fuss just to wear a dress. I was just glad to be getting a mum. But now, the whole buzz of it makes it magical. You know, that Walt Disney type of magic, that tingle inside." She closed her eyes. Her shoulders scrunched up as she gave out a sigh.

Alice, looking at Charlyyk, could only sigh with her. Alice, like the posse, knew how Charlyyk was changing. They might be small changes, but they were accumulating into a significant change. Everyone smiled at Charlyyk's febrile imaginative excitement.

Stella had noticed how Charlyyk's ears pointed forward when she was happy, and that was what they were doing now. She waited to see which way they turn next: to their upright position or straight backwards. Stella was beginning to understand how Charlyyk's eyes and ears changed with her moods. The talk Charlyyk had given her made her realise that she would have to start talking to the other members of the group, but what could she say to them? So, she had made her mind up to study them. She would have to talk about the things they were concerned with, just not anything that would bore them.

Bill Symonds listened to Harold's ideas for a wedding car and looked at Ted. "Alan Lyndd, he has the best selection of vintage cars. Rolls, Bentleys, Lagondas, not forgetting the Mercedes Nazi staff car. Leave it to me. I will talk with him."

Charlyyk went straight to her bedroom after dinner, just to get some peace from the constant phone calls. A half hour later, Bryn had joined her. He too needed to get away from the constant wedding banter. Charlyyk smiled at him, holding her hand out to welcome him to her little sanctuary. The smile was that of an innocent child. He snuggled up to her.

The morning run was no different. "Come on, it's not that bad." Helen was trying hard to justify herself to Bryn and Charlyyk. "They need to know the details about the wedding. Getting the right dress, matching hats—this is so important! It must not be taken lightly. The timing is so crucial!"

Bryn looked at Charlyyk, who was sniggering. "So what's so funny?"

Charlyyk gave a light-hearted laugh. "It's the same at school. The girls, even some of the teachers, they all want to talk about it." Charlyyk had to take evasive action to avoid a puddle, then got back in line. "The girls are bringing in magazines to show me all of the latest fashions. It's great. I love it."

Bryn gave her a nudge. "Turncoat. Traitor."

Helen pushed Bryn. "Leave her alone, bully."

At breakfast, the first phone call was not for Helen; it was Bill Symonds for Bryn. "Alan Lyndd said yes, if all of you would see him Sunday afternoon. Fret House." Bill gave Bryn the full details and phone number to make contact.

Bryn wrote it down. "Thanks, Bill. I will make contact with him."

Helen smiled at him. "Wedding business?" Bryn explained about the wedding car. Helen perked up on hearing it could be a vintage model. The image of herself sitting in the backseat was pleasing. "That sounds good. I would like that."

At the academy, the posse gathered around Charlyyk with more wedding items, to browse through. Julia showed her a copy of her mum's wedding list: something borrowed, something blue, something lucky, something new.

Charlyyk looked quizzically at the list. Julia explained what it meant. "My mum's wedding dress was her sister's—something borrowed. The garter she wore was blue. She carried a horseshoe for good luck in her bouquet, and her shoes were new. She matched all the criteria on the list."

Sandra was quick to point out, "It is supposed to be unlucky if you don't meet the right criteria."

Mike chuckled. "That's probably why my mum and dad keep arguing. They got married in a registry office on the spur of the moment." He moved in his chair to make himself more comfortable. "She put on a shift dress, put some flowers in her hair, carried a book of her favourite poems, and said 'I will'. That was that." Julia gave him a cuddle. Sarah took a sharp look at Charlyyk and winked.

The phone call to Alan Lyndd that Bryn made that afternoon gave Bryn the understanding that Alan Lyndd, was keen to meet the family. "Come for dinner and I can show you my collection of motors, maybe take a spin in some of them?"

Bryn agreed and set a time. "See you and your wife at twelve, Sunday." He quickly phoned Harold to inform him of the plans he had made.

After dinner, as they settled in the lounge, the doorbell rang. They were not expecting whoever this was. It was Father Stevens standing there. "Ah, Mr Collier, with all the talk in the village, I have taken this opportunity to offer my services to you and your wife-to-be."

Bryn opened the door to allow him access. "Please enter, Father."

Helen stood up when he entered. Charlyyk also stood up but positioned herself behind Helen. She still was not sure about him, so when they sat, she made sure she was the furthest she could be from him.

Father Stevens was first to speak. "Your sister Gwen mentioned that you were thinking of getting married, and I wondered what your plans were. I would love to offer you a service at our little church." He sat back on the sofa, looking towards Charlyyk. "But with all the media attention that has been given to you, the dean has asked if you would like to be married in a bigger church, with myself conducting the service?"

Helen smiled as she spoke. "Thank you, Father. We are still trying to work out the invitation list to see what will be required. Our family and friends are quite extensive. You are right to point out the media attention. Everyone will be stretching their necks to see what Charlyyk wears on the day. The village church would be overwhelmed. Had the dean any suggestions?"

Father Stevens raised his hands as if to welcome them to him. "There are four possibilities, but I would count them out as too far away, except for one. The dean admired the way Charlyyk handled herself at midnight Mass and thought the cathedral would be suitable for your big day. He would assist in the ceremony."

Bryn gulped. "I'm honoured at the suggestion, but it is a bit OTT, don't you think?"

Father Stevens smiled. "The dean believes that when the event takes on momentum, the cathedral will turn out to be just right for the occasion. Trust him. He has a lot of experience in these matters."

Helen's wide eyes and enormous smile could not hide her feelings. She liked the idea a lot. Father Stevens saw the pleasure it gave her. Charlyyk kept very quiet. "Don't worry, Charlyyk. You will not be gobbled up by our God.

He is spiritual, not physical. He will give comfort in the mind. He won't give you a kick from behind. And I will be there to protect you—that's a promise."

Charlyyk saw the meaning in how he had said those words. She smiled back at him. He was not bad after all.

Father Stevens started to leave. "Charlyyk, come and see me with your auntie Gwen one Saturday morning. I will explain our thinking about religion, but I promise not to attempt to convert you, only to explain how it works. I saw how frightened you were that first time you came to our church. That is not how we want you to see it, so come, and I will explain it to you."

On Saturday, a fresh buzz had settled among them. Helen had warmth inside of her. The thought of being married in a cathedral gave her that warm glow. It radiated from her.

Charlyyk felt more confident in being a bridesmaid now that Father Stevens had assured her their god would not come down on her.

Bryn was not comfortable. The wedding was getting too big; it was getting out of hand. But there was no going back, so he must face it head-on. He must talk with Catherine. She was the conscience that sat on his shoulder. He would hear her say, "Hu, hu, listen to me, Dad." That's what he would do.

When Harold and Gwen arrived, Charlyyk spoke with Gwen, telling her of Father Stevens and his offer. Gwen agreed she would go with her and promised her that the discussion was only to explain the workings of her God. That would be that.

Helen's excited news of them getting married in the cathedral set Gwen off in raptures, and the jungle drums were soon being beaten. Harold could only put his arm around his brother-in-law's shoulders and remove him from the disaster zone.

A dark cloud had descended over Bryn. He looked a forlorn man. He hated to be the centre of attention. He remembered how Kitty had paraded him around as if to say, "Look, he is mine."

The sound of Margret's voice had the girls rushing to convey the news to the new arrivals. Rachel soon had Charlyyk attention. Charlyyk's fingernails were now longer, and Rachel was keen to get some shape to them. "Wow! Look at them! Come, let's see what we can do with them."

All the women sorted through their handbags for their make-up bags. Rachel did no shaping, just applied polish for a bit of colour.

Thomas only needed to look at his dad to realise he was suffering big time. "Dad, let's go to the study." Sitting in the study, Thomas consoled his father. "You must have known what you were starting and that Auntie Gwen, Jane, and Tina Symonds would encourage Helen, let alone Rachel and Catherine. You had better let them have their day." Thomas wrapped his arm around his dad's shoulders. "So what are you going to wear, Dad? Your dress uniform? Now that would look good."

They carried on discussing what had gone on while Thomas was away. "That's incredible, Dad." Bryn played the video recording. Thomas stopped it and replayed the bit where Drenghaagh sat in the kitchen. "You can see where Charlyyk gets her looks from." Thomas used his artist's eye to see the sheer magnificence of the alien—how graceful he was in his full height and the way he moved. His golden hair flowed with the movement of his head. The silken clothes swirled around him. But it was the colours in his eyes and the way his ears moved that made the biggest impression. Thomas remembered something Rachel had said about Charlyyk: "There is so much to her you don't see in us humans. Her eyes talk to you. Her hands move like a conductor's baton, orchestrating a musical concerto."

Thomas studied the video again. "Do they all look the same, Dad?"

Bryn thought for the moment. "No, there were many differences in how they looked. Drenghaagh, who you can see in the video, had the look of a leader. Strenghaagh had a more passive look to him. His hair was lighter, and he was thinner in the face. There were two others *haaghs*. One looked older than the others. Then there was the *lyyks*. One was at least three inches taller than the others. There was Klyklyyk—she was the one that visited Michel and Clare. Her skin colour was greenish, not the pink of Charlyyk."

Charlyyk entered, carrying two mugs of coffee. She looked at the video recording. "He is like our dad, Thomas. He was concerned that I was OK."

Thomas moved his chair around and allowed Charlyyk to sit on his knee. "What were your concerns when you found yourself on the spacecraft?"

Her eyes changed colour and her ears twitched. "I was so frightened that they had changed their minds and

I was going to be taken away. But when Drenghaagh showed me that Mum and Dad were with me, I settled down. My fears evaporated." She cuddled Thomas. "I love my life here with you all. You are my family, my love, my life. They sensed it and are helping me to keep my dream alive. I now know what I have endured was for a reason. I am not happy with the loss of those I lived with before I met Dad, but I'm in a happier place than I was before."

Thomas could not help but cuddle her. "We would have been devastated if we lost you, Charlyyk. You have made this family a bigger, better family. We had been drifting apart since my mother passed away, and Dad was stagnating. Now look at him. We could not be happier. Helen is the icing on top of the cake. Catherine and I can build our dreams knowing you and Helen will keep Dad happy."

Bryn looked at his family. He felt proud seeing the love they were sharing. The wedding seemed so right. He told himself to allow what must be to be.

Charlyyk showed Thomas her fingernails. She was happy. They made her hands look so elegant. Thomas kissed her on the cheek. "You are going to be the prettiest bridesmaid ever."

Gwen came into the study and positioned herself behind her brother. She listened to Thomas praise Charlyyk. The contented look on Charlyyk's face gave Gwen much satisfaction. She kissed her own brother's cheek. "Margret has booked a table, at the Restaurant Milan for later. Would you all like a sandwich for now?" They all agreed. Charlyyk slipped off Thomas's lap and followed Gwen to help with the lunch.

"Dad, so what was the meaning of your abduction?" Thomas asked.

Bryn paused for a moment before answering. "Drenghaagh said that they needed to test the genetic changes that they required to live on the new planet they had chosen. They needed to send someone to live here for a period, to test the changes they had made. They needed to find a way to get somebody to look after her, so this very elaborate charade was thought up. Their new planet is like our Earth, with the same bacteria, and that is where their problems were, so the plate in Charlyyk's head made the experimental genetic changes. They came now to take Charlyyk home, but when he realised that taking her away would cause her grief, he just got up and left."

Thomas took great interest in what his father was telling him. "So the second meeting was to adapt Charlyyk to suit us?"

Bryn nodded and showed Thomas the ring on his finger. "These rings give us better stability when we are taken by the light source and returned, but what else we don't know. Charlyyk's ring has many functions. We do not know if ours have the same ability has hers, but the gadget that they gave us to check Charlyyk's health works on these as well."

Rachel came in to tell them that lunch was being served in the kitchen. Thomas took her hand and followed her, with Bryn close behind.

Around the table, the discussion carried on. Thomas had got bitten by the story, and it had left its mark on him. He started to relate the story to Rachel and Margret. Rachel's eyes were wide with the explanations, and she began to ask her own questions. "Charlyyk, were you not afraid of what they were going to do to you."

"No. Drenghaagh explained that it would only cause a little discomfort, mainly a tingling sensation. Klyklyyk said I would be a little disorientated. She was there to help me afterwards. When they put the armband on my arm, I was fine."

Harold asked, "Was it the same craft that took you to the planet you met Bryn on?"

"Oh no, that was a different craft altogether. That one belonged to the other aliens, the Gaintts. The flap to their nostrils was to protect them from the fine dust that exists on the Gaintts' planet. They are the same as us in every other respect except the facial changes."

Helen realising this was new information. "How did you know that, sweetheart?"

Charlyyk answered calmly, "Oh, the headpiece. It opened up memory cells in my head, and I started to recall some of my time before they placed me on that planet. But only little bits. It needs something to nudge it."

Bryn had been quiet. He was starting to get nagging thoughts in his head. "How could I breathe the air on that planet?"

Charlyyk looked at her dad. She closed her eyes, and her ears started to twitch. Standing up, she headed for the clinic. She returned with the gadget. She went to Bryn and held the device between his eyes. The device blinked blue to green. She said nothing, but went to her room and returned with the headpiece. Placing it on his head, she spoke to him in her native tongue. He replied in her language. Charlyyk said in English, "I think a visit to Michel's surgery could be in order."

Helen looked at Bryn. Her eyes were wide. "Are you implying that your dad could be fitted with a plate as well?"

Charlyyk took a sip of water. "Well, that could explain how he survived that ordeal."

Helen became concerned. "How about me?"

Charlyyk removed the headpiece from Bryn and placed it on Helen. She spoke in her native tongue, but Helen did not understand. Charlyyk removed the headpiece. "The jigsaw pieces are gradually falling into place. With each little nudge, another piece joins the puzzle, giving a clearer view of the overall picture."

Bryn carried on being quiet. The headpiece had shown him the shadow that he thought he had seen. Now there it was in his mind. Major Alan Carter had been right. The Gaintt was riding a large beast, similar in shape to a T. rex, but with hooved feet. Its tail was shorter but thicker, to balance it up. The neck was thick, the head pulpous. Its arms were long, with talons to them that could inflict severe damage on any animal. But how had it got there? Of course, the beam of light, but why? It did not make sense to him, so he said nothing.

The Restaurant Milan was so busy, the noise made everyone shout. Charlyyk just soaked it up, loving the vibrant atmosphere and the food.

She sat between Helen and Rachel, with Gwen opposite her next to Margret. It was girl talk all night, and she loved it. Rachel noticed how Charlyyk waved her hands about as if to say, "Look at how beautiful they are." Charlyyk was becoming the woman, not a girl.

On Sunday, Charlyyk woke after tossing and turning all night. The nag in her head was the welfare of her dad. What had they done to him? At four thirty, she got up and took her computer to the clinic. The disc was there. Setting it up, she placed it on the computer. Then she put her ring on the disc.

It was not Drenghaagh but Klyklyyk who responded. They talked for some time. Only when Bryn sat down with her did she realise how long it had been. He placed his hand on her shoulder but said nothing. What surprised him was that he could understand everything they were saying.

Klyklyyk soon dispelled Charlyyk's concerns. "We needed to place the plate in his head to make sure he survived. We had made many mistakes before, so this was the best way forward. No harm will come to him. In some ways, this will be good for you both. The gene changes were just so he could breathe and survive the time span. We gave him nutrients to sustain him." Klyklyyk's nod was to inform Charlyyk of a change in the conversation. "Helen's ring will only allow her stability if we need to bring her on board with the light beam."

Klyklyyk looked to her left. An elderly *haagh* sat down beside her. "Charlyyk, I am Helmhaagh. It is nice to be able to talk to you and your new father. Please, if you need to talk, contact us at any time. We will be here for you.

CHARLYYK

We are on a base station on the Earth's satellite which they call the moon. Don't be afraid. We have set up here to be at your service at any time. We sense that there is something big that is coming up in your lives. We are very interested in what it could be."

Charlyyk explained the importance of the occasion, and how it would secure her well-being. Helmhaagh listened intently to what she had to say. "It is quite similar to our joining together, although we have not a religion. A ceremony takes place, and there is the custom of giving each other a symbol of intent."

Helen was now awake and concerned when she could not find them. She knew they had not gone on a run, because their running kit was still there. She heaved a big sigh of relief when she did eventually find them.

Bryn explained how he had found Charlyyk and the concerns she had about their well-being. That was why Charlyyk wanted to know more about the plate they had placed in his head.

"So are you OK with that, Bryn?" the alien asked.

"Yes. It explains how I managed to survive for that length of time without food and water."

After breakfast, Bryn put the address in the satnav, and they were ready to go to Fret House. The drive through country lanes impressed Charlyyk. The beauty of the English countryside was in its full glory: small fields with hedgerows of hawthorn and hazel. Charlyyk's head moved around, taking everything in. There was a stud farm with Arabian horses that wandered about, grazing in the fields. Large old oak trees were sprinkled about. A hint of buds was just starting to appear on their branches.

A large Georgian house could be seen ahead of them with a long drive. A metal fence and copper beech trees bordered the driveway.

The drive up to the entrance had that stately house feel to it. A young girl stood by the large entrance doors. The canopy protruded out three metres, with two tapered porch columns holding it up.

As Charlyyk stepped down from the car, the young girl came forward. "Hi, I'm Annabelle. Mummy and Daddy said to come straight in."

The 10-year-old daughter of the Lyndds was very slim, with straight, mousy hair. The braces on her teeth gave her an awkward smile. Charlyyk warmed to her immediately. Annabelle did not concern herself about her awkwardness and was not shy. She had composure; she walked with an air of self-assurance. Charlyyk quickly stepped up to her and talked with her. "What a lovely house, Annabelle. The view of the countryside is fantastic."

"Yes. It has been in our family since the Battle of Trafalgar."

Helen and Bryn admired the way Charlyyk attached herself to Annabelle. They followed the girls and, as usual on these occasions, were led straight to the kitchen.

Joyce and Alan Lyndd were busy preparing the dinner. Joyce had a full hourglass figure. She stood five feet eight inches tall and her hair was honey blonde, straight out of a bottle. It was tied back loosely like Catherine wore her hair. She wore dark-blue jeans with a light-blue, long-sleeved blouse. A black-and=white chef's apron protected her. Alan was robust, with a rugby player's barrel-chested build. He was five feet ten inches tall and had fine sandy-coloured hair, thin on top. His round face was warm, with intelligent eyes. He wore white chino trousers and a light-blue twill shirt. Here was a couple who did not stand on ceremony.

Alan met them with a firm handshake. "Welcome to Fret House. My wife Joyce and I have looked forward to this meeting since Bill Symonds contacted us."

Joyce came forward, and Bryn introduced Helen, The two women were soon in deep conversation and had turned to what was cooking. Alan collected a bottle of wine and escorted Bryn to the lounge. The two girls had already left for Annabelle's bedroom.

Bryn relaxed immediately. He liked this type of man. He always felt comfortable with them. Alan pointed to some comfortable chairs. "I married into this; Joyce's family have owned this place since Trafalgar. Her ancestor, Philip Philpot, was an ordinary sailor on one of the ships in Nelson's fleet. The prize money they received after the battle was unusual. There was a storm at that time and many of the ships taken as bounty did not survive. But Philip's bounty was paid and was burning a hole in his pocket. By chance, he found himself at a gaming table. The stakes were high. The contest was between him and a landed gentleman. On the table were this house and the gentleman's wife. The gentleman lost. Philip Philpot then had a large pot of money, this house, and a mistress to go with it."

Alan pointed to a large painting hanging over the fireplace. "And there they are. They produced four children and lived a long, happy life together. The lady accepted that she had to stay with Philip Philpot or get thrown out. Women did not have much to say in those days."

Bryn, studying the painting, saw that the lady had given the circumstances her best effort. Judging by the way she was looking at Philip and holding his arm, she was enjoying the decision she had taken. Or perhaps that was just the painter's view.

Alan, watching Bryn, sensed what he had been thinking. "Yes, she made the best of her predicament. The story that the family told was that she turned Philip into a gentleman. He turned the farms around and made it profitable. The win-win situation they found themselves in grew out of the need to survive and to embrace whatever they could achieve from it."

Bryn was thinking about his own situation. Was it not the same for him and Charlyyk? Each had helped the other to survive.

Dinner was roast leg of lamb with rosemary and garlic. The girls had rainbow trout. Joyce told the story how she and Alan met. "Four of the girls and I from Roedean College went grape picking in France. We were there to learn about wine. I met Alan, who was there for the same reason. We had a healthy, romantic holiday, picking by day, singing around campfires at night, and lovemaking when we could. Afterwards, we did not see each other for two years. Then by chance, we met in Monaco at a Formula One Grand Prix meeting. We married six months later We started our own PR company. Now life could not be better."

After dinner, the Lyndds gave them a guided tour, ending at the garages. These had initially been the stables to the house. The cars were beautifully maintained; the bodywork sparkled. Charlyyk loved the smell of them. An old Bugatti, an open top in light blue, stood there. Alan started it up. The noise was loud, but the old, fruity roar it gave out had nostalgia written all over it. Joyce got behind the wheel and beckoned Charlyyk to join her.

Alan started up a 1920 Bentley, another open top, in dark green with black running boards and large wire-spoked wheels. Bryn, Helen, and Annabelle were soon sitting in it, and the two cars were heading down the lane.

The afternoon was all about the cars. Finally, they stood before a 1920 Rolls Royce Phantom II. It was black with red side panels. The upholstery was black leather. It had a fold-down roof like the coach-built prams of yesteryear. The gleam from it was majestic. Helen stood drooling over it. It was magnificent.

Joyce put her arm in Helen's. "So that's the one, then?"

Helen nodded. "Can we?"

Joyce smiled the biggest smile. "Yes, you can."

Bryn shook Alan's hand. "Can we settle the cost?"

Alan looked at Bryn. "This is payback time. Joyce had three bad miscarriages. and your late wife helped Joyce through them all. We are allowing you the use of this car as our thanks and as our wedding gift."

Joyce told Helen the full story. "I could not have boys. We just kept trying, and now we have Annabelle, who is well worth all the pain." The cuddle she gave her daughter showed the love she had for her. "Helen, we have been told by Bill and Tina how you met Bryn and how Charlyyk has come to love you. Although it was Kitty who helped me, we feel that she would approve what is happening to Bryn."

On the drive, back to Oakleaves, Helen seemed quiet. Charlyyk noticed and asked why. "The more people I meet, the more I find out how Kitty influenced so many families in this area. It really shows what a wonderful woman she was." Helen paused for a moment. "These are mighty big shoes I am stepping into. I just hope I can do them justice."

Bryn listened intently to what Helen had said. "When you meet some people, they seem to be eager to impress. They try hard to give an impression that they are better than they look or really are. But the Lyndds did not try to impress. They were 'we are what we are' type of people. That's how I saw you, sweetheart. You were always there. It just needed the realisation that a different you were in that hard shell—and my, was that not the truth."

Helen stared straight through the windscreen, feeling the truth of his words. Bryn was right; she had needed something to shake her out of her old self.

The voice of Charlyyk brought her out of her glazed trance she was in. "No one is perfect. We see things that are set before us, and it is normal to go on what you see as real. When you have to readjust, it is never easy. We were led astray on that planet. Now, as the truth emerges, we are making adjustments too." It was not an outburst. Charlyyk did not do outbursts. She always spoke as she saw things.

Bryn nodded. "Yes, but we should try to fit in the shoes we are wearing, not try to wear other people's shoes. I married Kitty and loved every minute I was with her.

But I also love every minute I am with you, Helen. Kitty was Kitty, and you are someone else. You might show similar qualities, but you are different from each other in many other ways." They drove into the drive and came to a standstill.

Charlyyk touched them on their shoulders. "Love comes differently to everyone. It depends on how you want to share it. I see you two share it well."

Helen covered her hand with hers. "Thank you, sweetheart. That was nicely said."

On Monday, the morning light had started to appear through the window before Charlyyk opened her eyes. Her dream had been of nice things, and she felt good about herself. A slight tingling sensation made her examine her hands and feet. She could not see anything unbecoming and dismissed it as a part of the changes she was going to experience.

During the run, she mentioned the sensation. Bryn listened. Helen suggested that she inform Michel.

Lunchtime at school saw Charlyyk and the posse talking about the meeting with the Lyndds. The drive in the Bugatti had been the highlight, not only for Charlyyk but most of the posse. *Top Gear* was what most of their parents watched, looking at new cars and how they performed.

Bryn's study had paper all over the work service. Helen and Bryn were trying to get a guest list sorted, and it just grew and grew. The arrival of Janet and Jane was a relief to Bryn. He that got up to make the tea.

Jane's level-headed attitude was what was needed. She cut the list by more than 30 per cent. The girls joined Bryn in the kitchen with the list. He nodded his approval. Where the reception was to be held was the next problem.

Janet laughed. "The barn! There is parking, it can hold two hundred, and there's no worry about noise. It's ideal."

Helen looked at Jane. "Gilmore's."

Bryn nodded. "Yes, that sounds good. I like that. And the date?"

Helen went through her diary. "Any date from 5th April onwards."

Jane said, "That's Easter weekend. Would it not be better on 12th April?"

Helen phoned Father Stevens. He said he would phone back with the dean's answer.

As they sat talking and drinking tea. Janet was caught up on Charlyyk. She had given Bryn a couple of articles she had written. She also gave Bryn the BBC's request for an in-depth interview. If they agreed, the interviewer would be Fiona Bruce, for her easy-going, unobtrusive style would suit this assignment.

The phone call came from the dean himself, confirming the date for the wedding. The rehearsals could be done in the village church, to save travelling. Helen was in full control. The phone call to Gilmore's was next. Her to-do list was getting shorter. "Invitations next," she said, looking at Bryn. Helen's worry started to evaporate; she saw the finish line, and she was feeling good. Jane, sitting beside her, made a list of what was next.

Janet saw what was going to happen when it was her time to marry James. She made mental notes, preparing herself for the inevitable.

Michel and Clare arrived ten minutes after Charlyyk had come home from school. Charlyyk looked pleased to see them. In the clinic, Clare took blood samples from Charlyyk, and a new diet sheet was produced. Then Clare took the gadget and checked her armband. The familiar blue and green lights appeared. "Nothing to worry about, Charlyyk." But Clare still gave her an examination. Michel watched with a satisfied smile. His protégée was doing well.

Michel explained the diet sheet and the reasoning behind it. "We have had some concerning results from the previous test, so I must ask you to adhere to this diet. No Kit Kats. The sugar and chocolate definite no-nos."

Charlyyk's eyes changed colour and her ears moved backwards. She was in her sad mood. She gave a nod of understanding. He said, "It is for the best until we can rule out the long-term dangers it could do to you."

Clare was nodding. "Michel is right. Some people can eat anything and not have any problems. Others could eat a nut and die. We just don't know enough to say, 'Eat what you want to.' These tests are important for your long-term well-being, so bear with us."

Bryn brought Michel up to date by explaining about the plate in his head. Clare went and collected the gadget. She put it on the ring Bryn was wearing. The blue and green lights appeared. Then she took the ring from his finger and placed it on the next digit. She held the gadget to the ring. A green and then a yellow light appeared. Each finger had a different colour. She returned the ring to the first finger. The blue and green lights showed. "So it is doing something, but what?"

Helen had come in and offered her hand. Clare copied the same procedure she had tried on Bryn. This time, each finger resulted in blue and green lights. "So, as they said, this ring just gives me stability," Helen said.

CHAPTER 19

WHICH DRESS

Helen liked the lighter mornings. The fields looked fresh; the grass looked greener. The buds on the branches had a hint of green to them. The runs had had the right effect on her. Janet and Jane had shown her a picture of a wedding dress, and the mental image of it draped over her pleased her. Running with Charlyyk, she described the dress to her. "It was a combination of silk and lacework, ankle length, with three-quarter-length sleeves. Lacework covered the breast, so a hint of skin showed through, and the veil was the same lace."

Charlyyk looked excited. "So what will I wear?"

Helen smiled. "We have yet to decide on that, but you will have your say. The final word is yours."

Bryn was running with Thomas. "We should make it back in time for the wedding," Thomas said. "I have spoken with Brent and his mother, who will be coming with Catherine and Amy. Amy is looking forward to being a bridesmaid. Catherine has been tied up with the TV coverage of the cricket, but she is up to date with everything. Jo has kept her well documented. Margret has

SPENCER CARVIL

donated some time to her over the wedding details. This is becoming quite an international thing. Australian TV companies have picked up on it, and Brent said that he has had requests from New Zealand for interviews."

As they arrived at the turn at the bottom of Bishops Lane, the girls waited for the men to catch up. "Come on, you two!" Charlyyk called. "You are letting the side down here."

Thomas caught up and gave Charlyyk a gentle tap on her bum. "We were talking about the wedding."

Helen looked at Bryn. "Were you, now?"

Bryn placed his hand on Helen's back. "You look surprised."

Helen laughed. "What gives you that impression?"

Thomas broke in, "I was telling Dad about Catherine coming to the wedding."

Helen took Bryn's hand. "I was just teasing" They carried on running hand in hand.

Thomas took hold of Charlyyk's hand. "Come on, sis. Let's do the last stretch together."

Gwen and Harold arrived at ten. The family sat around the kitchen table, some with coffee, others with tea and biscuits. The to-do list and the order it was to be accomplished in was the main topic. Gwen was adamant that the wedding invitations were a priority. "We must send them out as quickly as possible."

Bryn, Harold, and Thomas sneaked away, leaving them to it. Bryn showed the men the pictures he had taken on Sunday at Fret House. The 1920 Rolls Royce

Phantom II looked good in the photo, but, as Bryn was keen to point out, it had looked ten times better in the garage.

Margret was concerned about what Charlyyk was going to wear. Rachel had picked up as many wedding and bridal magazines as she could lay her hands on. Gwen had an old issue of *Vogue*. A Vivienne Westwood outfit was circled. It was in shades of red, looking like it had been made with offcuts, yet still very stylish. Gwen laughed. "She picked this out when Bryn first proposed to Helen, saying she would wear this to their wedding."

Rachel loved it. "Yeah, I could see her wearing that. Her rose-gold hair would really bring those colours out."

Margret pulled the magazine toward herself. "I agree. Those colours and that style would really suit her. The model wearing it has a skeletally thin frame like Charlyyk has."

Helen took a look. "Yes, it would suit her to wear in the evening. Any other suggestions?" The magazines were thumbed through relentlessly.

Thomas asked Bryn, "Why Fret House? It's a strange name."

Bryn told them what Annabelle had told Charlyyk. "The first owner was a local farmer, Tobias Fret. The family name was unintentionally altered by parish priest, who misspelled it at Tobias's christening, the original name being Pratt. By law, it had to stay as Fret thereafter. It was a common thing in those days."

The men wandered back to the kitchen and met up with the women over another cup of tea. It was agreed that Gwen and Harold would find some examples of invitations at the stationers in town.

Helen had the to-do list in front of her. She looked more settled. Margret and Rachel were going through the Yellow Pages for a florist. Gwen's favourite florist had retired, but she had advised Gwen that the best flowers were those in season—they gave the best effect on the big day.

Later that afternoon, Gwen called Helen to say that the invitation cards had been organised. The stationers had a printer to do special cards.

On Wednesday, the posse's main topic of conversation was the upcoming wedding. What was Charlyyk going to wear? Sandra and Julia had put together colour combinations to match Charlyyk's complexion and hair colour.

Stella sat with them, listening. Julia explained to her that the wrong colour could ruin a wedding photo. "One must not upstage the bride—it is her day, not yours."

"Oh, I see." Stella was getting to understand the thinking behind their advice to Charlyyk.

Sandra heard doubt in Stella's tone. She did not want Sandra to misunderstand what they were trying to do for Charlyyk. If Stella was going to be one of the posse, Sandra wanted to make sure she was not left in a state of confusion. "Not the photos with everyone in, but the main ones, the bride and groom photos. After, for the reception, she can wear what she likes, so long as she keeps to the main rule—you must not upstage the bride."

Charlyyk showed them the Vivienne Westwood dress she liked. *Vogue* had four pictures showing different angles.

Jan said, "Now you are just showing off. Do you know how much that would cost? You could be looking in the hundreds."

Peter looked over Sandra's shoulder. "What? It looks like it's made out of bits and pieces. My mum could do you something like that out of her scrap bag."

"Peter, you have not a clue," Sarah pronounced. "This is art. Look how it has been intricately put together. I love it, Charlyyk. I agree with Sandra that it would be fabulous at the reception."

Mike moved to stand behind Julia. "I like the pattern and the colour. You would look nice in that, Julia. It would make your smile even lovelier."

Julia placed her hand on his hand and gently stroked it. Her smile was mellow. She liked his praise, but she still felt sensitive about her birthmark.

Sarah kept an eye on how Julia reacted to Mike. She had not removed her hand. There was another stroke, then a squeeze. Sarah shot a look at Charlyyk and saw her knowing expression—Charlyyk had seen it too. Sarah could only marvel at how Charlyyk could tell by her nose how people felt about one another.

Sarah looked at Mace. She pondered why there was no chemistry between them. They had grown up and done many things together. She knew he loved her, yet he did nothing. She searched deep into her own feelings. *I know I love him*. She looked at Peter and Sandra. *But not like that*. Charlyyk was right. Brother-sister love was love, but not the love Sarah had in mind.

That evening at Oakleaves, Charlyyk brought up the question of the bridesmaid's dress. "Will I have a say in it? Or have I to wear what you choose for me?" It was not said in an indecorous way, more of "just wanting to know" kind of way.

Helen knew Charlyyk's ways. She did not do nasty; it was not her. "I thought we could go to London—you know, a girls' thing. We could do the bridal stores, eat dinner somewhere nice, and talk over dinner. In the afternoon, we could do more stores. What do you reckon?"

Charlyyk's grin nearly split her face in half. She was beginning to like London a lot, and this felt grand. "Can we go by train again, Mum?"

"Of course we can."

On Thursday, Bryn and Helen arrived at Carpenters' cottage at one o'clock. Helen spoke with Gwen about the proposed trip to London. Gwen had already put some thought into what stores they might visit and where these were situated. Gwen stressed that they should concentrate on two main stores, one in the morning and the other in the afternoon. "Give yourself time to try on a few dresses in each store. If it means we must go back another weekend, it will be worth the effort in the end."

The dress Helen had initially liked was stocked at the second store and not the first. "We will do it that way so you don't make rash decisions. We will have a little time to be sure we get it right," Helen explained. She told Gwen what Charlyyk asked her on Wednesday evening having a choice.

Gwen phoned the stores and confirmed appointments for Saturday. Helen booked a table at a restaurant. Everything was falling into place.

On Friday at school, Stella sat with Charlyyk at lunchtime. She was starting to talk with the posse, and they responded freely. "Thank you, Charlyyk. I always felt so insecure around other people, not knowing what to say to them. After that talk you gave me, I was still at a loss, so I watched everyone and tried to see what they were interested in. I realised that you don't try to talk about set topics, but about what comes up at the time."

Charlyyk chose a morsel from her lunch box. "That's what happens. Life throws up different things every day. Sometimes there is nothing to talk about of any significance, so you can just relax. If someone says something and you feel you can contribute, then say something. If you want to be liked, people have got to get to know you. How can they do that if you don't let them know who you are?"

Jan added, "None of us are the same. That is a good thing, not a bad thing. We may have alternative views. By discussing our ideas, we open our eyes to the truth. When we debate different subjects in our lessons, we develop a clearer view of what we are trying to learn. That also comes from talking to each other."

Spotty-faced Paul said, "That's OK for you, but when Stella or I try to say anything, we are ignored as though we were not here."

Sandra asked, "Is that because you were not sure what to say and did not stand up for yourselves? When you feel, strong and voice your opinion, like now, you are heard."

Paul looked at Stella. The look she sent back made him realise it was true—they did not push themselves strongly enough. Sandra continued, "You don't have to say something unless you have something to say. When you say what, you believe with a purpose, you will find that you are listened to, and with respect. Mace has a quiet personality. You don't often hear him say much. But when he does, we listen to him, because he contributes to what we are talking about. We know Mace has thought through what he wants to say and weighed up what he's heard."

Paul nodded. He saw the truth in Sandra's words. He remembered Mr Pearson remarking about a would-be jokester, "If you have no good words to say about someone, then it is best not to say anything at all. It is better to look a fool than to open your mouth and be proved a fool."

On Saturday, Charlyyk could not get back from her run fast enough. She crashed through the rear garden door to get to a hot shower. She was sitting at her dressing table, trying to dry her hair, when Rachel came in. "Let me help." Rachel soon was brushing through the rose-gold strands glistening in the morning light.

CHARLYYK

The over-enthusiastic Charlyyk could not keep still. The trip to London was apparently on her mind. Her clothes were already spread across her bed.

Rachel loved brushing Charlyyk's hair. She understood Charlyyk's eagerness to travel to London. Her new-found freedom made her want more—anyplace, anywhere, anytime. "Bring it on" was how Charlyyk looked at it.

As soon as Rachel finished, Charlyyk got dressed, her little tail flicking in erratic swishes. Charlyyk chose the emerald-green dress; it was easy to remove when trying other dresses on. She added white ankle socks and black patent court shoes, Rachel saw how Charlyyk had started to get her dress sense right, wearing the right clothes to suit the occasion.

Breakfast was simple and quickly finished. Charlyyk was a girl in a hurry. Slipping her Burberry camel coat on and picking up the little clutch bag, she was ready. Gwen's voice came through the front door, and Charlyyk was off like a scalded cat. She sat waiting in the Discovery. Rachel came to her. "I think you might need this." She gave Charlyyk the purse she had left behind on her dressing table.

Charlyyk's smile broke out. "Silly me." She chuckled.

Rachel reached in and gave her a hug. "Have a successful day, sweetheart. See you when you get back."

Helen and Gwen got into the car. Bryn drove them to the station. Then he and Harold collected his dress uniform. Bryn had left it in storage at his regimental barracks.

Charlyyk sat by the window on the train. She loved watching the countryside pass by. Her fellow passengers took great interest in her but did not bother her. She heard the sound of iPhones clicking as they took pictures of her, but none were in her face.

As she walked out of the station, people stopped and stared but did not mob her. She was feeling more comfortable going out and about. The taxi ride to Helen's mother's house took fifteen minutes. Elizabeth Bennett was waiting by her front door with Anna. Elizabeth slipped into the taxi beside Charlyyk, looking just as excited as Charlyyk was.

The first store was ready for them. An elegant middle-aged lady called Joan soon measured Helen and began giving Helen ideas of the type of dress she had in mind. The first three dresses did not suit Helen. Joan showed Helen two more dresses, but Charlyyk did not like them. "Too young, Mum!" Gwen and Elizabeth agreed with her. After four more dresses, Gwen noted what they liked, and they left the store.

The restaurant she had chosen for lunch was situated in a quite secluded back street. A young couple had started the business five years before. They specialised in fish. Helen had eaten there before. The building had two floors, and the top floor looked out across a quaint Tudor building that was otherwise hidden from view. The dining room was quiet. They could discuss dresses with no one bothering them. Charlyyk enjoyed the company of Elizabeth, catching up on events.

When they were ready, the next store beckoned. This was the store that carried the dress Helen had set her heart on.

A twenty-something young lady with a French accent attended them. She pulled out eight dresses that fitted the description Helen had conveyed to her. Gwen put aside the dress Helen preferred. After many dresses, she brought it forward again, and Helen put on the dress she had come for.

Helen looked breath-taking. The material draped just right. It flowed when she walked. Elizabeth was proud: at last, a mother's dream was coming true. The tears in her eyes were genuine.

Elizabeth had long resigned herself to accepting that this was never going to happen for her. Her career had over taken her life, to that point that she thought time had robbed her of this ambition. Elizabeth knew that it was through Charlyyk's agency that she had gained this joy, and she was going to cling to it.

She recalled how Edward had said, when he read the text message that Helen sent from Interlaken, "Careful. We must not push it. Let us hope the relationship grows stronger."

Gwen cuddled Charlyyk. "What do you think of your mum?"

"Fantastic. Mum looks really beautiful in that dress."

The sales assistant made Charlyyk hold her arms up and ran a tape measure over her. With a nod of her head, she left them. When she returned, she placed four dresses on the rail. One after the other, Charlyyk tried them on. Gwen was assertive, dismissing each one. "No, not right." Charlyyk agreed with Gwen. She did not feel right in them at all.

Another dress was brought in—a Jane Austen-style dress, something out of *Pride and Prejudice*. Charlyyk sort of liked it but was not sure. Looking in the long mirror did not help; her hairstyle did not go with the dress. It was not happening for her. She sat on a chair, looking despondent.

Elizabeth sat beside her. "There are other stores we can try. We have only seen two of them."

Helen finished being measured for alterations, closely supervised by Gwen. Helen settled up with the shop assistant, and as soon as Charlyyk was ready, they left. Helen hailed a cab and gave an address.

The taxi pulled up outside a boutique. Elizabeth ushered Charlyyk inside. Gwen showed the shop assistant the photo of the Vivienne Westwood dress. The assistant eyed Charlyyk up and down and was off. Soon she was back, a dress that Charlyyk recognised draped over her arm. Before anyone could stop her, Charlyyk disrobed. She stood in just her silk undies, dying for the dress to be put on. It did not take long. Charlyyk pranced up and down, twirling about. She loved it, and so did everyone else.

Helen took a video of the whole performance. Julia and Sandra had been right—Charlyyk's hair colour brought out the colours of the dress. It was as if this dress had been designed especially for Charlyyk.

Another assistant brought a pair of gold lace-up sandals with a little flat heel. They looked like something from classical Greek art. When Charlyyk put them on, they perfectly complemented the dress.

Elizabeth soon settled the bill, without anyone else noticing. They were too engrossed in Charlyyk.

CHARLYYK

Back at the Bennett residence, Anna admired the dress. Charlyyk was guarding it with her life. Holding it up in front of herself, Charlyyk twirled around.

Edward looked on with pride. He had never seen his wife so happy. When she took hold of Edward's arm, he could feel the pent-up excitement trembling through her whole body.

On the train, Charlyyk's grip on the dress bag did not let up. The one thought going through her head was showing it to her dad. She was in Neverland. Everything was spinning around; she was giddy with pleasure. She gave no thought to the bridesmaid's dress. That was out the window with the fairies. Today for her was what was in that bag.

Bryn stood in front of the long mirror in his bedroom. The dress sword was the last piece he put on. His Royal Gloucester dress uniform fitted him to a *T*.

Harold moved around him. "Bloody hell, Bryn, how do you do it? It looks no different to when you last wore it, collecting your gallantry awards. You were forty then!"

His medals were impressive. Two of them had gold bars and oak leaves. The gold bars meant he had been awarded the same medal before. The oak leaves meant he had been mentioned in dispatches. Standing to attention, he was the picture of manhood. From the crisp black trousers to the flat hat with a peak, he looked bold and magnificent.

When Bryn and Harold collected the travellers at the station, Bryn had changed clothes. It was a good thing.

The sight of Charlyyk rushing at him, the bag still held in a very tight grip, caused him to brace himself for the impact that was bound to happen. Harold took evasive action and kept three paces back. He knew how Bryn would swing Charlyyk around when she jumped him.

The conversation in the car was all about the shopping and Charlyyk's new dress. She spoke like a very young and excited child, almost blabbering. They could only laugh at her incoherent enthusiasm.

Later, in bed, Helen explained to Bryn the problems of finding a bridesmaid's dress for Charlyyk. "They made her look like Alice in Wonderland or a sugar plum fairy or an orphan from a Dickens book. The dresses just were not her. I could feel Gwen threatening to explode with frustration."

Bryn looked concerned. "So where do we go from here?"

Helen sighed a long sigh. "I really don't know." Another sigh. "I really don't know."

On Sunday at mid-morning, Janet and James arrived at Oakleaves. Charlyyk could not wait to show them her new dress. She was taking her clothes off before she reached her bedroom. James had seen this behaviour many times before and merely smiled.

Dressed in her new outfit, she paraded before them. Janet took as many photos as possible. She loved the whole experience. Watching her friend experience such an ecstatic feeling brought out emotions in Janet too.

Helen once again explained the problem of finding a bridesmaid's dress. Rachel and Janet discussed the matter. Janet texted Sam. The reply was simple: *I'm staying with Chance*. Janet showed Rachel and Charlyyk the text. Rachel just had to show it to Thomas. He said, "Good for her."

In Charlyyk's bedroom, the women attempted to find a style to suit Charlyyk. Janet set up Charlyyk's computer and surfed the fashion houses and their outlets. Charlyyk's thin frame and unusual complexion caused most of the problems. Helen's wedding dress was brought into their thinking, but no definite style was found to suit Charlyyk.

Janet and James left at five. Rachel had enjoyed their company, and continued the conversation she'd been having with them with Charlyyk and Helen at Carpenters' cottage.

Later, Thomas and Charlyyk launched a conversation with Michel. The diet tests had proved that some of the foods Charlyyk liked were not good for her. Chocolate was one of them. Saccharine had its problems too. Sugar she burned off; it was an easy source of energy for her. Michel was keen to stress that she was to be careful with sugar. It could become a problem for her later.

Salt was one of the things she could have, but moderately. Michel was worried about dairy products. They would not have been in her regular diet on her home planet. No issues showed up on her tests, but he still felt hesitant. "Keep your intake moderate for now."

SPENCER CARVIL

At the academy on Monday morning, the pictures on Charlyyk's iPhone garnered much attention. Rachel had made an effort to include the shoes in the picture. Julia, Sarah, and Sandra noted how Charlyyk's hair brought out the colour of the dress. The shoes matched the colour of her hair as well as bringing out the colour of the dress.

Jan, sitting with Stella, showed her how the dress gave Charlyyk's slim figure shape and proportion. Julia pointed out that backcombing on the top would lift Charlyyk's hair and give it some body. Stella saw how even simple things could make a big difference.

Julia pulled her hair back to show Stella the large birthmark that covered one side of her face. "When I allow my hair to grow long and brush it carefully to turn the ends under, it does not show so much. I cannot lose it, so I have to make the best of it that I can. Charlyyk does not worry. She just gets on with it."

Charlyyk sat listening to all the talk. She liked the attention they were showing her. One ear was pointing to the conversation Mike was having with Paul. Mike had looked in Paul's lunch box. "What food don't you like?"

"Why do you ask?"

Mike pointed to his lunch box. "There's nothing in there that's healthy, and you are what you eat."

Paul's face wore a look of doubt. "My mum always said that what you like does you good."

Peter asked, "Don't you ever look in the mirror?"

"Of course I do!"

Mike said sternly, "Don't you ask yourself, 'Why do I look the way I do?'"

Paul was not happy with what was being said. "But I enjoy what I eat."

"But you kept telling us you don't like people laughing at you because of your appearance," Peter pointed out. "You attend the same lessons with Mr Waverly as we do. He's always on about what types of food we should eat to keep us healthy. Are you asleep in those lessons?"

Paul pursed his lips angrily. He felt very awkward—and he had suddenly lost his appetite.

Sandra gave a sideways nod to Charlyyk, who passed her lunch box to her. Sandra showed it to Paul: vegetables, lettuce leaves, rye bread, nuts, and hummus dip. Julia passed her lunch box: sandwiches with salad fillings. Paul started to get the message.

Janet arrived at the cottage at lunchtime to show Bryn the article she had been working on. Margret liked the column she had placed in the *New York Times Magazine* on the watercolour exhibition in London.

What Janet was most eager to get going were the interviews for the BBC. "The production manager for Fiona Bruce said she would like to come on Friday night and spend some time with you all."

Margret looked a little disappointed. "As we leave, *then* something happens!"

Helen was looking in her diary. "Sometimes it feels as though we are on a carousel. One steps on and another steps off. It all seems quite necessary when it is happening."

Bryn looked at Janet's articles and the photos that went with them. "You can see the changes clearly. Look how her eyes are taking shape, and the face has become a little longer."

Margret looked carefully at the photos. "You must make a drawing of her, Thomas. A true artist shows the real person. I remember that first drawing you did of Charlyyk. We could compare them and see the real changes in her."

Rachel touched her husband's hand. "What a great idea. I would love to see that."

Margret turned her attention to Janet. "We leave Thursday morning for Liverpool. We will be back for the wedding. Is there anything we should discuss before then?"

Janet looked at her schedule. "I have made all the necessary changes to the programmes you asked for. The printers have assured me that all the printing has been done and is waiting for you. I hope the exhibition is a roaring success."

After dinner, Thomas asked Charlyyk to pose. "Just relax. This is going to be a ten-minute pencil drawing, very sketchy. I will complete it later with pen and ink."

The rest of them carried on as if nothing were happening. Helen made coffee and took it to the lounge. By the time she had seated herself, Thomas had finished his rough sketch of Charlyyk.

Charlyyk got up and looked at what he had achieved. "I like that, Thomas. You are so clever. You have not worried about getting it right first time. With all those pencil lines, I appear to be coming through a mist." She placed her arms around his neck and kissed his cheek.

Thomas finished the drawing in sepia-coloured ink on handmade paper. When he was done, Rachel produced the first drawing he had made of Charlyyk and placed them together. Even Charlyyk saw the changes.

The next day, Charlyyk was allowed to take the drawing to school to show the posse. Alice Vasey could not help but join them for lunch. The fine pencil lines still showed in the drawing, giving it character. She pointed this out to the posse. "We can see how Thomas has laid out his guide lines to get Charlyyk's features in their true proportions,"

Alice asked Charlyyk if she could show Thomas's drawing in her afternoon lessons. Alice had two of her most talented students in mind. They were in their last year at the academy.

Peter examined Paul's lunch box. "Now that's better."

Mike took a picture of Paul. "In a month from now, we will take another picture, and we will compare them to see what changes there are. In the meantime, we will check what you are eating."

Stella said, "What about when he is at home?"

"We need a programme of foods he should be eating at home," suggested Jan.

Julia did not live far from Paul. "I will go see his parents and have a word with them so we get it right."

Miss Vasey asked, "What's happening? Why is Julia going to see Paul's parents?"

Sandra said, "Paul needs help, and we have made up our minds to see he get that help, whether he likes it or not. We are tired of his bleating about nobody liking him because of his spots. Now he will have no excuses."

In the teachers' meeting room after lessons were over, Alice talked about the posse's concerns about Paul and what they had in mind for him. Tim and Wendy were interested. Wendy reflected on the changes in Stella during the last month. "I wish some of the other groups of students took the same interest in their friends as the posse does. It would make our life so much easier."

Louise Landon said, "I agree. Too many of them just want to ridicule others and not help. They seem to think life is just for laughs."

On Thursday, Margret, Thomas, and Rachel said their goodbyes to Charlyyk and made an early start for Liverpool. The pen and ink drawing was going with them. Margret thought it would be good to put it on show alongside the first drawing that Thomas had done of Charlyyk. Some of Janet's photos were also to go, to be shown in a separate exhibit from the watercolour paintings.

Bryn and Helen had much to get ready for the weekend. With so many adults in the cottage, it was a lot to keep up with the housework. Helen's life had changed, but she had met the challenges. With Bryn's help, they did not seem that bad.

Charlyyk put effort into the general chores. Helen always liked what she had to say as they worked. Yes, there were days, but overall life was good for Helen. She kept Catherine informed through weekly talks. The wedding plans meant that there was always something to do.

The thing that was most on her mind was the bridesmaid's dress. The weekend would be tied up with the BBC interview, so time was becoming important. Taking a break over a cup of tea, Bryn asked her, "Who else could help?"

Helen thought for a moment. "Janet and Sam tried to work out something, but as yet nothing." A worried frown appeared on her face, and her shoulders sank.

Bryn took her hands in his. "Let's get this weekend over. Then we will put all our efforts into getting this settled, no matter what the cost."

During the Friday morning run, the three of them chatted about the interview with Fiona Bruce. Charlyyk was not worried at all. She would be her usual self and take it as it came. Bryn also was not concerned. He knew Charlyyk better than anyone. He knew how she would respond and the straightforward answers she would give to each question asked.

Helen started to relax. Listening to them, she realised she must go with the flow or break under the pressure.

The posse also knew how Charlyyk would respond to the interview. They were more concerned about what she was going to wear. Julia worried about how she would place her hands and wanted her to practise to get the right pose. Sandra watched for other mistakes, like the angle of her body while sitting.

Peter asked Charlyyk questions as if he were Fiona Bruce. Mike and Mace thought up questions for him to ask. Jan and Stella looked on with bated breath.

Charlyyk kept smiling. She knew they had her best interest at heart. When the time came, however, she would react to how it plays out.

At a few minutes to five, the doorbell rang. Bryn opened the door, and a tall, elegant figure with a signature smile was standing there. "Fiona Bruce."

Bryn shook her hand and introduced himself. "Please come in." He took her bags and showed her through to the lounge. Helen was the most nervous, but Fiona had her soon at ease with her natural, relaxed manner.

Then Charlyyk stepped forward. Fiona's smile increased. She invited Charlyyk to sit with her on the sofa. Helen fetched some refreshments, and for an hour they got to know each other.

Charlyyk took Fiona on a guided tour of the cottage. She showed her the guest room, then Thomas's room. "Which room would you like?"

Fiona liked Thomas's room. "This will do me just fine."

Over dinner, Fiona made many notes. "I've read much of what Janet Stokes has written about you all. I am so pleased that the company has given me this chance to put my take on you."

After dinner, Janet and James arrived and much was talked about. Fiona found it useful to get as much information as she could beforehand, so as to ask Charlyyk questions she believed her viewers would wish to ask themselves.

On Saturday, when Charlyyk returned from her run, she found Fiona already up and working on questions. After breakfast, as the weather looked good, Fiona asked to see some of the places that Charlyyk liked.

A stroll around the area seemed a good thing to do. As they walked through the village, Sarah and Mace met up with them. All four walked up the lane to Parsons' farm. Charlyyk showed them the copse of trees on the hill where Bryn and Charlyyk had been delivered. They saw where she had found the alien footprint, down at the bottom of the lane to Dippers Meadow. All the time, Fiona asked questions.

Back at Oakleaves, Sarah and Mace gave their views about their time at school. Everyone enjoyed the experience immensely. Sarah and Mace left at five.

The camera crew were arriving on Sunday to do the filming. In the meantime, Fiona was making the most of her time with Charlyyk. Her producer came at six and Fiona filled her in on camera angles. During dinner, there was more talk about life and the challenges it had brought them.

Gwen and Harold arrived latter. For the rest of the evening, Fiona asked them how events had affected them.

On Sunday, Helen woke to find a card sitting on her bedside cabinet. It was addressed to her. With it was a box of Belgian chocolates. The neat handwriting took her by surprise, for it was not Bryn's. Opening the envelope, she found a Mother's Day card from Charlyyk. "*Sweetest*

Mum, I hope every day you share with me will feel like Mother's Day. My love always, Charlyyk X."

Bryn was now awake. He sat up in bed and put his arm around her. Helen cuddled into him. "So this is motherhood. I love it."

The morning run was just for Bryn and Charlyyk. Helen did not like to leave their guest alone. The camera crew arrived at eight and were soon set up. The weather had held up. Fluffy white clouds gave a good backdrop for outside views. A walk down to the village was planned, Fiona as casually dressed as Charlyyk.

During the stroll, Charlyyk's answers to Fiona's question were relaxed and given in Charlyyk's usual direct way. She would pause to think about one answer, then laugh and make fun of another.

Back at the cottage, the producer went over what had been filmed. They discussed how they thought the next session should go. Fiona wanted a shot of Dippers Meadow, and the crew were soon there.

A scene was set up by the stream. Charlyyk and Fiona sat under the willow trees, with the bulrushes as a backdrop. Some of the questions were repeated. They set up the next interview indoors. The subject was Charlyyk's time at school and how she found living among humans. As Janet, had published so much about her, there was little new material. The novelty was hearing it said in Charlyyk's unique way. The programme was scheduled to be shown over the Easter weekend, before the wedding.

Gwen and Harold helped Helen with the evening meal. After dinner, Helen managed to get Charlyyk on her own. She wrapped her arms around her. "Darling, that was the sweetest thing, you did this morning. Every day with you is a real pleasure."

Charlyyk gave Helen a hug of joy and buried her head in Helen's breast. There was no need for words. Helen felt the love Charlyyk had for her.

On Monday, the posse was anxious to hear about how it all went. Sarah and Mace gave their account of what they witnessed. At lunchtime, the conversation was much the same.

Sandra asked, "Any changes about the bridesmaid's dress, Charlyyk?"

"No, it is still not resolved."

Stella said nonchalantly, "What would you have worn if you were on your own planet?"

Charlyyk's eyes turned a different colour, and her ears twitched to a forward position. The posse watched carefully, knowing full well she was putting thought into action. A little nod meant she had thought it through. Charlyyk looked around at their pensive expressions. The smile she gave eased their concerns. She had come up with the answer.

"Thank you, Stella. That was just what I had not thought about. I had been so adamant that Earth was my planet, it marred my thinking."

Arriving home after school, Charlyyk spoke with Helen. "Stella asked what I would have worn if I were on my own planet. I was about to say, 'I *am* on my own planet', when I realised it could be the answer to our problem."

With that Charlyyk fetched her computer and set it up. She placed the disc on it and activated it with her ring.

Helen called for Bryn. As they gathered around the computer, the elegant features of Klyklyyk appeared. Nods and eye contact took place between Charlyyk and Klyklyyk. Charlyyk explained the difficulty. Klyklyyk nodded again with Charlyyk. Then the connection was gone.

Helen waited to hear what had been agreed, Charlyyk just smiled. "It will be sorted. No more to worry about."

Later that evening, a text message from Catherine asked them to meet her family at the Southampton Docks on Friday. She would give them details as to time on Thursday evening.

CHAPTER 20

THE INTENT

The days went quickly. On Thursday night, they received Catherine's text that the ship the Leany's were on would dock at eight on Friday morning. The Leany's had travelled by sea to give Catherine a little comfort and peace of mind. Because she was eight months pregnant, flight was not considered suitable. On the ship, there was a doctor on hand at all times.

Bryn arrived at Southampton Docks at ten. He saw activity but no passengers as yet disembarking. He parked the car, then made enquiries of the port officer. The officer said that the ship had just moored. He made some phone calls and then stated that Bryn could go aboard in about thirty minutes, after immigration and customs formalities had been completed.

When Bryn finally boarded, Catherine's smile was as big as her bump. Amy was three now and running around, giving Brent and his mother some headaches. Amy, seeing her granddad, made a beeline for him. Bryn was one happy fellow.

The drive to the cottage took an hour. Helen was waiting at the door. Introductions over, coffee in the lounge was the order of the day. It gave Helen a chance to talk about herself. Amy was up and about, dragging her granddad as if he were a rag doll.

Jo Leany was quick to ask for the local doctor to be contacted. "Catherine needs to be checked over. It has been a long trip, and these are delicate times." Jo had an uneasy sense of maternal worry at this stage of the pregnancy. Her feelings towards Catherine were those of a mother. She had come to respect Catherine for many things. Her determination for Brent to be his own man was top of the list. This had made Brent stronger. Brent had originally taken after his father, who had a soft attitude towards life. This had worried Jo. Now Brent was more the man he should be in her eyes—a true colonial man, rugged, who could stand upright when facing the world.

Helen had already been told by Margret that a doctor should be notified, and Helen had already taken care of it.

Jo had been to the cottage before and knew all about the clinic. It was not long before she was checking to see if it had been kept up to standard. Brent was aware of his mother's steely determination, when she felt the situation required it. When she was, sure all was fine, she changed to a soft, loving mum. It just took a little time to adjust.

The school bus arrived. Like a whirlpool, Charlyyk burst in, entirely and unashamedly loud. Brent managed to stand in front of Catherine to save her from being knocked flying. Charlyyk was so excited, she did not know who to hug first. Amy was the prime target. Jo and Brent were amazed how Charlyyk had grown; Skype views did not do her justice.

Amy took control of Charlyyk and was off on a new adventure. Charlyyk played with Amy until she tired, falling asleep in her grandmother's arms. Now Charlyyk could be herself and talk with the Leany's. Catherine's bump was the main topic. Charlyyk's hand smoothed over it in a very gentle manner. The kicks she felt brought out giggles and looks of wonderment.

It was what Charlyyk could hear going on inside Catherine's tummy that had her attention most. The heart of the child beat in a regular pattern. Taking in the scent that the baby gave out was another wonder for Charlyyk.

On Saturday, Charlyyk sat with Catherine and set the computer up. With the disc in place, she touched her ring to it. Brent stood behind Catherine, looking at the screen. The elegant figure of Klyklyyk appeared, and Charlyyk introduced Cat and Brent to her. There were the usual nods and eye contact, and then Klyklyyk was gone.

"Stay where you are," Charlyyk told them, and opened the door to the garden. In ten minutes the tall, lean figure of Klyklyyk entered the cottage. Amy did not flinch but went to her. She held out her hand in a gesture of friendship. Klyklyyk responded. Her very long hand reached down gently, and she allowed Amy to take hold of one of her fingers. Jo stood mesmerised.

To make them feel less intimidated by her height, Klyklyyk looked for a chair to sit down in. She took another gadget from her flowing gown and pointed the device at

Amy. After a nod to Charlyyk, she pointed it at her. She said, "This will give us the size to make the gowns."

Bryn and Helen joined them. Charlyyk made refreshments. For a while, they talked generally. One of Klyklyyk's eyes was on Catherine's bump the whole time. Then Klyklyyk nodded and left.

Jo looked at Charlyyk. "You would have grown to that height if they had not placed that plate in your head?"

Charlyyk nodded. "Michel said that. given the amount I was eating, I could have grown even taller."

Jo touched her hair. "When we first saw you, your hair was like straw. Now it so soft. Your skin was dry and leathery. Now it's soft and smooth. And I love your fingernails."

Charlyyk took a lot of pride in what Brent's mother was saying. "I spent luxurious hours in the bath with a lot of bath oils. I blame Catherine and Rachel for that." Her face took on a dream look and she sighed. She knew she had been spoilt. The face of Klyklyyk showed none of that pampering. The way Drenghaagh had touched Charlyyk on their first meeting showed he had noticed how different Charlyyk was.

Catherine laughed. "Are you purring, Charlyyk?"

Charlyyk cocked her head to one side. "You bet."

The week had gone by quickly. Catherine and Amy could not have been happier. Bryn was a punch bag to Amy. She could not stop jumping all over her granddad. The wedding witches popped in to make sure everything was running to schedule. The wedding dress arrived and was checked to make sure it fitted. The florist confirmed that everything was ready and delivery was at hand.

Only Catherine was concerned, as she could tell the bump had become more prominent. Jo fussed, making sure she was comfortable.

Easter was looming. The wedding would be the next weekend. Father Steven had arranged the wedding rehearsals, and Gwen had everything under control.

At the little parish church, Father Steven smiled at Charlyyk. "So you see, Charlyyk, it is spiritual, not physical. It is more in the mind. We use his teachings to guide our lives, to be better people. We look on at our fellow man as an equal, no matter what religion our fellow man follows. If man only did was what right for himself, anarchy would inevitably follow. Laws are there to give people an even chance to live a good life.

"As you know, some people don't believe in God. That doesn't mean they are bad people. Some are more Christian-minded than those who attend church. That's why we humble parish priests try to help those who walk an unsteady path. We give them guidance."

Gwen was pleased to see Charlyyk listening intently to Father Steven. "What do you think? Do you see what we see in our Lord, Charlyyk?"

From Charlyyk's pause and the expression on her face, Gwen knew she had not been convinced. "I can see the reason for laws. We have them at school. Laws control those who only want to mess about and disturb lessons. The church made laws to hold its parishioners to its will

SPENCER CARVIL

and to look after their needs. It's the praying bit I have trouble with. If I cook a bad meal, praying won't turn it into a good meal. It will still taste like crap."

Father Steven said, "That's correct. You are so right. It would be silly of anyone to expect it would. When you saw, your dad defending himself against that beast, what came into your mind?"

Charlyyk did not need time to think. "Where was I going to run to."

"And if that situation came up again tomorrow?"

Again, no hesitation. "I would attack the beast as well. It would be better to die together than for one of us to be left alive, wishing the other were still here."

Father Steven looked at her. He had thought he would win her around, but now he felt it was not to be. "How did you come to that conclusion?"

"I thought I had put my dad's life at risk. He had been taken to that planet on the chance he would rescue one of us—not specifically me, any one of us. If he had died, it would have been because of us. And I would have perished just because I did not know. So, at that crucial moment in time, it would have been about survival."

Charlyyk had not changed her ideas. She still saw things in black and white. Gwen saw that there was no way that they could modify the way she thought.

"Come, Charlyyk. We have stepped over the boundary of what we originally came here to discuss," Gwen said as she got up. Gwen offered her hand, but Charlyyk did not accept it, Charlyyk was not angry. The memories still flashed through her mind: recollection of horrible moments and painful cries. She had tried to bury them in the back of mind, but with a little nudge, there they were again, as large as life.

Gwen and Charlyyk returned to Carpenters' cottage. Harold always put things into perspective. This time was no different. A chocolate biscuit and a mint tea did the trick, and a cuddle settled the deal.

Charlyyk nestled up to him. "Don't tell Michel."

"As if I would!"

Gwen was feeling guilty that she had tried to convert Charlyyk and it had backfired. She should have let her be what she would be. It was her natural way, the way her logic set the path before her. "I'm sorry, Charlyyk. It was wrong of me to have put you through that."

Charlyyk took a sip of the mint tea, then turned and looked at Gwen. "How can I be something I'm not? Auntie Gwen, I see life so differently to you at times, but it does not make me angry. I love you for all you have done for me. You could strike me in anger and I would still love you. My people do not do anger. They try to understand why so that they can resolve issues with dignity, not conflict. That is why they are no threat to this planet."

Charlyyk placed her arms around Gwen and cuddled her. She gave her a tender kiss. "I love you so much, Auntie Gwen. I would lay my life down for you."

Harold gave them both a cuddle in a great big bear hug. "Come, Charlyyk, let's take you home."

On Sunday, Amy found Charlyyk drying her hair after her shower and wanted to help. Yelps emerged from Charlyyk as the brush in Amy's hands was handled like a tennis racket. Amy's forehand smashes smacked Charlyyk's head, but Charlyyk allowed her to carry on. The fun they were having could be heard all around the cottage. Jo came to Charlyyk's assistance.

"Granny, look! I'm helping Charlyyk."

Jo could only smile. She liked the way Amy and Charlyyk were enjoying each other's company. Later, Charlyyk took Amy for a walk to the village that ended in playing ball on the village green with Mace, George, and Sarah. Brian and Sergeant Wendy Bailey joined in on the fun. Harold and Gwen watched from the cottage. Liza Martin waved to them from her front door. She had not seen this amount of fun on the village green for some time. She took a video with her iPhone to show Jim later.

The Discovery pulled up outside of Carpenters' cottage. Bryn could not help joining in the fun. Catherine sat in the car with the door open, allowing Brent to stretch his legs. The noise had many of the residents coming out to see what was happening on the green.

Helen sat in the front seat of the car. She looked at Catherine sitting next to Jo Leany. She saw the pride in her eyes of her little family sharing each other. Cat reached between the car seats and took Helen's hand, placing it on her bump. Helen felt the movement of the child. She felt that she was now an integral part of this unique family. Could Charlyyk have survived if they had been a different type of family?

Father Stevens came out of the church to investigate what was happening. He walked down the path and leaned against the tiled porch. He too smiled at the raucous laughter that was being generated.

The Easter holiday was here. The posse had made plans to meet up, have a day in town, and go to Charlyyk's for a BBQ. Helen promised Rebecca that they would have a day of shopping. The girls would stay and look after Len.

Thomas and his charges returned from Liverpool in time for Easter Sunday. That morning, Charlyyk, Catherine, and Rachel stayed at Oakleaves. Everyone else headed for Winchester Cathedral. The banns were read out.

Thomas, sitting next to his father, whispered, "The last nail in the coffin, Dad."

Bryn knocked Thomas's knee with his knee, remembering that he had said the same words to Thomas when he was about to marry Rachel.

At the cottage, the two pregnant women had found a comfortable swing seat in the garden. The sun felt hot and became uncomfortable for them. Charlyyk ran about, looking after them. Digging in the back of the garage, she found an electric fan and soon had it set up to cool them. Charlyyk loved being able to help them, remembering what they had previously done for her. They had accepted she was different, yet treated her with love and kindness. The gap between them was big enough for Charlyyk to sit in. She was soon there, a satisfied smile on her face.

Catherine looked different. It was not just the bump. Charlyyk closed her eyes and let her mind drift. In her mental vision, Catherine appeared younger. Catherine's cheery smile put Charlyyk at ease. Charlyyk did not understand what was being said, but that did not matter. What mattered was the manner of speech—soft, reassuring tones.

Cat placed her arms around Charlyyk and gave her a cuddle. It was nice and warm, securely warm. That had never changed. Cat had been Charlyyk's first mum in a way—someone to cuddle when she felt threatened.

A gentle squeeze of Cat's hand brought Charlyyk from her thoughts. She turned to look at Cat. Rachel picked up Charlyyk's free hand and put it on her bump. The dual sensations of movement kept her looking at them in turn. Tucked between them, she felt she was almost the same as those two little lives.

On Easter Monday, the sky was clear. It looked like another hot day was in store for them. The runners made the best of the conditions underfoot. New grass was breaking ground, and the show of cowslips and primroses was magnificent in the early morning sun. Hazel catkins hung down from their branches, nodding spring's arrival. Lambs skipped about in the nursery fields halfway down Bishops Lane.

Charlyyk saw Janet working hard with James, keeping an eye on those bundles of fun. Janet was looking more and more like a farmer's wife. As Janet stood up, the sun caught the top of her head. The orange glow that radiated from it was like a burning beacon. Charlyyk's exaggerated wave was returned by them both.

For the rest of the run, Charlyyk bounced about like those spring lambs. The sun was on her, her nose scented the delicious smell of spring, and her ears were filled with the buzz of insects and the chirps of birds. Life was good.

She threw up her arms, jumped high in the air, and gave out a loud "Wheeee!"

Thomas caught up with her. Charlyyk jumped into his arms and wrapped her arms around his neck and kissed his cheek. "What have I done to deserve that?"

Charlyyk leaned back. "You were Thomas."

Thomas pushed his nose up to her nose and wiggled it. She was happy.

On Tuesday, Helen was all fingers and thumbs. Excitement was building inside of her, and she kept making silly mistakes. Charlyyk would nudge her and help to cover them. Helen could not be more thankful.

Charlyyk knew that this was not Helen's usual behaviour. Charlyyk phoned Sandra and asked if she could bring Helen over to see them. "It could settle her down and take her mind off the wedding."

Sandra thought it was a grand idea. "Just come. We are going nowhere. We will enjoy your company."

Charlyyk pushed Helen to the car. "Come on. It will do you good to talk with someone else for a change."

Rebecca and Len were pleased to see her, and soon Helen was her old self. Charlyyk sat with Sandra and Peter. Peter was spending a lot of time at Sandra's house since they had become an item. Julia had started to see more of Mike, and she did not feel cut off from her best friend.

Charlyyk was beginning to understand the changes that growing up brought about. She listened intently not to what they said, but more to how they said it, which told a much different story.

Stella's name was mentioned, which to Charlyyk's ears was good news. Her name had never been mentioned before.

Peter started to talk on his mobile. "The posse is meeting in town tomorrow."

Then Charlyyk's phone vibrated. Sarah and Mace had texted, "*Meet at the village bus stop 8 a.m. We are all meeting in town tomorrow. Luv u X.*" She showed the text to Sandra and Peter and nodded. The two of them knew what her nod meant. Even in the short time they had known her, they had noticed that each nod said something different. This was her approval nod.

By the time they returned to Oakleaves, Helen was back to her usual self. The sleeping arrangement had Catherine and Brent in the guest room. Thomas and Rachel were in Thomas's old bedroom. Amy was with Charlyyk and loving it. Margret and Jo were sleeping at Carpenters' cottage. Cat and Rachel had so much to talk about, Brent reckoned it was impossible to separate them. He threatened Cat he would move in with Thomas.

After dinner, Helen and Charlyyk cleared away the dirty things and discussed between them what was still required for the wedding. Suddenly Charlyyk turned and opened the door to the garden. The tall figure of Klyklyyk entered. Helen approached her and, without thinking, nodded. Klyklyyk smiled. "Helen, you are almost one of us."

"Thank you, Klyklyyk."

Another *lyyk* came in behind Klyklyyk, carrying the bridesmaids' dresses. "Let me introduce Saarlyyk," said Klyklyyk. They gave nods all round. Saarlyyk was a young *lyyk* about seven years older than Charlyyk. The two younger *lyyks* met amid a series of ear movements, changing eyes, and many nods. Charlyyk called for Amy, and the three of them left for Charlyyk's bedroom.

Klyklyyk sat down with the rest of the family. Brent and Thomas were in awe of her. Cat and Rachel were more matter-of-fact and asked many questions. Klyklyyk was fascinated by the two pregnancies.

When the bridesmaids entered, the family were amazed. The silk-like white material had no seams. The dresses draped over their small frames with style. The train of material that flowed behind them gave the impression that there were no restrictions. The lace had an art nouveau look of intricate designs and flowing curves. The necklines were loose, not tight, for comfort.

Saarlyyk said, "The material is spun from the seed husk of a plant. The conditions it grows in are unstable. This husk helps to keep the seed at a constant temperature, so the material will keep the girls warm when the air is cold, and cool when it is hot. The headdress is a unique metal that comes from a planet so far away, it took sixty of your planet's circles of your sun just to get there. As you will see on the day, it will make the whole dress radiate. I will wear something very similar when I give my intent to my *haagh*." The way her ears moved and her eyes changed colour showed how excited she was at the prospect of it.

Klyklyyk said, "Saarlyyk is my daughter. Her father is Drenghaagh." She gave a little nod to Charlyyk. "Charlyyk and the other *lyyks* in her group were alone in their lives. You would call them orphans? We feel that Charlyyk deserves something she can hold on to, and we see that she has it here. We owe her our gratitude for what she has achieved for us. This dress will be like her intent to you— as you say, our love to you. You are a part of our family, and if you need us, we will be here for you." With that, the two *lyyks* nodded and left.

Cat felt the material. It was so soft, Amy cuddled it. "Can I wear it to bed?"

Cat looked into her eyes. "No, darling, I don't think we should. Not until the wedding is over."

Brent was already on the phone with his mother, explaining what had happened.

On Wednesday, the walk to the village gave Charlyyk time reflect on many things. Images flashed through her mind at a hectic speed.

A police car approached her. Sergeant Wendy Bailey was in charge of it. "Hi, Charlyyk. They are at the bus stop already."

Charlyyk smiled at her. "Hi, Wendy. They must be keen."

Wendy nodded. "I see from the surveillance equipment that you had another visit last night."

"Yes. They brought the bridesmaids' dresses."

They bade their farewells and headed off in their separate ways.

The emergence of Charlyyk brought waves from the posse. She crossed the green and was met with hugs.

Mace was the first to speak. "You must have seen Mum. She was heading for Oakleaves."

"Yes, she stopped and talked."

Sarah asked, "She said you had another visit?"

Charlyyk nodded but did not speak.

George stepped between them and kissed Charlyyk on the cheek.

The bus arrived. They bought their tickets from the driver and sat at the rear of the bus. There were a few nods and hellos directed to Charlyyk, but not the frenzy she had started to get used to. It was as Michel had said to her at this time last year: "Once people get to know you and see you don't pose a threat, they will accept you. You can be yourself; you just have to be patient."

She felt the strong arm of Mace cover her shoulders. "You OK, Charlyyk?"

She smiled at him. "Yes, I'm fine. It's so nice to be able to walk about with some freedom. So often I've had to move quickly so as not to create a crowd. Now I find myself strolling at a more comfortable pace."

Sarah moved to allow more space, and the four of them settled down. "You were going to tell us about the visit."

Charlyyk told them all about it. As the bus pulled into the bus station, they saw the rest of the posse waiting. They strolled into town, laughing and fooling about. The group fell into pairs. Jan and George trailed at the rear. Mace was with Paul. Sarah talked with Stella. There was a satisfied smile on Charlyyk's face as she looked at the display in a favourite fashion shop.

Gwen felt the dresses. "How did they make them? It looks as if they were spun by a spider. There are no seams."

Amy did not mind getting dressed up again. It made her feel like a princess. As she glided about, Jo looked on with pride.

Margret sighed a big sigh. "How much would they have cost if you had had to make them?"

Cat was hanging on to Brent's arm. "All night in my dreams, I saw Amy walking down the aisle with Charlyyk. The dream just kept going around and around like a carousel at a fun fair, and I did not want it to stop."

Brent bent over and kissed Cat on the forehead. "You have taken me on an adventure which I don't want to stop, darling."

"That was your fault. You should not have looked so bloody handsome."

Thomas laughed. "I thought it was the fault of you being in hobbit land."

On Thursday, the weather changed. A low front had pushed the high front away, but the weather forecast for Saturday was fair.

Liza Martin was expected. She was bringing a friend. He was a top hair stylist in the movie world. Though she had left the industry, they had remained good friends.

When they arrived, Helen was surprised. He was a massive man with enormous hands. His gentle voice was a complete contrast to how he looked. Liza introduced him as Stefan Lennard. He soon had Helen sitting. He

CHARLYYK

fingered through her hair. "Yes, we can do plenty with this. Now I must see you in your dress."

When Helen returned in her dress, he stood back, then circled her. "We could do many styles, as you have left your hair to grow. Do you have a preference, or do you need guidance?" He went to his bag and took a sketch pad out. The deft strokes of his pencil gained Helen's undivided attention—page after page, front and back elevations.

Cat and Rachel stood close, marvelling at how those great hams of hands could draw with so much detail. They discussed each style carefully. "Yes, this one. It looks lovely, and the veil will sit nicely." Helen saw herself in how Stefan had drawn her.

Stefan picked up his bag and took out a bib. He covered her. Using a light spray of water, hairdryer, and brush, he soon had styled her hair. "There, something like that." He took the bib off and showed her herself in the mirror. The other women nodded in approval.

Stefan had fun with Amy, but nothing too elaborate. "She is only three," he observed.

Then he looked at Charlyyk's hair. "Now this is something else!" The colour and feel were very different. He gave the top of her head more volume and at the rear dropped corkscrew twirls. She felt very girly. Her little purple tongue poked out between her lips and moistened them. She tossed her head and looked in the mirror again.

Afterward, sitting around the kitchen table, Stefan talked about himself. "I'm Canadian. I have four sisters. Some winters, you spend a lot of time indoors. I found myself talking more about my sisters' hair and the ways they could wear it. That is how I got into styling. I found my way into television, then films. Liza and I worked together on many productions. It was like magic—you created people's fantasies. I could sometimes go over the top with my imagination."

Liza Martin confirmed his stories. "I had just got out of college and found myself on my first production set. Stefan, saw I was vulnerable and soon was protecting me. He became a father figure towards me."

Stefan promised he would be there on the wedding day with his team. He had created a new fan base. The girls loved his soft manner.

Bryn had gone to Carpenters' cottage, as no groom should see his intended bride in her dress before the wedding. He had been into battle many times, but he had never been this nervous.

Gwen loved her brother, and to have him there was like living a dream. Soon they were going over old times. Harold broke open a new bottle of Balvenie whisky. He knew well that it would make Bryn feel at home. But there was no need—this had always been Bryn's second home.

On Friday, Charlyyk, Thomas, and Brent had a good run. The drizzly rain did not deter them. They stopped to talk to James to confirm the stag do and were soon heading back.

Breakfast was noisy due to the nervous tension building up. They waited for the wedding gremlins to strike. Charlyyk had arranged to take Amy and spend the day with Sarah, Mace, George, and Jan. Brent and

Thomas were heading for Carpenters' cottage. The women remained in Oakleaves.

—⋘—

Saturday was the day of the wedding.

The morning sky was clear, and the warmth of the sun could be felt. A lone runner pushed hard; the lure of Dippers Meadow was too much for her. Looking around brought back memories of lovely, idyllic times. This was where her freedom had begun. While the family were sheltering her from the outside world, she learned so much here.

Charlyyk let her mind drift. New memories were starting to manifest themselves. The changes to her external body did not concern her, but she was excited about how her brains were developing inside her. She knew she had two brains; otherwise her ears and eyes would not have been able to function separately the way they did. Now she could feel the differences and manipulate them in a way she could not have done before.

Charlyyk's contemplation of the things around her brought a smile. She was a big part of this family, and they had shown her that they valued her. Being wanted and trusted was the key that had unlocked her heart to them all. The posse was also a big piece of this jigsaw. The puzzle had fitted neatly into place, making one large and fantastic picture, just as Dippers Meadow had done when it weaved it spell on her the first moment she saw it.

Back at Oakleaves, everyone was up and breakfast was laid out. It felt strange to Charlyyk that no men were there.

SPENCER CARVIL

Helen was pushing for everyone to finish breakfast. "Stefan will be here soon." No sooner she had said it than the doorbell rang. Stefan and two girls in their late twenties were waiting to enter.

"Morning, everyone. I hope that coffee is fresh?" He waltzed in. "This is Jackie and this is Toni—my girls." They found places to sit and tucked in to breakfast.

Breakfast finished, Stefan set up his salon in the kitchen. Charlyyk watched, her mouth ajar, trying to take it all in.

Liza Martin arrived and was greeted by Jackie and Toni as if they were sisters. Liza set herself up at the other end of the kitchen table. Stefan had made a list, and as one hairstyle was completed, Liza immediately did the makeup.

Charlyyk found herself answering the door and bringing in the flowers and the bouquet. Then it was her turn at the table. Stefan's hands smoothed over her. Charlyyk watching in the mirror how each movement created a different effect on her hair. She saw the joy in her own face as Stefan showed her how the corkscrew curls bounced up and down. When Stefan placed the headpiece on top, it all radiated and sparkled.

Out of this chaos came calm. Alan Lyndd arrived in the 1920 Roll Royce Phantom II. With white ribbons attached in enormous bows, it looked spectacular.

Harold arrived and took up Cat. Brent and Jo were already in his car. Thomas took Rachel and Margret in the Discovery and collected his father from Carpenters' cottage.

Charlyyk waved them off. The tension in the air was growing, and nobody could sense that feeling more than Charlyyk.

A taxi carrying Helen's father pulled into the drive. Helen greeted Edward with the special loving look daughters have on their wedding day.

Edward had to wipe his eyes. His daughter had long since grown into a woman and was not a young girl. He still could not believe this day had finally come. He gave Charlyyk a smile when he saw her standing beside Helen. He kissed her cheek, then squeezed her hand, knowing this wedding was her doing. He was so thankful to her.

During the drive to Winchester, Amy kept Helen amused with the small talk of a very young person. As they arrived at the cathedral, Helen was taken aback by the crowd that was waiting to see her. Press with cameras was in attendance.

Alan brought the car to a standstill, checked that everything was in order, and opened the door.

Charlyyk was first out of the car. She helped Amy and Edward. Helen was the last one out of the car. Charlyyk checked to see that Helen's dress was in order before she organised Amy so that Helen could take her father's arm.

Cameras flashed. Oohs and aahs sounded all around.

Janet had made sure she had a free day and hired a good friend to take the wedding photos. A few moments were taken to get the right positioning for the essential photos. The cameraman just kept clicking away, knowing Janet would expect nothing less.

Charlyyk and Amy walked behind Helen and Edward. The metal headdresses that Charlyyk and Amy wore sparkled in the sunlight and made the dresses sparkle as well. The crowd gasped at the effect created.

As they walked towards the large entrance to the cathedral, they heard more gasps from the waiting spectators. Charlyyk's senses made her turn around. To her pleasure, Drenghaagh, Klyklyyk, and Saarlyyk strolled behind her, looking magnificent in their silken robes. The nods they gave her showed their approval of how she looked. The crowd outside murmured as they saw the true height of the Laights and how majestic they looked.

They entered the cathedral entrance to the sound of the organ playing Felix Mendelssohn's "Wedding March". Gwen and Jane Parsons quickly helped the Laights to find seats next to Su Shi, Liu, and Major Carter.

As Helen stood next to Bryn, the smile on her face radiated a warm glow. her eyes glanced at Charlyyk with a look of "Hey, what do you think of your dad?"

Charlyyk's approving nod said, "Looking good."

Everything was going to plan. The rehearsals were working. Harold as best man stood beside Bryn.

Charlyyk looked around at the Martins, the Baileys, the posse, Wendy Butler, Alice, Mrs Landon. On the other side were the Parsons, the Stokes, the Symonds, Michel, Clare. Su Shi, Liu, Major Carter, Chance, Sam, Philip, and many more. She nodded to them.

Helen passed Charlyyk her bouquet. The ceremony had started.

Charlyyk helped Amy to get through the long service.

When the ceremony had finished. Charlyyk nodded to Drenghaagh. The Laights rose from their seats and made their way towards Charlyyk, the bride, and the groom.

Standing in front of the three of them, Drenghaagh held out his left-hand palm-up to receive their hands. He took the fingers that bore the gifted rings and placed all the rings together. Then he set the ring on his finger with their rings. Klyklyyk stepped forward and wound a silken band around them.

Drenghaagh looked them in the eyes and said with a gentle nod, "You each have given your intent. Now you three are one. May your life together be in harmony."

He nodded again, and Klyklyyk removed the band. "You are now and always our family."

Helen had started to understand the meanings of the nods. She looked at Charlyyk as the sense of being as one sank in. She saw the Laights were as happy as everyone around them.

The cathedral bells rang out as the newlyweds made their way out. Charlyyk walked behind them, the smile she wore telling everyone how proud she was. Amy looked around, making sure her mother was nearby. Cat nodded to her daughter to keep up with Charlyyk. The wedding congregation left their seats to follow the happy couple. The wedding photos were going to be very special, as the three Laights stood out from the rest of the congregation.

When the photo shoot had finished, the elegant Fiona Bruce stepped forward and spoke with Charlyyk. Charlyyk beckoned Klyklyyk to her. Klyklyyk explained to Fiona the reason for what had taken place. Then the three Laights stepped into an open space and, in a flash of light, were gone.

Fiona's expression as they evaporated showed her wonderment. She turned to Charlyyk and carried on with the interview with the professionalism of years of experience in TV presenting. "Charlyyk, did you know that your people were going to attend today?"

"No, but I am pleased they acknowledge us as family."

The vague images she'd had earlier at Dippers Meadow were opening up and becoming even clearer. Her brains were expanding. The restriction she had previously experienced was lifting. She knew much more than she had first thought she knew. What had held her memories at bay was crumbling, and she was taking charge.

Charlyyk took a deep breath, ignoring the flashes. She felt contented. She had her whole family around her—a real mum, dad, brother, and sister. Feeling the touch of Amy's hand, she bent down and cuddled her. Around her were all the people she loved.

Was she happy?

You bet.

Lightning Source UK Ltd.
Milton Keynes UK
UKHW011840220819
348429UK00001B/51/P